Acclaim for Grif Stockley and Gideon Page!

Probable Cause

"Build[s] to a dramatic courtroom finish ... Mr. Stockley is a talented writer."
—JOHN GRISHAM
The New York Times Book Review

"Homespun warmth and wry charm ... A down-home *Burden of Proof*."
—*Kirkus Reviews*

Expert Testimony

"The closest novel seen this year to Scott Turow's *Presumed Innocent*."
—*San Francisco Chronicle*

"Stockley has produced a delightful and intriguing human story. It is to be hoped he will use his newly found talent to dig into his past experiences as background for more such captivating tales."
—The Associated Press

Also by Grif Stockley
Published by Ballantine Books:

PROBABLE CAUSE
EXPERT TESTIMONY

RELIGIOUS CONVICTION

Grif Stockley

IVY BOOKS • NEW YORK

Ivy Books
Published by Ballantine Books
Copyright © 1994 by Grif Stockley

All rights reserved under International and Pan-American Copyright Conventions. Published in the United States by Ballantine Books, a division of Random House, Inc., New York, and distributed in Canada by Random House of Canada Limited, Toronto.

Library of Congress Catalog Card Number: 93-34194

ISBN 0-8041-1255-X

This edition published by arrangement with Simon & Schuster, Inc.

Manufactured in the United States of America

First Ballantine Books Edition: April 1995

10 9 8 7 6 5 4 3 2 1

To my daughter,
Erin Temple Stockley

"Whenever theology touches science, it gets burned. In the sixteenth century astronomy, in the seventeenth microbiology, in the eighteenth geology and paleontology, in the nineteenth Darwin's biology all grotesquely extended the world-frame and sent churchmen scurrying for cover in ever smaller, more shadowy nooks, little gloomy ambiguous caves in the psyche where even now neurology is cruelly harrying them, gouging them out from the multifolded brain like wood lice from under the lumber pile. Barth had been right: *totaliter aliter*. Only by placing God totally on the other side of the humanly understandable can any final safety for Him be secured."

—JOHN UPDIKE, *Roger's Version*

1

"CHET BRACKEN IS here to see me?" I ask in disbelief. Stuffed on a big lunch, I come awake and sit upright in my chair and stare at my telephone as if I expect it to pop up a picture of Blackwell County's one true whiz-bang, hotshot criminal attorney, Chester Theodore Bracken, an ugly, short man with jug ears the size of satellite dishes and a paunch he doesn't bother to hide. Bracken is the guy you call if you shoot Mother Teresa in a room full of nuns as she is being blessed by the Pope. Oddly enough, Bracken has showed up in my life unannounced once before. He had just picked up a client in the Hart Anderson murder case and rumbled through my office at the Public Defender's that day like a flash flood, intimidating me with his reputation and overbearing manner. It doesn't seem to have made much difference that I'm in private practice now. Why doesn't he just use the telephone like everybody else?

"He's not Jesus Christ, for God's sake!" barks Julia, our floor secretary and receptionist, her tone up to her usual snotty standards. "Are you gonna see him, or do you want me to say you're too busy crapping in your pants?"

If Julia weren't right so often, she'd still be intoler-able. As a relative of the owner of the building, she dresses and talks as she pleases. Today the magenta

1

sweater covering her breast implants is so tight her nipples look like rivets that have popped out of their holes from metal fatigue. At some perverse level, the lawyers on our floor like Julia and have grown attached to her, as one would a dog with a nasty growl. She can be a bitch, but she's *our* bitch. I look down at the blank legal pad in front of me. I had set aside this morning to work on a brief to the Arkansas Supreme Court, but what the hell, it's a loser anyway—a cocaine deal with the search being the main issue. If the money is right, the temptation is overwhelming to bag the client before he can slither out the door down to someone else's office. "I'll be right out."

"What's the big deal?" Julia mutters. "This guy looks pretty scruffy to me."

"Wonderful, Julia!" I exclaim. "Why don't you put down the phone and just yell it in his face?" Yet I know what she means. Outside of a courtroom, Bracken is a ratty dresser—cowboy boots the color of muscadine wine, ties that strain against his bulging neck like sprung mousetraps, and belt buckles that double as beer bottle openers. Still, I'd cut off my left arm to get the results he does for his clients. My friend Dan Bailey, a veteran Chet Bracken watcher, retells the story that Bracken is so prepared he can tell you what his clients ate for breakfast the day they got themselves into trouble.

In the reception room Bracken's appearance is, in fact, alarming. Scruffy isn't the word. His suit, a cowpatty gray, hangs on him; he looks like the family runt who has acquired a wardrobe of hand-me-downs. If he has been trying to lose weight, he should consider a career change as a barker for Weight Watchers. Otherwise he looks like a candidate for a bone-marrow transplant. Immediately, I think he must have AIDS and realize I haven't seen him around in two or three months. Despite the ghost he has become, Chet is a presence in Blackwell County legal circles, whether he is sighted or not.

"Mr. Bracken," I say with a forced, uneasy jocularity, "to what do I owe the honor of this visit?" I would feel awkward calling him by his first name. We are not friends or equals, merely colleagues in a suspicious profession. A couple in the waiting room stare at Bracken and me as if I am greeting royalty.

Bracken pushes up from his chair and says, "Page, you got a few minutes?" No handshake. No smile. He may not look like the Chet Bracken of three months ago, but he is acting the same.

"Come on back," I say, determined not to let myself be overwhelmed by him.

Seated in one of my chairs (the first time he came to my office at the PD's he stood the entire time), he asks, "Page, you know anything about the Wallace murder?"

"Only a little," I say. Leigh Wallace is a knockout brunette in her early twenties and the daughter of the minister of one of the largest nondenominational churches in the South who is on trial this month for the murder of her wealthy businessman husband at their swank home overlooking the Arkansas River.

"You got any interest in helping on the case?" Bracken grunts so quickly I wonder if I have heard him.

I can't believe he is asking me. Bracken has always been a one-man band, paying investigators and law clerks on a case-by-case basis. "What do you need?" I ask, trying not to sound suspicious. While Bracken is the best criminal defense attorney Blackwell County has to offer, his reputation is clouded by rumors of violent paybacks when he feels a witness has lied to him on the stand. (One informant supposedly ended up with broken kneecaps.) Yet, since nothing has ever been documented, the stories may be mere jealousy. We like winners in Arkansas, but we like to hate them, too.

"Right now I need your word that what I'm about to tell you will go no further than this room," he says, his voice earnest and low, "whether you come in with me on this case or not."

My curiosity raised by the hint of pleading in his tone, I nod and say, "Of course," noticing that the lines around Bracken's mouth look drawn so tightly they appear to be sewn on his face.

"I'm dying of cancer," he says hoarsely. "I'm on some painkillers, but I'm not going in for all the experimental crap and pretend I've got a chance."

Bracken's words send a chill through me that leaves me clammy. My wife, Rosa, died of breast cancer less than four years ago at the age of thirty-nine, and I've become spooked by the disease. It hasn't been a year since my girlfriend was in St. Thomas for a breast biopsy that ultimately proved benign but not before her surgeon (the same sawbones who mutilated Rosa) told us to expect the worst. Even though my experience with Bracken is that he is an obnoxious son of a bitch, I cannot imagine this intensely driven man dead. He can't be more than forty. "I'm sorry," I barely murmur. What is there to say?

Ignoring my sympathy, he says, "Anyway, I've got the Wallace case coming up, and I need somebody, if I don't feel up to it, who can talk to a jury the way I heard you did in that case with the nigger psychologist."

I feel my stomach muscles knot into a mass as if a tumor of my own is being formed. Bracken obviously has no idea I was married to a woman who was partly black. Rosa was a native of the northern coast of Colombia, and her bloodlines melded Indian, Spanish, and Negro ancestries. So, despite my eastern Arkansas upbringing, the word "nigger" is no longer in my vocabulary. At the same time I'm elated by his reference to the Chapman case. Bracken sets the standard by which all criminal defense attorneys in Blackwell County are measured. I feel as I did when I was seven and brought my father a note from Mrs. Harrod that I was the best reader in her second-grade class at Mulberry Elementary. "When is the trial date?" I ask, trying to conceal the excitement I'm beginning to feel.

"It begins on the twenty-fourth," he says, unfurling on his knees abnormally long fingers, which I realize now have been clenched. "I asked a couple of other guys, but they had a conflict."

My ego shrivels like the skin of a helium-filled balloon suddenly pierced by a needle. "What's the pay?" I ask, masking my disappointment with a question lawyers understand. Bracken commands fees the rest of us usually only dream about. Perversely, I think that with the money he is saving on medical bills he can afford to be doubly generous. My gall surprises even me. Here I am willing to haggle over money, and this guy's life is boiling away faster than a pan of water being heated by a flamethrower. Still, it's easier than talking about the pain he must be feeling.

"I'll give you a thousand a week," he says, slouched in the chair like an insolent teenager, "but it's gonna be nothing but asses and elbows from here on in."

I make a dollar sign on the pad in front of me. He's probably picking up thirty on this case at an absolute minimum. I'll be doing a lot more than waiting to see if he can't answer the bell. "I'll need two a week," I say, trying to sound casual, "to make it worth my while. No telling what I'll have to turn down."

For the first time Bracken visibly winces, either in pain or at the way I'm trying to hold him up. "Okay," he says, his face a web of tiny creases, "but I want my money's worth. I'm doing this one on the house."

I drop my Bic on my legal pad in amazement. One of the sayings about Chet Bracken is that he wouldn't know a pro bono case if one bit him on the leg. "Leigh Wallace should be loaded," I point out, "especially now."

Bracken says, his ears raising slightly, "I'm doing this one for her father. I'm a baptized member of his church."

Chet Bracken a Bible thumper? The thought of it is astonishing. There isn't a nonrational bone in his body, and Christian Life is hard-core fundamentalism. He really must be dying. Yet even my girlfriend has recently dumbfounded me by telling me she has started attending Christian Life. It must be something in the water. "I didn't know that," I say, sounding stupider by the second.

Bracken nods and says without a trace of irony, "You should try it, Page. Money isn't everything."

Feeling a little crass, I shift my pad an inch to the left. "I'm a Catholic," I mumble. Actually, this is bullshit. I've hardly darkened the door of a church since the Mass I was made to attend the morning I graduated from Subiaco Academy, a Catholic parochial school an hour from Fort Smith in the western part of the state. Rosa's death hasn't helped me answer any questions I have about religion. All the preaching in the world can't explain why a woman who had so much life in her had to die in agony before her daughter was even out of junior high school.

Bracken places his hands together as if we are all one

happy family and asks, "Are you sure you have the time to do this case?"

I hear anxiety in his voice. I wonder how much he has done to prepare. Bracken has the reputation of being a control freak. One story has it that on occasion he bribes the Blackwell County courthouse custodian to keep the temperature five degrees cooler than normal during a trial. There won't be any doubt about who will be the boss. I look down at my calendar for the rest of March. An ugly custody trial, a few appointments for new clients, a couple of DWI's, and three uncontested divorces. Pretty unspectacular. "I've got a few things," I admit, "but only one case that will chew up a whole day." As with almost every lawyer I know in solo practice who hasn't been at it a good while, it's either feast or famine. "What's the story?" I add quickly, before he changes his mind.

Bracken reaches inside his coat for his wallet, revealing a pink shirt and a tie that looks like a slightly surreal sunflower field. I wonder what kind of cancer he has. He hasn't even cleared his throat. "Damn it to hell, that's a good question," he says irritably as he peels off four five-hundred-dollar bills. "I've hardly gotten a word out of our client. It's a weird case, Page. Every time I try to talk to Leigh, she clams up. Usually, I can't get a defendant to shut up they give me so much garbage. I can't get her to talk. Frankly, I don't get it."

I look on in astonishment. I've heard of people carrying large sums of cash around, but he must have ten thousand on him. If he keels over in the street, there'll be a riot. "Maybe she shot him in self-defense," I say, recalling Leigh's picture in the paper. Some beautiful women photograph terribly; Leigh Wallace could model for any magazine in the country. She looks like that curly-headed Spanish-looking brunette who's always in

the Avon catalogs Julia keeps at the front desk. Leigh
has glittering dark eyes, a thin nose, a generous mouth,
and the kind of figure that ties up traffic for blocks.
Seeing her picture the day after she was charged, I re-
gretted my not-always-adhered-to vow to date only
women close to my age. But look what it got Art Wallace, who, like myself, was in his mid-forties.

"I'd settle for self-defense," Bracken says, handing
me the bills, "but the cops say there was no sign of a
struggle, and I can't get a thing out of her. The cops
nailed her on all the inconsistencies they've caught her
in and because there was no sign of a forced entry. It
appears she has gone to some length to establish her father's church as an alibi, but a neighbor saw her drive
by at the same time she was supposed to be in a
meeting. Hell, I don't know; I haven't felt like doing
much work lately."

Bracken must be going crazy. A notorious worka-
holic, he bugged me night and day during the Perry
Sarver case until he got the prosecutor to dismiss the
charges against his client. Some lawyers, the mediocre
ones, only go all out the last month before a trial.
Bracken knows only one speed. I can't imagine he
hasn't browbeaten his client to tell him her life story.
Cancer, however, isn't a disease that respects the work
ethic. Once Rosa started going down, she didn't feel
like doing much either. The depression was as bad as
the pain. What an ego this son of a bitch has. He ought
to be home in bed and probably has no idea he is depressed. "Were they getting along okay?"

"Depends on who you talk to," Bracken says gloomily. "She says they were, but a couple of neighbors say
different. They heard her yelling the night before he
was killed. She says it was nothing."

"I can't remember the weapon," I say, trying unsuccessfully to remember the article about the murder. It doesn't do me any good to read: I can't remember a word the next day, much less months later.

Distracted, Bracken nods as if he is on automatic pilot. "Three slugs in his chest and heart with a twenty-two-caliber pistol. Leigh claimed she didn't know anything about a gun. The cops figure she could have done a lot of things with it—from dumping it in the river to hiding it in her father's church."

"What about Wallace?" I ask, realizing Bracken doesn't have much gas left in him for this conversation. "Any enemies or unhappy friends?"

While Bracken reaches down to pull out a folder from his briefcase, I wonder what I'd do in his situation. Probably be on the phone to every quack in the country. He must have found an honest doctor who told him not to waste his time. Not a popular position in a society where you are supposed to fight on until the last blast of radiation. Hell, maybe I'd be going to church, too. But not Christian Life. All that right-wing stuff on abortion and men being the boss gives me the creeps, not to mention the nonsense about the world being created in seven days. I still can't believe Rainey, who is as liberated as any woman I know, is involved out there. It doesn't make any sense to me, but neither does dying at the age of thirty-nine. Bracken reads for a moment, then says, "I've had an investigator check him out, but nothing has turned up so far. Wallace made his money by functioning as a middleman between wholesalers and manufacturers all over the country. He had an office in his home. Perfectly legitimate."

I look past Bracken out the window at the mild March sunshine striking gold on the concrete ledge. His last spring. Yet there is not an ounce of self-pity or regret in his voice. Maybe religion has reconciled him to

leaving much too early. Who will miss him? Criminals.
Lawyers like myself, who dropped by the courtroom to
watch him try a case. His family, I suppose, of whom I
know nothing. So what if religion is a crutch? For all I
know, that's all he's got left.

"So what do you think this is all about?" I ask,
watching Bracken scan his investigator's report as if
something new might have magically appeared in it.

"Page, I wish I knew," he says. "Make a copy of the
file, get it back to me tomorrow, and we can talk. I'll
telephone Leigh and tell her that you'll be working with
me. Maybe she'll talk to you."

I take the file from him, shaken by how little confidence he has left in him. Normally, his arrogance is as
much a trademark as his jug ears. I'd be cocky too if I
got his results, but that is all gone now. His brusqueness
almost seems a smoke screen to hide the lack of progress he has made. I'm amazed that Bracken managed to
get her out on bond. Yet maybe it wasn't that hard. I recall reading that members of Christian Life flooded the
court with affidavits to the effect that Leigh Wallace
was no threat to flee the court's jurisdiction. Old hands
around the courthouse said there had never been anything like it in Blackwell County. The power of Shane
Norman, I guess. There are many influential members
in Christian Life, and not a few of them were contrib-
utors to Judge Shellnut's reelection campaign for municipal court judge. Still, he set bond at $500,000,
which didn't faze Christian Life in the slightest.
Twenty-four hours later Leigh was out, living with her
parents in the Christian Life compound in western
Blackwell County. After the case was bound over from
municipal to circuit court for trial after the probable
cause hearing, Chet didn't even bother asking for a re-
duction of the bond.

Bracken stands, looking relieved and tired at the same time, and surprises me by offering his hand. His palm is surprisingly soft as I feel his long fingers curl around my knuckles. "Leigh and an old lady from the church she brought home for lunch discovered Wallace's body, but once the cops got around to checking out Leigh's alibi, it didn't hold up, as you'll see from the file," he says, nodding at the folder on my desk.

I return the slight pressure, realizing Bracken has done almost nothing in the case. You get what you pay for, I think, but I know this doesn't apply here. Whatever his faults as a human being, Bracken has too much pride to lie down on a case if it is within his power to avoid it. The other side of the coin is that he has too much pride to say he is just too sick to do it right. "You think she did it?" I ask, suspecting Bracken, like myself, never asks that question of his clients. Unless you're arguing self-defense, knowing the answer to that question may ethically keep you from putting your client on the witness stand.

"Probably," Bracken says, grabbing his briefcase and leading me out the door. "For all I can tell, she could have been thinking about killing him every day for the last six months. We're lucky Jill isn't going for the death penalty."

A smart move on the part of Jill Marymount, Prosecuting Attorney of Blackwell County, I think as I walk beside Bracken down the hall to our reception area. There will be some not-so-subtle pressure on the jury, given Christian Life's influence in Blackwell County. No sense in adding to it. Life in prison for that beautiful body would be punishment enough, whatever her motive.

After Bracken is safely on the elevator, Julia looks

down at her watch and sniffs, "Damn, I thought he was asking you to marry him."

I hand her the cash to deposit for me, realizing now that Bracken didn't even ask for a receipt. I'll have Julia send him one. "He was," I say and explain.

Julia looks respectful for the first time in a month. "Surely he can afford a tailor."

I let that one pass and walk back to my office to study the file. I feel uneasy, wondering what I am getting myself into. I have the same mixture of dread and awe for Bracken that is supposed to be reserved for God. Where is the dread coming from? I can't quite pin it down, but more than likely it is that I won't come close to measuring up to him in a direct comparison. This is my chance to prove how good I am in the sight of the master, and I already feel my stomach begin to churn. Fear. Attorneys don't talk about it publicly, but the anxiety is so tangible it becomes like a separate organ in the body once you enter the courtroom in a big case, especially if you aren't as prepared as you should be. No profession except acting and politics risks greater public humiliation, a professor told my freshman torts class. That's why he taught, he cracked. As he pointed out, the public isn't allowed in the operating room with a surgeon during a triple bypass. Your mistakes in public can send men and women to their deaths just as easily.

As I squint at Bracken's terrible handwriting, I realize I am imagining myself giving the closing argument in the case and Bracken nodding with approval. How ridiculous! Bracken isn't that great. But he is. Right at the top of the heap, and there would be nothing more satisfying than to read in the pages of the *Arkansas Democrat-Gazette* the day after Leigh Wallace's acquittal a quote by Bracken that I was going to be better than he was. What an ego I have! The truth is, though, that I hope he is too sick to do anything but watch the entire trial.

"It's about time you got a decent-looking male client," Julia says so loudly the man sitting in the waiting room can't help but overhear.

"Mr. Blessing," I say, extending my hand, "would you like to come on back to my office?"

Richard Blessing stands and meets me at eye level with a firm handshake. Impeccably groomed in a slate green sports coat that I've seen at Dillard's, he smiles, showing a row of strong, gleaming white teeth that make my dingy molars seem as if they came from a pawnshop. "I hope you can help me," his voice betraying an anxiousness that is at variance with his self-confident appearance.

"I'll do what I can," I say, trying to get my mind off the file Chet Bracken handed me an hour ago. Over the phone yesterday Blessing had mentioned he had a products liability case he wanted to discuss. For about a year after I left the public defender's office I was an associate at Mays & Burton, a firm that specializes in personal injury cases. Before being fired with another associate during an economic downturn (we were losing cases so regularly, somebody had to walk the plank, and it obviously wasn't going to be one of the partners), I had learned enough about ambulance chasing to know I wasn't any good at it.

The dream of every lawyer in private practice is that a client will crawl in with a ten-million-dollar injury caused by the alcoholic president of a solvent insurance company. The problem with Mr. Blessing is that he looks as if he could run a marathon without breaking into a sweat. He has a strong yet sensitive face, with so much hair on his head he is probably running a fever. Yet every strand is in place. I resist the temptation to pat the ever-widening bald spot that sits on the back of my head like a dust bowl from the 1930s. Some guys have all the luck.

I lead him into my office and tell him to take a seat. To get the ball rolling, I ask him what he does for a living and he explains he is a men's clothing salesman for Bando's downtown. "Each guy's got to turn a minimum of a hundred fifty thousand a year, or we're a number on last year's spreadsheet," he confides. "You wouldn't believe the pressure to sell neckties to people who have a couple of dozen hanging in their closet already. The markup is terrific. We sell three-hundred-dollar suits that cost us maybe sixty bucks. If we can't move 'em, we'll knock off a hundred and then another hundred and still make money. If it's a good location, a store can clean up."

I notice a thread unraveling on the right arm of the sleeve of the russet blazer I got on sale this past spring at Bando's. Damn. I thought I was stealing it, and they probably still made fifty bucks. If this guy was injured, it wasn't his mouth. He's a talker. "You said that you thought you had a products liability case," I remind him, thinking he should have been a lawyer. He looks much slicker than the attorneys on our floor, but that isn't difficult to do, as Julia reminds us on a weekly basis.

"I think I do," Blessing says, frowning. "In my business image is everything. You've got to look sharp if you want to sell in the most expensive stores where they can really jack up the profit margin. If the customer is going to lay out good money for a pair of pants and a matching jacket, you can imagine he doesn't want to give his money to a guy who looks like a bum off the street."

I put my left arm over the offending thread. "Sure," I say. I went in Bando's once and was so horrified by the price of just the ties I had heartburn for a week. "It'd be like going to Alouette's and being served by a woman in curlers with grease stains down the front of her dress."

Nodding to signify that we're on the same wavelength, Blessing tugs at his lapels. "If the store is going to make seven hundred dollars off a suit," he says agreeably, "the customer should get something. It's only right."

Hell, yes, I think. At the very least he should be congratulated on his choice of store. Maybe even a lint brush thrown in for free. I think I'll wait awhile before I go shopping again. What is this guy's problem? Did his tape measure break when he was measuring an inseam, or what? Ah, capitalism. No wonder the Commies have such cold feet. "I'm not exactly sure how all this ties in," I say, wondering if I'm missing something. Any injury must be purely internal. With blue eyes the color of the inside of a flame and a diamond-hard chin, the guy could be a male model.

"Here's the deal," he says, his eyes suddenly out of focus. "My boss was taking me to a late lunch because of the great month I'd had in January, which is usually one of the toughest in the business, and he wants to try this new Indian place a couple blocks from the store. In February it's like being in a wind tunnel down there, and all of a sudden in front of my boss and about twenty other people my rug blows off into the gutter. I had to chase the damn thing. The way the wind was blowing, my boss said it looked like a little animal running down the street!" He jerks off his toupee and reveals a scalp as wide and barren as Death Valley.

Though I am trying desperately, there is no way to keep a straight face. I pretend I have to sneeze and reach for a tissue from the box on my desk to cover my face. I begin to laugh into it and nearly suck it down my throat as I try to draw a breath.

"It's not funny, damn it!" Blessing cries, throwing the hairpiece on the corner of my desk where it catches on a two-hole punch I use to make files. The toupee, a rich brown color, looks like some eyeless mutant creature dreamed up by a special effects person for a science fiction movie. I wait for it to begin to move toward me.

"Not funny at all," I get out without choking. "It must have been terrible."

Blessing grabs his hairpiece and crams it back on his head. Amazingly, it fits like a jigsaw puzzle piece onto his own hair, which rims his head like a bad paint job. "All of February my sales were down to nothing. I've lost all my confidence. Every time someone comes into the store I imagine this thing," he says, pointing to his head, "slipping down over one eye. After this happened, even the janitors were laughing at me."

I lean back against the wall and feel the bare skin of my own bald spot. The poor guy can't laugh at himself. If this had happened to me, I would have spent the rest of my life telling this story. Instead, Blessing wants to sue. "Actually," I say, "it looks incredible. You just popped it into place without a mirror and you can't even tell you have it on."

Blessing winces as he pats his hair self-consciously. "It ought to," he complains, "it cost fifteen hundred dollars."

Hell's bells. No wonder he's pissed. For that kind of

money you'd think they could have thrown in a bottle of Super Glue.

"Where did you buy it?" I ask, remembering there is a wig shop downtown that caters, judging by its windows, to African-Americans. I doubt if Mr. Blessing bought it there.

"At a place in Memphis called Wiggy's," he says, handing me a wad of papers. "There was an ad in the Sunday *Commercial Appeal* which guaranteed you couldn't tell the difference."

I look through the documents, searching for a contract. All I find are pages of testimonials from satisfied customers. There are pictures of wigs, and, curious, I look for one that covers up a bald spot. Wiggy's! I don't blame him for going out of town. It will be hard to keep my mouth shut. Since we are basically salesmen ourselves, lawyers love a good story. "Did you sign anything?" I ask.

"Something, I think," Blessing says, reaching for the papers on the desk between us. "The salesman who sold me mine said his had never slipped even a fraction of an inch in the two years he had worn it."

I study Blessing's hair, marveling at the transformation. He must have felt as if someone had somehow suddenly pulled his pants down. I tell myself I'd never wear a toupee, but if I looked like this guy, I'd think about it, especially if I were in his business. He's right. Appearance is important. You don't go into a clothing store to discuss the meaning of life. "Is there a booklet on how to care for it or some kind of warranty?" For that kind of money, you surely get more than testimonials.

"I know I got some other stuff," Blessing says, riffling futilely through the sheaf of advertisements, "but I can't find it."

Clients never bring in the right papers. "I want you to look some more at home," I urge him. "They could be important."

He assures me that he will, and after I let him wring his hands for a few more minutes, I escort him to the elevators. I'm not ready to sign up to argue this case at the U.S. Supreme Court, but I'll take a look at his papers. I've had worse cases. I might even get a free wig out of it.

2

AFTER WORK I swing by Rainey's house to eat dinner and get the scoop on Shane Norman and his Christian Life church. Until this past winter, my girlfriend's religious beliefs were as indecipherable as my own, but after having had a benign lump in her breast removed, Rainey, to my surprise, and not a little to my dismay, has gotten that old-time religion. As I pull up in front of her modest frame house, I try to rein in my feelings on this subject, as it is becoming a sore point between us. A lukewarm Episcopalian (God only knows what they believe) until her conversion, Rainey now talks about "Biblical inerrancy." If she weren't serious, I'd be sorely tempted to laugh at her.

Just a few years back we had our own Scopes monkey trial in Arkansas, a highly publicized battle in federal court over whether public school teachers should be required to teach "creation science," thanks to a bill pushed through the Arkansas Legislature by the fundamentalists. Gleefully, the media, smelling a circus, sent reporters from all over to yuck it up at our expense as the ACLU brought in Stephen Jay Gould, the heavy-duty Harvard rock sniffer, to testify about the probable age of the earth. Mercifully, the federal judge, a Methodist, ruled there was a lot more theory than science put on by the attorney general, who was obligated to defend

19

the statute with his own out-of-state scientists. Our AG, to his everlasting credit, had the good sense and political courage not to appeal.

When I remind Rainey of the trial, she gets an irritated look on her pretty, pixieish face and says, as usual these days, that I'm missing the point. She argues my worldview (so-called "logic" supported by scientists who are forever changing their theories) is culturally determined and can no more be "proved" than what's in the Bible.

Perhaps to serve as a buffer between us during this pricklish period, Rainey has invited my daughter, Sarah, to dinner with us and has already picked her up and brought her to her house. The less time Rainey and I spend alone these days the better we seem to get along. There was a time when it seemed we were on the verge of getting married, but at crucial moments one of us, as Paul Simon says, slips out the back, Jack.

Sarah, a high school senior and a daily reminder of her mother, who was a devout Catholic, comes to the door and whispers, her lovely face woeful, "We're having soup, salad, and cornbread." Virginal-looking (I can only hope on that score) in white sweats, she lets me give her a brief hug. Though we do not always understand each other these days, we remain affectionate, usually forgiving each other our respective generational baggage.

"Good," I say, meaning it. Rainey's soups are a meal in themselves. I follow my daughter through the living room and glance at Rainey's numerous bookshelves, wondering if I will begin seeing religious works in this eclectic stew of a library. My girlfriend is a reader, and last summer was on a kick when she zipped through the novels of a woman named Jane Smiley and pronounced her the greatest living American novelist. Other seasons she gobbles serious nonfiction works like chocolate-chip cookies. Thick tomes on Freud, Arabs and Jews, and racial discrimination are regular additions to the McCorkle collection. How an intelligent, well-informed woman can regress to such a narrow view of life's meaning is beyond me. Does a brush with death numb a person's mind to such an extent that she can swallow a book whole and not taste the indigestible parts? It seems so transparently childish I am amazed that Rainey can't see what she is doing.

I catch a whiff of curry as I enter the kitchen behind Sarah. Rainey, in Lee jeans and a man's workshirt, is peering into her refrigerator, which is covered with notices of do-gooder happenings: tickets for a silent auction for the Battered Women's Shelter, a note asking for volunteers to work in the food tent for an Arkansas Advocates for Children & Families benefit, a reminder of the next meeting of an AIDS care team. Rainey, a social worker at the Arkansas State Hospital, apparently can't get enough of human suffering. Maybe this new religious venture is a natural step, but before she gets on the boat and heads for Calcutta to work with lepers full-time, I'd like to make love to her just once. Charity begins at home, I have reminded her.

At various times in our tortured two-year relationship we have acted like passionate pre-sexual-revolution teenagers who stopped at necking on her couch, or best friends who have taken care of each other in our darkest moments, but never lovers. Watching her hips tug against soft denim as she reaches down for a bottle of salad dressing, I am reminded again how sexy this woman still is at the age of forty-two. Tendrils of frizzy red hair hang past her elfin ears and frame her full mouth, which today is painted pink, like the azaleas soon to bloom in her front yard. When her eyes, this

moment the color of blue-corn tortillas, flash with anger
or delight, my heart pumps a little harder. "Smells
great," I say, edging over to the stove for a look.

"Sarah cooked it," Rainey says, grinning, as she turns
around to face me. Her smile tells me that she adores
my daughter; no surer way to a father's heart. She has
been good for Sarah. Having raised a daughter of her
own, she is content to enjoy mine, and Sarah's self-
confidence has blossomed with Rainey's praise and en-
couragement. Over the last two years their friendship
has grown as steadily as Rainey's favorite oak, which I
can see budding outside the kitchen window. Rainey
and I would surely be married by now if our own
growth were as inevitable. If I dropped dead, I'd want
Rainey to take Sarah. I have a sister, but we aren't particularly close.

We all laugh at this obvious lie. Nothing Sarah and I
cook is more exotic than hamburger meat drowned in
A.1. sauce. "I made the salad," Sarah says with a grin,
taking Rainey's teasing better than she would if it were
coming from me. "Dad," she adds solemnly, looking at
my striped tie, "you dress like you're the manager at
McDonald's."

I look down at my shirt. It is a decent enough Arrow.
Orange stripes go with the tie. My pants, from Target,
are gray. "What's wrong with that?" I sputter. I thought
I looked pretty good today. Sometimes I don't match.

Rainey surveys me. "The one downtown," she says,
nodding at Sarah.

"What's wrong with that?" I say. I know who they're
talking about. Clean, polite, efficient, he always looks
presentable to me. "I take that as a compliment," I say,
preparing for the worst.

"I'm sure you do," Rainey says, winking at my
daughter.

"You're a lawyer!" Sarah exclaims. "You ought to wear suits."

I do sometimes, but if I know I'm not going to court, I can't bring myself to wear one. Suits I associate with weddings and funerals. "Having to go to work every day is bad enough," I say, knowing my defense is falling on deaf ears. "I'm not going to make it any worse. That guy probably makes a fortune."

At the dinner table I move our main topic of conversation from my clothes to the Razorbacks, which is appropriate, given the season of the year. How will the Razorbacks do in the NCAA basketball tournament? In the legends that surround the Kennedys, one that has stuck with me as the myths have accumulated is the story that among his other accomplishments, old Joe, the father of a president, an attorney general, and a U.S. senator, insisted that his children discuss world affairs at dinner. If table talk about geopolitics is a requirement of greatness, my daughter and I are doomed to the sticks.

"The best thing that ever happened to the Hogs was moving to the Southeastern Conference," Sarah pronounces, buttering cornbread that is soft as cake. "Playing Kentucky, LSU, and Alabama has got to toughen you up a lot more than blowing out TCU and Texas Tech."

I bite into cucumber and lettuce and chew. "I miss playing Texas," I say after I swallow. "God, we hated them." How boring my life would be without the emotions of resentment and envy.

Rainey, who is not a sports enthusiast but keeps up out of necessity, asks as she squeezes lemon into her iced tea, "Doesn't it seem strange that even though nearly all the players are black, people still care as much as they did when they were white?"

"We only care if they win," Sarah observes, looking
to me for my response. My daughter is at the age where
she challenges almost every utterance out of my mouth.
My relationships with other women, the way I practice
law, and my treatment of Rainey (who sometimes seems
more like a saint than a woman to my daughter) are all
put under a microscope and rarely seem to pass inspec-
tion.

I sip at a goblet of Cabernet red wine I picked up at
Warehouse Liquor. Ever since "60 Minutes" aired that
piece about how the French develop relatively little
heart disease, I have religiously drunk a couple of
glasses for dinner and have escaped criticism from the
two women in my life. Knowing I will get Rainey's
goat, I say, "If they win, we don't care what color they
are. That's what makes this country great. Winning is
everything."

Rainey, dainty as the first time I had lunch with her
at Wendy's (she had a salad that day as well), dabs at
her mouth with a cloth napkin she insists is ecologically
correct, despite the energy expended to clean it. "We're
great all right," she says sourly. "All the wealth in this
country, and millions of people don't even have health
insurance. With the cuts in Medicaid, I wonder how
people live as long as they do."

Content to be a white American middle-class male, I
savor the taste on my tongue. God, wine tastes good
with a meal. If the French weren't such snobs, they
could still civilize us. "Genetics," I say, undercutting
my excuse to guzzle more booze. "I'm beginning to
think your body gets a certain number of years no matter what you do to it."

"You don't believe that!" Rainey practically snorts,
shaking her head. "That would sound too much like
fate."

The truth is, I don't. Life will continue to be one random accident until, sooner or later, we peel a little too much off the ozone layer. "Did you tell Sarah I'm working with Chet Bracken on the Wallace case?" I ask her, moving the subject along. She is spooning her soup the way my mother taught me forty years ago in eastern Arkansas: move the spoon through the soup away from you as if it were a Ferris wheel and then bring it to your mouth. You don't look so greedy that way. Manners. An overrated virtue to people who don't have any.

"I would rather *you* breach your client's confidentiality," Rainey says dryly.

Sarah puts down her fork, and says in a high voice, "You told me once that Chet Bracken was a brilliant thug."

I look at my daughter and remember that is exactly what I said. What goes around comes around. "I meant some attorneys believe that about him," I backtrack, "but there's never been any proof he's ever done one thing unethical." Losing ground with Sarah, I turn to Rainey. "Did you know he's a member of your new church?"

Rainey sips her tea. "There're only five thousand members at Christian Life," she says, giving me an unusual deadpan expression. "I haven't met them all in the last four months."

I managed to keep Bracken's secret that he has cancer a total of two hours before I told Rainey, which is probably a record for me. I deposit information with my girlfriend faster than a squirrel stores nuts for winter. Rainey keeps her mouth shut, which is more than I can say for myself.

Sarah has consumed about an ounce of soup. She'd rather have red meat any day. She moves the spoon around in the bowl. "What case?"

I explain briefly about the Wallace murder and my client's connection with Christian Life. "I figured Rainey could fill me in, since she's started going to her church."

No longer feigning even polite interest in her food, my daughter pushes back from the table. "That's my dad," she says to Rainey. "What's a person for except for him to use to help win a case? And you're even fixing dinner for him!"

I raise my eyebrows to warn Sarah she is going a little far. Still, we have had this discussion before. My argument is that defense attorneys aren't given many weapons, and you have to make do with what is at hand. She says that lawyers like me hurt innocent people in the process and then act as if it couldn't be helped. Worse, according to Sarah, I seem to be more alive right before a trial and during it than at any other time. I seem to enjoy it too much. She's right. I do.

Rainey nods, apparently having made peace with herself long ago. "This way I can exercise a little influence over him," she says, as if I were not sitting across from her. "If you're not willing to help him, he won't listen at all."

I roll my eyes and pretend I don't know what they're talking about. In fact, not too many months ago I stashed in this very house a witness who needed to disappear for a few hours. She spent the night, and Rainey deposited her at the courthouse to testify the next morning. "So tell me about Christian Life," I say to Rainey, who nods as if she expected me to play dumb.

"Only if you won't make fun of it," she demands, her lips pursed, daring me to make some smart remark. "Why didn't you ask Chet Bracken?"

Sarah, who has not missed Sunday Mass in months after not going for a couple of years after her mother died, nods in agreement. At least I have a clue as to why Rainey has gotten religion. With Sarah I have no idea. Church seems to be a woman thing, mostly, is all I can figure. "I promise I won't make fun," I say, meaning it. Rainey can be a big help if she's willing to poke around for me. "Actually, I would have felt kind of weird asking Bracken," I admit. If Chet had started telling me about how Jesus Christ had changed his life, I would have tried to crawl under my desk. I can handle that kind of talk better from a woman.

"It's not like you think, Gideon," Rainey lectures me. "It's not hellfire and damnation." Rainey turns to Sarah, who is listening respectfully. "Your father has this image of a Jimmy Swaggart praying for money and promising to heal people. That's absurd! What Christian Life is about is helping people to accept the belief that God broke into human history two thousand years ago. Christian Life starts with a person just as you are right now, faith or no faith, and invites you, invites me, to witness the changes in the lives of the members of its congregation. People who are just starting are assigned church families. They are not blood families—just groups of about fifteen to twenty people who become your Christian Life family. It's incredible how persons in your family have changed their lives. Most of them weren't what anyone would call bad before. They lived ordinary, typical lives filled with the normal boredom, despair, and the sense of meaninglessness that accompany twentieth-century existence. Now their lives are truly God-centered, and they have a joy in their lives that is just thrilling to be around."

While Rainey is speaking, I am tempted to slurp my soup. When she gets started on Christian Life, she positively glows. It is hard not to be jealous. I never have been able to generate this kind of excitement in her.

Trying to conceal my irritation, I ask, "I don't get the connection between their lives and a literal belief in the Bible." I look at my daughter, who is listening intently. Mass, unless it has changed, is pretty much a cut-and-dried affair in the Catholic church.

"What happens if you let it," Rainey says, her voice soft and fragile, "is that God, working through your family, gives you the courage and will to believe that the Bible is His Word. It's simply through His grace that you come to accept the Scriptures."

I realize I have begun to resent the amount of time Rainey spends at Christian Life. In the last couple of months she has been up there at their huge complex for part of four or five days of every week. Christian Life is like a separate city within Blackwell County, but that's the point. A way of life, she says. It's difficult to avoid the conclusion that Christian Life is a cult, but Rainey flatly maintains there is nothing unusual about its doctrine or its leadership. Because of its size, she says, they break themselves down into "families" which nurture people like herself.

My daughter, who has never been shy before around Rainey until tonight, clears her throat and asks, "And you believe the Bible now word for word?"

Rainey smiles. "About ninety percent of the time I do. To help new members, they use the familiar metaphor of a trip. Joining Christian Life is like taking an unexpected journey. When you first begin it, you don't have the right clothes; you're anxious about what you're leaving; you're nervous about your destination. After you've been on it long enough, you learn how to be comfortable. That's where I am right now—I'm learning how to be comfortable."

I take my spoon and press it hard against the table, trying to contain my frustration. I've felt Rainey slipping away from me for months. Christian Life sounds like a day-care center for adults. All you have to do is check your brains at the door. Yet she has told me that a number of Blackwell County's movers and shakers are members now, including a number of attorneys who are partners in the biggest firms in the state. "Tell me about Shane Norman," I mutter. "What makes him so great?"

Rainey's eyes light up at the mention of Christian Life's principal minister. "I've actually met him only once," she says, giving me a rueful smile that is becoming familiar, "but as a preacher the man radiates peace. Even the Sunday after Leigh was charged, you couldn't tell the turmoil he must have been feeling."

I lean back in my chair so exasperated with her I can't eat anymore. I would be glowing a bit myself if five thousand people were showing up every week to hear me beat my gums. "Maybe he was at peace because his church raised half a million dollars for her bail by the next day."

Rainey gives me an indulgent smile. "Think how you would feel if Sarah were charged with murdering her husband. You'd be bananas."

I am capable of murder, but Sarah is not. She feels guilty if she accidentally steps on an ant. I start to make some asinine crack, but catch myself. Rainey will clam up if I'm not careful. "You're right," I say. "So have you heard any stories about Leigh's marriage while you've been there?"

"Don't ask her to snoop on her own church!" Sarah yelps at me. "It's not right!" She glares at me as if I had demanded that Rainey stake out the women's bathroom at Christian Life.

"It's okay, Sarah," Rainey says. "He's just trying to find out the truth about what happened."

I nod, ridiculously pleased that Rainey is defending me. "All I'm trying to do," I tell my daughter, "is get some information." At seventeen, Sarah is an idealist. I don't begrudge her this unrealistic phase in her life. I must have gone through one myself to run off and join the Peace Corps after college. Still, people like my daughter can be a pain in the butt, especially if they are charged with a crime. In my last big case I defended one who almost drove me crazy.

Sarah shakes her head. "You just want to hear something," she says, "that will make Christian Life look bad. You're mad Rainey's never home anymore when you call her."

A child shall lead us. "I have to confess," I say, glancing at Sarah before I turn to my girlfriend, "I'm a little suspicious of anyone who's made to sound quite so wonderful. He never turns out to be the superstar everybody says he is."

Sarah's voice takes on a high-pitched tone that signals she is mad enough to cry. "You're just like the media," she says to me. "Always criticizing, always looking for the dirt." She pleads with Rainey, "Don't tell him anything."

"Sarah," Rainey says, coming around the table to stand behind Sarah's chair and rub her shoulders as if she were a child who needed calming down instead of a spoiled, sulky teenager, "it's okay. Your dad knows he's got a standing invitation to get involved with me out there any time he wants."

Her dark eyes flashing at me, Sarah says, "The only reason you'd go is to get evidence for your case."

I stand up, wondering what I have done to my child. In conversations before, Sarah has accused me of using people, but she has never been so angry or so blunt. "I don't think," I say, throwing my napkin on the table,

"I'd make it to the inner sanctum in the three weeks left to trial." I head for the door. "Let's go home if all you are going to do is jump down my throat."

As I knew would happen, tears start down my daughter's cheeks. I still know what buttons to push. There may come a time when "guilting" her won't work, but practice makes perfect. "I'm sorry, Rainey," she says in a choked voice.

"I am, too!" I call from the door, waiting for Sarah. Sometimes she acts about three. I'm almost as mad at Rainey as I am at Sarah. I'm willing to bet my fee in the Wallace case that Rainey has been talking to Sarah about her coming to Christian Life. I don't mind her trying to proselytize me, but Sarah is another matter. Damn it to hell, who does she think she is? Sarah is my child, and I don't want anybody trying to feed her a load of crap. There is enough out there anyway without some right-wing nuts brainwashing her. Who the hell is Shane Norman anyway? In an earlier life he probably was some fly-by-night con artist who figured out that peddling salvation was an easier way to make a living. I may not be a genius or a saint, but I know bullshit when I see it. From the Crusades on down, with a Bible in one hand and a sword in the other, Christians who were sure they had a lock on the truth have murdered thousands of people. I'd rather my daughter's brain not be one of their victims.

"It's all right. Call me later," Rainey says, hurrying to the door.

I nod curtly, as Sarah runs ahead of me.

Sarah and I ride in an angry silence until we turn into our driveway. "You can be so closed-minded," she says, as she shuts the car door, careful not to slam it, knowing I will explode if she does. "Just because you don't believe anything doesn't mean other people can't."

Banging doors, yelling, any behavior except "Yes,
sir" or "No, ma'am" uttered with a respectful tone mi-
nus a snide expression were forbidden to me and my
sister, Marty, when we were growing up in eastern Arkansas. Even when my father was at his craziest, we
went around smiling like slaves who were working up
their nerve to ask for permission to marry someone off
the plantation. Only in the last couple of years have I
realized how much I intimidated Sarah when she was
growing up. I have begun to lighten up, but I am afraid
she will always be a little intimidated by me. "I believe
in something," I respond weakly. We covered this
ground last summer. Since religion has become important to her, it upsets her that I don't share her preoccu-
pation with it. I unlock the door, and we are greeted by
Woogie, a genetic disaster with his long legs and beagle
body and head. "Rainey asked you to visit Christian
Life, didn't she?"

I turn on lights in the den while Sarah reaches down
and pats Woogie's head. "What's wrong with that?"

I might as well sell the house and get a motel room.
"You're supposed to be Catholic. Your mother would be
spinning in her grave if she knew you were going to
join the Moonies or whatever this group is."

Sarah's jaw tightens. "God, Dad, you're impossible,"
she mutters. "Rainey wouldn't join something weird.
Besides, you don't know anything about Moonies anyway, and you know Mom wouldn't think it was the end
of the world like you do."

I throw myself down on the couch and watch Sarah
stroke Woogie's graying muzzle with her knuckles. I'd
even rather she be serious about a boy than get involved
with a group like Christian Life. First Rainey, now my
daughter. Why isn't it enough for the women I love to
get up and go to school or work and then come home

and plop down and watch the brain drain or even read a book? Life is complicated enough without getting heated up about whether some supernatural force is "breaking in" to human history.

Freud, if I remember my freshman psychology course at the University of Arkansas a hundred years ago, said that God is a wish and a pretty infantile one at that. An obvious conclusion if you think about it, given the rest of his psychology. As children, we can't get enough of our parents; as teenagers we can't get far enough away; and in marriage we look for them all over again. If he was correct, we aren't left with a particularly appealing portrait of the human psyche. But ever since the first ape saw his reflection in a pool of water, he has demanded a more grandiose explanation of his existence, Sigmund Freud notwithstanding. It is surprising he wasn't strung up by his tongue. If I tried to say something like that, the women in my life would burn me at the stake. Fathers, I have learned in the last couple of years, aren't supposed to commit heresy. Our job is to pay the bills and keep our mouths shut. "Do you want me to help you pack your bags?" I say, knowing how pathetic I sound.

Sarah's expression softens and she comes over to the couch and sits beside me. "That's what you're worried about," she says. "You're thinking you won't see me anymore." She pats my knee as if I were a child being comforted by his mother.

So, Rainey has been talking to her. I look around the den and realize how much Sarah has made it her own since her mother died. A year ago she persuaded me to buy an almost brand-new recliner for peanuts at a garage sale, and after my best friend Dan Bailey burned a hole in the coffee table before Christmas, she found another one at an antique shop and shamed me until, on

New Year's Eve, I broke down and bought it. Last winter a friend got her interested in ceramics, and now every flat surface in the room has some bizarre, gnomelike figure crouching on it. Not great art, but I don't know what's good unless I can read a label or a name. I'm not a visual person, as Rainey charitably puts it. I pull off my jacket and lay it beside me. "These groups can suck you in," I warn, "and before you know it you've become psychologically dependent on them." Great, I think. I'll have to pay somebody to kidnap her and then deprogram her.

"It's a church," she laughs, "not a concentration camp where they brainwash you. Rainey wouldn't be involved in anything like that."

"I should tell you that Chet Bracken's dying of cancer," I say, abruptly changing the subject. "That's why he's asked me to help him. It's a secret though."

Sarah's face softens, as I knew it would. "How much longer does he have?" she asks, her voice immediately anxious. Her mother's death was sheer agony.

He's going down fast," I say, milking this moment for as long as I can. "He's afraid he won't be able to do the trial."

"Has he got a family?" Sarah asks, biting her lip.

"I don't know a thing about him," I say, regretting I have told her. Why did I? Leverage, obviously. I know where my daughter is vulnerable. She was only thirteen when her mother died, and she still hasn't gotten over it. I'm pathetic, I realize. I didn't take this case because I'm sensitive to cancer victims. And yet, Chet's revelation has touched something in me. He has absolutely nothing in common with Rosa except that he's a fighter, too. Maybe there are more connections here than I am permitting myself to realize.

"That's so sad!" Sarah says, staring past me. "Isn't he young?"

You asshole, I think miserably. "Yeah, he's young."

With a somber expression now on her beautiful face, she goes to her room to do her homework, leaving me to sit in the den wondering why I'm so afraid of change. If I come down on Sarah too hard, she will resent me even more than she already does. Did Rosa go through some kind of religious rebellion when she was a teenager? She never mentioned it, or I wasn't paying attention. Regularly as clockwork, she went to Mass in Colombia and then here, so it never was an issue. Until her mother died, Sarah never missed, either. It's easy to have a perfect attendance record if you have no choice. After Rosa's death there was nobody to go with her, because I sure wasn't about to go thank God for taking Rosa away from my daughter at the beginning of adolescence.

I stare blankly at Leigh Wallace's file and think I should have faked it and taken Sarah to Mass these last few years. If I had, she wouldn't be so vulnerable now to the garbage that comes out of these fundamentalist churches. Who am I kidding? What could be more fundamentalist than the Catholic church? Abortion? Women in the church? The difference is these people at Christian Life take themselves so seriously. I never cared what Rosa believed as long as she agreed to use birth control. How she rationalized her faith didn't concern me so long as she did what I wanted. Guilt settles down around me like an occupying army as I remember how much pressure I applied to my wife not to have more children after Sarah.

I had just gone to work for Social Services as a caseworker and was making next to nothing, but Rosa wanted to stay home and raise our child. I knew that

would lead to more kids and told her that she had to
face the fact that I was never going to be rich. How
could that be? Wasn't this the United States, where everybody who wanted to work hard became a million-
aire? Reality set in after a year, and she went back to
work as a nurse. After ten years of marriage on a state
salary, I told her I wanted to go to law school at night.
Thrilled by my display of ambition, she began to talk
about the two more children we would have after I
passed the bar exam. Weren't all lawyers rich in the
United States? Poor Rosa. She'd still be working the
night shift. For the hundredth time, I wish she were here
to deal with her daughter. Our relationship has been on
a roller coaster lately. Woogie, who never changes, nuzzles in against my thigh. I rub his left ear gently. At moments like this, I think dogs are at the top of the
evolutionary chain.

3

CHET BRACKEN'S "FARM" is really no more than a few acres in the western part of the county. Though trees abound in central Arkansas, there are none around the structure that must be Chet's residence, unless I am badly lost. As I come upon an honest-to-goodness log cabin, my mind serves up pictures shown to grade-school kids of the pioneer experience at its hardiest: isolated huts hunkered down in the sod against the prairie wind. I have unlocked and relocked a second cattle gate and traveled, as directed, seven-tenths of a mile, so either I am about to surprise some unsuspecting family or I have for once followed directions to the letter. I pull up in the gravel driveway and think that I would plant some shade trees. Yet, perhaps Chet doesn't see the point. As exposed as this house is (despite the gates), I doubt that a young widow would want to stay out here by herself. I check to make certain I have Leigh Wallace's file and walk up the steps to the front porch, realizing that I am making all kinds of assumptions about Bracken's family. For all I know about him, he lives with his mother.

A boy of about seven comes to the door to answer my knock. "I'm Trey," he announces solemnly. "Are you Mr. Page?"

"That's me," I allow, smiling at this boy whose jug

ears seem to confirm his lineage more persuasively than any birth certificate. "Is your dad home?"

"Yes, sir, he's out back," Trey says seriously, offering me his tiny hand to shake. Trey's jeans are not totally clean, but his right hand is neither sticky nor grimy to the touch. For a child his age he has a surprisingly strong grip. I can imagine his father lecturing him to look the other person in the eye and, if he's a man, to squeeze his hand as hard as he can. The business of becoming a little Chet is about learning to deal from strength. The intimidation can be learned later. Yet, perhaps this isn't fair. This child has learned his manners, no more, no less. Still, it is unnerving to be greeted so firmly by a kid who barely comes to my waist. He leads me through the house, and though it is clean and picked up, it is difficult to imagine that a woman lives here. The living room is square like the main area of a lodge, lacking only deer antlers over the enormous fireplace to convince me that Chet uses this structure as a clubhouse for hunting and not as his principal residence. On the walls are pictures of ducks, geese, and other wildlife. The furniture is functional and sturdy. As much money as he has surely made from criminals, he could have three or four places like this scattered around the state.

"Mom," Trey solemnly introduces me as he leads the way into the kitchen, "this is Mr. Page."

Turning from the stove is a rangy, plain woman with short, graying hair, who is wearing an apron over bib overalls and a red long-sleeved jersey. She is stirring something on the stove that gives off a gamy scent. Given this rustic setting, I wouldn't be surprised if she announced we were eating bear meat. Anything smaller than an elk wouldn't seem fair competition for Bracken. She smiles pleasantly at me and says, her voice country but pleasant, "I'm Wynona Cody, Mr. Page."

Bracken's marital status, unclear before I came, still appears muddled. Is this his mistress or just a liberated woman? "How are you?" I ask, wanting to dig, but realizing the ground probably won't be hard at all in a few weeks. High-visibility lawyers like Bracken, who are always in the news with their clients, only seem to be all work and no play. Despite all the gossip about him, Bracken has kept his private life well hidden. I wonder what his "family" at Christian Life knows about him.

Wynona stirs the pot on the stove. "I hope you like Brunswick stew," she says, laying a blue lid over the pot on the stove.

Squirrel meat. I haven't had any since I was a boy in eastern Arkansas. "I remember my mother fixing it," I say, nodding. I remember how the meat used to stick to my teeth.

"Trey," she says, "take Mr. Page out back to talk to your dad and then come back inside. I won't be ready in here for a while."

"Yes, ma'am." Trey seems disappointed, but there isn't a lot of give in his mother's voice. Behind the friendly smile is a hint of steel. I wouldn't be surprised if it turned out to be Wynona who taught Trey his handshake. I follow him out a door off the kitchen and see Bracken sitting out on a deck that runs the width of the cabin with his feet up on a rail. A cooler is at his feet, and a beer is in his hand. "Dad," Trey says casually, "Mr. Page is here."

It sounds a little shocking to hear Bracken addressed so lovingly. Nervously, I clear my throat and look beyond Bracken to the woods no more than fifty yards away. The sun is about down now, giving the dense growth to the rear of the cabin a forbidding look. "Pull up a chair, Page," he says gruffly. He smiles at Trey, who grins and shoves his hands in his pants. "Trey, show Mr. Page how you can shoot."

Leaning against the wall is a .22 rifle that Trey lugs to the railing of the porch. He is too short to cradle the stock against his shoulder, so he steadies it under his arm and begins blasting at a tin can near the edge of the forest. The metal jumps as if it has acquired a life of its own as Trey sprays it around the shorn grass. Bracken watches with obvious satisfaction. I wonder what it would be like to have a son. I wouldn't trade her for anything, but Sarah has always been more than a match for me. Though Rainey disagrees, I have little to teach her except what to avoid when it comes time to choose a mate. Since her mother died, I haven't been the most consistent of fathers—too many nights I left Sarah alone while I went prowling around bars after lonely women who were eager to scratch a similar itch.

"He can sure pop 'em," I say admiringly.

"Can he try?" Trey asks, stopping after firing five rounds.

I haven't shot a rifle since I was twelve. My dad (before he went completely nuts and before my mother confiscated his guns) and I used to shoot turtles and gar off the St. Francis River bridge about ten miles from town. I was a decent shot then, but today only manage to hit the can one out of five shots. I offer the rifle to Bracken, but he waves it away. How much pain is he in, I wonder. It is easy to forget that he is probably doped up right now. With only a little time left, how can he think about law at all? What is death like? My mind resists contemplating its absence. Bracken doesn't have that luxury. If I were in his condition, I'd be tempted to say the hell with it and concentrate on keeping the cooler full. Other people are a mystery. Bracken may be spending the time he could be working on the Wallace case bargaining with God as if he were trying to cut a deal with a tough prosecutor. Given Bracken's reputation for insisting on absolute control, I'd like to be a fly on the wall during that conversation. The door opens, and Wynona waves Trey inside. Bracken looks up and gives her a warm smile. "We're lucky we're not counting on Page," he chuckles, "to defend Leigh in a shooting match."

She winks at the men in her life. "Y'all practice all the time," she drawls. "Be another twenty minutes. Come on in, Trey."

Reluctantly, the boy walks into the house, and I watch while Bracken unloads the rifle and checks the chamber. "Good kid," I say. "I thought he was gonna crush my fingers when he met me at the door."

Bracken reaches down beside him and picks up a rag from the floor and begins to oil the rifle. "It's hard to explain to a boy his age you're not going to be around much longer. They don't get it. Take a brew if you want."

For the first time, I feel some empathy for this man. Until this moment, his intensity and my own unacknowledged envy of his success had made us seem like beings from different galaxies. His need to dominate our previous encounters has repulsed me in a way that might say more about myself than him. He is successful because he leaves nothing to chance. I don't have his drive or single-mindedness. The fact is, I am flattered silly that he has asked me to help him, even if it means nothing more than sitting through the trial like a utility player on a team with an all-star infield. I lift the lid off the Igloo and pull out a Heineken. No light beer, but I guess there wouldn't be much point. "I don't get it either. My wife died a few years back, and I still haven't figured it out."

Bracken pauses from his labors to take a sip from his
can of Miller. "Dying young is going against the grain,
all right."

Going against the grain? Well, I didn't expect Chet
Bracken to burst into tears. I want to ask him about
what he's personally getting from Christian Life, but
now it seems an invasion of privacy.

"I read the file and copied it," I say, withdrawing the
Wallace folder from my briefcase. "If Leigh had kept
her mouth shut, they couldn't have charged her because
they wouldn't have had any real evidence. All they
would have had was a wife discovering her husband's
dead body and a neighbor's testimony they argued the
night before."

Bracken shifts in the green canvas chair at the mention of the case. He nods, his plain face gloomy.
"We've talked to everybody who claimed to be at the
church that day, and not a single one of them can testify
she was there during the time she says she was. Worse,
two people flat out contradict her story that she spoke
to them."

On Bracken's property there is a garden off to the
right of the cabin I hadn't noticed until now. Maybe he
does live here. "You think she could have been having
an affair and was supposed to be at the church and can't
bring herself to admit where she was?"

Bracken pokes his rag, which he has tied to a stick,
down the barrel. "Not at all likely," he grunts. "She and
Wallace had been married less than a year, and the word
is she was crazy about him. Her daddy complained she
was spending too much time at home with him instead
of being at the church."

So if she thought he hung the moon, why would she
kill him? At the edge of the woods, I detect some

movement. I think I'd be nervous at night out here. "Was Wallace a member?"

An ugly sound comes from Bracken's throat. "Not in good standing," he says, spitting over the railing into the yard, which is blooming with yellow forsythia and pink redbud trees. A butane tank only a few feet from the deck is mostly hidden by dense shrubbery, out of which arises a birdhouse for martins. "Shane Norman wouldn't have let his daughter marry Wallace if he hadn't joined his church, but right after they married, he quit coming much."

A small gray rabbit hops into the cleared field and cautiously sniffs the shot-up can. I am reminded of the days when my father and I used to hunt rabbits when I was a kid, and I look to see if Bracken will load the rifle. He yawns and looks down the barrel. "Maybe Wallace was playing around," I guess, "and she caught him at it."

Satisfied with his job, Bracken props the rifle in the corner against the beam supporting the roof. My father never fired a shot without cleaning and oiling his guns afterward. I think those acts of maintenance somehow gave him as much satisfaction as firing the guns. When his schizophrenia and drinking got bad (eventually he hung himself at the state hospital in Benton), my mother took the guns and gave them to her brother, telling my father someone had stolen them. He had to know what she had done (burglary of the home of a white person in a small town thirty-five years ago was as rare as a comet sighting), but, probably as a result of his illness, he preferred the theory that a crime had been committed. Bracken glances in the direction of the rabbit which has tentatively hopped a couple of feet toward the garden. "That's more of a possibility," he says, standing up and heading down the steps off the porch, "but we haven't turned up a woman in Wallace's past. By all accounts he was deeply in love with her, too." The creature sees Bracken and scampers back into the woods. Bracken turns and says somewhat sheepishly, "Live and let live."

I file away this story. Bracken, who chews up opposing attorneys for breakfast, won't even fire a warning shot at a rabbit. Perhaps dying is having a mellowing effect on him. It occurs to me that I am going to have the experience of watching a man die. It is a sobering thought. Rosa's death was not a good experience, but then I was too close. Maybe I can learn something at this distance. I follow him out to his garden where he shows me snow peas, spinach, onions, and broccoli Wynona and Trey have recently planted. He says the spinach especially will be delicious, as if he will be around to eat it. I want to ask him about his cancer but don't dare. I have been too intimidated by this man to presume familiarity I don't feel. Curiosity rather than sympathy is my dominant emotion, and though I'm beginning to warm to him, the myths about him shape my feelings to a far greater degree than this homey snapshot. Wearing beltless, faded blue jeans that are far too roomy in the back (they are in danger of sliding down his wasted shanks to his knees if he jams his hands in his pockets one more time), Bracken confesses he doesn't have the energy to do much more until the trial. "I had to browbeat Leigh to get her to see you tomorrow," he says, frustration working into his voice. "She's been about as useless as I am."

Embarrassed, I study the ground in the growing dusk. Only last year Bracken won outright acquittals in four first-degree murder cases in a row. His ability, the courthouse talk goes, has been exceeded only by his arrogance. Obviously, the specter of his own death has vanquished the Chet Bracken of legend. "I'm a little surprised somebody in that church hasn't tried to cover for her," I say, voicing a notion that has recently occurred to me. "They raised that bond money in a hurry."

Bracken bends down to pull up a weed. "I know Norman, and he wouldn't allow anyone to do that," he says sharply. "If she goes to prison, they'll have ten members there for her on visiting day the rest of her life, but nobody would be permitted to lie for her no matter how much it would help. We don't do things that way."

We. It is hard to take seriously Bracken's conversion. If he's so hot for it, how come he isn't in church tonight? Rainey was going. His sanctimonious tone sticks in my craw. Is he suggesting that I would suborn perjury? A decade ago, when Bracken was first making his reputation, the prosecuting attorney of Blackwell County claimed that he had bought a witness in a rape case but couldn't make the charge against him stick. I can't keep my irritation pushed down. "Joining a church doesn't make a person a saint."

Bracken smiles as if I had said something funny. He pokes at his teeth with the weed he has pulled from the ground. "I want you to talk to Leigh's father, too," he says mildly. "You're not going to get a feel for what I'm talking about until you do."

"I'll be glad to," I say, inwardly groaning at the thought. It is not only the Jim Bakkers, Jimmy Swaggarts, and Oral Robertses who have given Protestants a bad name. During John Kennedy's campaign for the presidency, Catholics were suspect in Bear Creek. Home during the summer from Subiaco, I was told more than once everybody knew the Pope would be calling the shots if he got elected. "Did Wallace keep a gun in the house?" I ask, wanting Bracken to focus on the murder itself.

Bracken leads me back to the deck. "Leigh claimed he didn't own one, and the cops can't prove he did, but that doesn't mean anything. I've got three guns in this house that were given to me." Apparently exhausted by our excursion to the garden, Bracken sinks gratefully into his chair.

Seated again, I watch the rabbit bound into the cleared ground and head for the garden. Bracken doesn't even bother to wave his arms. "As circumstantial as the case against her is," I point out, "maybe we could get a good deal for her."

Bracken reaches for another beer. "The sticking point is her father—he doesn't want her to have to spend a day in prison."

I finish my beer but decide against another one. How can a father believe his daughter is capable of murder? Sarah won't even kill one of Woogie's fleas. Bracken's hand shakes slightly as he brings the can to his mouth. "He thinks it's just a matter of time before some evidence turns up that takes her off the hook."

Wishful thinking is the only thing the brain is good for, according to my friend Dan. If not for that ability, there wouldn't be any reason to get out of bed most mornings. Trey bounds through the door, then, almost standing at attention, says formally, "Mr. Page, would you like to wash up before supper?"

I can't resist smiling at this kid and then remember what it is about him that is so unnerving. The child is being raised the way I was thirty-five years ago in the Delta. Form was substance, and substance form, and God pity the white middle-class child who didn't intuitively understand that. "Show me the way, Trey," I say, but turn to Chet. "Where were you raised?" I ask, guessing his answer.

"Helena," he says, pushing himself up from the chair. "About a mile from the bridge."

The bridge that leads to Mississippi, he doesn't have to say. I nod. "I'm from Bear Creek."

"I figured you had to be from over there, too, with that accent," he says, the barest hint of a smile on his face. We're practically brothers. Trey leads me through the kitchen past his mother setting the table and down a hall whose walls are covered with photographs. I pause and look at what has to be a picture of Chet in a Little League uniform. He is holding a bat in a kind of corkscrew stance that reminds me of Stan Musial. "That could be you," I say.

"Yes, sir," Trey says, not missing a beat. "You want to see the glove my dad played with?"

"Sure," I say. We pass the bathroom, which has been temporarily forgotten, and he leads me through a door at the end of the hall on the right. I haven't been in a boy's bedroom in years, but they haven't changed much except for the video equipment. Trey goes to a closet and pulls out a glove whose leather is so dry and cracked it is almost painful to the touch. "Dad played third base," Trey informs me as he hands me the glove to try on. "Did you know that Brooks Robinson was from Arkansas? My dad says he was the best ever."

I cram my fingers into his glove, remembering my days as a ten-year-old shortstop for Paul Benham Insurance. The first ball ever hit to me went between my legs. Every time we lost a game I cried afterward. Bracken probably went home and drove his fist through a wall. "He was incredible, all right."

"Trey!" his mother calls.

I slip the glove off and hand it back to him. Carefully, he lays it back in the closet. One way or another this kid will remember his dad. And his memories will be a lot different than most of ours.

Bracken says the blessing before the meal, but his wife and child do the talking. With the stew, Wynona serves biscuits and salad, and I eat until I'm bloated. As usual, I talk about Sarah and the travails of raising a teenage daughter who attracts boys by merely clearing her throat. It hits me that after a decent interval Wynona will be looking for another mate, and I wonder if Bracken feels bad when he thinks about her in the arms of another man. He seems content to listen, allowing his wife and son to carry the conversation. As I talk and am drawn out by Wynona (she titters sympathetically at my tales of paternal incompetence), I notice that Bracken is, in fact, content, period. Without a shred of self-pity, his homely face, reminding me, now I realize, of a young Ross Perot, is hoarding memories of his wife and son for the rough times ahead. "I would have had Chet invite Sarah," Wynona says, "if I had known about her."

"That's okay," I say, wondering what Sarah would have made of this family, "she's studying for a math test."

Actually, it is only a quiz, but she rarely begins to settle down before ten. She is on the phone, I would be willing to bet. Ever the little gentleman, Trey chews with his mouth closed and does not grab for food not within his reach. His table manners are better than my own. He asks, "Do you like being a lawyer as much as my dad?"

I chew, and signal with my hand that I will answer after I have swallowed. I have never thought one way or another whether Bracken enjoys his profession. With his success, how could he not? On the surface, he seems too obsessed, too relentless to be having fun. Yet, from experience I know the competition in trying a case acts like adrenaline, producing a high unlike anything else. "If I were as good as your father," I say, finally, "I probably would."

"He says he's going to heaven when he dies," Trey says, talking about what has to be bothering him. "Are you saved, Mr. Page?"

I look around the table, hoping to be rescued, but see I will get no help from his parents. Judging by their expressions, they are as interested in my answer as their son. I guess I don't believe in a heaven, so the theological implications behind this question hold no meaning. I want to claim this is a private matter, but children, like schizophrenics, have little trouble in crossing over boundaries that deter the rest of humanity. The silence is growing awkward, so I fill it by saying, "I've been baptized."

Like a professor who won't let a student off the hook with a general answer to a specific question, Trey asks again, "Do you accept Jesus Christ as your personal Lord and Savior?" His face is as open and friendly as if he had asked about my favorite baseball team. Yet there is a rote sound to the words, as if he has been practicing them.

Feeling trapped and resentful, I push back from the table, telling myself that it is not this child's fault. His parents should know better than to let him conduct an inquisition. If I have to endure a religious litmus test given by a child in order to work on a murder case, I'll pass. "When I was about your age, Trey," I say, trying to sound friendly, "my mother told me it was rude to ask questions about politics or religion."

Trey's face reddens, as if he is stung by my refusal to answer him, and he looks at his father for confirmation. "Nobody's trying to embarrass you, Page," Bracken says. "It's a sign Trey likes you."

This child is worried about my soul and whether his father and I (I must seem about to die to him, too, since I'm older than his father) will be friends in heaven. I have an almost overwhelming desire to lie to please this child, but I am irritated by his parents' behavior. I look at Wynona's bland face, hoping for a last-second rescue, but it isn't coming. Finally, I say, "I don't know what I accept, Trey." As brutal as it sounds, even this is a lie. I don't accept anything. And if his father weren't dying, he wouldn't be going to church either, I am tempted to tell this kid, but don't. I feel myself blushing furiously. Who am I to question the sincerity of Bracken's conversion? He obviously is already a changed man. The old Bracken wouldn't have any more let a rabbit into his garden (planted or not) than he would permit a prosecutor to badger one of his witnesses. Just because I'm incapable of change doesn't mean the rest of the world has the same problem.

"It's okay, Gideon," Bracken says, calling me by my first name for the first time. "That's what we're taught to do at Christian Life," he says, laying a napkin beside his plate. "But that question is supposed to come much later. Since my cancer was discovered, Trey understands there isn't much time."

As I sit there trying to sort through my feelings, the phrase "end times" rings in my brain. The world may be ending soon for everybody (it is for his father), and if his kid can't stop that, at least he can make sure we are ready for it. "I know it's hard to be asked that," Wynona says, her voice gentle, "but it would be confusing and dishonest to get on to him."

I push my knife around on the table. "Oh, I'm not upset." But I am. Nothing is more obnoxious than someone pushing religion on you, especially if it's an innocent kid. And with Rainey bleating on about it last night, I've had enough door-to-door salesmen to last a lifetime. The arrogance of it. Trey is watching me as if an ax murderer had declared himself. Still, I feel a grudging admiration for him. Even with your parents egging you on, it can't be easy being a little Billy Graham. My own failures with Sarah stand in stark relief. This kid is practically an evangelist; Sarah was lucky if I dropped her off at the front door of the church. It wouldn't have killed me to attend Mass more. It's not as if I were developing a cure for cancer and was just too busy to tear myself away.

Bracken begins to clear the table. "Would you like some blackberry cobbler," he asks cheerfully, "and some coffee?"

"Sure," I say. How can I be rude to someone who's dying? Wynona springs up to help him, leaving Trey and me to stare around each other. It is as if I had farted and everyone was determined to ignore it. How odd this all is, I think. After Bracken dies, what a story I will have to tell. Chet Bracken stories are legion, but nobody will be able to top this one.

Again, blushing furiously, Trey asks, "Maybe you can come to church with us this Sunday."

I look at the boy, astounded that a child so young would be this relentless. His eyes are somewhere on the middle button of my shirt. Doubtless, his parents have overheard him, but it is as if we were discussing baseball cards. Opening the refrigerator freezer, Bracken says, "Come on and go with us. It'll make your investigation go easier."

Extremely uncomfortable now, I lift the crystal water glass to my lips to give myself time to think. What can it hurt? "Actually, I've already been invited," I fudge, adding specificity to Rainey's open invitation, "by a

friend to attend your church this Sunday, so maybe I'll
see you there."

"Who?" Trey asks, a little suspiciously. This is too
easy. Yet his parents let him continue as if I were a pris-
oner of war in a country that knew nothing of the Ge-
neva Convention.

I tell them about Rainey, but, not surprisingly, in a
church with a cast of thousands, they have not heard of
her. Wynona has a way of listening sympathetically, and
I tell more about Rainey than I intended, managing only
to leave out my consternation that she has joined Christian Life. No matter. As she fills my coffee cup, she re-
marks, "You must feel she's deserting you because
she's gone so much."

"Exactly," I say, glad that someone understands. "She
might as well put her house up for sale." Wynona reminds me of someone's grandmother. I wonder how she
and Bracken hooked up. A plain Jane if there ever was
one, she wouldn't have caught Bracken's eye on a
crowded street. Since she is perhaps a decade older than
Bracken, she surely thought she had a husband for the
rest of her life. As Julia, my secretary, says, "Even if
you can find one halfway decent, he'll wear out so fast
and die you won't even remember what he looks like."

Chet, who has said little during the meal, sits back in
his chair. "There's only one cure for that. You'll have to
start going, too."

Damn. I look at Wynona, who nods. "She probably
can't tell you what it means to her. When you first start
getting to know your family, there's a kind of glow.
That's how me and Chet met. Trey and I were assigned
to be part of his family when he began coming regularly
six months ago."

My head spins to look at Chet, who gives a confirm-
ing nod and a sheepish grin. I guess I should have fig-

ured, but I'd never heard about Chet having a wife or family before. With those ears, Trey couldn't look any more like Chet if he'd had plastic surgery. "How long have you been married?" I ask, incredulous.

"Three months," he says, beaming at his bride. The kid calls him Dad, and Chet and Wynona look as if they have been married forever. Everyone seems happy. How can they stand it? The Lord's will? I suppose if you believe it's all for a purpose, you can endure anything, although I can't quite buy that.

As Wynona clears the table and does the dishes with Trey, we take our dessert and coffee and adjourn to the square, lodgelike room to sit in front of the huge fireplace and continue our discussion of the case. Chet gets a fire going easily, and yet it is obvious that he is tired and is not able to concentrate as I ask him questions about the case. Talk to Leigh tomorrow is his only advice. I drive home wondering if the only reason I was invited out to dinner was to have his kid browbeat me into going to church. Bracken is preparing for the next world; I've still got to live in this one.

As I drive I am thinking how hard it is to know another person. Chet Bracken the lawyer is one hundred and eighty degrees opposite from Chet Bracken the man. He was positively docile tonight. Was it the cancer? Clearly, he was exhausted. After dinner it was as if he were waiting for me to take charge. Perhaps that's what he really wants but is too proud to say it. Yet nobody was too proud to put me on the spot about religion. My skin crawls as I remember the kid's face. *Are you saved?* And they let him get away with it! Why am I reacting so strongly to this incident? It seems a matter of bad taste. Almost a matter of class differences.

It hits me that I am reacting as my mother probably would have. Nice people don't get in your face like that. It wasn't as if she were the Queen of England, but for the first time in a long while I remember that she and my father, before he went crazy, considered themselves and their friends far above the ordinary residents of Bear Creek. Her father had been a doctor, and she saw herself as a member of the eastern Arkansas aristocracy, with its disdain for emotional outbursts and theatrics of any kind. This wasn't so bad, actually. She and her friends weren't taken in by the demagoguery of Orval Faubus, who, as governor, on the pretext of preventing violence incited the state to wage a guerrilla war against school desegregation. How much of my mother's sense of who she was would have rubbed off on me if Daddy hadn't gone nuts and become a source of embarrassment? Yet perhaps tonight I saw vestiges of her emotional fastidiousness in my reaction to Trey. I know nothing of Chet's background, but in any case, he is way beyond a feeling of distaste for what is socially and aesthetically incorrect. Death, or the fear of it, I realize, as I hit the outskirts of town, will do that to you.

4

"IT's ALL A crock," Dan Bailey says cheerfully, "and you know it."

Dan, who became my best friend almost immediately after I moved into the Layman Building nine months ago, is obese, obscene, and remarkably immature. He stands at the window of my office, dreamily staring at the women in the Adcock Building across the street. Separated from us by the width of the avenue and the illusions of youth and middle age, they deliberately tease us, coming to the window and sticking their tongues out at Dan when he won't go away. I push Leigh's file into my briefcase. "If you'd seen Bracken's face at the dinner table," I say, "you might not think so."

"Acceptance, the final stage," Dan says, literally pressing his nose against the glass as he ogles my neighbors. "More power to him. If there is a God, Bracken ought to be punished for all the murderers and dope dealers he's gotten off."

I pull a yellow pad from a drawer and shove it into the case. The valise is bulging, like Dan. His neck, crammed into a too tight shirt collar, seems about to explode. "There's an inner peace about the entire family," I say. "Even Rainey."

Dan sticks out his tongue in the direction of the Adcock Building, a sign that he's been made to under-

stand his staring is not appreciated. I come around my
desk to see what's going on. A blonde in a tight sweater
closes the blinds. I'll probably be arrested for sexual ha-
rassment, and I barely saw her. "The mountaintop experience," Dan sighs. "It never lasts. Highs never do.
Physics 101. What goes up eventually sinks like a lead
balloon. They're able to sustain it longer because of the
group. New people coming in keep the fires burning for
everybody, but eventually they will go out. We all return to our evil ways, sooner or later." Smiling happily
at the memory, Dan cackles, "You should have seen that
blonde's chest. Just before you got over here she turned
sideways to the window just so I could check her out.
Julia looks like she got a couple of marbles put in compared to her."

I stand by Dan and look down at the street. Deserted.
Everyone is inside pretending to be working. "You
don't even believe there's a God behind the Big Bang?"

Dan bumps his swollen stomach against the window
ledge. "What we don't understand we call God. That's
why you don't ever read about preachers filing for patents."

Dan's zinc gingham broadcloth shirt has a grease
stain on it. Probably from the croissant he carried into
my office. By his own admission, he drives his rich society wife crazy. According to Dan, Brenda, by her
choice of a totally unsuitable marriage partner (himself),
proves irrefutably the perverseness of the human species. Accustomed to his logic, I cross my office and flip
the light switch. Dan will stay and talk forever if I let
him. "I don't read about many lawyers filing for patents
either."

"A complete lack of imagination is our only redeeming virtue," he says, silhouetted against the window. He
is beginning to develop the profile of Alfred Hitchcock,

double chin and all. "We're totally opposed to progress, creativity, and ingenuity. Once the human vocal cord was developed, unborn lawyers everywhere rejoiced, knowing the species had no further need to evolve."

I laugh, knowing that Dan, down deep, is one of the good guys, his cynicism a defense mechanism to deal with the chaos closing in around him. A man who has put up with as many divorce cases as he has can't be all bad. Brenda complains because they call him all night and on the weekends. In the office his patience is legendary, money no object. What could be worse than the pain of divorce? he asks, when I kid him about how many women are stacked up in the waiting room. The only bad thing about women, he says, is that they persist in marrying men. Nothing is more damaging to their self-esteem. My phone buzzes, and it is Julia with a message for Dan. I listen and sigh. "She says," I say to Dan, "tell Butterball it's Mr. Tatum again. His landlord has cut off his electricity, and he's having an asthma attack."

Dan looks at me in horror. "Will you let me take it here?" he asks, reaching for the phone. "It's the second time that son of a bitch has done this. By the time I get to my office, he might have hung up. The poor guy's on SSI, and every time he gets behind on his rent, he gets his heat turned off."

"Sure," I say, handing the telephone to him. "I was just leaving." I pick up my briefcase, leaving Dan to tilt at another windmill. Arkansas has, Dan tells me, the worst landlord-tenant laws in the nation and the distinction of being the only state in the country literally to criminalize the nonpayment of rent. Charles Dickens would have loved us, Dan has said on more than one occasion after cataloging our situation. In addition to the "criminal eviction law," Blackwell County has other

delights for debtors—hot-check laws whose enforce-
ment turns our overcrowded jails into debtors' prisons,
a recent law that allows landlords to consider tenants'
property abandoned and subject to seizure after nonpayment of rent, and now we are practically the only state
that does not recognize either judicially or by statute an
implied warranty of habitability in rental property.
"Nineteenth century? Hell, we're talking feudalism,
boy!" Dan cackles woefully about once a week.

Christian Life is not a collection of buildings; it is
like one of those new towns that seems to have been
created all at once. The flowers, trees, and buildings all
look freshly put down. I pull in behind Chet's Mercedes
in front of a two-story brick house whose trim is newly
painted. Given its location (western Blackwell County,
naturally), the mortgage on this property probably ex-
ceeds the national budget of some small countries.
"Shades of Jim and Tammy Bakker," I say under my
breath, noticing the exquisitely cared for lawn of Christian Life's senior minister, Shane Norman, who presumably lives here rent free with his wife, Pearl. For all I
know, however, they own the entire property outright
and charge the congregation rent on the acres of parking
that we passed on the way in. Ironically enough, given
its self-proclaimed Biblical literalism, from the outside
the church itself looks like a Greek temple, surrounded
as it is by columns vaguely reminiscent of pictures of
the Parthenon. With all the starvation and suffering in
the world, how do churches justify their wealth? Wasn't
Jesus poor? One of the church columns alone has
enough marble in it to pay for a well in Somalia. The
Vatican could sell its art collection and probably provide housing for a small country with the proceeds.
The trouble with people who have money and power

is that you are always expected to kiss their asses if you want any of it. Obviously, it pisses me off that I have had to drive out here. What in the hell is Leigh Wallace's problem that she can't make it down to Chet's office? Talk about kissing ass. And totally unlike Chet. An old story about him is that if he doesn't like a judge, he won't even nod to him or her outside the courtroom. Shane Norman must have really done a number on him. I'm not sure why I'm feeling so superior. I'd probably be groveling too, if I were in Chet's shoes and measuring time in perhaps weeks instead of years. The plan is for him to introduce me and then say he has to go to court.

Why he thinks I'll be able to induce her to talk is beyond me, but it's his money and his case. Unlike her father, Leigh may not accept Chet's eleventh-hour conversion and therefore may not be able to bring herself to trust him as her attorney. She didn't hire him; her father did. Norman may think Chet can steamroll her through to an acquittal when all she wants to do is plead guilty and throw herself on the mercy of the court. Representing children is a tricky business. It is easy to forget who the client is if you are getting the check from the parent. At least one thing is for certain: children are the same everywhere. Leigh Wallace may not like who her father has hired as her lawyer, but it hasn't kept her from moving back in with her parents According to Chet, she moved home two days after the murder.

As I meet our client, I think to myself that there are a few women (Michelle Pfeiffer in *Frankie and Johnny* comes to mind) who always look good under any circumstances. I suspect Leigh Wallace may be one of these women. Still, she has altered her appearance from the day of her husband's death. If I correctly recall her

picture in the paper the day of her arrest, she had
shoulder-length hair, was wearing jeans and a
sweatshirt, and looked ravishing. Today her body is
concealed by a long turquoise-and-beige Mexican-
looking dress, her dark, glossy hair piled up on her head
like some diva's. She looks spectacular but seems a decade older than her twenty-three years and a hell of a
lot more sophisticated than I expected.

Chet wastes no time in making his getaway, and she
and I are left alone like a mismatched couple on a blind
date. I look around the living room and barely restrain
myself from gawking. Somehow, I had expected the
walls of the home of a fundamentalist minister to be
decorated with religious art of the Jesus-flying-off-on-a-
cloud variety. Though I am hardly a connoisseur of interior design, even I have an inkling of the quality of
the wall hangings, tapestries, sculptures, and paintings
that are on display in the living room. Most, if not all,
have something of the foreign or exotic about them. My
eyes come to rest upon an oil painting of a scene I recognize from my Peace Corps days in Colombia—a famous Spanish fort in Cartagena that is a mandatory stop
for sightseers. "Gifts to my father," my hostess says in
response to my poorly disguised amazement. "Symbols
of gratitude from his mission trips on which he takes
Christian Life families to work for the poor."

"Have you ever gone with him?" I ask, letting my
eyes move to her face, thinking they didn't come from
the poor. She is perfectly made up and exudes a fra-
grance that suggests rose petals. Is this for me or for
herself? Chet hasn't prepared me for her at all. I expected her perhaps to be subdued, but there is something standoffish in her manner. Usually, criminal
defendants want instant reassurance you can help them,
whereas Leigh Wallace seems as if she could care less.

"Every year for the past five," she says, walking ahead of me into a formal dining room, "until this one." A massive mahogany table whose wood is nearly obscured by a Spanish lace cloth dominates the room, and I find myself wanting to touch the shiny surface. It is as if she is a tour guide who is answering the same questions for the millionth time in a well-rehearsed, detached voice.

I look in vain for pictures of her father perhaps exhorting the faithful from the pulpit or mixing cement for the masses in a foreign land, but there is not even a snapshot of a family dog. "Would you care for some coffee or something to drink, Mr. Page?" she asks, stroking the lace with her fingers. Though she has on a ring, an opal, I spy no wedding band. A silver bracelet adorns her wrist. Her red fingernails are perfectly manicured. Hardly the weeds of a grieving widow and certainly not the getup I had pictured of the daughter of a Bible-toting Jesus freak. In fact, Leigh's dark, dramatic features remind me of nothing so much as those of a well-to-do, haughty Colombian beauty. Even shop girls dressed to the teeth in the larger cities on the northern coast, and the ones who could afford it decked themselves out in a way that eclipsed their paler American counterparts. Though I am not particularly thirsty or in need of further stimulation this windy March afternoon, perhaps we could use something to break the ice. "Coffee would be great," I tell her and follow her into the kitchen, which gleams with copper pots and pans hanging from the walls like foreign artifacts.

The perfect hostess, she gives me a steaming cup of dark roasted coffee and offers me a piece of German chocolate cake. Accepting both, I make myself at home at her kitchen table. Sitting across from me, sipping at a glass of water, she asks, "Are you a Christian, Mr. Page?"

I suppress a sigh, remembering my earlier thought that she might mistrust Chet because of his Johnny-come-lately attitude toward fundamentalist Christianity. Fearful that the answer to this question guards the gate to a genuine conversation about the case, I push aside my desire to question its relevance. "Does Catholicism count?" I ask lightly, hoping to avoid an inquisition.

"There are Catholics," she says, "and there are Catholics."

"That's true," I admit, surprised she would know. I suspect it is not the Pope who bothers her but the ac-commodation made by any modern-day Christian to harmonize faith and science. Ever since Galileo looked through his telescope, the battle has been joined. My latest evidence of the fight, laughably sketchy, since I don't have anything to do with the church, comes from the popular press. Shamelessly summarizing years of scholarship mainly by European Catholic Biblical scholars, an article I read some time ago in *The Atlantic* on the historical Jesus put the matter bluntly: the four gospels in the New Testament are best understood as a collection of interwoven faith documents which put a particular theological spin on early Christianity (St. John, for example, was influenced by Greek philoso-phy). As accounts of the life of Jesus, according to the article, they contain very little history.

"Either you accept the entire Bible as the written word of God or you don't," she says flatly, her eyes fierce.

I wonder if poor Chet is cutting the mustard as a con-vert. The hypocrisy of people never fails to amaze me. Now that this Miss Ice Bitch is back home, she's holier than the Pope. It hasn't been very long since she was doing some serious backsliding of her own. According to the file, she had practically dropped out of the church by the time of the murder. I swallow a mouthful of moist cake to keep from saying that I'd rather be interviewing a boa constrictor. Get a grip, I tell myself. Murderers aren't usually Miss Congeniality material. Actually, behind this frosty facade, she may be scared to death, and that accounts for her snottiness. I decide to kill her, if not with kindness, at least with my own hypocrisy. "It looks like events are conspiring," I say in my friendliest voice, "to get me to see what Christian Life is all about." Briefly, I tell her about Rainey's apparent conversion and my conversation with Chet's stepson. I conclude by saying, "I'll be there Sunday."

Leigh Wallace's face softens a bit. Stories about women and children get women and children every time. "Don't expect to get everything from the Sunday service," she warns. "The place where you change is in your family, if you choose to participate."

"That's what Rainey says," I gladly acknowledge. "Can I ask you something about it?" I ask, feeling at last that the bait is set. "What bothers me about religion is that it seems like a feast-or-famine proposition. For example, Mr. Bracken says that after you were married your participation at Christian Life dropped way off. It seems like people get excited about Christianity and then drift away from it. Is that what happened to you?"

For a moment she does not speak, as if I have asked a profound question that demands reflection. "There really is such a thing as evil in the world," she says, without smiling.

If she weren't so serious, I'd have to laugh. It's not that I disagree, but the evil I know comes in human form. Her tone makes it clear that it might not be a bad idea to check under the beds when I get home tonight.

Feeling as if I were auditioning for a part in a soap opera, I ask, "Was your husband a part of that evil?"

Perhaps realizing she has sounded a little more dramatic than the situation warrants, Leigh gets up to cut a slice of cake for herself. "Art really wasn't interested in Christian Life. He joined just to get me to marry him. I quit going regularly to please him."

I'd like some more cake, but feel I ought to wait until I'm asked. "Wasn't that a natural thing to do for a while?" I ask, sympathizing with the lust of a dead man. Who wouldn't want to skip church to stay home with a woman who looks this good?

The piece she has cut for herself hardly seems worth the trouble. She moves some crumbs around on her plate. "There is always a choice about how a person lives. I let myself be lulled into believing I could be a Christian outside my family at Christian Life."

So far I haven't learned anything I didn't already know, but at least she's talking. So long as I stay on the topic of religion, she feels safe, but sooner or later, we are going to have to begin talking about his murder. "Do you feel somehow guilty about his death?" I ask. "I mean, if he had been interested in the church, maybe this wouldn't have happened?"

For the first time, Leigh recoils as if she had been hit. Ah, guilt. What would we do without it? I have wounded her, but she won't admit it. "Art had every opportunity to stay involved," she says mechanically. "He never intended to."

Despite her tone, her face looks sad, as if she has failed someone besides herself. I feel slightly more confident now. "Who do you think could have murdered him?" I ask, relishing the last sip of coffee. I'll take more of everything if I get the chance.

Leigh folds her arms across her breasts. "I have no

idea," she says coolly. "I've already been over this with Mr. Bracken."

I don't believe her. I may be wrong, but she sounds too defensive. "Just so I'm clear," I say quickly, "my understanding is that you told the police you had been at the church all morning that day you brought a friend home for lunch and found your husband's body."

Her cake is forgotten now. Rigid in her chair, she says, "That's absolutely correct." There is not a jury in the world who would fail to read guilt into her body language.

I hurry, afraid she won't let me continue. "According to Chet," I say, making him the bad-news messenger, "there is some dispute about this."

Leaning into the table between us, she answers, "Which is easily explained. The two women whom I saw and spoke with at Christian Life that morning are in their eighties. They often get their times confused, for obvious reasons. I myself was in error when I told the police I spoke with Nancy Lyons. I probably saw her the day before."

Like a hungry dog licking his dish, I scrape at the crumbs on my plate. This is weak even if you blow off the neighbor who remembers her driving past on her way home at nine-thirty. Several members confirm seeing her again at eleven-thirty, but nobody remembers her there between nine and eleven as she says. Since it was undisputed that Wallace died about an hour before an ambulance reached him (a fact confirmed by his autopsy), the police did not suspect Leigh initially, because they thought, with good reason, she had been at the church all morning. Mrs. Sims, the old woman Leigh invited to lunch, had told the cops Leigh had been with her at the auditorium listening to a missionary. But after Leigh had become the only suspect, the old woman admitted that she had not seen her since a little before nine, when the meeting began, until it was over at eleven-thirty. The police hypothesize that Leigh set it up to look as if she had been at the church for almost three hours. "Is it possible," I ask, avoiding her eyes so as not to challenge her, "that for a perfectly good reason you wanted to play hooky and stay home with your husband that morning and just didn't think it was the cops' business that you were home instead of at the church all morning?"

She stands and takes my dish and coffee cup to the sink. I should have stayed on the subject of religion until I had gotten my fill. "I'm sorry if you think I'm not telling the truth," she says, turning on the water.

"Maybe what happened that morning," I persist, "is that your husband wanted you to stay home, and you went to the church and put in an appearance and turned around and came home and then went back to show your face, and in the interval someone your husband knew came to the house and shot him."

Leigh does not speak. She seems to be looking through me. I feel as if I were a vacuum cleaner salesman who lost his customer during the demonstration of the third attachment. Damn. It is not as if I have suggested that she went home to worship a golden calf. "I think my mother is home," my hostess announces. She races into the living room as if we were adolescents who had been surprised necking when we were supposed to be doing our homework. I stand up. Since this conversation isn't going anywhere, I might as well meet the family. As I follow Leigh into the living room, I hear a buzz of angry words. Apparently, her mother had agreed to be out of the house and has returned home sooner than expected.

As it develops, Mrs. Norman is a friendlier, more vulnerable version of her daughter. Granted, she could lose twenty pounds (I could stand to knock off about ten myself), but the beauty is still there thirty years later in her face even if concealed a bit by the beginnings of an extra chin. "I'm Pearl Norman," she gushes. "So glad to meet you, Mr. Page. I hope you can help us."

I take her moist hand, feeling there is something deeply familiar about this woman. "I would very much like to," I say, glancing at Leigh, whose expression seems to evidence a slight distaste for her mother's effusiveness.

"This has been the most horrible six months in our lives!" Mrs. Norman wails. "Why, Leigh's never harmed a fly!"

"Mother," Leigh mutters, loud enough to be heard, "how do you know?"

Mrs. Norman, whose bulk is well packaged (I imagine an old-fashioned girdle squeezing and firming her soft flesh), positively gasps at such impudence, as tears form in her heavily made-up eyes. "You're our daughter, that's how!"

Embarrassed for her mother, Leigh laughs, but the sound coming from her mouth is sour and derisive, as if maybe her mother doesn't know her very well. Though I haven't yet met Shane Norman, I surmise that Leigh must be her father's daughter in temperament. Pearl Norman reminds me of a woman of an increasingly bygone era—the ineffectual, weak Southern belle who flutters her hands helplessly and expects a man to save the day. She is a bit of an actress but such a familiar one from my past that I feel right at home with her. She is also drunk, unless I am totally misreading the signs. Like any small community, my hometown of Bear Creek had its share of alcoholics, male and female, who went through most days pleasantly (or not so pleas-

antly) sloshed. She is not offensive; in fact, she is much
more pleasant than her daughter, who is plainly dis-
tressed at her mother's condition.

Leigh forces a smile. "I'll call you later in the week,
and we'll set another time."

I'm being needlessly run off. Pearl Norman would
stuff a bale of cotton in her ears if I asked her to.
"When does your father get back in town?" I ask,
standing at the door like a suitor who doesn't want to
leave. Maybe the old man can shed some light on his
daughter. According to Bracken, I won't understand
Leigh until I talk to him, anyway.

Halfway across the room, where she is lurking as if
she knows she will draw a reprimand if she comes too
close, Mrs. Norman pipes up, "My husband gets in day
after tomorrow."

"Where is he?" I ask her, unwilling to trust her
daughter even for a single fact.

"Peru," Mrs. Norman calls, edging closer despite the
dark looks coming from her daughter. "He and about
forty members of Christian Life have been there for a
week assembling a prefabricated health clinic."

At the mention of Latin America's most troubled
country, I feel a grudging respect for the first time for
Shane Norman. With the Maoist Shining Path revolutionaries assassinating thousands of Peruvians, I think
I'd send a CARE package instead. My own days in the
Peace Corps in Colombia convinced me that politics in
South America is truly a life-and-death matter. "Would
you ask him to call me?" I say to Mrs. Norman, who
has begun to remind me of the actress who played Aunt
Bee on the old Andy Griffith show. Her voice is all
quivery and anxious but full of goodwill and probably
gin. No mother and daughter could be less alike. What
I had interpreted as resigned hopelessness seems almost

like hostility in light of Leigh's attitude around her mother.

"Certainly," she says, gratefully coming to the door like a forlorn puppy being punished for shitting on the rug.

Leigh all but rolls her eyes back in her head. "Daddy doesn't know anything, Mother," she says. "Mr. Bracken has talked to him half a dozen times already. You know how busy he is right after he gets back from a mission."

Now that she is standing next to me, Mrs. Norman's perfume, suggestive of lilacs, overpowers the molecules between us. "This is your life at stake!" she says, her voice trembling at the indignity of her daughter's apparent indifference. "Of course he'll call you. He'll be back to preach this Sunday, and I'll make sure he calls you Monday. I'd like to talk to you, too."

Grateful for any cooperation in this case, I smile at Mrs. Norman. Drunk or not, she is the kind of mother who would stick pins in a voodoo doll if she were asked. To her, Christianity, as it surely is to many of its adherents, may be like medicine. If it doesn't cure, I doubt if she would be averse to trying another prescription, preferably one with a little alcohol in it. A practical people, most Americans demand results from their dogma. I drive back downtown, wishing I were defending the mother instead of the daughter.

5

"ARE YOU WASHED in the blood of the La-mb?" I wail in front of the mirror in the living room. I am standing alongside Sarah, knotting my tie as she applies her lipstick.

"Don't make fun," she says crossly, her lips flat against her teeth. "It's probably a lot more interesting than Mass."

Either my shirt is shrinking, or my neck is growing. I tighten the noose around my neck, dismayed by the turkey wattle I have created above my collar. The worry lines in my forehead, I tell myself, are a sign of character; my neck, increasingly a road map of cross-stitches to nowhere, is devoid of such nobility. I need to break down and buy some new shirts before I strangle myself. I probably deprive myself of ten I.Q. points every time I fasten the top button. "I'm just reciting from 'General William Booth Enters into Heaven.' I can't shake the feeling we're going to an old-fashioned revival meeting."

Sarah frowns, uncertain whether I am serious. When I came home for the summer after my freshman year at Subiaco, a Catholic boarding school in northwestern Arkansas, my older sister, Marty, went around the house reciting Vachel Lindsay's poetry until I learned it myself. Sarah probably thinks Vachel Lindsay is a rock group. Odd bits of my memory surface from time to time like debris washed onto a largely barren reef. Sarah pats her hair. "Let's go. I don't want to be late."

I goose-step out the door, leaving Woogie to wonder what is going on. I'm not supposed to be leaving the house on a Sunday morning unless it is with a tennis racket in my hand. "With a cast in the thousands," I say, gulping in the perfect spring day, "I doubt if they'll stop the service and hoot at us."

Heading for the driver's side, Sarah explains, "I don't want to have to sit in the front row."

Inside the Blazer, I hand her the keys. "Me neither. They'll probably be able to tell we're Catholics and make us stand up and denounce the Pope." Sarah must feel some guilt or maybe is nervous. Do they wave their arms and speak in tongues? Full immersion for baptisms? We have been remarkably sheltered from the peculiarities of other faiths. I feel a little nervous myself.

Rainey is not reassuring when we pick her up. "Wait and see," she says, grinning, when I ask her what to expect. She looks great in a peach sweater over a blue skirt, pearls, and heels, dressed up in a way I don't usually see. "They have these giant spotlights in the ceiling that crisscross the congregation looking for people who've been identified as sinners. I've told 'em your dad's coming," she tells Sarah.

Sarah doesn't believe this, but asks, turning up Darnell Road, "Do they really know we're coming?"

Rainey leans forward from the backseat and places her hand on my shoulder. "No," she says and gives Sarah a reassuring smile she does not see. "Not really." By my willingness to attend, I have earned some points. She and Sarah know I am more curious about Shane Norman than his message, but women have been trying to reform men so long it is almost a genetically programmed response.

"I met Pearl Norman the other afternoon," I say to Rainey, risking her newly reacquired goodwill, "and if I'd struck a match, we wouldn't be worrying about a trial. Does she have a reputation for getting snockered, or is this a recent phenomenon?"

Sarah groans (here I go again), but Rainey reluctantly admits, "I hear it's a problem that's persisted for most of the marriage."

I wince, feeling a degree of sympathy. I might get drunk too if I had married a saint and my daughter was about to be tried for murder. "That's tough," I say sincerely. "She seems like a very warm person." Unlike her daughter, I don't add.

"She's warm all right," Rainey says, her voice cold with disapproval. "I've been told she gets out of control on occasion."

Out of control enough to waste her son-in-law? I doubt it. Damn, women can be tough on each other. For a social worker, Rainey isn't showing much empathy. Pearl isn't pulling her weight on the road to the kingdom, so a pox on her. Chet didn't mention Pearl Norman. Nor has Rainey. The party faithful always want to hide their warts. "How'd she handle her daughter's murder charge?" I ask, knowing Sarah will revolt if I keep pumping Rainey too much longer.

My girlfriend shrugs. "About like you'd expect. Poor Shane has a lot on his shoulders."

I square my shoulders to the seat, so my daughter won't explode at me. Shane, you saint, you!

To give the man his due, Norman does not disappoint. For all our fears, the service is hardly exotic, though a little unusual for a Catholic fed a more formal diet. Sarah is instantly captivated by the music and amazes me by singing out from the printed songsheets as if she were Amy Grant. An electric guitar, drums, and a trumpet accompany the songs, which are uptempo with soaring melodies that even I can follow. There are, of course, no hymnals, no official dogma to choke down. The words (on the order of "You Light Up My Life") don't matter as much to the two song leaders, a boy and girl barely older than Sarah, as the enthusiasm with which the audience sings them. The first fifteen minutes of the service are given over to this couple, who seem right out of the cast of "Up with People," which performs occasionally in Blackwell County.

Seated in comfortable theater seats toward the back, we are too far away to see faces (I wish I had brought my binoculars, but I didn't have the guts—at this point it feels a lot like a concert). The mood of those around us is happy, even joyful. The men in our section are wearing suits or sports jackets and the women suits or dresses (we are, after all, in affluent west Blackwell County), but I see a conspicuous absence of furs and lavish jewelry. The rare times I've been in an established Protestant church in Blackwell County, many of the women looked as if they were auditioning for a fashion show.

Though at this distance I can't tell if Shane Norman has contributed to his daughter's spectacular looks, the man impresses me with his apparent humility. I had expected him to come strutting out like some superstar. Instead, he is restrained, even perhaps a trifle shy, as he stands with his head bowed while the youth minister, a kid in his twenties, prays and then reads from the Old Testament. Dressed in a dark business suit, Norman comes forward and reads the familiar text from St. Paul's letter to the church at Corinth. " 'Though I speak with the tongues of Angels ...' "

There is none of the pleading, almost whining, tone of the TV evangelist in Norman's voice, which has a tenor's pitch. It is pleasant, sincere, and without the heavy-handedness I feared. Rainey, to my left, whispers, "Don't expect a stirring sermon. That's not what this is about."

Indeed, it's not. Norman gives us a brief account of his just completed mission trip and impresses me by how much credit he gives to the crew of Peruvian workers that assisted them. "They worked themselves silly, a lot harder than we did. . . ."

The formal sermon, taken from the Scripture, is on the power of love. It is the love of God, Norman asserts, that makes faith possible. "We Christians have difficulty believing the Bible is the word of God," he says gravely, standing beside the pulpit, "because we haven't grasped God's commitment to us. We don't feel it; we're scared to death of it. We want to live free of God's love as if it doesn't exist, because we don't want the intensity and the personal challenge of a relationship with God. We want to live floating on the surface of life, avoiding risk and pain. But it is God's love that makes all things possible. . . ."

I cut my eyes to the right and see that Sarah is so focused on Norman's words it's as if he and she were the only ones in the building. Ever since Sarah began to write me letters from the campus of Hendrix College where she attended a summer program for gifted and talented high school students, I have begun to notice an intense desire for some kind of spiritual bond. The Roman Catholic church may have just lost a member, I think, as she twists at a lock of her hair, a characteristic sign of anxiety. What will I do if she joins? Norman's words, which have an appeal even to a hard-bitten agnostic like myself, don't make sense. If there is a God, where is the evidence that He, She, or It loves us? I know Norman's answer. It's in the Bible. Free will notwithstanding, my eyes and ears tell me a different story. So does my brain.

Norman goes on to talk about the kind of love that is supposed to exist in each "church family," and I feel a grudging interest in what he's saying. The "family" at Christian Life replicates to some degree the extended family Americans no longer enjoy. Deliberately, each family has been given older members, children, "aunts," "uncles," etc. All are taught to care about each member, and each member learns to care about the group. I can tell by her expression that Sarah is eating this up. Our two-person family must seem impoverished to her. With only a grandmother and some aunts and uncles in Barranquilla, Colombia, no brothers or sisters, and my sister, whom I rarely see, Sarah has no close relatives.

Norman asks those three families to stand up who made the trip with him to Peru. Approximately forty people stand up, including women and children. With the Shining Path on the loose, I can't imagine why they would risk sending children, but Norman anticipates my question by explaining that Christian Lifers, once they truly understand what it means to be in a Christ-centered family, no longer fear death. We, he preaches, were dead before we began to live in relationship with each other; heaven will be a community, centered around God. " 'In my father's house, there are many rooms, and I go to prepare a place for you. . . .' " Norman recites, describing heaven.

Having heard this passage repeatedly trotted out at funerals to comfort grieving family members, I concede that it is a nice touch. Norman uses it to build enthusiasm for a committed and shared lifestyle. Christian Lifers practice on earth what will be made perfect in heaven. Family transcends biology. The Apostles were Jesus' real family. . . . I turn to Rainey, who is seated on my left, and whisper, "Does he split families up?"

"Sometimes for a while," she says, her warm breath against my ear. "If it's one that's really dysfunctional, they can learn from others who are in sync."

Norman concludes by thanking the congregation for its massive and continuing support for Leigh. He reminds them of the trial date and asks for everyone's prayers. Leigh probably sits down front with her mother to keep an eye on her. I wonder if Pearl lays off the sauce on Sundays in deference to her husband. I have no hope of speaking to Leigh even if she is at this service.

Surely Chet has told Norman how uncooperative she is being. If I had to place a bet right now, Leigh shot her husband in a fight over the church, and the guilt is eating her up. She doesn't want to hurt her father's ministry, so she is claiming innocence. Unless somebody (and it doesn't look like it's going to be one of her lawyers) wakes her up, she may be facing a long stretch in Pine Bluff. If she would come clean, I have no doubt that considering how much Jill Marymount, the prosecutor, fears Chet, we could whittle this down to manslaughter in a plea bargain and get her back on the street in less than three years. As it stands right now, Leigh's clinging to an obviously false story is ridiculous. I can't imagine that Chet hasn't had a come-to-Jesus meeting with her, and she is too smart not to get the point. Something weird is going on, but I'll be damned if I can figure it out.

After a few announcements, the collection plates appear. (Dan Bailey said that the only good thing about weddings and funerals is that they don't put the bite on you.) This church doesn't need my money, but with

Rainey and Sarah flanking each side, I feel pressure to give something, and drop in a five-dollar bill. Rainey tears off a check, but I can't see the amount. Looking around the vast structure I marvel at the number crammed in here and don't see an empty seat. I wonder where Chet and his family are sitting. Probably in the front row. There had been a service at eight-thirty as well, which Rainey said was also full. They are considering adding a third Sunday service. Rainey whispers, "You didn't have to give anything."

"It won't break me," I mumble against her ear. The music alone was worth five bucks. While ushers move the plates from row to row, a woman with hair down to her butt sings a couple of solos. She is accompanied by a guy on acoustic guitar and is dynamite.

Sarah, who has been motionless throughout, punches me with her elbow and says softly, "Isn't she incredible?" I nod, as usual amazed at the level of talent in Blackwell County. We've got musicians who could make it anywhere.

After another prayer, Norman asks that anyone who feels moved to profess that Jesus Christ is his or her personal Lord and Savior should come forward at this time. As the band plays "Amazing Grace," I feel myself tensing up. If Sarah wants to go, I can't very well drag her out of the place kicking and screaming. She watches closely as a couple of women in their twenties walk quickly down the aisle. The song played on guitar is electrifying. Maybe it is the atmosphere, but this version is even more moving than the one sung years ago by Judy Collins. The emotion in the place is overwhelming as she warbles, " '. . . that saved a wretch,' " and then when notes go up high during " 'like me,' " a chill runs down my spine. With tears streaming down her cheeks, Sarah turns and says, "I have to go, Daddy."

For an undeniable instant I am tempted to get up with her, but I know I won't. "Don't you want to think about it?" I say more loudly than I intend, but she shakes her head and pushes up from her seat.

Rainey grabs my hand and squeezes it. "She'll be okay."

I watch forlornly as Sarah walks quickly down to the front. I don't doubt the sincerity of her feelings, but this is so obviously simply naked emotion. Damn these people! They're slick as politicians. If you're psychologically vulnerable at all, they suck you right in. This is like some boy trying to get in her pants. Come on, baby, I love you, and it'll feel so good if you'll just come on down. Hell, I know she's searching for something. You're supposed to be, if you're her age and not brain dead. But this is the kind of act she'll regret sooner or later when she wakes up and realizes what happened. Yet who am I to say? My life since Rosa died hasn't been such a success. What answers have I given her?

She doesn't need a Ph.D. in psychology to figure out that this country's culture is long on form and short on substance. An attention span of thirty minutes is more than enough to get you by. If you're lucky, you can make a nice living and worship the free enterprise system, but Sarah better not get too excited about it because it'll make her sick at her stomach when she really sees how much humanity has fallen between the cracks. The truth is, I haven't got anything to offer her but my own anxieties. Death and taxes, you can count on them, Sarah. Wow, Dad, did you make that up? My love for Sarah will be worth at least a couple of lines on a Hallmark card at Christmas when she's grown up and got a family of her own but is pretty cold comfort right now to a seventeen-year-old girl who admits to lying awake at three o'clock in the morning wondering why she's alive and her mother is dead. Down front there must be twenty-five men, women, and children. Norman says a prayer, and asks them to remain after the service for a while.

"If you want to go on home," Rainey says kindly, "I'll wait for her and get us a ride."

"What is he going to do?" I ask, feeling more morose by the moment. We are on our feet for the last song. "She'll probably come home with a cross branded on her forehead," I say pathetically.

Rainey giggles at such nonsense. "He'll ask if they want to begin participating in a family that meets here a couple of times a week. If she does, one of his assistants will take some information from her, and they'll match her up by Monday and give her a call."

I strain to catch a glimpse of Sarah, who has been moved off to the side with the rest of the group. They'll probably want her to turn over her paycheck from her part-time job. "Maybe I should wait, too. I need to introduce myself to Norman, anyway."

As Norman gives the benediction, Rainey shakes her head. "I wouldn't try to approach him now. Call him tomorrow."

Why? I wonder. It seems to me he would be more accessible in the afterglow of bagging converts, especially the child of one of his daughter's lawyers. Still, Rainey has a better feel than I do for the way business is done around here, so I nod, glumly resigned to seeing Sarah only a couple of more times the rest of her life. I stare down the aisle again trying to find her, but with the service over, my view is blocked by the hundreds of people heading for the exits.

"Gideon!"

In the parking lot I look up and squint in the direction

of the bright noon sun. I can't believe it. "What are you doing here, Amy?" I ask, dumbfounded.

"What are you doing here?" Amy Gilchrist asks, a smirk on her elfin face. Amy is an old friend from law school who made it into the prosecutor's office and was on her way to trying major cases when she became pregnant and had an abortion, incurring the disfavor of her boss. She is now in private practice with a group of lawyers almost as motley as our crew in the Layman Building. Lively, sarcastic, and humorous, Amy is scrapping for clients as hard as I am.

"God only knows," I say, surveying Amy's figure. "I'm really just visiting because a friend invited me." I am embarrassed to admit I came with Rainey and that my daughter is still inside getting hotboxed by the head cheese. Amy seems always on the verge of carrying too much weight for her compact frame. Still, perhaps because she is so likable, the total effect is pleasing to the eyes. Dressed in a knee-length black-and-white-checked skirt and a long-sleeved white blouse, she seems more chaste and modest than usual.

"Being seen at Christian Life isn't an indictable offense," she says, giving me a frank once-over, too. "As you can see, some of the best people in town are members."

From time to time, I had thought about violating my self-imposed pledge not to date women so much younger than myself and asking Amy out. I can't imagine it now. Why is she coming out here? Yet why shouldn't she be? It hasn't been that long since she admitted to me she'd had an abortion in the last year. As traumatic as that must be, that would definitely get you to wondering if your compass was pointed toward north. "That's true," I admit.

"Don't be a stranger," she says, as I get into the

Blazer. I wave as I drive off, wondering if when I get home there will be a note from Woogie to the effect that he has run off to join a Christian dog sect.

"SARAH'S AN IMPRESSIVE young woman," Shane Norman tells me the next morning in my office. "Since so many other kids her age are concerned only with themselves and their friends, which is natural from a developmental point of view, she's quite extraordinary."

I unwrap a lemon drop and slip it into my mouth. Unlike his daughter, Norman is sparing no effort to cooperate in Leigh's defense. Having called Chet at home last night, who told him to talk with me as soon as possible, he was waiting for me when I got to work. His wife is a no-show. Still on the booze, I guess. "She's been searching pretty hard for most of the last year," I say cautiously, not wanting to offend Norman. I was relieved to find out when Sarah came home yesterday that Norman had not put the hard sell on her. After learning she was Catholic, he responded by telling her that as much as Christian Life would be delighted to have her, she needed to think a little bit more about whether she was truly ready to leave her Roman Catholic faith.

"Most kids, not all, don't feel a spiritual need at that age," Norman says, as if he were talking to a colleague. "When you find one like Sarah, every word becomes important. They take you so seriously that you feel under the gun to find just the right tone with them."

Disarmed by his apparent genuine humility, I say,

"You should try being her father. She's pretty sensitive these days. Everything I say or do goes under a microscope."

Norman, now that I see him at a distance of less than fifty yards, is attractive in a craggy sort of way. His jaw juts out sharply, and his cheekbones are prominent under a high forehead that is crowned by a widow's peak of brown hair. He doesn't look a thing like Leigh except in his dark eyes. "We forget sometimes," he gently reminds me, "that kids that age are just as hard on themselves."

I wait for the inevitable "Do you accept Jesus Christ as your Lord and Savior?" but decide I won't get it from this guy. Dressed in a blue business suit and fancy silk tie, he could pass for a bond lawyer. I have to give the man credit. He seems genuinely interested in Sarah's welfare at a difficult time in his own life. I realize I have been feeling like an errant member of his congregation, when, in fact, he needs much more help with his own daughter than I do with mine. I say, "I'm sure Chet and Leigh both told you I visited with her last week. Frankly, I haven't learned a whole lot, since Leigh didn't have much to say."

Norman rubs his mouth with his right hand as if his lips are burning. Shaking his head, he says, "Surely, if Leigh is involved, it had to be self-defense. Her husband wasn't at all what he seemed."

The lemony taste of the candy is irresistible, and I crunch into it. My teeth are congenitally bad, so I might as well finish them off. It dawns on me that Norman is assuming that Leigh is lying. He thinks she did it. I am amazed that he could think his own daughter capable of murder, but why not? He raised her. "Leigh admitted the only reason Art joined Christian Life was so he could marry her."

Norman, who only moments before seemed so benevolent, says angrily, "Leigh hardly participated in anything at church after they married. He couldn't have been any more effective in separating her from Christian Life if he had been the Devil himself."

I take another lemon drop from my drawer and begin to unwrap it. The little pleasures are as addictive as the large ones. From the frown on Norman's face, I have no doubt that he believes in a literal Devil and an all-consuming hell. "But she says she was at Christian Life at the time of the murder."

Norman shakes his head. "Nobody yet can back up her story."

I watch Norman's face as he fights for control of his emotions. I wish Leigh had showed herself capable of having them. I say what I'm thinking. "You're convinced Leigh shot him, aren't you?"

Norman stands up from his chair and goes over to the window. "I know she's lying because I called her at her house that morning about ten. Art answered the phone and said she was at the church, but I heard her voice in the background."

I suck on the lemon drop in my mouth while Norman gazes out the window. I wonder if he, like Dan, is mentally undressing the women in the Adcock Building. Surely not. Chet hadn't told me Norman called Leigh. I wonder if he even knew. "Tell me what you know about Wallace," I encourage him. "He sounds like he got his hooks pretty good into Leigh."

Norman turns from the window and comes back to his seat. "If you had known my daughter before she met Art, you would understand how different she is."

For the next fifteen minutes he paints a picture of Leigh that is very sympathetic to somebody who thinks his own daughter is wonderful. From almost the moment Leigh was born, she was a "daddy's girl." After two girls (Alicia and Mary Patricia, now married and living out of state), Pearl was hoping for a boy, and, in truth, so was he; but when Leigh was born, he somehow bonded with her in a way he hadn't with his two older daughters. Maybe it was because Pearl paid her less attention, or that Leigh was more an extrovert like him, but whatever the reason, his youngest daughter took to Christian Life like nobody else. "Preachers' kids can be a pain in the ass. . . ." (the word "ass" sounds queer coming from Norman), and Alicia and Mary Patricia rebelled in many little ways, but Leigh never did. As far as he knew, Alicia doesn't attend any church, and Mary Patricia, he says, his face clouded with disapproval, has become a Unitarian or something absurd like that. Until she married Wallace, Leigh was a delight. Every spare minute was spent at Christian Life. She had been to Thailand, Mexico, Haiti, Taiwan, and El Salvador with him and loved every minute of it. "I tried to make her feel guilty about how she separated herself from us," he says without apology, "but nothing worked. She was obsessed with him."

It occurs to me that Norman's parenting techniques are more sophisticated than my own. The difference is that he thinks he is entirely correct. Sarah accuses me of manipulating her if I even look at her hard. "How did she meet Wallace?" I ask, watching the time. Knowing how much I like to talk about Sarah, I try to move him along. We could be here all morning and never get her out of college. It is easy for me to identify with Norman. He worries as much as I do. I probably bore people talking about Sarah. Strip away the religious gloss, and he and I have a lot in common.

At the mention of his dead son-in-law's name, Norman frowns. "I sent Leigh to Harding to keep her away from men like Art, and he found her anyway."

I nod, resisting my desire for a third lemon drop. "How?" I ask, curious. Located in a small town north of Blackwell County, Harding is a strict Church of Christ school with as many rules as the game of bridge.

Norman sighs and crosses his legs. "Art was originally from Crossett. He had been invited by a friend who taught in the business school to deliver a couple of lectures on opportunities in international business and saw Leigh in the student center. He didn't stop pursuing her until they were married a year after she graduated, and, believe me, that took some doing. The man quit a successful career with Chase Manhattan Bank in New York and started his own business down here."

I lean back in my chair, intrigued by this story. Crossett, a mill town in southern Arkansas that owes its soul to the Georgia Pacific company, is a long way from the Big Cave. "I take it Art began coming to Christian Life."

"Religiously," Norman says, without a trace of irony. "I had gotten Leigh a job with the church after her graduation, and he joined as soon as he moved back to Arkansas. What a con artist! Within a month after the wedding, he had stopped all but minimal Sunday attendance, and within three months so had Leigh."

There is a mixture of anger and sadness in Norman's voice as it trails off. "Art fooled me as badly as he did Leigh. The only problem I had with him was the age difference, and it didn't bother me the way it bothered her mother. The man could charm the pants off a snake though, and I was convinced he was sincere. If he hadn't been killed, I think he would have had Leigh moved to New York inside another six months."

I rub my tongue over my sugar-coated teeth, marveling at Wallace's persistence. When he was killed, they hadn't been married quite a year. "Do you know of any enemies," I ask, realizing for the first time I'm talking to one, "that Wallace could have had?"

Norman gives me a bleak smile. "Other than myself, you mean?" He laughs, but the sound coming from his throat is not a merry one. "He could have had a million. Who knows? He could have been running drugs into the country with all the overseas contacts he had."

I smile to take the sting out of my words. "So could you." I sit up straight in my chair and feel my back protest. How do people stand surgery on their spines? It hurts mine just to sit erect. "My point is," I say quickly, "we've got to come up with something specific if Leigh's to have a chance. Self-defense would be okay, but there was no sign of a struggle, and besides, she already gave the cops and everyone else a different story. I suspect you probably made some calls about Art before he married your daughter. What did people say about him?"

Norman licks his lips. He has refused my offer of coffee or a soft drink, so if he wants something, he'll have to ask. "That he was ethical, smart, a whiz at numbers," Norman admits. "I was told by one guy Art Wallace had a great future at Chase."

I pull our investigator's report from its envelope. Wallace was a real chamber of commerce poster boy. Sure, he made bad loans, but back then Chase was practically begging the Third World to take their money. At any rate, there is no evidence that some foreign operative tracked him to Blackwell County and snuffed him because at some point Chase wanted its money back. My recollection is they finally said to hell with it and wrote off billions. "Do the police know you called Leigh around ten that morning?" I ask, trying to keep

my voice light. Talk about the proverbial nail in your
coffin. "You said you heard her in the background. Was
she crying, laughing, or what? Maybe it wasn't Leigh."

Norman seems to be staring at my diplomas as he
considers my questions. I feel self-conscious, since I
have been out of law school less than five years.
Bracken must have hyped me. Finally, he says, "It was
Leigh. I'd know her voice anywhere. She has this giggle when she's excited . . ."

His voice dies, and I guess aloud what I've suspected.
"You think she was in bed with him?" My question
sounds crude. I know how I would feel. This guy is her
father, and a Holy Roller at that. Your child's sexuality
is taboo, but surely he has thought the same thing: that
Leigh went home to get it on and somehow things
turned bad. If this were Sarah, I wouldn't want to be
thinking about it either. Yet, the cops found nothing: no
drugs, no gun, no weirdness of any kind. Still, she could
have put anything she didn't want the cops to see in the
car and dropped it off somewhere on the way to Christian Life when she went back at eleven-thirty. If Leigh
did kill her husband, though, why was she giggling an
hour before his death? Norman must think this information will incriminate her. It might save her life.

"She obviously was close by," Norman says finally.
"It was the kind of laugh she had when she was caught
being bad as a child. I've confronted her, but she denies
she was there. It's ridiculous for her to say that!" He
adds, "I haven't lied to the police about this. They just
didn't ask the right question."

I have a mental picture of Leigh, and it is a hot one.
She and Art making it to beat the band, when the old
man calls. She might have been blowing him while he
was talking to her father, and this prompted the hysteria. (My mind goes back to phone calls Rosa and I re-

ceived when we were having sex. Coitus interruptus we called it. Hi, what's going on? My husband is eating me, but aside from that, nothing much.) Poor Shane. He can't even pretend his daughter isn't lying. Would I lie to protect Sarah from a murder charge? Surely so. But Bracken says Norman doesn't do things that way. "Why were you calling her?" I ask, trying to shake the idea of Leigh's naked body from my mind.

Norman's face flushes. "I was checking up on her. She had promised to come hear the missionary from Guatemala we had been supporting, and I didn't see her Acura in its usual parking place when I was coming from one of our morning Bible study classes, so, damn it, I called her."

I lean back in my chair and study the lock on the main drawer in my desk. Norman is obviously embarrassed he is having to acknowledge he harassed his daughter, and I give him a moment to compose himself. I can imagine myself doing the same thing. It must have been maddening to watch her slip away from him. "What did you say to him after you heard Leigh's voice?"

Norman sighs and ducks his head like a ten-year-old. "I called him a son of a bitch. He just laughed and hung up."

Norman is such an obvious murder suspect I want to laugh out loud. Why didn't Chet clue me in? Norman must have an ironclad alibi. Surely Chet has checked it out. I push my drawer in and out. It catches on all the junk I have crammed into it. "What could have happened afterward," I propose, "is that Leigh felt guilty and they had an argument, and he made fun of you and Christian Life, and she shot him. Is that possible?"

Norman shifts uneasily in the chair as if his bladder

is sending him signals of distress. He swallows with some difficulty. "It's possible," he agrees.

"Have you told Chet this?" I ask, knowing he hasn't. Damn clients. They hire you to help them and then never tell you the truth.

Norman wags his head. "I kept hoping someone would verify her story, and either Chet hasn't been around much or I haven't been around."

Weak but understandable. With this information, Norman thinks he has been holding the key to the prison door. Now that time is running out, he is finally spilling his guts. But why tell me instead of Chet? I wonder if he is beginning to lose confidence in Chet. I am. Pissed, I lecture him, "There's no way we can help you and Leigh if you don't tell us the whole story, no matter how bad it makes either of you look. Do you understand that?"

Norman gives me a sickly smile. He is not used to being talked to like this, but he takes it. "Of course you're right," he says, clearing his throat. "Tell me something. Is Chet all right? He said he's in remission, but he looks bad to me."

I have just preached a sermon on honesty, but it doesn't work both ways. "I guess he's okay," I say breezily. "He hasn't complained to me."

Norman looks behind me at my diplomas. "He says you're really good."

I shrug, but inwardly I am ridiculously pleased. Bracken's good opinion is worth a lot. Yet he couldn't very well say that he had hired a guy who, outside of a couple of cases, hadn't particularly distinguished himself. Also, I doubt if he told Norman I was at least his third choice. There is some dishonesty here, but this is no time for true confessions. "We're only as good as our last case," I say, trying to seem modest. Actually, I don't believe this. If you only take the easy ones, your "won and lost" record is meaningless. At the Public Defender's we measured our success by how much time our clients actually did in comparison with what they could have pulled when they were originally charged. Only if you are a Chet Bracken does it make sense to look at your record of outright acquittals or dismissals. The problem with this case is that the Chet Bracken of six months ago doesn't exist any longer. How could Chet not have gotten from Norman that he called Leigh the morning of her husband's death? He must really be slipping fast. What else don't I know about this case?

We talk a few more minutes, but I do not get anything else useful. I walk Norman to the elevators, realizing he hasn't mentioned his wife even once, and head for Dan's office. Poor guy. I have to feel something for him, too. If Pearl truly has been a hooch hound their entire married life, no wonder he's been so strict with the girls. Keep 'em down on the farm as long as possible.

Dan is on the phone but hangs up as I come in. "I'm thinking of having liposuction," he says, "but it costs a fortune. I should have become a doctor. You don't really believe that crap about doctors asking their nurses to be present when they examine their female patients?"

I close his door and take a seat. Dan's office is gross. The air smells like the alley behind the Layman Building that receives the exhaust fumes from a Chinese restaurant that has just opened on the first floor. Boxes, files, law reviews, bar association magazines, books, and food compete for space in Dan's office on a no-holds-barred basis. My files are admittedly disorganized, but anything that enters Dan's office has less chance of being found than a ship sailing into the Bermuda Triangle. "You're not serious about liposuction?" I ask, somewhat alarmed. Dying is the only way Dan is going to lose weight, and even that might not do it. He's joked he wants to be buried with a box of Hostess cupcakes and a case of root beer.

"They say the pain is terrible," Dan says gloomily. "Jesus, I can't even stand to have Brenda cut my toenails."

The thought of Dan's prissy society wife agreeing to perform such a mundane task makes me smile. "Get this," I tell him. "Bracken hasn't told Norman that he's about to croak."

Dan rolls back the cuffs of his shirt two folds, revealing fat, hairy wrists. "Why the hell not?" he muses. "He's setting himself up for a malpractice claim and incompetence of counsel charges if Leigh doesn't get off."

"His estate," I remind him. "I wonder if I've got some duty to tell Norman about Bracken. The truth is, Chet hasn't done shit on this case, and Norman tells me just now that he called Leigh at home the morning of the murder and heard her voice in the background. The cops don't know this yet, but it's just one more thing that can cook Leigh's goose. Chet didn't know either."

Dan reaches in his desk and pulls out a Snickers. It is not even ten yet. He offers it to me, but I shake my head. As he peels off the paper, he says, "If I were you, I'd have a heart-to-heart with Bracken. If this case is headed for the toilet, you're the one who's gonna be flushed."

I begin to wonder if I have made a serious mistake in agreeing to second chair this case. A neon sign inside my head is blinking the word "sucker." This was to be my ticket to the big leagues. The way it is shaping up it looks like a bush-league game for last place. I fight back a momentary wave of panic. As Dan ingests the chocolate in two bites, I am reminded of the night he called from the jail to tell me he was arrested at a convenience store for stealing a Twinkie. Some people can't tell the truth even if you hand them a script. Dan, for all his faults, can't tell a lie. "On top of everything else, Norman admits he can't find a thing on Wallace either," I complain. "Other than stealing Norman's daughter under false pretenses, Art was a model citizen. Even Norman admits nobody had a motive to snuff him except himself. Of course, he was smiling when he said this."

Dan wipes brown goo from the corners of his mouth with a dirty handkerchief. With all his practice, I think he'd learn to hit the target. "You check out his alibi?"

I shrug. How can Brenda stand to make love to him? She is no Barbie but hardly a Petunia Pig either. "He says he called from the church."

Dan finds a corner of his handkerchief to blow his nose. "That one didn't wash for Leigh," he points out. "Who all saw him that morning? You just said he hated Wallace's guts."

If I had been in his position, I would have hated my son-in-law's guts, too, but I doubt I would have killed him. Norman isn't a real suspect, as far as I'm concerned. He has far too much to lose. Even assuming he lost his temper big time, the image he has of himself wouldn't allow him to shoot the man his daughter loved. As different as Norman and I are, I think I understand the guy. If Sarah marries a rich creep, I'll get her the best divorce lawyer his money can buy. Sooner or later, despite the woman-obey-your-husband garbage fundamentalists love, Norman, I'm convinced, would have come around to trying to talk Leigh into a divorce.

I reach behind me and open a window to let in some air. Dan has a great view of the Arkansas River. He tells me he will switch offices any time I want. He'd rather have my view any day. "Come on, Dan," I say mildly, "get real. Norman's a lover, not a fighter."

Dan reaches into his desk again but only to pull out a paper clip. He straightens it and begins to pick his teeth. "How else was he gonna get his kid back? To Norman, Wallace was the Devil incarnate. What could damn a person more in a preacher's eyes than a man who uses God for his own ends, especially if it involves the person he loves best?"

Dan is forgetting that preachers are supposed to hate the sin but love the sinner, and that usually precludes murdering him. I breathe deeply. There is a slight odor of mildew in the room. Some of these boxes have probably been sitting here for years. I indulge Dan, knowing he has to get this crap out of his system or he will never shut up. I point out, "But Norman wouldn't set up Leigh to take the rap."

Dan, loving the role of the great hypothesizer, says, "Norman wasn't setting her up. He calls her at home, makes her feel guilty. She goes back to the church, and he slips out and goes to their house and offs Wallace, thinking she'll never be charged, but the cops screw it up because they can't figure out who else to nail. Norman thinks this will be a snap, but he gets the best criminal defense lawyer in town anyway. What he doesn't know is the best is eaten up with cancer and can barely answer the bell."

From Dan's window I can see a barge coming into view. He's got a point. Preachers have been known to commit murder for more sordid reasons than protecting their daughters. Not too long ago I read about a minister who killed his wife to run off with another woman. Yet, Norman, like myself, I realize, would try to talk somebody to death before he would shoot him. To humor him, I say, "I'll check his alibi, but surely Chet has already done that much."

Dan runs his tongue over his teeth to get every last bit of sugar, chuckling, "But talk about biting the hand that's feeding you."

I protest, "I haven't bitten it yet." Actually, it's Bracken who is bothering me more than anything. Even if he has been sick, I can't believe he has done such a sorry job. I realize I have been intimidated by his reputation. If I'm going to keep from making a fool of myself at the trial, I'll have to stop acting like I'm the messenger boy in this case. To give Chet credit, he isn't hiding his lack of effort from me. In fact, he is practically rubbing my nose in it. Why? Can it be that he wants me to take over the role of lead counsel and can't bring himself to say so? Men are harder to read than women. In our sex, the ego is like a five-hundred-pound gorilla guarding the door to the rest of the psyche. Women are more vulnerable. "By the way, the wife's a lush. She's functional, but she keeps her tank topped during the day. She was lit the afternoon I saw Leigh, and Rainey confirmed she has a problem. Norman didn't mention it."

Dan grimaces. I have confirmed his prejudices. He says, "Of course not. These guys go halfway around the world while their families go to hell in a hand-basket."

Julia sticks her head in the door. "Can't you stay in your office thirty minutes by yourself?" she scolds me. "I thought you were having a heart attack in the crapper. Mrs. Chestnut's been waiting for ten minutes while I've been trying to find you." Julia looks at Dan and shakes her head. "That's how Elvis died, straining on the pot. That's how you fat boys check out a lot of times, you know."

Dan grits his teeth, pretending to strain. I stand up,

trying to remember Mrs. Chestnut's problem. Some kind of contract dispute. I follow Julia into the waiting room for my client. "Thanks for looking for me."

She turns and grins. "It was just an excuse to see Dan. It's like visiting a preschool every time I go back there."

Mrs. Chestnut is a sweet-looking old lady with old-fashioned puffed sleeves and a floral-patterned skirt that almost touches the floor. Jewelry and pearls give her a nice rich look. Though she was extremely vague about her problem over the phone, she expressed the hope that she wouldn't have to go to court. I hope so, too. I can't read a contract without yawning. She sits primly in my small office, and I wish, not for the first time, my furnishings were classier. Judging by her clothes and her address in western Blackwell County, I wouldn't mind probating her estate.

"An acquaintance gave me your name, Mr. Page," she says, smiling pleasantly at me. This is the kind of woman who takes a cruise every summer and whose major interest on board is the stock-market report. Money has a way of announcing itself, even to me.

"Good," I say hopefully, glad to hear my name is getting around. "What can I do for you?"

A timid smile comes to her lips. "I signed up Bernard Junior for spiritual development classes," she says, her voice delicate and shy, "and I've been extremely disappointed with the results."

Sometimes, I think I'm losing my hearing. This is one of them. What on earth? Bernard Junior must be hooked up with a correspondence course with one of those New Age groups in California. Maybe Dan can enroll, too. "Is that a grandson?" I ask.

"Absolutely not," she says, looking me in the eye, daring me to laugh. "Bernard Junior is a pit bull."

I fight to retain control of myself. This is a gag Dan and Julia are pulling. The potential for spiritual development in the humans who frequent this office is almost nil. Pit bulls may have a little better chance, but not much. Still, I can't risk not taking this woman seriously. She could be loaded. "I wasn't aware anyone in Blackwell County," I say, not believing I'm saying this with a straight face, "gave, uh, pets classes in spiritual development."

"Oh yes!" Mrs. Chestnut says firmly. "And it's not for just any animal. Canines only. And then only dogs over five pounds."

No chihuahuas need apply. She is serious. There is too much dignity in her voice, even if she is totally and certifiably mentally ill, for this to be a lie.

"Who does this?" I ask. Somehow, I don't see this presumably capitalistic endeavor as a part of corporate America. "I've seen ads for obedience school but never for spiritual development." Each time I say the words I realize I am close to hysteria. I wish I had the nerve to ask if I could record this interview so someone would believe it.

"Purely word of mouth, no advertising," Mrs. Chestnut says. Carefully groomed, with every hair in place, she is attractive for someone surely in her seventies. "Not every dog is accepted."

Woogie probably couldn't get in. He meets the weight limit, but beyond that, I doubt if there's much to work with. Undoubtedly, I'm a bad influence on him. I can't bring myself to take any notes. "Did Bernard Junior make any progress at all?"

Mrs. Chestnut shrugs dejectedly. "At first he seemed to," she says, "but after about the third week he was back to his old self, scratching and licking his privates, that sort of business." With this revelation, Mrs. Chestnut wrinkles her nose at the thought of Bernard Junior's backsliding. "It was as if he just didn't seem to think it was worth it."

I know the feeling. If virtue is its own reward, we need new door prizes. I try to sit as erect as Mrs. Chestnut, but no dice. My spine could be stretched on a rack for a week but it would still look as if I were slouching. She seems to be reluctant to tell me who fleeced her, so I ask, "Were you told what the classes consisted of, or was that a trade secret, kind of like the formula for Coca-Cola?"

"Oh dear me, no!" Mrs. Chestnut informs me, a frown of disapproval crossing her face. "We were allowed to observe the first hour. Unfortunately, Bernard Junior went to sleep during the introductory lecture, but we were told that was to be expected at first."

As if I were talking to a normal person, I hear myself sympathizing, "I've nodded off at a lecture or two myself." Unfortunately for my clients, law school was one big snooze, which, come to think of it, was full of Bernard Juniors.

Mrs. Chestnut complains, "I spent five hundred dollars; and to watch him now, you'd swear he didn't get a thing out of it. The instructor said sometimes he even kept Bernard Junior in during the exercise period, but I can't see that helped him."

Five hundred dollars! That would buy a lot of Puppy Chow. The think method. Right here in River City. "How many were in a class?" I get the feeling that Bernard Junior might have been the only one to pay tuition.

"Just five at a time," Mrs. Chestnut says. "Small classes for small minds, Mr. Von Jason said."

Not in the presence of Bernard Junior, I hope. That would crush a spirit, no matter how many classes he attended. I can't bring myself to talk about fees. "Would you like for me to make a phone call and see if I can get your money back?" I'm not putting anything down on paper. As soon as I do, it will probably start showing up on billboards all over Blackwell County as the most elaborate pre–April Fool joke ever played.

Eagerly, Mrs. Chestnut digs in her purse and hands me a business card. In script it says:

Canine Spiritual Development
By Appointment Only   Jason 683-9888

Keeping a somber expression in place (this could be me someday sitting across the desk, I have decided), I dial the number and push the button on the speaker phone so Mrs. Chestnut can hear. A male voice, cultured yet friendly, instructs that Jason is busy teaching a class but not to worry: he will call as soon as possible. I manage to leave my name and number without giggling.

"That was Jason's voice!" Mrs. Chestnut says excitedly. "He's always talking in the third person."

Why am I not surprised? "Why don't you call me tomorrow?" I say, standing to indicate the interview is over.

Mrs. Chestnut looks disappointed but asks, "How much do I owe you?"

I shake my head. "If I can get your money back with a phone call, there won't be a charge." What am I saying? I should have told her my fee was two thousand dollars just to get rid of her.

I walk her to the elevators. In the hall she says, "I know you think this is silly, but Bernard Junior is really my best friend. Nobody wants to listen to an old woman. My children are so busy, and all my friends talk about is their illnesses and their children's divorces, which seem endless, and it seemed the least I could do for Bernard Junior. After all, we send our own children to Sunday school when they're practically babies, and Bernard Junior is smarter than a lot of children his age. Would you like me to bring him next time?"

The door opens, and I say hastily, "I don't think that'll be necessary." All I need is a pit bull attacking clients. "I'll call you when I hear something."

In the reception area in front of a handful of clients waiting for other lawyers, Julia asks loudly, "What'd she want? Unlike your other clients, she seemed harmless enough."

How reassuring Julia is. You'd make an ideal prison matron, I think, but do not say. "I've got to make a phone call," I lie, fleeing to my office. "I'll tell you later."

Back in my office, I pick up Jason's card and marvel at the human animal's capacity for self-deception. Have I been kidding myself about Chet? Like more than a few successful lawyers, he has a reputation for doing whatever it takes to win a case. But maybe he is too near the end to care. Death is supposedly good for concentrating one's mind. In his case, however, it seems to be having the opposite effect. When I get him on the phone, he professes not to be surprised that Shane hasn't told him everything. "Now that we're coming down the home stretch," he says, his voice calm, even a little flat, "Shane's having to admit to himself that Leigh probably killed her husband. Memories, don't you find, always improve dramatically the last couple of weeks before a trial? He's only human. If it were my daughter, I'd forget a few things myself."

Though my own thoughts aren't radically different, I am frustrated by his failure to react more strongly to the information I've given him. "You realize, of course, that Shane had as much reason to kill Wallace as Leigh did?" I regurgitate Dan's theory without assigning him credit.

In a slightly patronizing tone, Chet responds, "So you think Pastor Norman decided on a little frontier justice after he and Art had their chat?"

Irritated by his manner but beginning to feel foolish, I push my feet against the edge of my desk and practically ram my chair through the wall. I know this theory is farfetched, but what else do we have? A jury won't acquit Leigh because she is a preacher's daughter. "All I'm doing is suggesting that you check his alibi," I say as evenly as possible. "You probably already have."

Chet answers quickly, but without any inflection, "He was at the church."

I wonder how much medication he is taking. His voice reminds me of mental patients I have represented. No affect. Maybe he is just trying to calm me down. You don't yell at an excited child to get him quiet. "I assume he can prove that," I say, knowing how strident I sound.

"Shane Norman is not a murderer," Chet replies, his voice firm for the first time. "Surely you've figured that out."

Every instinct I have about this case agrees with him, but lawyers are supposed to be more than fortune-tellers. "This isn't 'What's My Line?' " I yelp, my patience running out. "Either he's got a solid alibi or he doesn't. Let me check it out, okay? I'll . . ."

"You'll do no such thing!" Chet says, cutting me off. "You'll embarrass the hell out of me if you go charging up there. I'll look into it again."

I can't believe what I am hearing. When has Bracken ever worried about being embarrassed? One of the reasons he's been so successful is that he's never had the slightest qualms about whose cage he's had to rattle in order to defend a client. If he is worried about how Norman is going to view this, he has no business trying to represent his daughter. I feel my sense of deference drying up in a hurry. "That's fine with me, but don't you think you ought to tell Norman how sick you are?" I ask, deliberately baiting him. "I'd want to know if I were the client."

"I'm all right," he says abruptly. "Do me a favor, okay? Let's not get too carried away. Just because we don't have rabbits popping up out of a hat doesn't mean you have to feel you've got to stage a mutiny. I appreciate your enthusiasm, but you're still the understudy. If you can't live with that, I'll get somebody else."

Chastened by his tone, I back off. Both Sarah and Rainey tell me that I have a tendency to overreact. Patience, it is pointed out, isn't one of my virtues. I remind myself that Bracken knows a hell of a lot more about this business than I do. If I were handling this case by myself, with only two weeks to the trial, I'd be running around like a chicken with its head cut off. I have forgotten how cool Bracken can be under pressure. If I could shut up, I might learn something. "I'm sorry," I say, hoping I sound appropriately meek. "It's just that I kind of feel like we're out on a sailboat on a hot day waiting for a breeze, and about out of drinking water."

"Well, second-guessing me at every opportunity," Chet mutters, "isn't going to make that feeling go away."

He suggests that in the next couple of days I reinterview the witnesses who saw Leigh on the day of the murder and see if he and his investigator have missed anything, then meet him on Wednesday afternoon at the crime scene. Mollified, I hang up, wondering how close

I came to blowing it. Probably not very. Aggressiveness
is not a sin in Chet's book. At least it didn't used to be.

Though I feel more comfortable, I can't shake the
sense that something is out of kilter. Not only does
there seem to be no movement in this case, I can't see
a theory developing that will generate any forward motion down the line. I am like a seminarian who keeps
having heretical thoughts. My mind keeps drifting back
to Shane Norman. Could Chet be protecting him somehow? It makes no sense that he would, but still I wonder. I'd like to free-lance a little in this case, but I don't
dare. If Chet got even a whiff of what I was doing, I'd
be gone quicker than a wad of spit on the Fourth of
July. So what is going on with Chet? It could be that the
painkillers are slowing him down, or maybe he's so
damn preoccupied with dying that he isn't thinking
straight. For most lawyers that wouldn't be an unrea-
sonable explanation, certainly not for me. However, the
mystique of Chet Bracken is such that I expect him to
shrug off a little thing like death. Maybe I'm the one
with the problem.

As I am about to leave for the day, Julia buzzes me.
"I forgot to tell you," she says, "that Mr. Blessing
called while you were at lunch. He said to tell you he's
on the seventh floor at St. Thomas. He'll come see you
when he gets out."

Blessing? I rub my eyes and finally remember: the
guy whose hair blew off and ran down the street.
"That's the psycho ward."

"He's nutty as a fruitcake," Julia says regretfully.
"Such a good-looking guy, too. There's always something wrong with men."

"How'd he sound?"

"Crying like a baby. He said not to come by."

"Thanks, Julia," I say and hang up. Poor guy. I turn

off the light in my office, wondering if a normal person would lose it this badly because his wig blew off. I head for the elevators. Who is normal? Nobody I know.

7

MR. HECTOR TYNDALL may be in his early seventies, but I'm not sure I'd want to go one on one with him in any athletic contest. Besides having less of a gut and a firmer handshake that I do, in his den, where we are sitting, are literally dozens of athletic trophies in a number of sports dating back from over fifty years ago to almost the present: swimming, track, skiing, tennis, golf, even pistol shooting. Not a team player, this old geezer, completely bald and split-high like a center on a basketball team, has enough metal in this room to start his own mint. "I came in third in the hundred-yard dash in the whole country in my age group five years ago," he brags.

I sip at the glass of bottled water he has offered me ("The real secret to a healthy body is keeping the bowels open—I drink eight full glasses of water a day just like they tell you, and that keeps things moving on through"). After talking to church ladies all morning, I find Tyndall a breath of fresh air. Even if his story about seeing Leigh drive by in the direction of her house the morning of the murder at nine-thirty is unshakable, I'd rather waste my time with him than the two ladies who swear they didn't see or talk to Leigh between nine and eleven-thirty. I thought they were going to cry when I questioned them. Tyndall is dogmatic about what he saw, but at least he's interesting. He's a former distance man in high school, and I have to respect the guy. After a sluggish winter I can't run the length of a football field now without puffing. "I didn't know they had competition in that age bracket."

Tyndall tips back his glass. "That's what's great about this country," he says. "If you have the money to travel, you can find someone to compete against your whole life."

Not a philosophy to warm the heart, but along with his water, it obviously has kept him going. "How can you be so sure about the time Leigh drove past?" I ask, leaning back in the recliner. Along the way, Tyndall has made some money. Not only is this neighborhood rich, Tyndall's home is lovely. Though he is on the side of the street away from the view of the Arkansas River, he does have a swimming pool, and I figure his house must be in the half-million-dollar range.

"Because I jog the same time every day," he says, his pale blue eyes staring at me without hostility. Talking to lawyers isn't everybody's idea of fun. The old ladies were defensive and upset by my questioning; Tyndall seems to enjoy it. According to Chet, he is a widower; I wonder if he gets lonely. "I stretch out before and after. Once I hurt my arch and couldn't run for three months. I've stretched out ever since. Leigh and Art lived east of here a few doors down. I remember that day, because it was odd she didn't wave, and she was always friendly, even to an old fart like me. I'll be honest. A woman that good-looking you look forward to seeing even at my age. I didn't think anything of it until the cops asked if I had seen anybody drive by that morning. Since I spend my time in here or out back by the pool, I didn't see anybody but her that morning. I was in the front, cooling down from my run, and that's what I told 'em."

There is no moving this bunch. Even without her father's story, it is clear Leigh is lying her ass off by claiming that she was at the church between nine and eleven-thirty. "Did you know Art?"

"Hardly at all," Tyndall says. "He jogged some in the afternoons. I saw him in church occasionally."

"No kidding," I say, dumbfounded by the number of people who attend Christian Life. Tyndall doesn't seem the type, but then neither does Chet Bracken or Rainey. "I didn't realize you were a member."

Tyndall grins, showing a set of dingy teeth that look to be his. "They take old people."

Until recently, that's mostly who I figured went to church. I wonder if he knows any gossip, but to his credit, he discourages me by saying he really doesn't know much about anyone there except a group he sees regularly, which I take to be his "family." I thank him and leave, but not before giving him a card and asking him to call me if he happens to remember anything else about that morning. He flips it on the table beside his chair as if I were not the first person to make this request, but to get rid of me he says he will.

The only people left for me to interview are the couple next door to the Wallace house, and I park the car in front of the empty home, feeling I'm wasting my time. I'm not going to find anything new. Still, if Chet gets worse and I have to try this case, it won't have hurt me any to have talked to the witnesses.

According to the statement they gave to the police, Ann and Bobby Wheeler overheard an argument between Art and Leigh the night before Art was killed, but it doesn't seem like much to me. (My Rosa, true to her Latin temperament, could sound emotional just talking about taking out the garbage.) True, the subject matter was Shane Norman. Supposedly, they heard Leigh yell at Art as they were getting out of the car that she was "sick of him bad-mouthing her father." Art had said something unintelligible while slamming the door but ended the exchange when both looked up and saw they were being watched.

On this pleasant afternoon, I am met at the door by an attractive redhead in her early thirties wearing sandals and an aqua jumper over a flowered jersey. I have called ahead, and she invites me in as if I were a neighbor down the street instead of somebody who conceivably could be grilling her on cross-examination. Her husband, a tall, distinguished-looking man who could pose as a male model, is a little cool, but the woman offers me a drink, which I regretfully decline. We sit in their living room, which has more floor space than my entire house. I sometimes forget how much money there is in Blackwell County. People who have it don't take out ads on TV. They have talked to Chet's investigator already, and the husband especially seems to regard my visit as an unnecessary intrusion, which it probably is. "We didn't hear much," the husband volunteers. "I'm not sure it was even a fight."

This is good news, and I dutifully make some notes. Mrs. Wheeler adds, "I never heard them argue before."

These aren't the kind of people who want their names in the paper except on the society pages. Who knows what they'll say at the trial, but as long as I'm here, I might as well see what I can get out of them. I ask Ann Wheeler, "How well did you know her?"

This is the right person and question to ask. "A lot better than my husband did," Mrs. Wheeler says, daring him to shush her. "We became friends. Leigh was about as sweet as you could get. She sometimes came over for coffee in the mornings. Art would get jealous if she was gone an hour. He liked her right under his thumb."

The husband places a hand on his wife's knee as if to restrain her. I pretend not to notice. "How'd she react to it?"

Ignoring her mate, Mrs. Wheeler leans forward and says, "I think she was so used to it that it didn't bother her; apparently her father had treated her the same way. Leigh didn't have it in her to rebel like she said her sisters had. I think unconsciously she married Art hoping he'd rescue her from her father. Actually, Art probably was a lot like him. To hear her describe her father, and then listen to her talk about her marriage, Art and her father could be the same man. It was almost spooky."

Crowding her on the long couch, Mr. Wheeler whispers urgently in his wife's ear, but she shakes her head. "I've tried to talk to Leigh a half-dozen times since all this happened, but it's like she's been kidnapped. I didn't say much to the police or your investigator right afterward, because I didn't want to get involved, but this just isn't right. Leigh couldn't have killed Art. She just couldn't get that angry at anybody. There was a lot of emotion in her, but it was completely repressed. Besides, she worshiped Art like he was some kind of god. Actually, I thought he was kind of cold, and so did you," she says, turning to her husband.

Mr. Wheeler is plainly uncomfortable. He is immaculate in his chino trousers and olive blazer, and his kind doesn't become involved in a murder trial, but his wife has put him on the spot. "We had them over a couple of times, but he didn't say much. Since they never reciprocated, the friendship was between Ann and Leigh," he says, in a low voice. "Art seemed okay to me. He just kind of sat back and watched Leigh, but when he was

ready to go home, there wasn't any doubt about who
was boss."

Unlike his own home, fortunately. "Were either of
you home for any portion of the morning Art was
killed?" I ask, double-checking the police statement and
Chet's investigator's report.

Neither was, but Mrs. Wheeler isn't through. "You
ought to get in touch with at least one of her sisters. I
know her father's a famous preacher around here, but
he was obsessed with Leigh. Mary Patricia came to visit
not too long before Art was killed. Leigh brought her
over, and she gave me an earful about the father. Any
sign of independence in them he hated. Christian Life
was like a prison for them; they never got to go anywhere else. According to her, their father didn't pay any
attention to them until they were almost teenagers, but
he didn't make the same mistake with Leigh. He started
taking her everywhere with him when she was five
years old."

I sit there, watching the husband glower at his wife.
There is no stopping her. I ask, "What was Leigh's reaction to her sister telling you this?"

Ann Wheeler makes a face as if the memory pains
her. "She just laughed and said she had loved it. I truly
believe she did, but it had its price. She felt a lot of
guilt when she stopped going to church all the time.
There was a real battle going on inside her between Art
and her father, and Art was winning."

Mr. Wheeler can't stand it any longer. "You don't
know anything from anyone's point of view except
Leigh's. Most kids would love to have had a close relationship with their father. Leigh's sisters were probably
just jealous."

I look around this big house for signs of children, but
there are none. I change the subject to lower the temper-

ature. "I talked to Mr. Tyndall before coming over. Is he reliable?" I ask, hoping the wife will trash him, too.

Mrs. Wheeler nods. "According to Leigh, he practically built Christian Life when it was first beginning. In fact, he's Mary Patricia's godfather, Leigh told me, and he and Shane Norman are still close." I think of Tyndall's trophies. The guy bragged about his running, but didn't mention his connection to Shane. Why in the hell not? If anybody had a reason to lie for Leigh, that old guy would. I think of Chet's comment: "We don't do things that way." Well, maybe not, but it seems odd that he wouldn't have volunteered his connection with Christian Life. Perhaps he kept an eye on Leigh for Shane and didn't like what he was seeing. I don't know what to make of his omission. It is probably meaningless, but with Chet acting as screwy as he has been, maybe it's significant. I stare blankly at the Wheelers, realizing, not for the first time, how little confidence I have right now in the man who has hired me to help him. I can't avoid the feeling that this case is like watching a play being done in a foreign language that sounds like English but isn't quite. Until now, I've thought that if I just listened hard enough, I would be able to pick it up, but clearly, that isn't happening.

Glowering at his pert and increasingly loquacious wife, Mr. Wheeler stands up, ending the interview. He's had enough of this conversation, and I have no choice but to take my leave as gracefully as I can. I have undoubtedly ruined this evening for the Wheelers, but there's nothing to spice up a marriage like a good fight. The wife seems slightly disappointed, but I can always call back for more information when Mr. Tightass isn't around between now and the trial, if she wants to cooperate.

Outside, parked in Leigh Wallace's driveway, I find

waiting on me Chet and the cop assigned to assure minimal damage to the crime scene. I don't see what the big deal is after all these months unless the prosecutor is going to try to take the jury on a tour. Chet looks exhausted, but gives me a nod as if to say that we'll talk later about what I've learned. "Gideon, this is Officer Brownlee. He's our nanny for your tour," he adds superfluously.

I shake Brownlee's hand. All arms and legs and so young that I wonder if he has a driver's license, Brownlee grins as if being in the presence of the state's premier criminal defense attorney has been more excitement than he can stand. "Nice to meet you, sir," Brownlee says politely. The kid has a nice smile.

"My pleasure," I say, winking at Chet but meaning this pleasantry sincerely. Unlike some lawyers, I like cops, and the older I get, the more I like them. Every profession has its bad apples, but try giving lawyers a gun and a nightstick to carry around, and we would quickly acquire a worse reputation than we already have. You don't have to be a psychologist to realize that if you give people the power and opportunity to abuse others (as cops unquestionably have), some of them will inevitably oblige you. But so will a convent of nuns.

Like all the homes out here, Leigh's home is monster size. I'm glad I don't have to make the mortgage payments on an empty house, but it would give me the creeps to keep living in a place where my spouse had been murdered even if I had done it. Nice double-wide yard, I notice enviously. Woogie would be in heaven pissing on all these shrubs. However, given my live-and-let-die approach to yard work, it would surely look like a desert inside of a month if I owned it. As we enter, immediately to our right off the foyer are a living room and adjacent dining room the size of a train station. They could have hosted the Blackwell County Bar Association meeting in here. Why do people buy what they least need? Because they can, I guess. "Great party room, huh, Mr. Page?" Brownlee says, gawking at the scene before him.

I nod. The place looks like a museum. The walls are covered with exotic tapestries, paintings, and engravings, the quality of which I'm not fit to judge. We would have been happy to get an Artmobile full of this stuff where I grew up. I am in awe of the solid oak dining room table, which could seat a busful of schoolchildren, but I'm glad I wasn't part of the crew that wrestled it in here. I can feel a hernia coming on just thinking about it. Even though Chet has been here before, he remains impressed. He whistles, "We're not in Kansas anymore, Gideon." He knows as well as I that while a few eastern Arkansas farmers may have had homes this size, almost none looked like this on the inside. He leads me to a room off to the right.

"This is where he bought it," he says, pointing to a desk located next to a window looking out on the lawn and the Wheelers' house next door. I've seen the pictures. Art was seated in his chair behind the desk when he was shot. According to the autopsy report, he died instantly from a bullet through his heart. According to the report, the time of death was between ten and eleven-thirty.

I stand in the doorway waiting for some brilliant insight, but feel only a slight headache from hunger. I like the office, too. It has a fireplace, books, and photographs on the wall that Wallace must have made during his business trips. Besides imposing architecture of Third World banks, there are kids on burros, Latin American campesinos, Asian peasants. It is nice to think that Wallace got out in the countryside a bit.

There are also pictures of more than a few women. Without a doubt, Wallace had an eye for female beauty. There is one portrait of an Asian teenager that is unusually arresting. Her gentle, round face is dazzling in its luminosity. With eyes the color of washed graphite, she glows with a beauty so serene it is difficult to associate it with youth. Of all the women he encountered, how odd he found the one he wanted in a state as obscure to many Americans (until Clinton's election) as the country of Albania. It is easy to forget that Wallace was from a small town in the state almost equally as obscure to Arkansans. His pictures of Leigh are gems, her face expressive, alive, and joyous in a way I've yet to see. The portraits of her are enough like the others that I have to assume Wallace made them. If so, the proof of her love for him is staring me in the face. Her face radiates happiness.

"Even if she doesn't go to prison," Chet comments from the window where he is studying the pictures, "how does she put her life back together?"

I think of the tug of war between father and husband. Depending upon how a person looks at it, either her life is over or she's gotten a second chance. If we can somehow get her off, she may never leave her father's side again. "Maybe being married wasn't all that different," I say quietly, thinking of the comments I have heard this afternoon. Despite their best intentions, how many women, I wonder, swap one form of domination for another?

We are here to look for evidence that will help our client, but I know I am just going through the motions. If somebody other than Leigh killed Art, surely it had to be somebody he knew well enough to invite back to his office. I can't help thinking the evidence is somewhere outside the house, not in it; but that's the mind of a lawyer at work, not a forensic investigator. Yet, according to the police reports nothing has turned up in the lab—no exotic grass stains in the carpet, no unusual bullet pattern. Naturally, the absence of physical evidence will be used against Leigh.

Brownlee appears in the doorway. "Come check the view," he invites us.

Chet smiles at the cop. As a watchdog, he isn't much. "Go on," he says to me, "it's not bad."

I follow Brownlee down a hall and through French double doors onto a deck that overlooks a swimming pool and below that the Arkansas River. "Nice, huh?" Brownlee says, leaning over the railing.

Real nice. We are on the second floor, I realize. They probably ate dinner on the deck when the weather was nice. Spring is here today in all its glory. The air is soft and without the soaked-cotton-ball effect of a humid Arkansas summer. Between the pool and the water is fifty yards of no-man's-land of thick brush, containing perhaps a .22 pistol. On paper there has been a search of the area, but it looks as though Leigh would have gotten all scratched up if she had tried to hide a gun down there.

"Makes you wonder why rich people kill each other," Brownlee says, his eyes on the drained pool beneath us. "If they can't get along, why don't they just divide up the loot and move on?"

Good question. The problem is, few people really think of themselves as rich. To Brownlee and me, this looks like heaven on earth, but Wallace probably figured he was just barely ahead of the rat race. It turns out he had credit life insurance on the house, but it's hard to believe a woman would kill her husband just to avoid a mortgage payment. No other insurance policies, no significant bank accounts. Down on the river I can

barely make out a speedboat. It is growing dark, but the
urge to be outdoors is irresistible. "They don't have any
more sense than we do, just more money," I tell
Brownlee. A comforting thought, but not one I really
believe. Down deep, I've always had the feeling they
know something I don't.

I go back into the house and find Chet sitting in the
kitchen with his head between his knees. Damn. I
wanted to tell him what I learned from the neighbors,
but it will have to wait. "Are you okay?" I ask, glancing
behind me to see if Brownlee is coming. This would be
a hot story for a cop to spread around the station: the
great Chet Bracken can't even hold his head up. Maybe
it's just as well. I'm not so sure I would trust him anyway. Why? Is it because he is sick, or because at some
level I don't think he is being straight with me? I'm not
sure.

Chet looks up at me in obvious pain, but struggles to
his feet. "Yeah," he grunts.

I still don't know what kind of cancer he has. This
doesn't seem the time to ask. I have begun to like the
man, but he doesn't invite sympathy. "I'll go tell
Brownlee we're leaving."

He nods, and two minutes later I watch his Mercedes
creep away. The real question I wanted to ask remains
unanswered: How good is Shane Norman's alibi? Actually, I realize now that the question I really want to ask
Chet is: Are you somehow covering up for Norman? I
don't have the guts at this point. Why? I can't explain
it. Fear, I suppose. He's like some kind of god to lawyers of my ilk. I need to get over that, but so far I
haven't quite managed it. Besides, he'd bounce me off
the case quicker than some of the checks I've written
since I've been in private practice. Brownlee, bursting

with vitality, watches for a moment. "That guy may be a hotshot, but he looks like death warmed over to me."

I can't disagree. If he croaks before the trial, will I get this case by myself? I want it in the worst way. But there is too damn much I don't know. The best I could do is second-degree murder and that seems like a remote possibility at this point. People will say that Chet would somehow have won it. I lie, "That's what happens when you hit thirty, Brownlee."

He grins. In his early twenties, he is safe from old age and death. Sure he is.

8

THURSDAY NIGHT. MY daughter's night to open cans, for
surely what we do can't be called cooking. Yet food is
the furthest thing from her mind. I sit at the kitchen table while she checks a pan on the stove. Always the op-
timist, Woogie, whose culinary requirements are almost
as simple, watches hopefully beside my chair. "I feel so
sorry for Pastor Norman," she says. "All that he is
doing, and his wife is an alcoholic, too."

I reach down to pet Woogie and decide my sympa-
thies lie with Pearl Norman, who sounds as if she has
been starved for attention ever since she married Shane
and especially since Leigh was born. "It could be that
she has a genetic predisposition toward alcoholism," I
point out. "And I suspect she feels lonely a lot of the
time."

Sarah, judgmental as only the young can be, will
have none of it. She tosses an empty box in the trash.
"She doesn't have to drink," she says blithely. "She has
a choice."

I feel a bump on Woogie's head and wonder if it is a
tumor. Surely not. "It's not that easy," I say, finding this
conversation an uphill battle. My daughter has many
virtues, but at this stage of her life, tolerance is not
among them. During her grandfather's lucid periods, he
knew that alcohol and schizophrenia didn't mix well,

118

but that didn't stop him from drinking. I haven't always known when to quit either. People drink for a reason. It may not be a good one, but nobody promised that the species wouldn't have its perverse moments.

"Maybe not," Sarah replies, "but you have to admire the strength that enables Pastor Norman to endure her drinking and do so much, too."

Woogie settles down on the floor, and I rub the arthritic knuckle on my left hand. I have my own bumps. Shane Norman doesn't seem the type to endure much of anything. "Maybe," I can't resist saying, "she drinks because of him."

Sarah puts her own spin on my remark. "I can see how she might feel inadequate," she says, putting a lid over the pan. "It would be hard to feel you could ever do enough to help a man like that."

Sarah, Sarah, Sarah. How much of this crap will I have to endure? It's not as if Shane Norman is on the cutting edge of anything. I complain, "What bugs me is the insistence on the literal belief in the Bible. I just don't see how you and Rainey can swallow that."

Sarah slowly turns the knob on the oven as if she were performing an experiment for her chemistry class. My mind goes back to my sophomore year in high school. My biology teacher, who had a stutter, told our class after we summarily covered the theory of evolution in five minutes, "You can believe you came from mon-mon-monkeys, but the 'h' if I-I-I do." We all laughed, but somehow even then it didn't bother me to think my ancestors swung down out of trees. Sarah says, "You can't explain the world any better. If the world was originated by the Big Bang, who or what began that? Where did that first little something that originated the universe come from? Nobody knows. Something can't come from nothing, can it?"

I sip at a can of Miller Lite and futilely try to think. This is why I have given up the Big Questions. "I don't see how," I admit. "Sort of like, what began in the beginning?"

"God did," Sarah says firmly. Holding a spatula so old it precedes her birth, she turns over ground beef in the skillet. We are having spaghetti again.

"But surely not just six thousand years ago," I say, shaking my head. "No reputable scientist believes that."

Smelling the meat, Woogie begins to whimper. I doubt if he's lost any sleep over the Creation. I stroke him with my foot to hush him. Sarah says, "That's not true. In our creation science trial even the judge who ruled in favor of the evolutionists admitted in his written opinion that no scientists have been able to explain away the discovery of the existence of radioactive polonium haloes in granite and coalified wood that call into question the inference from carbon dating methods that the earth is ancient."

Good Lord! What's she talking about? They are already working on her. I don't want to get into a scientific argument I'm sure to lose. "Even assuming you're one hundred percent right, you just can't isolate the one blip that nobody understands and say that justifies disregarding the overwhelming body of knowledge on the subject."

Stubbornly, Sarah shakes her head. "It's not knowledge; it's theory. You just want to be on the side that appears intellectually respectable. You're worried about what people think. If a bunch of Harvard scientists came out and said they had just discovered evidence that the world was only about six thousand years old, soon you'd start saying the same thing."

I get up to set the table. She's probably right. Most lawyers are suckers for authority figures. That's how we earn our living. I feel a little tension in the room, but she doesn't appear to be getting angry. "Maybe that's true," I admit. "But they all say the earth's several billion years old."

Sarah drains the boiling water from the spaghetti, and a cloud of steam rises from the sink. A documentary on Channel 2 a few weeks ago portrayed the earth dramatically cooling down after its fiery formation. Needless to say, this one re-created the beginning of life without reference to the book of Genesis. Vapor rises into the air that condenses into rain. Lightning flashes, and somehow chemicals interact, and—*poof!* life begins. It makes more sense to me than some giant in the sky scooping up clay and molding a human who comes to life. "You're just afraid of looking silly," she says benignly, dishing the noodles out onto the plates. "It's more comfortable for you pretending you sort of understand science when you really don't. All you're doing is taking someone else's word instead of the Bible's."

I bring the meat over to the table. She's right again. I still don't understand why the earth rotates. No Clarence Darrow or even a William Jennings Bryan, I'd be a liability to either side of a debate on the subject. Actually, I'm more interested in how much time Sarah will be spending away from me than what she is being told, which, obviously, is quite a lot, if she already has been briefed about the evidence at our own monkey trial. Since Sunday she has spent a couple of hours every day out there, even though Norman told her she should wait. "Citing authority is about all lawyers know how to do," I concede. "One good precedent is worth ten pages of legal arguments."

Tasting the spaghetti, Sarah seizes the opening I've given her. "And the Bible is the oldest precedent you could possibly cite."

Dan, my childless expert on child rearing since Rainey's defection, tells me the more I argue (even if I knew what I was talking about), the more she will resist. But I want to cry out the obvious, which she surely knows: the first monkey trial showed how badly eroded the Bible's authority is for the purpose of demonstrating the origin of life, and the trial in Little Rock wasn't any different. I mutter, "It's old, all right." I guess I do care about appearances. I don't want Sarah to be so out of step with the mainstream that she spends her life trying to defend something most of the country outside the South discarded long ago. She is too young to get stuck with such a narrow outlook on life. I thought people were supposed to be liberal when they are young and turn into conservatives when they get old. Maybe the country has become so threatening with its steady diet of violence, drugs, and sex and out-of-control economic problems that some kids will jump at the chance to bypass the complexity and uncertainty of reality for some definite answers. I know Sarah's answer already. The Bible is God's truth.

Sarah puts down her fork. "What you can't or won't see is how meaningful the Bible becomes when it is believed," my daughter lectures me, "and not just taken as metaphor or statements of faith."

Despite Dan's injunction not to argue, I protest, "But for something to be meaningful, surely it has to make sense and be true." As my voice gets high, Woogie stirs restlessly under the table. He doesn't like conflict either.

Sarah moves her glass of milk around on the placemat as she responds, "When Jesus died on the Cross for us, it didn't make sense, did it?"

I suppress a sigh. Shut up right now, I tell myself. A total no-win situation. She wants to argue with me. It will be a test to see if she already knows enough to beat the old man. What she doesn't know is that it will bruise our relationship, and that's the last thing I want to happen. I'm already losing Rainey. I can't afford to lose Sarah. I try a question, myself. "Isn't the reason Jesus died a question of theology?"

"No!" Sarah practically shouts, her food forgotten. "It's what gives my life meaning."

I have lost my appetite. Maybe all of this is rebellion. I am not going to fight with her. If she wants to become an evangelist, I'll try to learn to live with it. I'm just afraid she is going to miss so much of life. The world is a larger place than Christian Life, our house, and her school. "You're going to end up like Leigh Wallace," I say stupidly, my voice trembling. Who am I kidding? Of course, I dread the thought of her cutting herself off from the twentieth century; it's ridiculous to pretend otherwise. True enough, so much of what exists is banal or even hideous, but at least some people weren't afraid to think and experiment. Why throw them out?

Sarah gets up from the table, knocking her chair back against the wall. "That's the most absurd thing you've ever said!" she storms at me. "If Leigh hadn't turned her back on Christian Life, she wouldn't be in the situation she's in now."

I stand up, too, and take my plate over to the sink. "Most people can't live all their lives shut up in a little cocoon. Not at your age. Now is the time for broadening yourself, questioning things. The way you're going about this is to shut yourself off. For God's sake, Christian Life is a fortress. It might as well be patrolled by security guards. That's not living; that's hiding."

Sarah follows me over to the sink. "I suppose what you do is real living, huh?" she yells. "After Mom died, you'd have brought a prostitute to the house if you thought you could've gotten away with it. You make a living defending people who spend their lives doing evil things, and then you use people who care about you to help get them off. You finally find one woman who's good for you, and you risk giving her AIDS and jerk her around like a puppet! If that's what you call living, who needs it?"

Sarah is way over the line. I don't claim to be a saint, but I'm not much worse than most people I know. I turn on the hot water full blast and squirt some detergent into the sink. I am so mad right now that if I say anything, I might regret it the rest of my life. I realize now I have told Sarah too much about my cases over the years. Dumb as a rock, I got involved once with a woman who later died of AIDS. Everything I could possibly do wrong during that case I did, but I didn't expose Rainey to AIDS; and, even more than anything else, it galls me to realize Sarah assumes I would. "What makes you think I've ever slept with Rainey?" I ask, my voice calm as I can make it.

Sarah, who is leaning against the refrigerator, says, "I'm not that naive!"

"Not that it's any of your business, young lady," I say, turning to face her, "but we haven't, and you have said just about enough for one night."

"I'm going up to the church!" she says, checking her watch.

I slam the sponge into the sink. "What is so wonderful about that goddamned church? Before you fall too much in love with him, you might as well know that Shane Norman had as much reason to kill Leigh Wallace's husband as she did."

Sarah looks at me as if I had called her mother a whore. "What are you saying?" she asks, her voice now shaky.

I back off, knowing I shouldn't be discussing this

subject. "I'm not saying anything except people aren't always what they seem, and the sooner you learn that, the better off you'll be."

Sarah's eyes are enormous. "Do you have any evidence he's involved?"

"That's none of your business!" I say harshly, ashamed to admit I couldn't prove right now that the man came within five miles of Art Wallace the day he was shot. "And don't you breathe a word of this to anybody, you hear me!"

"Yes, I hear you!" she yells and bursts into tears as she runs out of the room.

"Good!" I holler after her. My voice sends Woogie slinking away after her. What is her problem? Anger that her mother died, leaving her to be raised by a not-always-model father? She has really pissed me off. The trouble is that a lot of what she says is true. Granted, very few of the women I dated after her mother's death were candidates for a convent. Although criminal defense work doesn't usually put one in contact with the cream of society, I doubt if most of my clients have had the energy to engage in nonstop evil. I admit I haven't always done right by Rainey, but she has backed away a time or two herself.

Sarah wants everything to be black or white, and even though I would like fewer shades of gray myself, it doesn't work that way. Maybe she didn't ask to be born during the last gasp of the twentieth century, but I didn't either. The only thing I know to do is to slog through it one crisis at a time. I shouldn't have mentioned Shane. That was stupid. Still, she's got to learn that the only people who don't have feet of clay have been dead for centuries. Norman may not be a murderer, but he was an overbearing son of a bitch who tried his best to smother his daughter. Even if Leigh is guilty, as far as I'm concerned, Norman has some blood on his hands. If he had let her lead her own life, perhaps she wouldn't be facing a murder charge.

In a few minutes Sarah returns, her dark winter coat over her gray sweats. At least Christian Life doesn't require designer clothes. That might be the straw that broke the camel's back. "My ride's outside waiting. I'll be back by nine," she says, her voice containing the bare minimum of civility. She is no longer crying, but her eyes are red.

"Is your homework done?" I ask, exercising my prerogative, though she is almost a straight-A student.

"Yes, sir," she says, unsmiling. "Would you like to check it?"

She hasn't said "sir" to me this year. "I doubt if that's necessary," I reply sarcastically. Damn. I want my daughter back. I thought Christianity was supposed to be about love and acceptance. For a moment I am tempted to tell her to go to her room, but all it will do is convince her even more that I am the Devil.

After she leaves, I call Rainey, who starts the conversation by telling me she is about to go to Christian Life, too. "I've tried my best not to let this bother me," I say, feeling I'm getting the bum's rush, "but I confess I'm really beginning to resent your meddling with Sarah's religious faith." There is a long silence on the other end, and while I haven't quite said what I intended, I'm not sorry I've said it. I didn't mean to sound so pompous, but damn it, I want someone else to feel a little guilty, too.

Finally, Rainey says, more evenly than I expected, "All I did was tell her about Christian Life and invite her to attend. She wasn't bound and gagged last Sunday."

I squeeze the receiver in frustration. "She's a seventeen-year-old kid who got caught up in a wave of emotion. The Bible isn't any more literally true in some places than a Grimm's fairy tale. It's not science; it's myth, and you know it as well as I do. I'm sick and tired of pretending it doesn't matter to me what she believes, when it's clear she isn't thinking rationally about this."

Rainey remains maddeningly calm. "Faith isn't rational, Gideon. That's what scares you about it. The idea of Sarah having enough faith to commit her life to something other than a career or a man frightens you to death. After all, you can't commit yourself to anything or anybody, because you can't get over your wife dying sooner than she should have, and you're terrified of losing someone again.

"As long as Sarah remained under your thumb, it was easy to be wise and tolerant, but the moment you can't control her you want to blame me. If you think Sarah isn't thinking with her head as well as her heart, you're sadly mistaken. Of course she is. For the first time in her life she's being offered something more than, here, take a number, buy this, buy that, and keep smiling until you find a job and a husband. Sure, we're taking a risk. At Christian Life we know we're ridiculed. You saw *Inherit the Wind*. The character based on William Jennings Bryan was made to look like a senile old fool, and people such as yourself haven't gotten any kinder since then. Sarah's not dumb. She knows you're upset by this, and she knows that you'll react by making her feel as guilty as you possibly can."

I feel myself on the verge of throwing the phone through the kitchen window. I have never heard Rainey sound more condescending. There have been times when I thought she was going to be the answer to every problem I've had since Rosa died. We used to talk about everything; she was the one person who would always be there no matter how bad I showed my ass. Once, when I was fired, she offered to dip into her savings. I've been there for her, too. During her breast-cancer scare, I was the one waiting at the hospital for the surgeon to come out of the operating room. Granted, I nearly wimped out when she first told me and probably would have if it hadn't been for Sarah, but I was there. I've listened to innumerable complaints about the state hospital and worried more than I ever admitted that she would lose her social worker job when the in-patient census was drastically reduced. Now, however, she is not the same person. Although she was never dogmatic before, these days she is almost a zealot. It seems every conversation we have revolves around Christian Life. "Maybe you ought to let Sarah speak for herself. I haven't made her feel guilty. As a matter of fact, she's up at the church right now. For all I care, she can move in so she can be there twenty-four hours a day if she wants to."

Rainey laughs, as if I can't possibly be serious. "You want to cut her throat for going up there at all. If you would let her go gracefully, she'll come back. Kids her age have a hard time staying committed to anything. There's so much else for them to do."

I shout into the phone, "That's exactly what I'm trying to say. If she were our age, she would at least have tried to live a normal life. Now she won't even be able to say she tried."

Rainey's voice becomes impatient. "That's just dumb. You're overreacting as usual! You make it sound as if she wants to become a preacher. Listen, I have to go. Calm down, and she'll be all right."

Never have I heard her so patronizing. Her smugness is making me sick to my stomach. "This is in confidence," I warn her, "but I'm going to tell you what I told Sarah. Before you write him in as saint of the year, you need to know that the great Shane Norman is a suspect in his daughter's murder case."

There is stunned silence on the other end. Finally, her voice shrill, Rainey says, "I simply can't believe that!"

It is my turn to laugh. I say savagely, "Why the hell not? You can believe God took one of Adam's ribs and made a woman out of it; you can believe that after six days of making a world God needed a rest, so he called the next day Sunday. The trouble with people like you is that you think it's perfectly wonderful to pick and choose your beliefs. If it makes you feel good, you can swallow a whole book. In the real world insensitive slobs like me don't have that luxury. While you've got your eyes squinched shut reciting some prayer to give you more faith to believe what Norman tells you to, dumb clods like me have to consider the very real possibility that he shot dead his son-in-law. Maybe, though, I ought to just take his word that he didn't do it. If I just pray hard enough, any disturbing thoughts I have about the man will go away."

Rainey asks so quietly I can barely hear her, "Do you really have some evidence he might have done it?"

I bluster, "You know I can't go into that, but tell me what I should do, Rainey. If there is enough evidence that Shane Norman killed Art Wallace, should I just sit on it, and let your beliefs guide me in this case? If he says he is innocent, do you think that ought to be the end of it? After all, he's telling you to swallow the Bible whole. Shouldn't his word that he didn't kill his son-in-law be enough?"

She says weakly, "I just can't believe he is capable of murdering anyone. You don't know him. I know what your point is, but until I see some evidence, I just can't accept he might have killed Art."

I laugh triumphantly. "Evidence! What do you want evidence for? There's a ton of evidence the world wasn't created in seven days, and you couldn't care less about that. If Leigh goes to prison for the rest of her life for a crime her father committed, I guess that's okay, because facts only matter when you want them to."

"You're not being fair," Rainey says, her voice almost fading out. "It's not the same thing."

Who is fair? Is anything or anybody fair? "No, I guess you're right," I say sarcastically. "Unless you can look it up in the Book of Genesis that Shane Norman killed Art Wallace, it could never have happened."

Rainey says, her voice tremulous, "I have to go."

With this, she hangs up, leaving me feeling almost gleeful. It's about time she and Sarah learned they can't have it both ways. They've both been so obnoxious it's made me want to puke. Even if Norman's got an alibi, they'll never feel the same way about him again. Even if the son of a bitch didn't have the guts to do it, he had murder in his heart. That's got to be a sin in his book. Shades of Jimmy Carter. These people drive me up the wall. The phone rings, and I pick it up, knowing it is Rainey. She's decided she wasn't in such a hurry after all. She's too smart to stay in la-la land indefinitely. "Hi!" I say, more cheerful than I've been all day.

"Gideon," Chet says, his voice scratchy but full of life, "we've finally got something on Wallace that might lead somewhere. I'm down at my office with my investigator. Can you come down? I'm finally feeling a little better."

"Sure," I say, looking at my watch. I've had the feeling Bracken has been avoiding me. It's about time I heard from him. "I'll be right there."

I scribble a note for Sarah. For once this week she will be waiting up for me. Woogie, sensing I'm going out, thinks he may be getting a walk and begins to bark and jump up against my legs. "You're not going," I explain. "No!"

Frightened by my tone, he slinks away into the hall. Though I am glad that Chet seems to be finally doing something on this case, I am disappointed he isn't calling me to tell me about Norman's alibi. Woogie turns and gives me a look that leaves no doubt he is pissed off at me. Lately, somebody's always mad about something in this house.

DOWNTOWN IS NOT a fun place after dark, and tonight is no exception. What little life there is gives me the creeps. I am no stranger to criminals, but the older I get, the more I like to see them sitting politely by me in a courtroom filled with cops. The shadowy figures walking the streets tonight are possibly candidates for future clients because there is absolutely nothing going on here after 6 P.M. that will find its way into the hands of a tax collector. The dream to revitalize the downtown center dies harder than the Terminator. As I drive down between the Layman and Adcock buildings on my way to Chet's office, I view the remains of the latest mall. A Wal-Mart would have to open up down here before real shoppers would come back downtown, and that is about as likely as Paul Simon doing a concert in my living room.

Bracken owns his own small one-story building near the courthouse, but with its barred windows, it looks more like a reconverted bunker from World War II than a law office. Dressed in jeans that fit him only slightly better than the jeans he was wearing the night I ate dinner at his place, he lets me in the heavy metal door, saying, "Glad I caught you at home."

I have been to his office once before, on the Sarver case. The law books in his library, overflowing before, seem to have multiplied. In fact, there is little in his office except books. Lawyers as famous and rich as Bracken usually cover their walls with crap that lets clients know how great they are. His walls are bare. Who will get his books? He probably pays more in updates and supplements than I make in a year. Many criminal lawyers, myself included, hate research. Judging by his library, Bracken must love it. I go to the law library at gunpoint. "No problem," I say as another man walks into the room. As little direction as Bracken has provided, I would have driven to Memphis for this conversation.

"This is Daffy McSpadden, my investigator on the case," Chet says, introducing me to a short, dumpy guy in his thirties with slightly crossed eyes. He is wearing a gray suit and striped tie and, except for his eyes, looks normal enough, until I notice his feet. He is wearing sandals. Though I get only a glance, I swear his toes are webbed. Surely not.

"How are you?" I ask, unable to call him Daffy. His hand feels like the skin of a reptile. This is one guy who didn't get his job on his looks.

Instead of speaking, he nods, which makes me fear that he can emit only quacking sounds. I look uneasily at Chet. Maybe he is beginning to suffer dementia. Daffy seems like a character out of a Batman movie. Chet commands, "Daffy, tell him what you've run across."

Daffy nods eagerly as we seat ourselves at a small conference table in the library. Speaking in a rapid monotone, he says, "Among Mr. Wallace's other business interests, all legitimate so far as I've been able to tell, is evidence of a deal for pornographic videos produced in the Netherlands which probably went sour with a buyer in New York. Wallace found a distributor in San Francisco who later accused him of cheating on the price. The distributor, who reportedly has connections with some pretty tough customers, was obviously leaning on Wallace to come up with two hundred thousand dollars in cash to make things right. Wallace was acting as broker on the money transaction but apparently not an honest one."

Art, you old sleazoid, I think. Yet a little extra profit on that kind of deal would be easy enough to conceal. It's not the kind of market that puts out a big Christmas catalog. "How do we know all this?" I ask Daffy, but it is Bracken who answers.

"I had him," Bracken says, nodding at Daffy, "do some digging on a series of phone calls Art made to San Francisco the month before he died. On the surface it appears legitimate, but if you represent enough crooks, you begin to sniff a distinct odor. The paperwork behind the calls didn't check out; and, with a little work, Daffy heard enough rumors about the buyer to guess at a connection. I wasn't certain about the skimming until Leigh admitted it to me this afternoon after I confronted her. She said Art had been threatened, but she was afraid to tell me. Art said they would come after her, too, if she talked. He was still trying to come up with the cash when he died."

I lean against the table and look at Daffy's crossed eyes with grudging respect. "The cops don't know about this?"

Daffy answers, with a snicker, "Are you kidding? They might have spent five minutes checking out his phone bill."

Poor Leigh, I think. No wonder she looked so grim. If I were in her situation, I'd keep my mouth shut, too, and count on Chet Bracken to do his magic. "Why didn't Wallace pay off?" I ask Chet. "I thought he was loaded."

Daffy volunteers, "Two hundred thousand takes a while to come back from the laundry. The problem is that some guys get their feelings hurt when they're taken and aren't very understanding of international currency laws. Wallace knew how to keep his money working, but that kept it from being as liquid as his creditor in this case would've liked. Rub-out guys aren't paid to have a lot of patience."

Rub-out guys. Great. I'm out of my league. Is this for real? The closest I've gotten to international currency was down in Colombia in the Peace Corps, and it seemed like play money, it bought so little. I look around Bracken's library a little dazed. I didn't sign on to spend the rest of my life wondering if I'm going to have an unexpected dinner guest some night. I ask stupidly, "Do we call the cops?"

Across the table, Daffy coughs politely, and Chet tells him he can go home now. "I've got sole custody of my five kids," Daffy explains. "I need to get to the house."

Five kids! I have to wonder what the ex–Mrs. Daffy looks like. And the children. Chet accompanies him into the hall and reaches for his wallet. I suspect Daffy is not averse to working off the books occasionally. With that many mouths to feed, he doesn't have a lot left over to feed Uncle Sam, too. Chet walks back into the library and gives me a wan smile. "So you want to turn this information over to the police, huh?"

I lean back in the leather chair and try to think. "We can't protect her."

Chet sits down across from me and pushes his thick brown hair back from his forehead. "I'm sure not going to be around," he says, grinning sourly at his own black humor. "Look, this doesn't add up, no matter how you do the math. Wallace was killed with a twenty-two pistol. What kind of hit man uses a popgun? The cops searched the house and found nothing. There was no sign of a struggle, no forced entry. Wallace was hardly the type to invite his killer inside for a cup of coffee and then draw an *x* on his forehead for him. He would have fought like hell. If Wallace was really worried about his health, don't you think the cops would have found a weapon or two around his house?"

I rub my eyes, trying to keep up. By this time of night, my I.Q. is in the single digits. "So she's making all this up?"

Chet looks down at the papers in front of him. "Maybe the death threat, I don't know. It's not like I can call up the distributor in San Francisco and get him to go on David Letterman to talk about this deal. Maybe Leigh's getting a little desperate. Maybe she made up the threat because she's scared the porn business will come out in court, and pull her father and mother into the slime. This could really be a problem for her family."

People are weird. She's on trial for murder, and she's worried about her daddy's reputation? "Maybe Shane knew about the porn stuff and killed Wallace," I suggest, taking the opportunity to raise the subject of Norman's alibi. "I could see that a lot quicker than him killing Wallace because he was keeping Leigh away from the church."

Chet fidgets in his chair. As his face becomes thinner, his ears seem to get larger. "That's garbage," he says curtly. "He's seen a lot worse than what Wallace was involved in."

Perhaps so, but not where his own daughter is concerned. God damn it. I feel my face burning. The son of a bitch still hasn't checked out Norman's alibi. What has Norman got on him? Chet must have confessed to some crime and has had to cut some deal. So much for confidentiality between priest and penitent. Norman could leak information about Chet in a million different ways, and Chet won't be around to save his reputation. But surely Norman wouldn't risk his daughter's freedom this way. What in the hell is going on? I realize I'm beginning to think of Norman as a thug instead of one of the most respected men in the state. The odd thing is that I like the man. In some ways he and I don't seem all that much different. Hell, yes, I could murder someone. And so could Norman.

"So what do we do with this?" I ask, watching Chet take a beer from a cooler he has beside his chair. I wouldn't mind a beer right now, but, feeling like a junior law clerk, I don't ask.

Chet makes a face as he untwists the cap from the bottle. "At this point we'll follow it until it dries up or we run out of time. Even if it turns out to be worth less than dog crap, we've got to throw some sand in the jury's face. Shit, we don't have any choice. This is all we've got at the moment. I want you to go to San Francisco and see what you can find out about the distributor. If we have to put Leigh on the stand with this story, we need to know a hell of a lot more than we do now."

Why should I go? I'm a lawyer, not an investigator. "Can't Daffy go or someone else? There're a million guys who'd love a free trip."

Chet shakes his head and takes a long draft before he speaks. "What I'm mainly interested in is you finding someone out there whom we can qualify as an expert witness to testify that Leigh and Art had something to worry about. An investigator won't have that kind of credibility. I'd go myself if I were in better shape."

With the trial only little more than a week away I feel
I'm being gotten out of the way. From a defense stand-
point, it's not a wild-goose chase; Chet is right. We've
got to give the jury a reason to acquit Leigh, but it is as
if there's something here Chet doesn't want me to find.
The main tent is in Blackwell County, not San Francisco. "Shouldn't we be asking for a continuance?" I
ask, searching his face for clues.

Chet looks down at the table and winces as if he had
just discovered some kind of flaw in the wood. "We
wouldn't get it. Besides, I may not have that kind of
time. Trust me on this one," he says, glancing up at me
with an attempt at a smile. "My track record is pretty
damn good. I may not even put Leigh on to testify, but
we've got to be prepared to go with this story if we
have to."

My mouth feels dry, but for some reason I decide not
to ask for anything to drink. This case feels terrible.
Yet, I can't argue with him. He has won acquittals for
some clients for whom I would have been satisfied to
accept a plea bargain of life imprisonment. I warn him,
"I've got to be back no later than Thursday night. I've
got a custody case to get ready for Friday I told you
about."

Chet nods absently and slides me a file. "My Visa is
in there, and so are Daffy's notes. I'd like to see you
gone by tomorrow night." He stands up, dismissing me.
"I promised Wynona I'd get home early. Call me tomorrow when you've had a chance to decipher Daffy's
handwriting. I won't be coming into the office."

Wondering what's on my calendar for the next two or
three days, I let myself out of the heavy, fortresslike
door. I can put off an uncontested divorce, and Dan,
who owes me one, can make an appearance for me in
municipal court on a DWI I know is scheduled. As I

pull away from the curb, I feel a strong need to discuss this recent turn of events with Dan. I don't understand what Chet is doing in this case. As good for nothing as Dan can be sometimes, he provides a decent sounding board.

I take Skyline Drive along the Arkansas River, knowing he and Brenda will be through with dinner and watching TV, which is all they do until bedtime, so I probably won't be interrupting anything. With money on both sides of her family, and none on his, Brenda keeps Dan on a short leash, although why she doesn't cut it altogether probably neither of them understands. He says they were put on earth to make each other miserable, and from the expression on her face when she answers the door, tonight is no exception.

"Sorry not to call first, Brenda," I say, without an ounce of sincerity in my voice, "but I need to talk to your old man if he's not yet comatose."

Brenda, who is smaller than Dan but not by much, jams her hands into an old gray cardigan sweater she is wearing over extra-large sweats and stares warily at her husband's best friend. "Come on in," she decides. "He's still awake. But just barely."

I look down at my watch. It is not quite eight o'clock. Married love: almost as exciting as bachelorhood. She leads me down a hall toward the back of the house. "How are you, Brenda?" I ask, pleased as a life insurance salesman to gain entrance. My theory is that this would be a relatively happy union if they would quit trying to conceive children and try to buy a couple instead. Brenda can afford it. If they would, then Brenda could quit trying to make Dan grow up and turn her attention to kids who at least have a chance of maturing.

For an answer, Brenda says, her voice rich with the

snideness she is famous for, "I hear Sarah has found Jesus."

The carpet in the hall is so lush I nearly stumble. "I guess there are worse ways to spend your time," I say, unwilling to incur Brenda's full wrath, but also unwilling to deny my own flesh and blood. I can kick my own kid around, but I'll be damned if I'll let somebody else.

As usual, Brenda has the last word. "I can't imagine what they'd be," she says, leading me into the den. "Gideon's here," she informs her husband over the sound of a documentary on what appear to be dolphins and other sea creatures. My theory is we love animals because they can't talk back. If they could, there'd be no end to their grievances against us. Wholesale slaughter not the least of them.

His head bent low over a bowl of cheese dip, Dan looks up with a sheepish expression. He has assured me he is on a strict diet. "Come to check on me, huh?" he says, grinning. "It's gotten so bad in this country that you can't even lie to your friends without them getting suspicious. Want a beer?" he says, punching the remote.

Beside Dan's recliner, separated by a small table, is a couch that makes into a bed. As good friends as Dan and I have become, I have been in this room only a time or two before. Dan prefers to escape, and Brenda's parties don't include me. I can feel Brenda's disapproval radiating next to me. "Love one." I'd drink an entire case if I thought I could get her goat.

Dan lifts his obese body half out of the chair and reaches to his left to open a door to a small refrigerator. "Take your pick," he says. From where I'm standing, I can see a six-pack of Miller Lite and at least as many soft drinks in cans. If he had a microwave in here, they could rent out the rest of the house.

"I'm going to bed," Brenda announces, and Dan climbs out of his chair and pads across the room to pacify her. Obviously irritated, nevertheless she lets him kiss her on the cheek and pat her wide shoulders. Like so many fat women, she has a pretty face.

I go take a beer. "Good night, Brenda." I am tired and do not plan to stay long, but Brenda doesn't have to know that.

She murmurs something I can't pick up, and Dan disappears down the hall with her. I sink down on the couch and grab a chip from the bag of Lay's beside me. When he comes back, I say, "I didn't mean to spoil her evening."

Dan shrugs, an embarrassed grin coming to his lips. "We got a TV in our room. She'll be okay. What's up?" he asks, arranging himself in his chair. He speaks softly as if she might be listening through the wall. How do retired couples stand each other all day? Dan says he and Brenda can't get through a weekend without at least one fight. Considering how long people live nowadays, it's surprising there's not something called eldercide.

"You gotta promise to keep your mouth shut," I warn him, but before he can open his mouth, I fill him in on my visit to Chet's office. "What the hell do you think this is all about?" I ask, when I am finished.

Dan moves in on the cheese dip he had temporarily abandoned. "Bracken's sending you on a wild-goose chase," he says instantly. "He's protecting Norman, obviously, and doesn't want you sniffing around the church, because as soon as you do, you're gonna find that nobody saw him during the time Wallace was killed."

I sip on the Miller Lite after crunching into the chips. I could add a couple of pounds tonight easy. "That doesn't make any sense. Why would he be protecting Norman?"

Dan wipes his mouth on his sleeve. "Somehow Norman found out about the porno, probably from Leigh," he guesses, "and killed Wallace. As bad off as Bracken is, it'd be easy for Norman to convince him that Wallace was truly evil and deserved to die. For all we know, Norman has convinced Bracken that this is his ticket to paradise. This is Bracken's last case. He doesn't care that he's covering up a murder. He just wants to go to heaven. Hell, it wouldn't be the only time he's pulled shit like this."

I tap the can against my teeth. In a case that forever earned him the enmity of a former prosecutor, Chet hired a psychologist who had the reputation of fashioning his theories to fit the facts and won an acquittal for a major child abuser. Then there are the stories about violent paybacks. Though Dan and I are on the same wavelength, I try to play devil's advocate. I argue, "But the guy just converted to Christianity. The last thing in the world he would do is get involved in a cover-up."

Dan dips a chip into the cheese. "Who in hell could be worse than a guy that profits from porno and corrupts his wife? Wallace sounds like a scumbag to me, and while these Bible churches preach love, they love the Old Testament's eye for an eye."

I sip at the beer, trying and failing to think of a decent reply. Violence is the easiest thing in the world to rationalize. Every time a handgun is sold in this country, somebody does that. Norman is no idiot. He easily could have heard about Bracken's reputation for taking revenge. Chet probably told him. Even if leopards could change their spots, it wouldn't happen overnight. I look at Dan, who is chewing thoughtfully and staring at the wall above the TV. "Why would he ask me to help him? Somebody who's trying to pull off a cover-up like this isn't going to want another lawyer looking over his shoulder."

Dan snorts, and when he speaks his voice is full of condescending mirth. "Lawyers like you and me are the perfect cover. Bracken knows his reputation. He can say night is day and get guys like you and me to believe it. When it comes down to it, he knows you're not going to question him. He's the great Chet Bracken. The only thing that can screw this up is him dying before the trial."

I put down the beer can. "Where this breaks down," I say, "is they wouldn't expose Leigh to a conviction."

Dan rolls his eyes. "What conviction? Leigh's probably in on this, too. Where do you think she came up with the story about the death threat? Bracken fed it to her. By the time he gets through with Wallace's reputation, the jury will be glad he's dead. Hell, he'll probably have you giving the closing argument while he sits back and pulls your strings. The guy's slick as pig shit. He's got you believing he just stumbled on Wallace's porno deal. Look at the way he had his investigator discover this a week before the trial. He made you think that weirdo broke this case himself! Bracken probably rubbed his nose in it until he nearly suffocated."

Dan belches. I lean back in my seat to get away as far as I can. "What do you think I ought to do?" I ask, stung by his assessment of us. Hell, he's right. Around Bracken I've been acting as if I were a first-grader afraid to raise his hand to ask to go to the bathroom. Yet Dan and I are hardly the first persons in history to be intimidated by a forceful personality. Demagogues are made, not born, and in the South it has been a specialty.

Dan says, "Enjoy the ride. You don't have any proof anything unethical has happened. Actually, if you put yourself in Bracken's place for a moment, there's no funny business going on at all. After all, it's a real stretch to think Shane Norman would murder anyone, especially if he just converted you to Christianity. So, naturally, Chet doesn't want to smear him, and who can blame him for that? Norman has just opened the gates to eternal life to him, and now Chet is supposed to argue he's a murderer? Get real. Our mentality is the reason the tabloid industry is alive and well in the United States. We're happiest when somebody is making up some dirt about the rich and famous. We tell ourselves the most improbable gossip must be true because we're jealous and envious of their success. Chet's got to send you to San Francisco. What other leads are there?"

Tired, I rub my eyes, wondering which of Dan's versions makes more sense. Like any decent lawyer, he can argue both sides of a case. "So you really think I'm off base?" I ask.

He grins. "Hell, no. I think this case stinks worse than I do."

Ten minutes later, I am hustled out the door by Brenda, who reappears in her robe and slippers, looking like that old Vicki Lawrence character on TV. "I've got to talk to my husband before I go to bed," she tells me, daring either of us to argue.

Having heard enough of this, I drive home, my head spinning. Dan should have written a book on the Kennedy assassination. The only person who isn't implicated, according to him, is Billy Graham, and if I mentioned his name, Dan would have me checking his alibi, too. The problem with conspiracy theories is that they are an awful lot like the astrological predictions I read every day in the *Democrat-Gazette*. They have this amazing way of coinciding with our desires and prejudices. Dan couldn't be more hostile to religion if he had been forced to watch Jim and Tammy Faye every day for the last twenty years. I realize that I'm not much different. You see all this stuff on TV and expect the worst out of everybody when the reality is that people are different.

Most of us have a line we refuse to cross. The man who preached about the work being done in Peru to help poor people wouldn't shoot down his own son-in-law in cold blood; arguably, the greatest trial lawyer Blackwell County ever had wouldn't orchestrate a murder. Even if there were some benighted, bloodthirsty kingdom of heaven to gain, they have too much to lose on earth. For one thing, the risk of discovery is too great. People have a compulsion to talk. I'm living proof of the way people run their mouths. Chet has cross-examined too many informants not to know that. When all is said and done, he wouldn't want his kid to wake up one morning and, while looking for his baseball glove, find instead a newspaper article about how his stepfather cast doubt in his final case on all he had accomplished.

The truth is, jealousy accounts for the negative talk about Chet. No one has proved he has ever suborned perjury or arranged a single payback. So why do I feel so bad about this case? I think back to the one case Chet and I worked on together when I was at the Public Defender's. What was the difference? He was as subtle as a steamroller, and that's always been his reputation. In Leigh's case it is as if he were working with an archaeologist's hammer, tapping here, tapping there. It could be his illness. Dan has confirmed what I have already suspected. The problem is that I don't know what to do about it.

At home, Sarah is full of herself. Before I can tell her about San Francisco, she begins to talk about what the youth of Christian Life are doing. "They don't take ski trips or have lock-ins; they help a lot of people," she says, instructing me as if I were a slow student. "I'm not just talking about the foreign work trips. At the shelter downtown, for example, we baby-sit the kids while the parents go look for work."

Go look for a bottle of Ripple, I think sourly. "Is there security down there for you? Even many of the homeless won't stay in places like that because they're too dangerous."

Seated on the couch with her English book, Sarah strokes Woogie until he is almost purring. "There're tons of kids around. But it's not a social thing. We're not down there to show off or hang out with friends."

When I tell her that I am leaving for San Francisco, she becomes anxious (as I knew she would). It's okay for her to run around, but she likes the old man to stay put. "What for?" she asks. "Isn't this kind of at the last minute?"

I collect the day's residue from the coffee table: the *Arkansas Democrat-Gazette*, an empty Coke can, the junk mail, including a plea from Greenpeace, one of Rosa's favorite charities, which can't take the hint after three years of silence from her. "That's one of the weird things about this case," I say. "It's not making a lot of sense."

Sarah's back visibly stiffens, as if she is daring me to fight her again. "I've thought a lot about what you said about Pastor Norman. I know you can't understand it, but a man who radiates so much joy and peace just isn't capable of murder."

I open my mouth to argue. Every man wears a mask at some time in his life. But do I really want my daughter to become as cynical as I am? Suddenly, I feel like an asshole. I knew I didn't have any proof that Shane was involved, so why did I say it in the first place? Am I so weak that I have to accuse a man of murder because I am jealous of him? Obviously. How pathetic! "You could be right," I say insincerely. "Sometimes defense lawyers try so hard to get our own clients off we forget other people are entitled to a presumption of innocence, too." I paste a smile on my face, wondering how disillusioned she will become if it turns out that Shane is the murderer. I don't want to destroy her capacity for a less radical kind of faith, but I may not be able to have it both ways. Fearful she will pick up on my hypocrisy, I change the subject. "Can you stay here, or can you find a friend?"

"I'll call Rainey," she says quickly.

Most kids her age would love to get their parents out of the house so they could have a party. Not Sarah. I know she is nervous about staying by herself. I came in late too many nights after her mother died for her to have a sense of security. "You can have a friend over to stay," I say, thinking of Sarah's best friend, Donna Redden. Sarah hasn't mentioned her in a couple of weeks. "What about Donna? Wouldn't her parents let her?"

Sarah wrinkles her nose at the thought. "I don't see Donna much these days. I'll call Rainey. I saw her leaving the same time we did."

Naturally. I try not to sigh audibly. "Rainey's probably a little mad at me."

Sarah is on me like Woogie on peanut butter. "What did you say to her?" she yelps.

Too damn much, I think. "Pretty much what I told you," I lie. I can't bring myself to admit that I accused Rainey of interfering with her faith. "I don't think it's such a bad idea to be prepared for the worst."

Sarah heads for the phone in the kitchen. "Daddy, you're just incredible," she says coldly, dialing Rainey's number.

I've been called worse. "Let me talk to her after you've asked her."

I eavesdrop as Sarah talks to my old girlfriend. Sarah's voice changes tone, becomes happier as she rattles on about her new "family." I sit at the table, pretending I am reading Daffy's notes. "It's great," Sarah says. "One of the men about Dad's age hasn't missed a mission trip in six years. He had everybody in stitches. I was afraid I'd be scared to talk, but they all made me feel so comfortable, I jumped right in."

Woogie comes over to the table, and I reach down to pet him. I wonder if Sarah will ask me to let this guy adopt her. Doesn't she remember I was in the Peace Corps? That was two solid years, and I didn't have a "family" supporting me. But I guess it doesn't count, because we didn't run around screaming "Praise Jesus!" at the top of our voices.

By the time Sarah hands me the phone, I am mad again, but I try to fake it. All either of them will do is patronize me. "Is it okay if she stays?" I ask. "I'll be back Sunday."

"Of course," Rainey says. "You know it is."

Her voice sounds so smug and sugary I want to vomit. "If anything happens to me, I'd appreciate it if you'd call my sister. Sarah has her number."

Rainey laughs. "You're so dramatic. It's safer to fly than to drive downtown."

For an instant I am tempted to tell her this case

stinks worse now than it did when I talked to her a couple of hours ago, but I don't feel particularly credible at the moment. "Thanks," I tell her. There are worse things than hard-core Christians, I tell myself, and hang up.

10

"THAT'S YOUR FLIGHT!"

It is good to hear Sarah's voice rising with an emotion other than anger. It seems as if ever since I have heard of Christian Life she and I have fought. My hands full, I nod with my chin at the gate. I still can't believe Sarah is awake at this hour of the morning. Anything to get me away from her. A few people are still disappearing into United's flight number 1639. Nuts. I've made it despite my best intentions. I hand my ticket to the woman behind the desk. My travel agent, Julia, neglected to obtain a boarding pass. The United representative, a stern, chubby-cheeked girl who appears to be only slightly older than Sarah, looks at me disapprovingly but hands me back the paper. "It's almost boarded!"

Sarah walks with me to the boarding line as if I were a child who needs to be reassured. I do. "If we crash," I say mournfully, "remember I've got two hundred thousand dollars in flight insurance. Get Dan to sue the hell out of them, anyway."

Sarah giggles nervously. "You're not going to crash."

Easy for her to say. She has only flown once. Her mother and I took her to Colombia to visit her grandmother when she was a kid. "Maybe you can go live with your *abuela* in Barranquilla," I tell her, rolling my r's. When I spoke Spanish in the Peace Corps, I could see the campesinos literally wince at my eastern Arkansas accent. "Marbel would love it." A good Catholic, she'd put a stop to Christian Life in two seconds.

Sarah nudges me to give the flight attendant my pass. "I'll be fine."

Since she is not eighteen, a guardian would be appointed for her if the plane vaporized. Dan won't let her give the insurance money to Christian Life. "I think you're our last passenger," the flight attendant says in an accusing tone.

What's the big deal? Somebody has to be last. They would have been more than happy to overbook this turkey. I hug Sarah hard and take a good look at her. Even in gray sweats, sleepy, and without makeup, she makes the flight attendant look like an undercooked bread stick. "Be good!" I say needlessly. She'll spend all her time at Christian Life.

Embarrassed, Sarah pushes me away. "You said you might be back as early as tomorrow night."

Aware how melodramatic I sound, I grin stupidly at the frowning flight attendant. If Shane Norman was a doting father, what am I?

In twenty minutes we are above the clouds, and I breathe easier. What I can't see won't hurt me. Sure. It's been a while since I've flown, and I watch, fascinated, as my seatmate, a long-haired cowboy complete with black Stetson, boots, and a belt buckle almost the size of a Frisbee, inserts a credit card into the phone attached to the back of the seat in front of us. "Wilma, don't forget to walk Buttons for me," he pleads. Damn. How can people afford to fly, much less call long distance from the plane? This stuff used to be science fiction just a few years ago. I think he is trying to impress the young blonde on the aisle. It won't take much. She

is as white-knuckled as I am. Our flight attendant
("Don't call them stewardesses," my politically correct
daughter reminded me as we were driving to the airport), a buxom black woman, with the nail on her pin-
kie finger painted gold, passes me nothing but a cup of
coffee on this first hop to Tulsa. The rest of her fingernails are the color of old blood that proctologists warn
signals colon cancer. This trip is going to be bizarre.

Reggie's Bar in San Francisco isn't exactly jumping
(I count only two customers at a table in the corner),
but then, it is only two in the afternoon. I have managed
to check into a hotel near Chinatown and find the address on Columbus Avenue Chet has given me. "I'm
looking for a man named Harold Broadnax," I say to
the guy behind the bar. The bartender is above average
height but is distinguished by the largest handlebar
mustache I've ever seen. It makes the guy on the "Today" show look as if he drew his on with a pencil. At
a distance of a hundred yards this man must resemble a
seagull.

Birdwing gives me a hard look as he wipes the bar in
front of him and says, "I don't know the guy."

I am thirty minutes early, so I decide to walk around,
since Birdwing gives me the creeps. Chet hasn't given
me a lot of information about our contact. Broadnax, an
ex–sheriff's deputy in Blackwell County, supposedly
knows somebody who can help us. Instead of heading
outside, I ascend the stairs to the second floor, the
Vanna White Club. Though Blackwell County is not totally devoid of female impersonators, they are not on
every street corner, and since I've never seen one except on TV, now is the time to complete my education.
The sign on the street is enticing, and a blow-up of
seven performers in the hall leaves no doubt.

At the top of the stairs, I hear what sounds like the voice of a carnival barker. If I am so curious, why haven't I done this before? Behind the counter an Asian guy lets me in for half price ($7.50) since the show is almost over. The club, dimly lit except for the stage, has few customers, so he leads me to a table in the second row where a waiter appears and takes my order for a beer. On stage, which is a narrow platform that leads down to a spacious dance floor, is a fat guy about my age in a platinum wig and pink evening gown telling jokes. He asks, "Are any of you old enough to remember the show 'Queen for a Day'?" The sparse audience is composed of mostly couples, tourists like me, I guess. A few raise their hands. Our MC puts his hands on his hips and delivers his line: "Hell, I knew I was going to be a queen for life!"

This gets a few laughs, and even though I know the MC is a man dressed like a woman, it is already difficult to think of him that way. Though his voice is deep, his mannerisms are so feminine I find I am beginning to think of him as a woman. "I'm one of the lucky few who's always known what they wanted to be since they were a kid. Honey," he says, winking at a guy at a table directly in front of him, "I didn't just play with Barbie, I wanted to be Barbie!" After a couple of more jokes on this order, our MC tells us to put our hands together and welcome "Miss Lynn Leopold, our own Louisville Slugger!"

Accompanied by a drumroll, out comes a man or woman—I can't tell. If born a male, Lynn has had his share of hormone treatments because only his jaw seems too firm for him to be taken for a woman. In fact, Lynn is stunning: wearing a red dress slit on both sides, revealing tanned thighs, he or she launches into a credible version of "New York, New York," and sways back and forth to the music on five-inch red heels. In this person's eyes throughout the song there is a hurt look that won't go away. Despite the jaw, she has a pretty face with glittering dark eyes that try to smile. She has a little cleavage (possibly pushed up, but maybe hormones), and as she dances by the table in front of me, I feel the faint stirring of lust. What the hell is going on? I know she isn't for real. She stops in front of a couple's table to my right and begins to sing to the man. In his thirties, bespectacled, bald, he looks as uncomfortable as I'm feeling. His wife, a trim brunette wearing an Atlanta Braves baseball jacket, seems to enjoy it enormously, a story to tell to their friends. ("Bill nearly wet his pants while this beautiful creature came on to him right in front of me!") Actually, beneath the sickly grin, Bill seems about to turn four shades of red. I notice Lynn doesn't quite touch him. If Bill is a good old boy, he may have to prove himself somehow, so there seems to be a fine line she doesn't cross.

Afterward, our MC is back. "Where is everybody from?" he asks. Familiar with this question—this group looks as if it usually vacations in Branson, Missouri—the audience surprises me by yelling out places like L.A., San Diego.

Through his gown, our MC scratches his crotch and smiles maliciously. "Well, that just goes to show if you put too much pressure on the sewer system," he cackles, "anything is liable to pop out."

The crowd loves it. A transvestite Don Rickles. The next performer is Marvin the Mambo Queen who does something that is strangely reassuring. An ugly little Latino, Marvin marches out on the stage with his makeup kit, gown, and wig and proceeds to get dressed to the accompaniment of some furious banging by the house percussionist and the keyboard man. Watching this guy, I sense more diversity in the performers than I would have suspected. Were it not still the afternoon, I would be willing to bet my return ticket home that Marvin has a day job and dresses up for entertainment. As he dons his long black wig, completing his transformation from an ugly Latino into an ugly Latina, I have the feeling that our MC and Lynn take themselves a lot more seriously.

Afterward, our MC brings everyone out on the stage, a total of seven in an array of gowns and dresses, and they parade around as if they were trying out for the Miss America pageant. My eyes are drawn again to the Louisville Slugger. She is more than a female impersonator, her sad eyes proclaim. Finally, the music ends, and except for the MC, who begins to shake hands with some of the couples, they dance off the stage. If Chet has sent me out here to divert me from the real action in Blackwell County, he is accomplishing his goal. I've never seen anything like this in my life.

As I head for the stairs, the MC calls after me, "Gideon, what's your hurry?"

I nearly knock over one of the tables in my shock. I haven't told a soul my name. I turn, and see this big man, his arms bare and ugly folded across his chest covered with taffeta and sequins.

"How do you know me?" I stammer, squinting in the smoky haze that is like the fog bank outside.

He comes toward me, and says in a low voice, "You cross-examined me once. Not bad for a rookie public defender. Search and seizure. You kept a couple of grams out of evidence that day."

I think back, my eyes stinging in the gloom. Of course. This is Harold Broadnax. Beneath the makeup, the false eyelashes, the mascara, the man's round face takes on a sardonic expression that I think I recognize.

How weird! He was one tough deputy sheriff. Automatically, I extend my right hand and then feel foolish.

Harold grins and then crushes my hand as if it were a paper sack. "You're early," he says loudly. "Give me ten minutes to change and we'll go down to the bar. I got an hour until the next show."

So off-balance I feel physically disoriented, I mutter, "Sure," and stand by the entrance trying to assimilate what I've just seen. Over in the corner of the stage, the Louisville Slugger has reappeared and is talking animatedly to a good-looking young guy I hardly noticed until now. He places his hand inside one of the slits and moves his hand up her thigh. I watch, transfixed. I wonder if she has had surgery. With his free hand, he begins to gesture wildly, and after a few moments, she turns on her heel and again strides dramatically off stage. Despite my best intentions, I feel cheered by his rejection and catch myself only after I have allowed myself to gloat that the young don't always finish first. How can I be jealous of a man who comes on to a female impersonator? The male ego never rests. I'd compete against a dead man if somebody threw his corpse on top of my grave.

Harold comes out the same entrance that the Louisville Slugger disappeared into, and I wonder if they watch each other change clothes. This infantile thought lingers in my brain all the way down the stairs. What is sex? I don't seem to have a lot of control over my reactions right now. Harold, his baritone voice booming against the walls, says playfully, "I saw you looking at Lynn. She's been the downfall of many a poor boy."

"Harold," I say, finally recovering my tongue, "what in the hell are you doing in San Francisco?" I know I sound a little shrill. Still, I've got good reason. How many other ex–deputy sheriffs wear gowns and eye shadow? Maybe more than I know.

"What comes naturally," he says cheerfully as we enter the bar. He is wearing jeans, an Arkansas Razorback sweatshirt, and Reeboks. "How's Chet these days?"

I have been in a gay bar, I realize belatedly, as we turn the corner downstairs. Birdwing just blinks his eyes as we take a seat at the bar. I am not totally unsophisticated (or so I thought) about these things. Skip Hudson, my best friend before he moved to Atlanta last year, is gay, and when he finally came out of the closet, I went to a gay bar with him a time or two. "Not so good," I tell him. After what Harold has revealed about himself, there doesn't seem a lot of room for pretense. "I don't know what he's told you, but he's dying of cancer. That's off the record."

Harold, his makeup still in place, winces and orders us a couple of beers. I remember now. He beat a guy within an inch of his life who was harassing a friend of his, and Chet somehow got him off. There wasn't even a trial. Until that incident no one even suspected Harold was gay. He resigned from the Sheriff's Department, and no one ever saw him again. I guess Blackwell County was about to find out a lot more than it wanted to know about its gay population. "Damn," he says soberly, "he was one hell of a lawyer."

I nod. I'm not sure what he is now though. I look around the bar to try to see if I should have picked up on its identity, but it seems pretty ordinary. There are a couple of Forty-Niner posters on the walls, a TV, even bowling trophies behind the long counter. Mainly there is booze. I am disappointed. I was looking for more atmosphere. Small talk seems too awkward, so I ask, "You know what we're looking for?" Harold, without the wig, has a big meat-ax of a face. He is beginning to go bald worse than I am, and he looked better with the mass of hair to distract from his features. I had forgotten how ugly he is.

"I owe Chet," he says, sipping on a Moosehead. "As you might expect, this is sticky. Other than run-of-the-mill porno, there's no proof of anything, only rumors. Tim Hogan, the guy who runs the operation your client's husband ripped off, understandably likes to keep a low profile as much as possible. The best I've been able to do on short notice is arrange for you to talk to an investigator for an insurance company who's gone on record claiming Hogan hired someone to torch a competitor's porno inventory. Since it was a kiddie-porn operation, nobody got too upset. Not even a civil suit came out of it. No criminal charges were filed, but this gal tells a good story."

Harold reaches in his hip pocket, pulls out a worn leather wallet, and begins to go through it. I look up as two tourists, obviously husband and wife, their cameras banging against their chests, come in and quiz Birdwing on directions. He points upstairs, and the female grins and nudges her mate in the ribs. I can almost see the goose bumps on the guy's arms from where I'm sitting. I wonder if women get off on this stuff more than men. Harold hands me a dog-eared piece of paper, and I squint to make out the address. "She'll meet you at a restaurant in Chinatown at five tonight," he says, downing his Moosehead. "It's only a couple of blocks east of here. I told her it's your treat."

I think of the wad of fifties Chet crammed into my hand last night. My wallet's so thick I look like I've crapped in my pants. I look at the address. Jim Chu's.

"Is this a bunch of crap?" I ask, hoping for an honest answer.

Harold shrugs. "You tell me. Chet's a magician. I've

seen him, and I'm sure you have, too, point so many fingers during a closing argument that you get cross-eyed just watching him. Misdirection is every defense attorney's stock-in-trade, but he's the best I've ever seen, and I've watched some big names work out here."

I nod, wanting to ask Harold whether he thinks I should be trusting Chet to tell me the truth. Yet this man is not the person to ask. He'd be on the phone to him as soon as I walked out the door. Whom can I ask? Bracken has been such a loner that I haven't got the slightest idea. Maybe I can come in through the back door. "He doesn't like to lose. Did you ever hear the story about him paying back a witness who lied in a case of his?"

Harold grins. "The word got around, too. You didn't hear any more tales about informants coming forward after that with stories about what they supposedly had learned from his clients while they were in prison. Even if you didn't know what was going on at the time, he was always about five moves ahead of you. I thought I was headed for some serious time, and before I knew it Chet had my charges dismissed and handed me a check that included my severance and retirement pay. It wasn't until I moved out here that I learned he had threatened to have the biggest coming-out party in Blackwell County history if the prosecutor didn't drop the charges. Shit, he would have done it, too. He believes in total war."

"That's for sure," I say, watching Harold's face as he relives some memory. Bracken never rests and never will. The odds that Chet has been planning out his moves in Leigh's case for months go way up. Once again the feeling that I am being jerked around by strings two thousand miles long washes over me. Who is Chet trying to fool in this case? Me, I guess. But maybe somebody else, too. As soon as I get back, I'm arranging my own come-to-Jesus meeting with Leigh Wallace, and then Chet and I are going to the mat over Shane Norman. If Norman doesn't have a solid-gold alibi, we're going after him or I'm off the case.

Harold stands and offers his hand. "I've got to get back. Do me a favor and keep my job quiet. I've still got family in Arkansas."

"Sure," I say, and thank him. A minute later I am in the street, gawking like the rest of the tourists. I didn't get a description of Jessie St. Vrain, but I guess she won't have any trouble picking me out. I'm the hick who's already got a tan. Though it is cool and breezy, I could live with this weather. No humidity. After San Francisco, central Arkansas will be like a swamp. I walk around before stopping by my hotel to check in with Chet. The number of panhandlers is distressing. We like our poor to be invisible in the South. With the wad I'm carrying, I could feed half the city tonight and lose ten pounds at the same time. Not a single Asian beggar so far. We'd do better if we turned over the United States to the Pacific Rim countries. Why aren't Asians in charge already? Yet, there's not a chance. The Pope'd have a better chance of being elected president.

"Sir, do you have a couple of dollars you could spare?" asks a shabbily dressed Caucasian of about sixty as I pass by the City Lights Bookstore.

Embarrassed by his politeness, I can't even bring myself to acknowledge him, and hurry on. These guys don't look like the drunks we have back home. The famed homeless, I guess. This very man may have had a decent job but got laid off, I tell myself, though I can't quite bring myself to believe it. The prejudice or fear is too strong. A lifetime of being told that a man who isn't working is committing an unforgivable sin kicks in, and I feel a familiar contempt welling up like poison gas. Only bums or blacks don't work. With a rush of anger, I remember the day I was fired from Mays & Burton. I made off with a paying client and went into private practice the same afternoon. Not everybody has a license to steal. I turn around and look for the man again, but he is gone, melded into the crowd of tourists and locals.

Before returning to my hotel on Powell Street, I wander around Chinatown gaping at the Chinese (do they let Koreans in Chinatown?) businesses and walk in a store and pick up a Chinatown T-shirt for Sarah for the grand total of three dollars. She will like the strange script. For all I know it says "You're dead meat, white asshole," but she will be pleased that I actually picked out something for her myself. For the last couple of years I have gotten Rainey to do my shopping for her. As I wait for my change, I remember a couple of weeks ago I heard a report on National Public Radio about how in New York Chinese immigrants pack themselves like rats into an apartment to save enormous amounts of money. Then, in "Doonesbury," there were a week's cartoons on how disciplined Asian kids are and how white kids just can't fathom working that hard. If this is the future, it gives me the willies. The United States probably had its mortgage foreclosed on yesterday and I missed it. The best thing about the heartland is that we don't know how bad things are.

A little tired, I go back to the Fairfield Hotel and try to check in with Chet, but his secretary tells me he is at a late lunch. As little as he apparently eats these days, he can't have gone far, but when I call him back later he is still out. He probably is asleep on the couch in his office. I think of calling Sarah, but she will be at school. Relax, I tell myself. Everything is fine. If I don't calm down, before long I'll be acting like a drunk who insists on making a nuisance of himself by calling his friends long distance in the middle of the night.

Since I have time to kill, I call Julia to see if I have any messages. She tells me Rich Blessing called. I try to reach him at Bando's but am told he is running some errands and won't be back until tomorrow.

At five o'clock I am waiting for a chair at Jim Chu's, when a young kid who looks like John-Boy from the old "Waltons" series comes up and sticks out his hand at me. "Gideon Page?" he asks in a clear, unaccented soprano voice. He is wearing a dark pinstriped suit without a tie. I stand up, towering over this kid, and for once crush somebody else's hand. Usually it's the other way around. Probably a messenger from the investigator's office telling me she will be late. That's okay. I'm enjoying the crowd, a mix of tourists and Asians, as Sarah has warned me to say. Rugs are oriental, people are Asian.

"That's me," I admit, wondering what it is about me that sticks out like a sore thumb. I'm wearing a gray, fifty percent cotton, fifty percent wool suit I got on sale at Dillard's. Granted I'm not much of a clotheshorse, but I look better than most of the tourists who are coming in wearing anything from Bermuda shorts to college sweatshirts.

"I'm Jessie St. Vrain," she says, "and I'm starving."

I try not to look surprised. Is everybody here androgynous? "Good," I say. "We're eating on my boss's money."

We sit at a table against a mirror, and I can't get away from wondering whether Jessie is really a woman. Harold, I remember, used the word "gal," but I'm beginning to wonder if that holds much significance around here. Shit, maybe this is Richard Thomas's son or daughter. Jessie's lips are full but unpainted. John-Boy wore more makeup than this woman. Jessie is mercifully oblivious to my confusion and treats me like a visiting cousin. "Have you gotten to see anything? Ride the cable cars? We could have gone to Fisherman's Wharf, but the prices are such a rip-off."

I look at the menu. More expensive than home but not bad. I close it and get what I always order at home: sweet-and-sour pork. My tastes would put a lot of people out of work, Rainey has observed. Jessie, obviously a veteran, makes several suggestions and sighs in frustration at my choice. She orders squid. "How do you know Harold?" she asks, pouring us each a cup of tea as if we were a long-married couple who know each other's routines. "Isn't he wild? I just love his show, especially that little one they call the Louisville Slugger. If you do only one thing, you should catch it."

Afraid to admit I already have, I say, "I've known Harold a while. He said you have an interesting story."

Jessie gives me a frown, as if I have committed some horrible breach of etiquette. "Have you got to be someplace at five-thirty?" she asks, disapproval in her green eyes.

"Not at all," I concede. Lighten up, I think. My plane doesn't leave until tomorrow afternoon. Jessie is like a Mexican businessman. We're supposed to entertain each other before we do a deal. I order a beer for me and sake for her. What the hell? I tell her I found the Louisville Slugger attractive, too. "It made me feel a little weird though," I confide. "I have enough trouble with the opposite sex without having to worry if it's truly opposite."

Jessie laughs, revealing lovely teeth. I decide she is pretty in an unusual way. I haven't been out with a woman who is as petite and graceful as she is in years.

Perish the thought. The last thing I need to do is go to bed with her. Even the idea of masturbation in this city makes me break into a cold sweat. Dan told me, not entirely joking, that I was running a risk by changing my underwear. I suspect that is a risk I'll take. As she spoons her soup, Jessie begins to tell me her life story. She is divorced but no kids. A frustrated artist, she draws in her spare time, and proving it, she whips out a pad and pen and sketches my face while we are waiting for the rest of our dinner. While she draws, she tells me she has lived everywhere except the South. "No offense, but I've avoided it like the plague. We drove through Alabama and Mississippi once, and you just seem so backward and poor. Granted the prices here make you think you're living in Russia, but the diversity is just fantastic!"

I smile, trying to avoid feeling defensive. I'm here to persuade Jessie to testify, not start a new Civil War. Still, I can feel my hackles rising. Condescension toward Southerners is a lifelong obsession of mine. "Yeah, the Rodney King thing," I say, getting into my Arkansas Delta accent, "made me want to load up my old pickup and five kids and move on out. It's hard not to get nostalgic for the old days when you see a beating like that."

Our waiter, a frazzled Asian kid who seems accustomed to moving at the speed of light, throws on the table two egg rolls that resemble dried dog turds. Jessie downs her sake before attacking her portion. She smiles to make sure I'm joking. To keep her going, I show a few teeth. She says, "I'm afraid I'd just vegetate even in a place like Atlanta. Mainly, you just have two races, still living separate and unequal, African-Americans oppressed as ever."

Since we are eating in a ghetto made up of a race that

as far as I know has never had a governor and seems to wield little political power, I observe, "Tell me about it. That black mayor in Atlanta rants and raves, but you know how crackers are down South. It's a living hell all right."

Smiling shyly, she tears off her drawing, signs it at the bottom, and pushes it at me. I'm astonished at the likeness: I've been told I look a little like Nick Nolte but never took it seriously until this moment. "Not bad," I tell her, trying not to squint. I don't want to ruin the effect by putting on reading glasses.

The drawing somehow serves to bring about a truce, and we eat our meal in relative harmony. I tell her about Sarah and her current flirtation with fundamentalism. As expected, Jessie expresses horror, but I wouldn't be surprised if her own beliefs weren't just as extreme, if "Doonesbury" 's Boopsie is any guide to California. At least Sarah hasn't told me she is into "channeling" yet. I don't want to start a fight, so I don't ask Jessie about her religion and am relieved when she doesn't relate any out-of-body experiences. After dinner she reads me her fortune: " 'You find beauty in simple things. Do not neglect this gift.' "

She smiles, and I wonder if I am one of the simple things. I read her mine. " 'A wise man and his tongue are never parted.' "

Draining her third sake, she says, with a snicker, "Only with great difficulty."

Jessie suggests that we talk at my hotel and takes my arm in a proprietary way as we walk back toward Powell Street. I confess I am nervous. From a distance she looks so much like a boy I know we are taken for a homosexual couple. Because of my acceptance of Skip, I thought I didn't have any prejudice, but I feel myself blushing when I get a glance from tourists.

"There's a couple of 'em," I can imagine them saying. But maybe they are thinking, "Nick Nolte—I didn't know he was gay."

Inside the Fairfield Hotel, I feel sweat soaking my undershirt. "You want to talk in the bar?" I ask, my voice sounding plaintive even to me.

Looking up at me with her clear emerald eyes, she murmurs, "I'd feel better if we talked in your room."

A bellman, an Asian guy in his early twenties, catches my eye and grins. He must want a tip to keep his mouth shut. I'm not doing anything wrong, I want to scream at the top of my voice. I take my hands out of my pockets as if this somehow will indicate my good faith. "Okay," I sigh. "Let's go."

Feeling as though the entire staff of the hotel is watching us, I follow her onto the elevator and keep my eyes on the floor until the door shuts. On the sixth floor there are no guests roaming the halls, and I unlock the door to my room, relieved not to have encountered one. Like a couple returning from a night on the town, we both head for the bathroom. Though my bladder feels like an overheated inner tube, I defer, and she says companionably, "I'm about to bust."

Hoping things won't get any stranger, I look around the room, wondering how to get as far away from the bed as possible. There are two chairs, and I drag them over to the window and place them a yard apart and sit down. Though I have brought a pint of bourbon, alcohol is the last thing this little party needs right now. Once she leaves, I may not even go out for ice.

When Jessie comes out of the bathroom (fully clothed, thank goodness), I point to the empty chair across from me. She yawns, and I steal a look at my bed, glad it looks as hard to get into as an aspirin bottle. Finally, she sits down and looks out the window onto the city. "There are some bad people living in this town," she says, and begins to tell me about her investigation of the arson of a business in Oakland called Bay Videos. "The company I work for won't pay off on the excuse the place was torched. The owner of Bay Videos was screaming he was making money hand over fist and had no reason to burn down his own place. He said from the beginning that Jack Ott had done it and tried to kill him, too, but the cops yawned and went back to sleep. They don't put the demise of a porno store at the top of their list to investigate thoroughly. Though a couple of people could have been killed, no one was, so basically the cops' position is that this is a private matter for our lawyers if they want to get into it."

I write the name "Jack Ott" down on the hotel stationery. It was Jack Ott whom Art Wallace had ripped off. I ask, "So did Jack Ott do it?"

Jessie leans forward with a conspirator's smile and says, "I'm coming to that. I begin to check out Bay Videos' story and sure enough, I start hearing the name Jack Ott. To make a long story short, Jack Ott is one of the biggest porn distributors on the Coast, and Jack likes to make his money the old-fashioned way—by eliminating the competition. Now, the kind of stuff these guys deal in would undoubtedly be considered obscene and therefore illegal in Arkansas, but here, by our enlightened community standards, it's just considered a little strong. Nobody who's actually in the business likes to make any noise, because the feds get involved once it starts moving interstate. That kind of bust is great PR for the FBI."

I begin to doodle. I am already losing the thread. "So if nobody's talking for the record, what's the point?"

Jessie reaches into her pants pocket and pulls out a

small tape recorder. "I got the guy who actually torched the place for Jack on tape. You want to hear it?" she says, her voice rising like Sarah's when she's excited.

"Give me a little background first," I say, dumbfounded by her claim. John-Boy never got into these contretemps. "Why would a guy like that say anything in an investigator's presence that would implicate himself?"

"Well"—Jessie grins, standing to take off her suit coat—"that's a long story, too, but suffice it to say Robert Evatt didn't know what I was or who I was, or that I always wear a wire. Want to see?" She begins to unbutton her blouse.

"No, no, I believe you," I say hastily, horrified that perhaps she has been taping our conversation. "So you've been recording us, too?"

She nods, not embarrassed in the slightest. "I like to have a record." She presses the play button, and I hear a boozy male voice that is impossible to understand against a background noise of rock guitars and other conversations. I get a few words and actually hear the name of Jack Ott, but that's all. When she turns it off, I shake my head. "I didn't get it."

Undaunted, she rewinds it. "You've got to listen to it more than once. The guy that burned Bay Videos was scared shitless of Jack Ott. You can hear it in his voice." She plays it again, twice more, and I begin to pick it up though I can't quite get every word. " 'Hell, yeah . . . I . . . burned Bay Videos . . . for Ott. . . . You don't quit . . . him. . . . He wanted me . . . to off the guy . . . but he got out.' "

I stare at the tape, wondering if this is admissible to show that Art Wallace truly had something to fear from Jack Ott. Coupled with Leigh's testimony that Art had told her that he was in trouble for not coming up with the two hundred thousand he skimmed from Ott, a jury might be persuaded to believe someone else had killed him. I doubt if Robert Evatt will volunteer to repeat what I've just heard. "So where is Sir Robert now?"

Jessie reaches again into her bag and hands me a piece of paper. "He's dead. Drug overdose." I put on my reading glasses and hold the article up to the light. It is a brief story from a January *San Francisco Chronicle* and says just enough to confirm her statement. "If my partner and I think it will do any good, would you be willing to come to Arkansas for the trial and bring your tape with you?"

Jessie rewinds the machine and grins at me. "Is it true that people go barefoot in public?"

"Just in the summertime," I say. This woman is a piece of work.

"Well, why not?" she responds with a sly smile. "What else do you want me to do? I can hot-wire a car, disconnect a burglar alarm. I can even crack a safe."

I put down the paper and stare. Is she pulling my leg? Probably not. I wouldn't be surprised if this woman had done some time. "Just testify," I say. "Just testify."

She looks disappointed.

On the flight home the next day the winds out of Denver bounce the plane like a yo-yo. ". . . encountering a little turbulence . . ." the captain tells us in a glum voice that on a routine flight would suggest he is merely battling a hangover.

"A little, my ass!" shrieks my seatmate, a copy machine sales manager from Oklahoma City. "It feels like this damn thing's attached to a bungee cord."

Next to a window, I look out to see if we are about to slam into the Rockies. Since nothing but soupy yellow clouds are visible, I force my attention back to the file in front of me and to the custody trial I have on Friday. Ordinary hatreds between a man and a woman. As bizarre as the Leigh Wallace case has become, there is something comforting about a case that consists largely of garden-variety malice.

"Somebody, get me a towel, damn it!" my seatmate pleads. Queasy myself, I keep my eyes glued to the page of notes in front of me and try not to breathe. Get me home, Lord, and I'll never leave again.

11

"IF EITHER OF you insists on trying this case," Teresa Mason, the guardian ad litem appointed to represent my client's child, says, her eyes flashing, "I'm going to recommend foster care. Wayne, your client beat this child black-and-blue, and, Gideon, your client let him, and I've got the records from Cook County Social Services to prove it."

I want to lean over and kiss Teresa. She has done her homework. I was prepared to win this case and have nightmares the rest of my life. Wayne Oglesby, glancing over at our clients seated with their witnesses on opposite sides of the courtroom, blusters, "They're not admissible. It's all hearsay."

Teresa, who must be a third of Wayne's size, scoffs, "Give it up, Wayne. I'll just ask for a continuance and get them certified. You know the judge will grant it if I ask him. I just got them in the mail this morning."

Wayne, an ex–tight end for the Arkansas State Indians, swells up like a toad, somehow reminding me of Jabba the Hutt in one of the Star Wars movies. I know he is thinking that Teresa is a meddling little bitch, but thank God for lawyers who take this role seriously. Both Wayne and I have known that neither of our clients was fit to have custody, but we were prepared to tear little Bobby McNair apart this morning in the name of representing them.

"What do you want?" I ask Teresa, knowing I can shove down my client's throat whatever she recommends. Salina McNair can no more resist the male species than Dan can stay on a diet. Away from dominant, brutish men, whom she attracts like flies on fresh roadkill, Salina is a marginally decent mother; however, she won't or can't protect her son from the hideous guys who seem to line up at her door. In my bones I've known this for the last month, but pretended she only needed one more fresh start, despite watching the dynamics between her and the asshole who insisted on coming to my office with her each time I interviewed her. Over Teresa's shoulder I get a glimpse of him now, all draped around Salina. He would have locked Bobby down in the cellar after a week, and she would have told herself, "Gee, all of a sudden, Bobby likes to play where it's nice and dark."

"Salina's sister will take him," Teresa says firmly. "The home study's not bad, but each of your clients will have to kick in for support. She can't do it by herself."

"No fucking way," Wayne grunts under his breath. "He'll never go for it."

"That's okay with me," Teresa shoots back. "Tell him the social worker in Chicago has promised me she will file criminal charges for assault if he gets custody."

Wayne picks at a herpes cold sore as big as a dime on his lip. He knows this may be a bluff, but it is something his client will have to think about. His distaste for Teresa is obvious, but she couldn't have him more firmly by the balls if she were holding on with a set of pliers. Rick Crawford, the chancery judge who appointed Teresa to represent the kid, would believe her over Wayne or me even if we had the entire United States Supreme Court as character witnesses for our clients. "Let me go talk to him," Wayne mutters as he gets up.

I can't resist winking at Teresa as soon as Wayne's back is turned. Teresa is one of the better-looking female attorneys in Blackwell County, and is happily married, with four kids. She glares at me. "How can you represent a woman like that, Gideon?" she hisses at me as I start to push up from my chair to go talk to Salina. "She should have her cunt sewn shut and you know it!"

The fierceness of her words shocks me as much as her profanity. Teresa and her husband, a pediatrician at Children's Hospital with a national reputation, appear regularly in the society pages of the *Arkansas Democrat-Gazette*. I shrug. "Women who want custody of their kids don't seem at first blush public enemy number one."

From a manila folder Teresa throws out on the table pictures of Bobby that turn my stomach. His buttocks look like hamburger meat. "I haven't seen these," I say, feeling my face turn warm.

Teresa shakes her finger at me. "Your client doesn't have any business even trying to raise a hamster."

I finger the pictures, trying not to wince. "She's had a hell of a life herself," I say weakly. Actually, I do not know this, but only suspect it from some of my client's comments.

"That doesn't give her the right to let her child suffer like this," she says harshly. "I'm not kidding. She should be sterilized."

So should about half the population of this country, I think, having had enough of Teresa's righteous indignation. It must be nice to be on the side of justice all the time. "I'll go talk to my client," I say, and scoot away before I shoot off my mouth.

Ten minutes later, we announce to a relieved Rick Crawford that we have a settlement. He tells our clients to make sure they pay Teresa's fees within thirty days, and I walk back to my office, relieved I have lost another case and telling myself for the tenth time since I have been in private practice to turn down all but childless divorce cases with ironclad prenuptial agreements.

"Why, Mr. Page," Leigh says, displaying only mild surprise, "I didn't know we had a meeting set up." Though it is after two in the afternoon, she looks fresh and crisp, and, as usual, is dressed as if she is ready to go out on a moment's notice. What is different is her hair. When I had seen her before it was up. Today it is down past her shoulders and more gorgeous than ever. She is wearing a pure silk emerald green shell with padded shoulders over a tan skirt. Even her belt looks expensive. Maybe Art laundered a lot more money than we know.

"You didn't call me back," I remind her. In the background I can hear her mother's voice on the telephone. "Why don't we go for a ride? I need to talk to you, and I don't think you want your mother present."

She gives me a quizzical look. She has seen the deferential version of the faithful sidekick and probably likes him better, but she nods. "Just a moment."

I try to look into the house, but my eyes don't have the time to adjust to the dimness before she is back striding past me out the door. It is a brilliant spring afternoon, the kind of day that makes me wish I had a job out of doors. After this morning's travesty, I ought to try to get one. The best thing about Arkansas is that even its most populated areas are within fifteen minutes of the country in any direction. Since we're out in the western part of the county anyway, I head for Pinnacle Mountain, only a short drive west. No one will mistake us for an illicit couple looking for a place to neck. No McDonald's employees I know have girlfriends who look this classy. "Why didn't you call?" I ask, trying not to sound like a rejected suitor. I realize as soon as I ask that my feelings are slightly hurt. I pride myself on being able to get clients to talk to me. I didn't expect her to fall in love with me, but I assumed she would keep her word. Just like a man, Rainey would say.

"I've been talking to Mr. Bracken," she says carefully. "I'm sure you know that." I glance over at her, but she keeps her eyes on the road.

I decide to wait to respond until we are at the park. I want to see her face when she is speaking. I tell her where we are headed, but she has no comment. Surely Chet has told her that I have been to San Francisco. It is all I can do to keep my mouth shut.

I turn off the engine in one of the parking spaces near the picnic tables, remembering one Saturday long ago with Rosa and Sarah. Sarah was about nine years old, and it was her first ascent to the top. We treated it as if we had climbed Mount Everest. An ache comes into my heart as I remember the exhilaration we all felt as we came down. I turn off the motor and ask, "You ever climb Pinnacle?"

"Sure," she says, her face softening for the first time. "My dad used to bring me out here lots of times. The best thing about being a preacher's kid is getting to see your father. His days off were in the middle of the week."

The park is virtually deserted, with only a couple of cars in it. Too late for picnickers, too early (I hope) for the teenagers who come out here to smoke and hang

out. We get out and both wander around, each of us
locked for a moment inside our own memories. Eastern
Arkansas, with its rich Delta soil nourished by the Mississippi, for the most part, is flat as a table top, and it
does not take much of a climb to impress me. Leigh, in
four-inch heels, is hardly dressed for an assault on a
peak I've seen five-year-olds conquer, but such is the
mystique of heights that we both search the brush for
the trail that leads to the top. She could easily be taken
for my daughter, I realize. Not for the first time I wonder if I have smothered Sarah as much as Norman has
smothered Leigh. Sarah is still angry at me. Though she
pretended to have gotten over our fight the night before
I left for San Francisco, she said barely two words after
she picked me up from the airport. How much am I
really like Norman? Probably more than I care to admit.
He got Leigh a job in the church to keep her close; se-
cretly, I've dreamed for the last year that Sarah would
attend law school at UALR and come into practice with
me. Norman and I both use guilt in the same quantities
the Nazis used gas. I think Leigh is protecting her father. As disgusted with me as she is right now, I'm not
sure Sarah would be so charitable.

I sit on one side of a picnic table and watch Leigh
staring at a squirrel that is eyeing her with an equal
amount of curiosity. Could she really have murdered her
husband? At the moment, nothing seems more unlikely.
Bending down and clucking at the bemused animal, she
seems about ten. Finally, it scampers away and she
comes to the table, smiling as if she had tamed it. I say,
hoping to catch her off guard, "I didn't learn anything
in San Francisco that will convince a jury you were at
risk."

She does not respond but places her hands over her
mouth as if she is becoming nauseated. "Art wasn't a

lot different from your father, was he?" I say, and tell her my belief that they must have hated each other. "It must have seemed like Art was fighting for your body and Shane was fighting for your soul."

Parting her hands, Leigh gives me a fierce look. "My father didn't kill my husband, if that's what you're thinking."

The bench is hard. There is no getting comfortable on it. I follow up quickly. "But you're worried that he might have, aren't you?"

When she doesn't say anything, I plunge ahead. "He was furious that morning at Art because you hadn't come to church. He knew you were home, and when you went up there to pretend to check in, he went to the house and killed Art."

Her beautiful face is flushed. "That's ridiculous!" she shouts at me. "My father is incapable of killing anyone."

She is breathing too hard for me to belive she is convinced of that. "You know how jealous he was of Art," I say. "He thought he was the very personification of evil, and that's what you now think, too. What was it you stayed home to do with Art that morning? Was it sex? Is that what you're ashamed to tell?"

She begins to cry. Somehow she has to open up to me. I tell her, "My own daughter and I have become incredibly close since her mother died. I feel so helpless right now, because it seems like I'm about to lose her— ironically, to your father's church. Could I kill somebody? I think I could, but if I couldn't, I suspect the reason is that I don't know anybody at the moment who I can say is evil. If somebody abused her, hurt her, I doubt it would take me long to work up some uncontrollable anger. Did your father know about Art's pornoskimming plan? Is that what tipped him over the edge?"

Leigh reaches into her purse for a tissue. Her hands are shaking. Most women look terrible when they cry. Instead, her eyes have become more enormous and beautiful. "I don't see how he could," she gets out.

With the trial next week, it is now or never. I fear that someone will drive up, but it is quiet and peaceful, beyond words. In the distance I can see a park ranger's truck stop down by the entrance. I say, "I know how attached your father is to you. He lost your sisters, and he was about to lose you. He probably loves you more than he loves your mother, Leigh. And Art stood for everything he hated. Your dad knew how the world seduces people, and he spent his life building a fortress so you could be safe from it. He didn't want you to marry Art, did he?"

Leigh's breasts rise and fall under the silk. She shakes her head. "He wanted me to delay the wedding, but he couldn't find anything specifically wrong with Art. He did say that if Art really loved me, he wouldn't mind waiting until we got to know each other better."

Men in their forties don't have much patience. We see too many heart attacks in our age bracket. I stand up, unwilling to inflict the bench on my butt any longer. "Shane hired an investigator to try to turn something up, didn't he?" This is pure speculation, but not out of the realm of possibility. Shane, like Chet, doesn't seem the type to leave much to chance if he can avoid it.

Leigh brushes her hair away from her neck. Though it is gloriously mild, doubtless she has begun to feel warmer since this conversation began. "Art told me after we married that he thought Daddy had done something," she confesses. "He said somebody was looking into his business. Naturally, he assumed it was Daddy, but he was never able to confirm it."

I glance up at the mountain, fearful that someone is

suddenly going to come walking out of it. Turning back to Leigh I say, "A pretty logical assumption, don't you think? After your sisters left the church and the state, I imagine he was paranoid about his favorite daughter. And after you married Art, his worst suspicions were confirmed." She looks down at the ground. There is something she hasn't told me, but it may be too difficult. All her life she has been dominated by middle-aged men. She may have had her fill of us. "What about Art?" I ask. "Was he worried about your father?"

Leigh wipes her eyes. "Not physically," she said. "Three months after we were married, he told me I had been brainwashed by Daddy. He said Christian Life was fine for people afraid to live in the real world. He said our family groups were essentially spies, part of the thought police that Daddy used to control our behavior."

I watch the park ranger's truck drive slowly toward us. If he sees Leigh crying, he may stop. "He never took Christian Life seriously, did he?" I ask.

"He said he did," Leigh says, her voice bitter, "but I didn't believe him." She turns to watch as the ranger creeps slowly past us. He waves. I wave back. It is too lovely a day to go looking for trouble. I don't know what the pay is, but I wouldn't mind the job, cruising around the parks in perfect weather, hoping to catch couples making it in the backseat.

Leigh, I see, has some of her father in her. There is an unrevealed vein of anger at Art I haven't tapped into yet. "You wanted to believe him," I say, encouraging her. "That's pretty obvious."

She wets her lips, and her voice becomes high with indignation. "My husband was a con artist of the first order. He could make you think black was white before you knew it. Of course I wanted him to believe in Jesus Christ. What was wrong with that?"

Am I the one being conned? She sounds so convincing my reaction is to doubt her. Still, I ask, "Did he make you doubt your faith?"

Leigh's voice takes on an accusing tone. "He could ridicule something without you even realizing that's what he was doing. Before I knew it, I had begun to question the book of Genesis."

Her look of astonished anger seems genuine. I try to put myself in her place. Despite her exquisite beauty, she has never lived in the world like a normal woman. My supposition until now has been that anyone who looks like this can't be naive. I realize I have been applying the same standards to Leigh that I apply to Sarah and to Rainey, but their situation is not even remotely similar. If Sarah and Rainey did not want to take the Bible literally, there is no one on earth who could talk them into it. "You had to realize at some point Art was calling into question everything you and your father had lived for," I say, not quite asking a question. What better motive for murder? If her actions weren't a crime, they would be easy to justify. A jury made up of Christian Life members would probably acquit her in five minutes or at least would keep her out of jail.

Leigh looks pained as she admits, "It wasn't as easy to see that as you think. For the first time in my life, I guess, thanks to my husband, I began to rebel against my father. Art was subtle about it at first. It was only right before he died that he really began to criticize Christian Life."

I watch as the ranger drives back by. He waves again. What a tough job. "Was Art open about it?" I ask, wondering how much of it was getting back to Shane.

"No," Leigh explains. "You'd have to have known

Art. In public he was charming and would give a million excuses for us not being up there more. In private, he made fun of my father."

The prosecutor's office would have a field day with this information. It is as damaging to Leigh as it is to her father. It hits me that it is not out of the realm of possibility that Leigh and her father could have planned this murder together. They certainly had a motive. Perhaps at the last moment someone is going to step forward to support Leigh's alibi that she was at the church the entire time. "Where has your mother been in all of this?" I ask, struck by how little Pearl Norman figures in her account.

Leigh shrugs as if the answer is obvious. "Mother's been out of the loop for as long as I can remember."

I'm put off by her apparent callousness, but I think I can understand. She's been looped for years, is what she means. You learn to maneuver around a parent like that and pretend things are normal. Two cars come roaring toward us. I know there is more that she needs to tell me, but it will have to wait, as an ancient Volkswagen and an equally old Dodge Dart swing in next to the Blazer. Six teenagers equally divided between boys and girls spill out and come toward us. They look like punks to me, though Sarah is constantly telling me I judge kids too harshly. The guys instantly begin to give Leigh the eye. Their girls, dressed in jeans, pale in comparison. Though the age differences are clearly obvious (Leigh looks older than twenty-three), one of the guys can't resist saying to her, "Hey, why don't you drop this old fart and come with us?"

My manhood is threatened, but I can't very well fight a kid, especially not one this big. Though I am an inch under six feet, this boy goes at least six feet two inches and looks in a lot better shape. My first and last fight in the last thirty years (less than a year ago) cost me a tooth. I am too young for a full set of dentures, so I mutter, "She doesn't want to spend the afternoon changing your diapers."

Naturally, this gets everyone's attention, and I'm quickly surrounded by three kids whose ages barely add up to my own. Wonderful. In the course of twenty seconds I've gone from being a lawyer who has finally conducted a decent interview to becoming a hopeless jerk. "I think pops wants his ass kicked," the smallest kid says, clenching his fists.

I could probably whip him if I got lucky. Leigh looks frightened, though it seems extremely unlikely that she is in any danger of being harmed or raped. The three girls who came with the boys are plainly unhappy with the turn of events, even though they are silent. Their expressions range from disgust to jealousy. I wish one of them would announce that she will be organizing a sexual boycott if there is trouble, but the silence grows as I rack my brain for a suitable reply. Finally, I come to my senses and allow us all to save face. "I'm not looking for trouble," I say. "All I'm trying to do is take this woman back to Christian Life, where I picked her up an hour ago."

I have said the magic words. The least attractive of the girls, a dumpy blonde in denim overalls with hair the texture of straw, says, apropos of nothing, to her surprisingly sexy neighbor on her left, "I got an aunt who goes there. She says the minister's really cool."

Without missing a beat, Leigh says, her voice strong and confident, "He's my father." She doesn't add that she suspects he is a murderer or that she is believed to have shot her husband through the heart. Nor does she add that one of her lawyers thinks the other one may somehow be involved. I would be willing to bet my

false tooth that none of these kids has ever heard of
Leigh. My bias against this motley crew is so strong it
is next to impossible for me to concede they know
much beyond each other's names. Most information
among the young, unless it is gossip, is baggage whose
weight they consider excessive. The group parts like the
Red Sea, and my client leads me to the safety of the
Blazer.

Whatever closeness Leigh and I achieved (and I have
at least the illusion that she has confided in me) van-
ishes. We return to her parents' house like a couple on
their first real date, which didn't quite work out. I feel
I was near some information that would explain her to
me. My remaining questions go ignored as she insists
upon returning to the Christian Life compound. Instead,
she protests mildly, "Why'd you say something smart to
that boy? They could have hurt us."

I look over at her to see if she is serious. I am so
frustrated I'm about to burst. The last hour has convinced me she is covering up for her father in some
manner, but I don't know how to get it out of her. I
can't remember the last time I felt this irritated with a
client. "Was I supposed to kiss his ass?" I say crudely.
"I suppose I should have told him to be my guest."

Shocked by my reaction, she seems to cower against
the door. "Men are such bullies," she complains. "You
don't sound any different than those boys."

"You're forgetting I backed down," I remind her.
Bullies, are we? Is she talking about her father or Art or
both? As we hit the traffic near town, I try again. "What
did Art bully you into doing?"

I look away from the road to see her reaction. For an
instant I see anguish in her eyes, but she says nothing.
What was it? I know there is something she wants to

tell me but can't. I blurt out, "I think you know your father killed Art but you won't admit it."

In her eyes is the dumb fear you see in an animal's face when it realizes it is trapped. "Daddy didn't kill Art!" she says shrilly.

I don't believe her. I stop the Blazer in front of her parents' house and get right in her face. "You're going to have to choose, Leigh. I know you think Chet can get you off. But with the way the evidence is stacking up now, that isn't going to happen. I know how much you admire your father, and except for one horrible moment, he may be the most wonderful man in the world. But you don't want to spend the rest of your life in prison for a crime you didn't commit. Unless his alibi is rock solid, we're going to have to go after your father."

Leigh shakes her head and pushes her way out of the Blazer. As she runs around the front of the vehicle, I see her mother coming toward me down the walk. As before, she has the florid complexion of someone who has been drinking. Seeing the look on her daughter's face, she pleads, "Where have you been? What's wrong?"

Leigh stops on the grass between the curb and the sidewalk. "Nothing, Mother," she says stubbornly. "Just go back in the house."

Mrs. Norman looks at her daughter and then at me. "What happened?"

There is no doubt in my mind whose side Pearl Norman will come down on. From the beginning, she has struck me as the kind of woman who would call her child a liar before she would believe an allegation of sexual abuse by her husband. Afraid Leigh will recite our conversation to her word for word, I say, "You understand my relationship with your daughter is confidential, Mrs. Norman."

Pearl Norman blinks away the technicality. "Leigh is my daughter, Mr. Page."

"And she is my client," I say firmly, watching her face flush. Where was she during the murder? I'll find that out, too, but the truth is, I can't imagine Pearl Norman firing a gun any more than I can imagine my own mother doing it. She seems too helpless, too dependent on men to be able to kill one of us. "If you want to help Leigh's case, you won't pry."

It is as if Barney Fife had cussed out Aunt Bee. Her lips quiver, and ninety-proof tears begin to gush as if a dam had burst. She turns and rushes back into the house with Leigh following closely behind. She is as protective of her mother as she is of her father. Damn. Another conversation like this one, and I'll be watching this case from the back of the courtroom. I drive off as frustrated as a teenager who didn't even get a goodnight kiss. With this weather I can't bring myself to return to the office just yet and decide to make the afternoon a total waste by looking for Jason's spiritual development center.

If I can get Mrs. Chestnut's money back for her, maybe she will adopt me and I can forget all this nonsense about making a living. I have not been able to bring myself to return her call, but while I was in San Francisco, Julia said she had called with the address of Jason's school: 10000 Darnell Road. Since it is the only address in the last five years I've been able to remember without having to look it up, I consider it a good omen and head west again. In five minutes I see the sign, but instead of spiritual development, it promises Personality Enhancement in freshly painted letters. Maybe Jason has begun to doubt his own abilities and has begun to settle for more modest goals.

I can hear dogs barking as soon as I get out of the

car. I enter a rectangular wooden building and am met by a smiling young man behind a desk who asks if I am here to pick up Clarence.

I clear my throat and look around the room. It has the hosed-down look of a vet's office, but I can hear opera music in the background. I am hardly a fan (the golden oldies on Cool [KOLL] 95 are my speed); nevertheless, I hear the familiar Toreador song and realize I'm humming along with it. Maybe this is the key to my own spiritual development. I am tempted to confess to being Clarence's master if it will give me the opportunity to escape. Somehow, I am having difficulty asking for Jason. All of a sudden I feel as if I am here to get my hair done. "No," I stammer, "I'm just here to talk to, uh, Jason for a minute. Is he free?"

The young man, who has the smile of someone enjoying a drug high, looks at his watch. "You're in luck," he says, beaming at me. "He's just finishing a class right now."

Three P.M. right on the money. School's out. I hear excited howls over the music. Why should this class be any different? Time to boogie. "Great," I say. "Can I go on back?"

"I better take you," he says, standing up and extending a hand. "I'm Harvey," he says. He, too, is dressed like a McDonald's manager. We look as if we each work a different shift, but otherwise we could be father and son. "I like your tie," he says.

"Target's," I admit. "I have four or five almost just like this," I say, shaking his hand which, like mine, is small for his size. I glance down at his tie. It is striped like my own. No flower jobs for me and Harvey. We're from the old school and proud of it.

The fact that we are dressed almost identically must be reassuring to Harvey, for without another word, he leads me back through a kennel where there must be fifteen dogs in small cages. I get claustrophobic just looking at them. Every time I have had to board Woogie, he loses weight. I might get a little depressed myself. No table scraps here. Harvey yells over the din, "You interested in a class?"

I am captivated by a toy collie in the corner. He looks so friendly I want to take him home, but another dog would break Woogie's heart. A man might as well bring a mistress home to live alongside his wife. For an instant, I think Harvey means for myself. "Sort of," I say ambiguously. "How often do they have them?"

Harvey leads me through a back door into an area that has several empty pens. "It depends on the interest. Jason will have a class with as many as five. But fewer students than three, and there's not much interaction."

I smile and get a sinking feeling. As I have feared, this is for real. The music, which has been so loud I can barely hear, ceases, and I respond, too loudly, not believing I'm having this conversation, "We learn best from each other all right." Actually, there are not a lot of role models for Woogie in our neighborhood. My law-abiding neighbors keep their dogs penned and don't let them outside except on leashes. When I take Woogie for a walk after work, he gets a free shot at all the flower beds, hydrants, and trees he wants. My hometown of Bear Creek in eastern Arkansas had no animal-control law (or if it did, it was unenforceable), and I can't bring myself to accept the notion that central Arkansas insists upon such trappings of big-city life. However, the first time I have to bail Woogie out of the pound I suspect I will be convinced.

We exit the building, and I look to my left and see a man about my age squatting down in the dirt, talking seriously to a cocker spaniel. Jason, I presume. I strain to hear what he says, and catch the words, ". . . having too many negative thoughts, Clay."

Clay, a buff-colored fatty with wet, friendly eyes, wags his tail at the mention of his name. He looks pretty happy to me. Negative thoughts have a way of energizing me, too. Some of us in the animal kingdom may not be educable. "Jason, this man would like a word with you," Harvey announces, not particularly loath to interrupt work in progress.

Jason looks up and gives me a glance that makes me glad I am not Clay's owner. "There are no bad dogs," he says. "Only bad owners."

I am not quite so optimistic about four-footed creatures, but I hold my tongue, figuring this conversation will be difficult enough. I introduce myself: "I'm Gideon Page." I look around, since Jason does not rise to shake hands. I notice I am standing in an enclosed yard that actually is quite pleasant. Three large elm trees provide shade over half the area. Even in midsummer it would be possible to survive out here if one were of the canine persuasion.

"I need to get back up front," Harvey announces cheerfully, apparently oblivious to the lack of communication rapidly settling in between his boss and his boss's visitor.

He walks back into the kennel, while Jason scratches Clay behind the ear. At least the man seems to like his pupils, which is more than I can say for a lot of teachers. "I know who you are, Giddy Page!" Jason suddenly hisses, still squatting on his heels like some Eastern mystic. "I'd swap every lawyer in this country for one of these," he says, stroking Clay's back like a lover. "Who have you lawyers ever made smile except criminals and greedy corporate thugs? You'd scrape the paint off your mother's toes before she'd been dead an hour if you thought you could sell it. Why, this lovely creature," he said, looking soulfully into Clay's eyes, "brings more pleasure to people in five minutes than your profession has brought throughout the entire existence of its long, depraved history."

How does he know I hate to be called Giddy? "Mrs. Chestnut wants her five hundred bucks back," I say, deciding that Jason is one of those people who plays defense as little as possible. "She isn't at all satisfied with the work you did on Bernard Junior."

Jason leans backward to look up at me, and I realize the man is terribly deformed. I thought he was squatting on his heels, but, in fact, he is standing as upright as he will ever be. He is a dwarf, as humpbacked as anyone I've ever seen. As vitriolic as his personality is, it's impossible to feel sympathy for him (as if he gives a damn), but I do understand his attitude a little better. No lawyer has ever loved him. The canine population (if Clay is any example) would elect him president by acclamation if they could vote. I'm not sure the country would be worse off if a couple of million lawyers suddenly decided to emigrate.

"Bernard Junior was a rare jewel," Jason says, glaring at me. Clay emits a low growl as he senses his teacher's distaste for his visitor. "Bernard Junior had the soul of an angel. He was all heart. Mrs. Chestnut is an old prude. Just because he liked to lick himself didn't mean he wasn't advancing metaphysically. Pit bulls are so full of life and vigor that it would be a crime to expect to curb habits that have been programmed genetically. You think we humans wouldn't do the same if we were physically able? Jealousy. Pure jealousy. Mrs. Chestnut was green with envy, and you can take that to the bank."

I think of Mrs. Chestnut's delicate, sweet old face,

and realize I have some doubts about Jason's sanity. "I don't think a judge would come to the same conclusion."

"Of course not! Judges are lawyers! Talk about a conflict of interest, Mr. Giddy Page. I've never heard of one so brazen." No longer growling, Clay rolls over on his back to let his teacher work on his stomach. His eyes seem to roll back in his head in pure ecstasy.

I feel uncomfortable looking down at Jason and squat down on my heels to get at eye level with him. He is wearing green swimming trunks over black tights, sandals, and a T-shirt with a picture of Lassie. "Okay," I sigh. "What did you teach Bernard Junior?"

Jason drums his fingers on Clay's midsection and Clay's lips recede from his teeth. I could swear he is grinning. "Acceptance of his lot in life," Jason says without hesitation. "Imagine having his physique and jaws and never once being allowed to rip off the head of a cat. He's as bored as a lion in a zoo. He kept nodding off, but I understand that. If I had to live with Mrs. Chestnut, I couldn't stay awake either. How do I teach a class? Lectures, music therapy, lots of individual attention. I know what you're thinking, Giddy Page. They don't understand. How naive of you! Do your muscles understand a back rub? Does your mind understand Beethoven's Ninth Symphony? Of course not! But even as coarse and self-absorbed as the mind of a lawyer is, you surely and without a doubt get the message. As Marsh McLuhan preached decades ago, 'the medium is the message,' and I, Jason Von Jason, am the medium."

Jason Von Jason? Why not? I look enviously at Clay, whose teeth are twice as white as my own. I concede I've never looked so happy. If Jason could get on TV and pitch Slim Whitman records, he probably would make a fortune. No judge will have the patience to listen to this case for more than thirty seconds. Besides, Jason is the type to counterclaim for a million dollars. And win. I stand up. "If Mrs. Chestnut hasn't gotten a Ben Franklin from you in three days," I bluster, "she won't have any recourse but to sue."

Jason looks up at me and says scornfully, "Sue. Betty. Jane. Martha. You lawyers are the least imaginative species on the planet. Go bore a cockroach to death, Giddy Page. What kind of dog are you torturing?" I think of how bored Woogie must get during the day. He seems as if he accepts himself though. I don't dare answer Jason. He'd crucify me. "Some kind of poor mutt," he guesses, "who looks like a giraffe."

A chill runs down my back. Considering Woogie's legs, Jason isn't far off. Maybe I ought to ask Jason if Leigh killed Art. As I leave through the front of the building, Harvey, smiling beatifically, says, "Bring your dog for a visit. I'm sure Jason would love to enroll him."

I wave but keep silent. I've learned my lesson.

12

"CHET BRACKEN'S WAITING for you in your office," Julia says in hushed tones as I come up to her desk from the outside door. Uncharacteristically, she is speaking as if someone had died. "What have you been doing? You smell like a puppy farm."

I look at my watch. It is just after four. Leigh didn't waste any time calling him. My stomach begins to bubble with anxiety. He is going to be furious that I went out to see Leigh on my own. Last night, when I got in from San Francisco, I left a message on his answering machine that I would call him as soon as my custody trial was over. Now my plan to see Leigh and then confront him doesn't seem like such a good idea. "How long has he been here?" I ask, looking at my shoes. I might have stepped in something in the schoolyard.

"About ten minutes," she says, now a little nervous. "I took him on back. After the money he gave you, I kind of felt it was okay. He asked."

Julia obviously is a graduate of the take-no-prisoners secretarial school and makes it a point of honor never to apologize. This is as close as she will come, and so I accept. "No problem. How did he seem?"

Julia squints at me as if she is trying to understand something. "A little hostile. Is he well?"

I wave her off and try to keep from running to my office. What all did Leigh tell him? Shit, this is as good a time as any to lay my cards on the table. He is sitting at my desk with the light off, his head resting against his arms on top of the desk-top calendar. The expression on his face when I hit the switch does not reassure me. "Are you trying to blow this case?" he demands as I take a seat across from my desk like some scared client. Pulpy, plum-colored circles under his eyes make him look as if he were in his fifties, but his voice rushes toward me like a freight train. "What in the hell do you think you're doing?"

All the frustration I have been feeling on this case finally boils over. I smack my desk with the palm of my right hand. "As far as I'm concerned, the odds are at least even that Shane Norman is involved in this murder, and if he's not, he sure as hell looks like it. Though she won't admit it, Leigh suspects it herself. She told me that Art believed that Shane had him investigated before they got married and tried to persuade her to wait."

Chet shakes his head and gets up to shut my door. I am practically yelling at him. Chet's neck is swallowed by a pink Oxford shirt and a green tie with penguins on it. If he weren't dying, I'd laugh. Julia sneers that he dresses worse than I do. He leans back heavily in my chair and says, "That doesn't prove shit!"

I rest my elbows against the corner of the desk, realizing how utterly passive I've been in this case. "Norman hated the man. Don't you get it? Wallace was stealing his last daughter from him and turning her into an atheist who would make fun of him. Leigh had been Shane's favorite since she was five years old. Art was a bastard, and nobody knew it better than Norman. For all we know, he may have even found out about the child porno deal."

"None of this makes him a murderer!" Chet thunders. "Look, I know this man. There is absolutely no way he killed Art Wallace. Do you hear me?"

I hear him all right, but his words ring with all the authority of a carnival barker. His curiously blank expression and outraged tone don't match. I wonder if he may be concentrating on controlling the pain he may be feeling. "All you know is that Shane Norman saved your soul, and that has blinded you to the fact that the man was, is, and shall remain until the day he dies a human being who had a real reason to want his son-in-law dead. Damn it, will you at least check his alibi?"

Chet stares at me as if he is seeing me for the first time. I think I am about to get fired. So much for inheriting his cases and being known as his heir apparent. "That won't satisfy you," he says, his voice cold and mechanical. "If he can prove he was at the church, next you'll claim he hired somebody to kill Art."

I seize the tiny opening he gives me. "No, I won't. There's no evidence to support it. If it had been a hit man, Art wouldn't have been sitting behind his desk. Like you've already said, it wouldn't have been a twenty-two pistol. At least check it out," I beg. "Norman told me himself that he thought Leigh would have left the state with Art in another six months. In the same conversation he admitted he could be thought of as Art's enemy."

Chet slumps in his chair. He says morosely, "Shane would think the cancer has gone to my brain once he got over being insulted."

I can't believe my ears. "When have you ever worried about insulting anyone? Leigh is our client, not Norman. Let me check it out," I insist. "I'll just pretend I'm trying to nail down Leigh's story."

Chet loosens his tie, a needless act if there ever was

one. "You're not dealing with an idiot. He'll know what you're up to as soon as you start poking around." He hesitates but promises, "I'll handle this."

I don't believe him. Norman has become like a god to him. "You're going to have to," I say firmly, "or I'm quitting the case. We have no business representing Leigh if we can't give her our undivided loyalty. It's a clear conflict of interest."

Chet flinches as if he is in pain. Probably no one has ever talked to him this way. Most likely no one has ever needed to. "You're right," he says finally. "I'll do it."

"The sooner the better." I feel a sense of relief. For the first time I realize he probably has asked for help on the case because he sensed the dilemma he was in but couldn't bring himself to face it squarely. From now on, I need to be more aggressive, not less. He's been looking for somebody to stand up to him, and until now I've been entirely too deferential. For the next fifteen minutes I tell him about my trip to San Francisco, concluding, "For what it's worth, and it doesn't seem much, the investigator is willing to come testify."

Chet, who has listened intently, nods, saying, "We can do a lot with this. A local jury would love to believe some thug from California killed Wallace."

Damn it, he still is looking for a way out of having to check out Shane. Unaccustomed to sitting in the chair I provide clients, I shift around trying to find a comfortable spot. No wonder they are always squirming. My conversation with Harold Broadnax comes racing back to me. Bracken points so many fingers during a trial you'd think he was a freak in a carnival. "It's better than nothing," I admit.

Chet grunts noncommittally and pushes himself out of his chair. He looks like a scarecrow. He says wryly,

"Thanks for the conversation. I've got to run by the pharmacy. I know the way out. I'll call you."

I am afraid to press him further. The son of a bitch. He knows I'm right. Shane Norman is like some sacred cow that roams the streets while people starve. I stew in my office for a minute and then go try to find Dan to run this latest development by him. Maybe I am overreacting. I don't think so, but if anyone will tell me, Dan will. He is not in his office, and I buzz Julia. "Where's Dan?" I ask, realizing how rare it is to see her on the defensive. It is good for her.

"He was headed for the crapper," she says, snickering, "but he wouldn't admit it. He's been gone fifteen minutes. Maybe you better check on him. You know how the King died."

"I doubt if Dan is on as many drugs," I say dryly. I'm sure Julia is referring to a magazine account that Elvis was on the commode when he bought it.

"You never know," Julia chirps, her voice malicious, "people fool ya all the time. By the way, Chet Bracken is starting to get on my nerves good. He looked like he was about to puke his guts out when he came by here on his way to the elevators. You're making the guy sick to his stomach."

Out of the mouths of babes, I think. I concede, "I've been known to have that effect."

"Tell me about it," Julia agrees. "Most of your clients look a lot more worried coming out of your office than when they went in. Here's Humpty Dumpty now. Hey, Dan, you the one been stinking up the joint? The cleaning people are having fits, according to Uncle Roy. They're wanting to charge extra to do the crappers on this floor. It's like there's mass food poisoning every day up here. If you guys would get paying clients who could afford their own toilets, we wouldn't be having this problem."

I try to imagine Dan's expression as Julia interrogates him. Julia's main qualification for her position is her bloodline. Her uncle, Roy Rogers (not the cowboy, she was quick to assure me), owns the building. "Up yours, too. By the way, Zorro is panting for you, as usual." I wore an old black suit I found in my closet one day last week, and I've been Zorro ever since.

"I hope there aren't too many people in the waiting room, Julia," I say, fascinated as usual by the horror show. Julia will be working here until she is ninety. What a joy she will be then.

"As of this moment," Julia yelps into my ear, "I'm off duty, Zorro, so button it up."

I look down at my watch. It is exactly five o'clock. Asking Julia to stay five minutes late is like asking one of the lawyers on the floor to add more paper to the copier. Don't waste your breath. Dan wobbles into my office, patting his stomach. "I think I swallowed a hand grenade at lunch," he moans. "What's up?"

An upset stomach doesn't prohibit him from wandering over to the window to check to see if any of our female neighbors from the Adcock Building are about. "Shit," he mutters, disappointed. He turns and plops down in the chair across from me. "Why do they leave so early?" he says. "No wonder this country is going down the tubes. I didn't expect to see any of them standing there naked. I just wanted a memory to tide me over till I return to this hellhole. Is that asking too much of life?"

I am too wired to bullshit and tell him about the last two days. Dan has been the main advocate for a conspiracy between Shane and Chet. "He's scared shitless what he'll find. What in the hell do I do?"

Dan shifts in his seat as if he is trying to ease out a fart. "You really talked to Bracken that way?" he asks admiringly. "I didn't think you had it in you."

I prop my feet up on my desk. "I didn't have any choice."

Dan shakes his head. "While you were in San Francisco, I thought a lot about this case. You're reacting the way you are because you'd like to see Shane take a direct hit. Why? Your kid. You resent the hell out of Norman because he's stolen Sarah away from you. It's natural, and I don't blame you, but let's face it: murder is not how the guy makes his living."

To say I'm perplexed is an understatement. It was Dan who first hatched this theory. I pick up a paper clip from my drawer and begin to straighten it. Is he right? Perhaps. But that doesn't mean Shane couldn't have done it. Preachers aren't immune to violence. Hell, when I was in the Peace Corps, one of the most famous Colombian revolutionaries was a Catholic priest. "So I'm biased," I ask, trying not to sound irritated, "what's your excuse?"

Dan chokes off a belch. He seems about to explode. I wonder if he's been talking to Brenda about the case. Probably. She throws a wet blanket over everything. Dan grins. "You know how I am about conspiracies. Hell, I think Jackie had Jack bumped off because she was sick of him screwing around."

"Supposedly, I was hired," I say sarcastically, "in this case to help get Leigh off. I'm getting the distinct impression that while I was out of town the rules changed. Maybe even before I left."

Dan places his right hand over his stomach as if it were a seismograph attempting to measure an earthquake. "You gotta admit you're dealing with a club you're not a member of."

I smile for the first time all day. If nothing else, Dan is good at pointing out the obvious. "Tell me something I don't know. The judge probably knows more about this case than I do."

"Who you got?" Dan wants to know. I can see his stomach jumping from the other side of my desk.

"Grider," I say. "It'll be a circus." George Grider is the kind of judge who lets lawyers in his courtroom savage each other like wild animals. He is intelligent and comes from an old Blackwell County family but seems to get some kind of perverse pleasure out of the hostility that is generated in the courtroom. Twenty years ago he was a prosecutor, and he generally comes down in the middle with his rulings on evidence and procedure. The trick is getting him to come down at all. My guess is that he likes the publicity that his hands-off approach spawns.

"A mud bath all right," Dan acknowledges. "Maybe you ought to tell Chet *adios* on this one. It looks like he wants to stick you with his first loss so he can go out a winner."

"If he would let me, I could win this damn thing!" I practically shout.

Dan stands up and leans against the wall. Apparently, he feels better if his stomach is pointed downhill. "Maybe that's bullshit, too. He might not be sick at all."

There Dan goes again. "He's sick all right," I say. Still, I'm in the dark about that as much as I am on everything else. "But he could live another two years, as far as I know."

"Hell, Leigh probably did it," Dan says. "Women have a million reasons to put us out of our misery. The surprising thing is that you don't see it more often." He grins at me. "You know, I forget what an ambitious fucker you are. You pretend to be a sap like the rest of us on this floor, and yet behind all that eastern Arkansas cornpone, you're eaten up with this stuff."

I have to bite my tongue. The bottom line is that you're a talker, not a doer, my friend, I think. "Not like Chet Bracken used to be."

"You're working on it," Dan pushes himself to a vertical position. "I'm out of here. I think I'll go have my stomach pumped."

Dan's wrinkled shirt bulges out over his pants like a plastic garbage bag. "Rosa used to say that's not a lot of fun."

Dan winks at me. "Hey, I'm stupid, but I'm not crazy. I'll just go home and eat until I pop open."

I grab my coat. I might as well leave, too. On the freeway, I realize just how much Bracken has got my number. He knows how much I want to stay in and do this case. Shit, if he knows that, he also knows whether Norman has an alibi. But maybe not. I don't trust anyone on this case, including myself.

In the waiting room a guy as bald as an egg stands up and says, "Mr. Page, I just got out yesterday from St. Thomas. I found the papers you wanted."

Rich Blessing? I stammer, "Good to see you. Let's go on back to my office, and I'll take a look." He falls in step alongside of me, and I steal another glance at him. Without his toupee, he didn't have much hair, but now he looks like a retired caretaker for a nuclear power plant.

"How're you feeling?" I ask, turning on the light in my office.

"Better," he says, handing me an envelope. "I was having a nervous breakdown because of my toupee. I began dreaming I kept having to chase it. My doctor got me admitted to the psychiatric wing at St. Thomas, but now that I'm out, I've decided to make a clean sweep of it," he says, pointing to his head.

Given permission, I take a good look. Sweep, hell. His skull looks like one of Woogie's dog bones. "Whatever helps you make it through the night," I mutter, before I realize how bad I sound. I open the envelope and find, among more testimonials, a warranty. In the third paragraph, in big block letters, it says: DO NOT WEAR IN WATER OR OUTSIDE ON DAYS WHEN WIND IS EXPECTED TO EXCEED TWENTY MILES AN HOUR. "How windy was it that day when it came off?" I ask, handing him the document containing the warranty.

"Practically a hurricane," he says cheerfully as he begins to read.

I let him read in silence and watch his face fall. "I never saw this."

"We could try to argue the salesman misrepresented it to you," I say, my heart not really in it.

Blessing stands up and shrugs. "He didn't. Actually, I don't think I want to sue now. After a week of being on the funny farm with some really sick people I realize how inconsequential hair is."

"Good," I say, and hand him all his papers. I'll get rich next time. I've got a more important case to worry about. I just hope Blessing can make a living.

At home I have trouble concealing my rotten mood. It is Sarah's night to cook, but when I look in the refrigerator to take out a beer all I see are food stains and a quart of milk three days past the date on the carton. As Sarah comes into the kitchen, I complain, "Why aren't you putting stuff on the list?"

Sarah pushes up the sleeves on her wind suit and washes her hands in the sink. "I don't see your handwriting up there either," she says mildly. "Bad day, Daddy?"

I stare at her back. That kind of remark would have been considered impudent when I was her age. It seems as if I have no control over anything. Beginning with the custody deal this morning, followed by my meeting with Leigh this afternoon, and then just now with Chet, I have no power to affect events. I say candidly, "I think I'm upset because the more work I do on Leigh's case, the more I'm convinced she's covering up for her father, and yet there doesn't seem to be anything I can do about it."

Drying her hands on a dish towel, my daughter turns and admonishes me, "If there's no evidence of his involvement, you can't do anything."

I pour myself a glass of water instead of the beer I want. I shouldn't be talking to her about the case, but I can't seem to resist rubbing her nose in it. "You've got to promise to keep quiet about what I'm going to tell you, but I've found out this afternoon your pastor had every reason to want his son-in-law dead." I launch into an abbreviated version of my conversation with Leigh and add the highlights of my talk with Shane before I went to San Francisco. "Shane Norman is a lot more likely suspect than his daughter," I conclude, knowing I've exaggerated a few things, but not by much.

"You're going to argue in court that he's the murderer!" Sarah guesses, her voice high enough to shatter the glass in my hand. "That's so wrong. You'd destroy an innocent man's reputation to win a case. You're horrible, Daddy!"

Without thinking, I slap Sarah across the face. Instantly, I regret it. I haven't spanked her since she was five years old and ran out into the street. Still, I am sick of her high-and-mighty attitude. "You don't know what you're talking about!"

Stunned, for an instant she stands watching me, unable to comprehend I have hit her, then bursts into tears and runs from the kitchen into her room. "Sarah!" I yell, but she shuts her door. I can't believe I have raised a hand to her. Yet she has no business talking to me like that. I go to her door and open it. She has thrown herself face down across her bed. I look around her room. Clothes are strewn on the floor; Coke cans are everywhere; even the collage of her friends on the wall by her bed is askew. She is still such a child. "I'm not the lead counsel in this case. Chet has no intention of making the argument that Shane Norman is implicated."

"But you would!" she says in a choked, muffled voice.

"If I thought he might have done it, of course I would!" I say firmly. "That's my job." She is silent, and I see her shoulders shaking as she sobs against her pillow.

She doesn't move. I want to hug her, but I know she is too angry to let me. She will forgive me. She always does. I say, "I'm so sorry I slapped you, babe! That was terrible. Listen, I'm going to the store. We'll eat when I get back." I leave the room and shut her door. To hell with a list. We always get more than the items we put on it.

At Harvest Foods, filled with remorse, I wander the aisles almost aimlessly, unable to decide even between one or two percent fat milk. Sarah is by far the best part of my life, and I have hit her like all those parents I used to see when I worked child abuse and neglect cases as a social worker for the Division of Children and Family Services. What has she done except defend a man she respects? But what Sarah will never understand is that a defense attorney doesn't have a lot of choices. If your client is going to have a chance, you better be prepared to show the jury some smoke and mirrors. Shane Norman, I am convinced, can take care of himself. If he's innocent, this trial won't hurt him much. Waiting in line while the manager breaks in a new checker, I realize how much rationalization I am doing. Unless Chet pulls off a miracle, one way or another, Norman is going to be devastated by this trial.

At home I am greeted by Woogie but not by my daughter. Woogie jumps up against me as if I have been gone for a year instead of an hour. He needs his toenails clipped. The last time I tried to do it myself I made him bleed, but I am loath to spend the money. Sarah and I need to spend some quality time together and not mention Christian Life or the trial. Since I have been back from San Francisco, until tonight I've hardly talked to her. She has either been out (at Christian Life) or I have. Maybe we should just put up the groceries and go out for a steak. Food is still a bond between us. She doesn't mind spending time with the old man if he comes across with the right bribe.

After I put the groceries down on the table in the kitchen, I go to her room to tell her we're going out, but she isn't there. "Sarah?" I call, knowing as I do that she isn't in the house. Where could she have gone? She doesn't have a car. The phone rings, and I pick up the receiver by her bed. "Sarah?" I guess.

"It's me, Daddy," Sarah says in a voice so low I can barely hear her.

"Hey, babe, where are you?" I say, enormously relieved. "Do you want to go out and get a steak tonight? We don't need to cook."

"I'm not coming back home tonight. I'm staying with a friend from Christian Life."

She is punishing me for slapping her. "This is a school night, Sarah. You've been gone enough as it is." I try to lighten my voice. I don't want to argue with her. "I thought we'd go out and get a steak."

"Listen," she says, her voice high with emotion. "I'm almost eighteen. I'm not a child anymore. I don't have to do what you say."

I nearly drop the phone. Never has she talked to me like this. No child has ever been more obedient. I have never had a moment's trouble out of her. In fact, Rainey has remarked that Sarah has been almost too perfect. "Legally, you're wrong," I tell her crossly. "Until your birthday, you're still a minor." Though this is technically true, it's meaningless. "I'm very sorry I slapped you, but this isn't going to help matters any if you begin acting like this."

Sarah's voice becomes firm. "I'm not being kidnapped, so don't start acting like a lawyer, please."

What am I supposed to act like? Who does she think she is? I've put food on the table, bought her clothes, been a taxi service, not to mention raised her single-handedly since her mother died. I make an enormous effort to control my voice. "Do you think your mother would approve of how you're acting? The least you can do is tell me who you're staying with so I won't worry about you."

Sarah gives a little cry of frustration. "Don't try to guilt me like you usually do, all right? It won't work. And I'm not telling you where I am, because I don't trust you not to come get me. I'm staying with a friend, okay?"

Guilt. I've always used it. For the last year she has sniffed it out every time. For God's sake, why shouldn't she feel guilty? This is inexcusable. It's that damn church. "At least let me talk to one of the parents, so I know it's okay."

There is silence for a moment. In the background I think I can hear a radio or maybe a tape. It sounds like that stuff they played the Sunday I went. "It's just a couple of friends who have an apartment. They don't live with their parents."

"At least one of them is a boy," I suggest. "That's what this is about, isn't it?"

I can see Sarah rolling her eyes. "I knew that's what you'd think! You just don't understand anything about me. That's why I left. You don't want to understand. You think all these people are deluded sheep who can't think for themselves, and that's just not true. You think it's just about belief. You don't get it that faith and love are inseparable. We don't use each other at Christian Life. That's practically all you do. You don't care about people; you just care about winning. That's become your Bible. I don't want to be like that."

Left? Does this mean she won't be coming back? "What time," I ask carefully, "will I see you tomorrow?"

She stammers, "I-I-I don't know. I'm okay though."

The phone clicks in my ear, and I tear back into her room to see what she has taken. I throw open her closet door and see there is nothing left except a couple of dresses she never wears. I go through her drawers and find almost nothing. Practically the only thing left in her room is a poster of Tom Cruise from the movie *Top Gun* and the collage of her friends, none of whom she has mentioned since she started this Christian Life business. She must have called someone immediately. My heart begins to race. I can call Shane Norman and ask him to track her down. Somebody in her so-called "family" surely can find out where she is. Yet, as I am looking up his number, I realize that Christian Life has thousands of members, and he won't know off the top of his head who to call either. And what do I say? I slapped my daughter because she defended you and she ran off, and I want you to bring her back? Instead, I dial Rainey's number, thinking Sarah may have mentioned somebody to her.

Rainey answers on the first ring, and I yell, "Sarah's gone. Do you know any of her friends from that church?"

"What are you talking about?" Rainey asks, sounding alarmed. "What do you mean she's gone?"

I lower my voice and quickly run through the last hour and a half.

"Gideon, have you lost your mind?" Rainey says, when I am finished. "I don't blame her for leaving. It makes me sick to my stomach that you would even consider trying to implicate Shane without any more evidence than this. You're slandering one of the most decent human beings I've ever known. And I can't believe you slapped Sarah. What is wrong with you? Were you drunk?"

I eye the six-pack on the counter and think I'm going to be soon if I have to listen to any more of this self-righteous crap. "It didn't leave a mark," I defend myself; but I feel terrible. "I guess I shouldn't expect you to understand. You've been such a perfect parent. And, no, I wasn't drunk."

I wait in silence while Rainey takes in my snide comment. Her daughter, Beth, went through a rebellious period of her own as a college student. She is now a contented first-grade teacher in Mississippi, again close to her mother, but at one time they were barely speaking. I know what Rainey is thinking. She never hit her daughter in the face. I can't believe I slapped Sarah either. She's right. I must be losing my mind.

"I know this is killing you," Rainey says. "But if you try to drag Sarah back home tonight, you'll regret it the rest of your life. I know you think she's being brainwashed, but it's not like that at all. As sincere as I think Sarah is about Christian Life, this is directed at least as much against you as toward something else. Believe me, I know."

I lean back against the wall in the kitchen and think what else I can say to hurt the people I care about the most. Beth, I recall, thought Christianity was a con game run by, I believe the phrase was, "mostly male prostitutes in the service of Mammon." I rub my eyes, exhausted. "What have I done?" I wail.

Rainey says quietly, "Right now, Sarah sees you as the antithesis of everything good. I know this will hurt your feelings, but right now she sees you as tainted, even corrupt. You personify for her the compromises human beings make with the Devil."

My heart begins to race. I can't stand any more of this. That's ridiculous! Sarah wasn't like this before she started going to that church. Granted, she didn't think I was perfect, but I sure didn't have horns and a tail. What in the hell do I do that every attorney in Blackwell County doesn't? "This is ludicrous. I can't begin to touch the stories about Chet Bracken. What makes him such a saint and me such a sinner?"

Rainey's voice grows softer as mine becomes louder. "He's accepted Jesus Christ as his personal Lord and Savior."

I want to smash the phone against the wall. If I hear that phrase one more time, I'm going to get some dynamite and blow Christian Life to kingdom come. She is so blind! Shane Norman is probably a murderer, and the man he hired to represent his daughter is letting him get away with it. I stop myself. I don't trust Rainey any longer. How incredible! This is a woman with whom I have entrusted every doubt I've had for the last two years. "Chet's a candidate for one of the apostles, all right," I say sarcastically.

"Give Sarah some time," Rainey advises me, ignoring my last remark. "She'll come home. I'll try to find out tomorrow where she is and make sure she's okay."

Her voice is a little too soothing. I think Rainey already knows, but Sarah has sworn her to secrecy. Yet I don't have the slightest proof. Like Dan, I see conspiracies everywhere. "I'd appreciate that," I say dryly. "What about starting tonight?"

"If I can," Rainey says after a pause. "I've got a meeting up there in a few minutes, so I'll ask around a little."

For a moment I want to tell her not to bother. I am embarrassed. I have never had a moment's trouble from Sarah. She is my greatest success. I feel I have failed Rosa. If she were alive, Sarah would be home now. "Thanks," I mutter.

"I'll call you tomorrow," Rainey promises, "unless I run across some information. It's possible she may call me."

I hang up, feeling more depressed than I have since my wife died. I take out a beer and walk out in the backyard to let Woogie do his business. I should take him for a walk, but I don't feel like it. When I come back in, I put away the groceries but realize I don't feel like eating and decide to go out. The house is driving me crazy. I'd like a real drink. I put food in Woogie's bowl and check his water. He gives me a sad look as if to say, Is this all the attention I get? I reach down and pet him, but I can't stay here a moment longer.

I decide on Kings & Queens, a club on the south side that, despite its name, is definitely not a hangout for homosexuals. Like a dog returning to his old haunts, I set the Blazer on a familiar course down College Avenue while I brood on my daughter's actions. I shouldn't have slapped her, but she shouldn't have run off. Have I kept too tight a rein on her? I don't think so. She dates whomever she wants, has a 1 A.M. curfew on weekends, spends her money from her part-time job on the weekend at a video store however she pleases. Spoiled like most kids (we pretend to divide the chores but neither of us really cleans the house), she nevertheless makes do without a car and doesn't demand money for clothes. The fact is, I don't have a thing to complain about. She knows that we're at the lower end of middle class and I am still paying loans off from my belated law school debt. She wants to go out-of-state to college, but it will depend on scholarship money. Why am I worried about college? At the rate she's going, she will end up as a janitor at Christian Life. Surely Rainey is exaggerating. The antithesis of everything good! Since when does trying to find out the truth make a person corrupt? Give me a break, Sarah. Yet is that what I am really doing? Or is it the way she says—am I just trying to win? What Sarah won't realize is that our system of justice is set up that way. It's supposed to be adversarial. From the battle in court with all its lawyers and procedural rules the truth is supposed to emerge. Do I want the truth or do I merely want Shane Norman to lose his luster in my daughter's eyes? The truth is, it wouldn't break my heart at all to find out Norman killed his son-in-law. I feel a hardness somewhere inside me from all of this I can't seem to break down.

Kings & Queens does not cater to your yuppie lawyer and "bond daddies," but over the years has attracted a loyal, albeit eclectic, clientele because of its total commitment to a delicate mix of crossover country music and golden oldies that range from Willie Nelson to Vicki Carr. Throw in the cheapest hard-liquor prices in the county, a modest cover to discourage a crowd that is too young and rowdy, and you have a nice environment in which to pick up a woman—something I have done on occasion in the not-too-distant past. Granted, it has been a couple of years, but Kings & Queens is like the drinking water: unless something busts loose, you can count on it.

Inside, I am not disappointed. Some things never change. The smoke and noise level I would recognize anywhere. The crowd looks a little younger, probably because I am a couple of years older. Over the din of conversation I can make out an old Dave and Sugar hit. I make my way to the bar, which is dotted with a few empty spots, and grab a stool next to a couple of women who look like schoolteachers who have vowed never to teach junior high kids again. The decor of Kings & Queens, unchanged since I started coming here after Rosa died, won't win awards for originality, but still commands my attention. Royalty and their families are everywhere. What we don't have, we love. Unhappy or not, they (Diana, Charles, Fergie, Andrew, Elizabeth, and Philip) stare down from every wall at their Arkansas admirers in what I decide is perpetual amazement that their most unroyal deeds attract such ardent attention from the most republican of their former subjects. I order a bourbon and Coke, not caring it will be the house brand. For some reason, cheaper bourbon mixes the best or maybe just seems the sweetest, which apparently is all I require in the way of taste.

"Why get fancy?" the older of the two presumptive

teachers asks when she hears my order. She gives me a smile that says she isn't saving the seat for anybody.

Why indeed, I think, giving her the once-over. No ring (this could be girls' night out), frosted short hair; she is wearing a long-sleeved green turtleneck and dress jeans. Either she went home to change or is the playground supervisor. Yet maybe teachers dress more casually these days. "No sense trying to fool anybody, is there?" I respond, pleased I don't have to think of something clever to break the ice. Her younger partner is prettier, but given her lockjawed expression, she won't be running for president of my fan club any time soon.

For the next thirty minutes I compete head to head with Lockjaw for her friend's attention (Jennifer spelled with a "J," she says with a practiced smirk, no doubt having used that line more than once but still getting a grin out of me—she has no idea how easy-to-please I am tonight). Finally Lockjaw gives up and calls it a night, pissed, but obviously not for the first time. Men spoil everything, her parting glance says. If I had known, I would have brought a friend. Preferably somebody with rabies.

Jennifer, who turns out to be an accountant for a wholesale food club, and I seat ourselves at a table and share some nachos and cheese dip while we trade selected poignant vignettes from our pasts. She donated one of her kidneys to a twin sister who died from cancer anyway; I tell her about Rosa. Realizing she has topped me (I would have been glad to donate a breast), she lets me talk, which is progressively easier to do as the bourbon slides down. I tell her about a former divorce client who served her husband rat muffins for breakfast; on the dance floor I regale her with the continuing saga of Jason and his spiritual development classes. Steadily drinking Dos Equis (our table is beginning to resemble a missile silo with multiple warheads), she laughs appreciatively.

In my arms, slow-dancing to "Bridge over Troubled Water," Jennifer feels nice, her body warm and as user-friendly as buttered toast. I used to be pretty good at this once. I am almost six feet tall, with only a slight paunch, and most days I can look myself in the mirror without wincing until I put in my contacts. Then I can see the warts. True, the bald spot on the back of my head looks, according to Dan, like spreading tree blight (what are friends for?), but Jennifer, with her slightly pug nose and weak chin, doesn't appear on the verge of launching a campaign for Mrs. America. Actually, compared to what else is out on the dance floor we stack up fairly well. The hard-body competition is agreeably thin, if you throw out a couple of women who could be hookers judging by their makeup and out-of-season sundresses that reveal more than repair work. Jennifer's body, pressed against mine, is, if not overly firm, not of the Jell-O variety either. Up close and personal, she looks around my age. Staying away, for once, from the subject of Sarah (usually, by this time I have whipped out my wallet and showed off her senior class picture), I work into the conversation that I have never been through a divorce, a fact that surely must be alluring to a single female patron of Kings & Queens.

"I've never been married," Jennifer says, as we leave the dance floor hand in hand to return to our drinks.

I look down at her, amazed by this disclosure, feeling in some vague way she has again topped me. "Imagine," I say, bumping her slightly, "two middle-aged adults without a single child-support check to show for it." We sit down and drink. "How come?" I ask, drunk enough to stick my nose where it doesn't belong. We're not exactly at the point where we exchange life stories. "Doubtless, you've had plenty of chances."

She smiles a little more brightly than necessary. "It's not that I don't enjoy men, but I guess I've never liked the odds."

Enjoy. I smile, too, pleased at my good fortune. I want to go to bed with this woman, but I'm not in the mood to listen to any bitter stories. Around nine, after we've danced again, I ask, "Would you like to come to my place?"

Obviously considering, she waits until we are back at our table to speak. She reaches down and finishes off the last of her beer. I should have ordered a six-pack and a bucket of ice. "Thank you, but you seem a little too sad, Gideon. I appreciate the offer though." After picking up her purse, she reaches up and lightly kisses me on the cheek and then slips away, leaving me to find our waiter to pay the bill.

Me, sad? I thought I had been witty and charming. I drive home in an alcoholic daze, on the lookout for cops. All I need to cap this perfect day is a ticket. Damn.

At home the only thing on the machine is an incomprehensible message from Pearl Norman. Skunked worse than I am, she is saying something about "tryin' ever since Leigh was ten . . ." to do something. Most of it is her crying into the phone. I run the tape twice, and then erase it to get away from the sound of her voice. Her self-pitying whine reminds me of my father's voice when he was on the sauce. Jesus Christ. An alcoholic and a schizophrenic. No wonder my mother shipped him off to the state hospital. I felt terrible I never went to see him, but I was glad he was gone. Embarrassed the shit out of us sometimes. The asshole! "Drunk and crazy, drunk and crazy," Marty would hiss under her breath at him at the dinner table. I'd sit there scared to death he'd understand, while mother tried to act as if nothing was wrong. Glad those times are past. In the den on the sofa I sit as still as I can to make the room stop spinning. Woogie hops up beside me to wait for Sarah. Good boy. No wonder Leigh and Shane try to hide Pearl. I would, too.

13

I AWAKE TO my doorbell ringing at four in the morning. Though my head is pounding and my stomach quivering with last night's liquor, I am relieved. Knowing it is Sarah, I get up and stumble to the door in my underwear. Brave watchdog that he is, Woogie follows me, barking deliriously. Thank God I didn't bring what's-her-face home with me. For the life of me, I can't remember her name. I haven't drunk that much in years. So what if Sarah has come home out of guilt? What's wrong with that? How can we be moral without feeling bad when we screw up? I can feel myself smiling, understanding how the father of the prodigal son felt. I won't say a word—just tell her I'm glad she's home. If she wants to rant and rave a little, I'll endure it. For a while.

I flip the porch-light switch by the door and open it to find Leigh Wallace. What the hell is going on? I jump behind the door. In these thin boxer shorts I might as well be standing in the nude. I yell, "Come on in. I'm going to get some clothes on." Why in the world didn't she at least call? Don't people think I own a telephone?

"I'm sorry about this," she calls after me, "but I couldn't stay at my parents' home any longer."

It is chilly in the house. I flip on some lights and hit

216

the thermostat. I'll make coffee when I get some clothes on. When I reappear, dressed in jeans and a sweater, I find her in my kitchen by the pantry, presumably looking for coffee.

"I hope I haven't awakened your daughter," she says, staring at me as if I were a ghost. Well, she doesn't look so great either. Swallowed by shapeless gray sweats and tennis shoes, she seems smaller than I remembered. Her face, devoid of makeup and lipstick, is a little unnerving in its austerity. I have never seen her when she didn't look perfect.

"She spent the night out," I say, unable to summon the energy to explain. My mind isn't quite functioning yet. I find a jar of Taster's Choice and fill a pan with water. "Why don't you have a seat?"

She goes to the kitchen table and sits, apparently convinced I can boil water without her assistance. How odd this is, I think. I wonder if her father knows she is gone. Our daughters are both in trouble, though Sarah obviously doesn't think of it like that. Woogie goes to Leigh and jumps up against her legs. A substitute sister. Acceptance is his long suit. Smiling, she reaches down and pets him as if he were some magnificent breed of animal. "I haven't been telling you the truth."

Better late than never, I think. With only five days until the trial starts, it's nice to think I might know what the hell is going on. Aware that I stink worse than the bottom of a trash can filled with whiskey bottles and cigarette butts, I putter around the sink. If I get too close, she may pass out from the fumes. Woogie smells better than I do. "So what *is* the truth?" I ask, prompting her when she doesn't speak. This is a strange place and time for a murder confession, but maybe not so unusual in this case. Confessing to her father may be just too difficult. I can't imagine Sarah confessing to me.

Tears begin to slide down her face. "I wasn't up at the church in the middle of the morning like I said," she says, sniffling, and dabs at her eyes with a wadded-up tissue she is holding in her right fist. Woogie nestles against her feet as if he can sense her distress.

Tell me something I don't know, I think. Still, she has got to start somewhere. My hand is trembling from too much alcohol as I measure out a teaspoon. "Want some Coffee-mate and/or sugar?" I ask, trying to appear relaxed. Finally getting to the bottom of this case has speeded up my heart. After last night, I need all the jump-starts I can get.

She shakes her head and again bends down to pet Woogie. What would we do without animals to comfort us? I pour boiling water from the pan and deliver her coffee to her and then cross back to the sink to pour my own. A little of me goes a long way this morning. When she doesn't speak, I prompt her, "As you may realize, this isn't much of a surprise."

She sips at her coffee and makes a face. Probably too strong. Well, too bad. I would have met her at an I-Hop if she wanted. "Do you remember asking me if I had been doing something I was embarrassed about?"

I nod, tasting my coffee. God, this stuff could power a tractor-trailer rig. "Yeah," I say, as offhandedly as I can. This will be hard enough for her to admit without me starting to pant in front of her.

"The morning of his death, Art had persuaded me to make a video," she says bitterly, "without any clothes on." She studies her mug. It is one of those mugs they send you for pledging money to Public Radio. Embarrassed for her, I look away and sip my coffee. She fills the growing silence. "He said he wanted me to dance for him." With these words she begins to cry, but it is controlled, as if she has promised herself to get it over with as quickly as possible.

I wait as long as I can to see if she will reveal more without my having to humiliate her by asking questions. The things women do for men! I think of the performance of those female impersonators. True, they were paid, but I had the impression they would have danced for nothing. "You must have loved him a lot to do that for him," I say, coaxing her to continue.

Fiercely, she says, "You have no idea! I can't believe I was so stupid."

Woogie, now her protector, glances up from her feet at me as if to say that I should not even look as if I intend to hurt this woman. I have no desire to add to her already considerable distress, but my job is to represent her, not act as her therapist. "It must have taken a lot of trust," I sympathize. Art must have been quite the salesman. As wretched as I feel, I notice I am becoming slightly horny. She must have looked magnificent. What was Art going to do with it? If he had no qualms about serving as a middleman, did he intend to market his own wife's private video? Surely not. Yet people have done worse things. If Leigh killed him over this, a jury might be understanding. Talk about justifiable homicide.

Leigh wipes her eyes. "When we first got married, I was so repressed that I wouldn't let him see me naked. We made love in the dark for the first month."

God only knows the guilt she must be feeling. I sip my coffee. It doesn't seem so strong anymore. No knowing what Shane had told his daughters about the human body. For two thousand years preachers have said that lust is evil. With my experience so far, a good case can be made in their favor. What a battle was being waged! Did Shane, I wonder, have any idea? "You must have had a pretty strict upbringing."

Leigh smiles wanly. "My sisters had it worse." Her own coffee is untouched. Caffeine is probably the last thing she needs. "They never even saw a PG movie until they turned eighteen. By the time I was their age, I had seen a couple. But I never was allowed to watch MTV until I was married, and the first time I saw it I was terribly embarrassed."

I try to imagine the journey she has made since she met Art her last semester in college. Her sisters rebelled, so why shouldn't she? How difficult it must be to try to keep your child from being exposed to lust in an age when toothpaste and sex are marketed together. I think of that ad with the woman running her tongue back and forth over her teeth. Ummmm, good. So much for "Brusha, brusha, brusha, New Ipana toothpaste." To make sure I understand, I ask, "Was it Art who filmed you?"

Leigh, even now, blushes. "I wouldn't have let somebody else do it. What I wanted to tell you is that the film disappeared during the time I went back up to the church and then came home and discovered Art's body. I looked for it, but I couldn't find it."

Her voice has taken on a slightly hesitant tone as if she is doubtful I will believe her. I don't know what to believe. The implication is that Art's killer has the tape. But how could he or she know Leigh had performed a nude dance on tape unless he or she was there? I doubt if the windows were open while this was going on. "Art could have moved the tape after you left, which means it might still be in the house and the police never found it."

She nods. "It's possible, but I was only gone forty-five minutes."

I am buying into this story, I realize. It may be a total

crock, designed at the eleventh hour. "Why have you waited until now to tell this?"

Leigh begins to cry again. "If this comes out, it will kill my father," she says, her lower lip trembling.

Trying to think, I choke down some coffee. Is it possible Art called Shane back and told him what he had done with his daughter, and Shane came to the house and killed him? Surely this has crossed her mind. "It could have been your father. He might have called back, and Art, in anger or hubris, might have told him."

Her features collapse, and it dawns on me that she believes her father murdered her husband. "Art treated Daddy with such contempt!"

If this is what happened, I have to take her down this path as far as possible, so she can't talk herself out of it later. "Had they argued?" I ask, as if I were talking to her for the first time. Perhaps, in a sense, I am.

Leigh brushes her hair from her face. She has it pulled back in a ponytail, but some of it has begun to escape. If she has gotten any sleep tonight, I can't tell it by the way she looks. Her normally beautiful skin looks puffy and loose under her eyes. Her voice becomes anguished. "Art argued with Daddy in a way nobody else dared. Just the week before he died, he told Daddy that anyone who believed the earth was only six thousand years old was an utter fool. That the scientific evidence against the Bible being literal truth was overwhelming. He said the New Testament merely represents the efforts of some of the followers of Jesus to convince others that He was the son of God, and is no more hard evidence of the Resurrection than a man preaching on a street corner."

I had prepared myself for much more, but Leigh has spoken in such hushed tones I realize that even this little snit of Art's must have seemed like someone daring to urinate on a shrine. Art had done no more, as far as I can tell, than espouse, albeit in a forceful way, the view of mainline Christianity. Yet, perhaps to Shane, and obviously to his daughter, he sounded like the anti-Christ. Doubtless, Shane had heard much harsher attacks on his brand of Christianity even from within the Bible Belt itself. Still, his daughter's soul was at stake. "How did you react?" I ask. "I take it you were there."

Leigh's face flushes, the memory of it too much. "Daddy had stopped by the house to ask me to come to church to hear one of our missionaries. Art was so rude I thought I was going to faint."

Poor Leigh. Rudeness, not false dogma, is the ultimate sin in the South. "Did you agree with Art?" I ask.

Leigh betrays her feelings by stammering, "Art . . . knew so much. He read all the time."

It is Leigh who has betrayed her father. Could his murder of her husband have been directed at her rather than having been on her behalf? I have given up trying to understand my own motives and assume everything I do is selfish these days. I want Sarah back, not for her sake but for my own. The fact is, she seems happier than she has for months. Just because fundamentalism may not serve her for a lifetime doesn't mean it isn't meeting some need right now. "I can understand if Art was trying to persuade you to believe something a little different," I say gently, "than what you were raised with. It happens to all of us."

Leigh's face is full of sorrow. "Daddy realizes I'm losing my faith, and it is just about to kill him."

The irony is that my own daughter has traveled in the opposite direction. I tap my empty cup on the kitchen table I've loved so well since Rosa and I bought it at an antique sale in Hot Springs. It is oak, weighs a ton, and will outlast us all.

Leigh, exhausted now or perhaps just sad, rests her head on her knuckles. Shane has her body back but not her mind. Yet, if she is acquitted, she may never leave again. After all, the maiden voyage was a disaster. This is one woman I would like to know in five years. I feel a wave of tenderness as I look down on her tousled hair. From this angle she reminds me so much of Sarah. But I don't dare comfort her. Even as smelly and gross as I am now, anything I do could be misinterpreted. And as lonely as I feel, I would be quick to misinterpret a gesture from her. Once I slept with a key witness in a big case and almost screwed it up royally. This one is hard enough without doing that. I smile at my own ego. Any shudder I might produce in a woman right now would be from horror, not ecstasy. "You need to go home," I say gently, "and try to get some sleep."

She raises her head and nods. "Daddy's probably called the police."

The irony is too great. In a moment of anger I thought about calling the cops, too, and claiming Sarah had been kidnapped. What a disaster that would have turned out to be. Sarah never would have forgiven me. Briefly, I tell Leigh what has happened. She listens sympathetically. Sarah is in a place emotionally Leigh may never occupy again, and I sense in some way she envies her. "You've got to come down to Chet's office today so we can prepare your testimony for Thursday."

She bites her lip. "Can I stay here the rest of the night?" she asks, sounding like a little girl. "I don't want to go home. I feel too weird now being under the same roof with him."

I look at my watch. It is close to four-thirty. "You have to promise to call first thing in the morning and tell your parents where you are."

For the first time she yawns, her chest swelling under the gray sweatshirt. "I promise I won't be any trouble."

I stand and lead her to Sarah's room. "My daughter's room is going to be a mess," I apologize, forgetting how bare she has left it. When I hit the light switch, my emotions almost get the better of me and I say in a soft voice, "Or used to be."

I go find her a clean towel and washcloth and inspect the bathroom. It is passable. It was Sarah's turn to clean it this weekend. Fortunately, she usually does a little better job than I do, and if Leigh doesn't inspect it too closely, it will do. Standing in front of my mirror, I am repulsed by what I see. If my eyes had any more red in them, I could donate them to the blood bank. As I pick up the only hair I see on the sink, I can imagine Pearl Norman on her hands and knees scrubbing out the commode in her own home until it gleamed with an alabaster sheen. Her house was spotless, and I realize that Pearl reminds me of my mother, who lived in an age when it was okay if all a woman knew how to do was cook and clean house and take care of her husband and children. At least it was permissible until her husband died. I go to say goodnight, and Leigh thanks me for letting her stay. "We have to talk to Chet today," I remind her.

She ducks her head. "I can't tell people," she wails, "that I let myself be filmed dancing without any clothes on. I just can't do that to my father."

I try to contain my frustration by glancing around my daughter's bare room. It is as if I were trying to rent it out. How strange! Leigh is facing life in prison for a crime her father may have committed, and once again she is worried about his reaction. My daughter runs away, and I haven't done anything. "We'll make the jury understand," I tell her gently, "the kind of influence Art had over you. By the time Chet is through with his opening statement they'll hate Art as much as your father did."

Leigh sits down on Sarah's bed, twisting her hands in her lap. "I can't implicate my father!" She begins to cry. "It's my fault all this happened!"

I lean against the doorjamb of Sarah's room and marvel at the guilt on this girl's shoulders. Our battle isn't going to be with the jury; it will be with her. "You won't be implicating your father," I say, disingenuously. "Only he can do that. You'll just be telling the truth."

For the first time the words come tumbling out: "I think Daddy killed Art!" she cries, tears streaming down her cheeks. "I don't think he meant to, but I think he did it!"

Despite the stench coming from me, I go sit down by her on the bed and put my arm around her shoulders as she sobs against me in gasps that rack her whole body. How can I not believe her? If this were Sarah, I wouldn't have a choice, and I have not smothered her nearly as much as this girl has been. Would Sarah risk her life and lie to protect me? I'd be lucky to escape being burned at the stake. "You know your father wouldn't want you," I say, patting her shoulder, "to run any risk of being convicted." I say it, but not convincingly at all. Despite all the alleged emphasis on the redeeming power of love emanating from within the walls of Christian Life, I am no longer certain that punishment isn't Shane's agenda. In his heart perhaps he knew even before she did that Leigh was past the point of no return, and this was his way of keeping her. What did Chet say—that Christian Life would have ten people there on visiting day for her?

Leigh wipes her nose on the sleeve of her warm-up but doesn't speak. I would feel better if she got angry.

I get up and say, "We'll talk about it later. You need to try to get some rest."

"Thank you," she answers, and I leave her sitting in Sarah's room.

I slip off my pants and get into bed, trying not to think about what she is sleeping in. How can I think of sex at a time like this? I ought to be put to sleep. I lie awake wondering if I am being conned. What happened to the video? Was there one? Maybe we shouldn't allow her on the witness stand. Up to now, I thought we ought to pick the most conservative jury possible, but how is a Bible thumper going to relate to a woman who dances nude an hour or so before her husband is murdered? Somebody ought to be punished, and it's too late to teach her husband a lesson. Did Shane Norman do this? There is no evidence that he did anything except have a good reason to hate his son-in-law. Chet has got to confirm Shane's alibi today, or I will. I feel the bed sag slightly, but it is just Woogie, probably confused about the night's events. "Welcome to the club," I say, reaching down to pet him as he curls up beside me. "Somebody's in Sarah's bed, but it's not her, is it, boy?"

For a response, he burrows against me. I'm not much of a substitute. If Leigh stayed another night, he'd be in there with her. Damn. I wonder if I'd try to join him. Why can't I think of her like a daughter? For the same reason Art Wallace couldn't, I guess. Incredibly, when the bed moved, I hoped it was Leigh. Sure. What could be more attractive than a whiskey-breathed, smoke-stenched, middle-aged sad sack? As my old track coach at Subiaco used to say, "Page, if you had a brain, you'd be dangerous." Still, it is nice to know my self-esteem is still intact. How boring life would be if I couldn't make a fool of myself.

At six my alarm blasts me out of a sound sleep. How

could I have even closed my eyes with all that caffeine? I stumble into the hall to go to the bathroom and notice Sarah's door is open. I can't resist the urge to peek but it is too dark to see anything. After I piss, I go into the kitchen and find a note by the coffee pot from Leigh telling me that she will call my office later. I wait until seven and then call Chet and tell him about my overnight visitor. "You've got to determine today if Shane could have killed Wallace!" I almost yell at him. "We're almost out of time!"

He responds calmly. "Come on out for breakfast," he invites me, his voice strong. "Wynona would love to cook for you."

"Okay," I answer. I hang up, nonplussed by his manner. How can he be so calm? He has screwed this case up, and all he can think about is breakfast. It must be the medication.

Woogie wanders into the bathroom while I am shaving and looks up at me as if to ask, "Where's Sarah?" The few nights she has spent the night out in the past he has wandered from room to room obviously looking for her. This morning has been no exception. "She'll be back soon," I say, without conviction. How could I have slapped her? We'll both remember it the rest of our lives. I had no business doing that. The phone rings, jarring me out of my growing self-pity.

"Have you heard from her yet?" Rainey asks, her voice concerned yet determinedly upbeat.

I beat down the feeling that she is ultimately responsible for Sarah's departure, confident that Sarah is likely to call her before she calls me. It is odd to be estranged from the woman who has meant so much to me. If we had gotten married instead of backing away each time at the last moment, maybe none of this would be happening. She wouldn't have all this time for another "family" if she had a real one. It's hard to escape the conclusion that Christian Life is what people do if there's nothing good on TV. As bitter as I feel, I manage to avoid delivering myself of this sentiment. Like the comments of a rejected boyfriend, it would be taken as so many sour grapes. "Not yet," I say evenly, and tell her I'm going out to Chet's.

From her tone it is clear that Rainey is hurting for me. Missing from her voice is the accusatory, sanctimonious tone from last night's conversation. "She'll call you today," she assures me, though she doesn't sound as confident as I would like.

Still wary of her, I resist the temptation to tell her that Leigh was over here and spilled her guts. Nothing I can say right now would convince Rainey that Shane is involved in his son-in-law's murder. "You seem more understanding today," I say hopefully.

"I want Sarah to come home for you," she says, "but please realize that if you try to make the jury think Shane killed his son-in-law when you really don't have any proof he did, I'll never feel the same about you again."

So much for biting my tongue. "I have a job to do!" I screech into the phone. "You know that! And since when have you been worried about your feelings for me? Ever since you started going to Christian Life, you haven't spent five minutes thinking about me, and you know it."

"That's not true," Rainey responds, her voice no longer under control as it was. "It's been hard for me. I've loved you, and I know my involvement with Christian Life has hurt our relationship. I know what things cost. There have been times when I wish I could just back things up to a certain point and start over again. But finding that tumor in my breast changed my life.

Either the world is a random series of events held together and perpetuated by blind instinct, or it is a meaningful place created by a loving God who cares infinitely for us and who commands us to love each other. My response is the latter, and because it is, I can't pretend I'm not affected by your decisions about people important to me, no matter how you choose to justify them."

Rainey is a bit breathless by the time she has finished. She isn't much for speeches. I am moved by what I have heard. I've simplified her just as I have simplified Sarah. But my choices aren't so easy. "What if Leigh is innocent and she goes to prison the rest of her life, and I could have done something to prevent it? How do I live with that?"

"How do you know she is innocent?" Rainey asks, her voice betraying her frustration for the first time.

"How do you know there is a loving God?" I shout into the phone, and hang up, angry and frustrated. Lawyers and preachers aren't that much different. We are both advocates for our clients. We marshal all the evidence, facts, theories, and arguments, and do our best to convince juries and congregations, After we sit down, you either believe or you don't. But if I had told Rainey that, she would have said it was blasphemy.

14

As I PULL into Chet's yard, Wynona and Trey are coming out the door. "How are you, Mr. Page?" Trey calls from the porch. It is easy to forget this individual's favorite snack is probably Animal Crackers. Dressed in jeans, a lightweight nylon jacket, and high-top tennis shoes, he looks like an advertisement for the All-American kid. Not for the first time I wonder what it would have been like to have had a son. Now that I'm making a botch of Sarah, I doubt it would have been any different.

"Fine," I tell him, inspecting his mother, who smiles cheerfully in the chilly spring air. It must be at least ten degrees cooler once you get away from concrete and office buildings. I want to tell him that I haven't been saved yet, surprising myself by the amount of irritation I am feeling. It might be lack of sleep, but it could be a lot of things this morning.

Wynona, in the bib overalls that must be her uniform, tells me, "I'll be back to cook up some breakfast for you and Chet after I take him to the bus stop. He got up too late to walk."

Trey grins, pleased at his mischief. It's not much, but it's probably all he can get away with, having Wynona as his mother.

"You don't have to go to any trouble," I say politely,

but the truth is that I am starving. I've burned up some calories worrying, not a diet I'd recommend.

Trey marches up to me and sticks out his hand. This kid, I decide, through no fault of his own, could get on my nerves. Like the first time I was out here, his grip is firm, and he looks me in the eyes as if he is deciding whether to offer me a partnership in his law firm. When I was his age I was so shy I wouldn't answer to my own name. "Hold your head up, son," my father used to command me, but with little success. Even when I was little I must have sensed he wasn't quite right in the head, although he was still making a go of his drugstore. "Dad's out on the back porch. He likes being outside in the morning."

It is so peaceful, I wonder if Chet will be buried on his property. Is that against the law? Surely not. We are in the country, but modern life has so many laws and regulations I wouldn't be surprised if there isn't a statute on this, too. "I can see why," I say, more to Wynona than Trey. "It's just great out here."

"Just go on through the house," Wynona says as she opens the door to the Mercedes.

"Thanks." I smile, feeling like the amiable flunky. I am trusted with the silver, but I am increasingly weary of my second-banana status. I know more than Chet does about this case. Who am I kidding? I probably know exactly what he wants me to know, no more, no less. In the kitchen Trey's cereal bowl has already been rinsed. Wynona probably made him do it himself. I wonder if she and Chet still make love. If he's in pain, he may not even think about it. Rosa and I stopped making love a month before she died.

I pass through the kitchen door and find Chet sitting on the steps that lead off the deck. With his back to me, he looks like a teenager, but as he turns around, he seemed to have aged since I saw him yesterday. The energy to stay alive seems to be cutting new ruts in his face on a weekly basis. His eyes have the dim look of someone who has insisted on living over a century. He is wearing one of those sleeveless jackets over a blue flannel shirt, jeans, and brown work boots, so I assume he won't be going into the office today. "Wynona told me to come on through," I say, feeling a need to explain my presence in his house. I am less comfortable with this man each time I see him.

He pats a place on the wooden floor by him as if he doesn't trust his voice to carry. "Have a seat."

Though the chairs we sat in last time are in easy reach, I sit down on the step by him and see that he is carving the figure of a woman who bears a remarkable resemblance to Leigh. He holds it up to me, asking nonchalantly, "You know who this is?"

"Our client," I say. "I wish she were this malleable all the time. That's an incredible likeness." The figure reminds me of a stylized totem, yet somehow Chet has captured Leigh the day he first introduced me to her. All made up, with her hair piled high on her head and jewelry flashing, she looked like a member of the Spanish aristocracy. A far cry from what she was wearing this morning.

Chet grunts and puts the four-inch figure aside. Solemnly, he says, "I got Daffy to double-check Shane's alibi between eleven and eleven-thirty. According to a former secretary who worked in the church office, Shane said he had something to do over at his house and left about quarter to eleven and came back in just before Leigh called, which was about an hour later. Pearl was off in Benton that day visiting her sister, so unless he has someone else to vouch for him he has some explaining to do."

I knew it. It is all I can do to keep from thrusting my fist in the air like some demented jock on TV after a touchdown. To hide my feelings, I look toward the woods, hoping, I suppose, to see the rabbit that visited Chet's garden the evening I was here. With spring bursting forth in every direction, the woods seem alive but offer no visible sign of warm-blooded life. It is remarkable to me that Chet, who has no fear of man or beast, is so reluctant to confront the man who has become, in my eyes at least, the primary suspect. Everybody is afraid of somebody. Maybe, it occurs to me, Shane has a lot more on Chet than the other way around. No telling what Chet has confessed to him. There are a lot of stories about Chet that I've pushed aside since I've taken this case. A minister is supposed to keep the confidences of his flock, but Chet may be thinking that Shane might not be quite so circumspect if he were doing a stretch in the Arkansas state penitentiary in Cummins. Ministers worth their salt know enough dirt to break up half the marriages in their congregation and send the other half to jail. Chet may not give a rat's ass what the legal community says about him after his death, but Trey and Wynona are in a different category. Their good opinion is important to him. "This isn't much to go on," I say, squinting in the morning brightness. "What about his car?"

Chet folds up his knife, which looks surprisingly ordinary to have done so much intricate work. "Nobody remembers," he admits. "It's been too long."

My stomach rumbles loudly, either in hunger or in protest against last night's dinner of alcohol and cheese dip. It needs something hard, as my sister Marty, obese since adolescence, used to say. I hope Wynona cooks some meat. "Shane could have been working at home in his own house the entire time," I conclude, wondering if Chet is trying to humor me, since I have been so vehement that Shane is a suspect. It seems as if we have reversed roles. Why, after all this time, has he finally pinned Norman down? Obviously because of me. But now that I have what I want, I'm not sure I trust it.

Chet pushes himself up from the steps. "You want some coffee?"

I spring to my feet. He's the one with cancer. "I'll get some for both of us." Coming through the kitchen earlier, I noticed half a pot. After this morning's earlier fiasco, I'm glad I don't have to make it. I thought I had discovered a new energy source. He nods, and I retrace my steps and run into Wynona as I go through the door.

She smiles, her pleasant face growing on me. "Trey tried to get me to let him stay home and listen. He wants to be a lawyer, of course."

Anticipating my mission, she hands me two coffee cups while I think about her son. More lawyers this country doesn't need, yet the schools keep flooding the market. Half of us in Blackwell County can probably qualify for food stamps. "How's Chet?" I whisper conspiratorially.

"Not so good," she says, her voice dropping to match my own. Standing next to her, I can detect her scent. She smells like Palmolive soap. "He's living to get through the trial."

Now is my chance to ask what kind of cancer he has, but before I can, Chet comes through the door. "Planning my funeral?" he asks, but his voice is gentle, and the way he looks at his wife I can tell there is no malice behind his words.

She bumps up against him, letting him feel her warmth. "Gideon was saying"—she winks at me—"that he would like to sing."

Embarrassed, I try to keep from smiling at the thought, but since they both chuckle, I grin, too. This black humor is contrary to my image of them, but I realize I don't really know them. When our mother was dying with cancer of the pancreas, my sister and I acted as though she had a stomachache. The doctor surely told her the truth, but, as if it were a shameful odor, we never acknowledged it in her presence. The last time she went into the Baptist Hospital in Memphis (and never came out), we all pretended she was going in for more tests. I let Wynona fill up our cups and begin cooking while I sit down across from Chet at the kitchen table.

Chet reaches out and touches his wife, who responds by bending over and hugging him gently as if he were made of glass. There is a calm sweetness between the two of them that is as real as the smell of frying pork. They have something I don't have and can't even imagine. All the scientific evidence in the world can't destroy the bond between them. Clearly connected to their faith through Christian Life, their love for each other, for this moment at least, transcends pain and memory. The cost seems high to me, but watching Chet's face as his wife nuzzles him, I can't say it isn't worth it.

Our breakfast is conventionally good, and there is plenty of it, though I am really the only one who eats. Serving us first, Wynona picks at a plate from the stove, while Chet manages only a couple of bites of his eggs and a half a piece of toast. Now is the time to ask him about his cancer, but I lose my nerve. Though he is permitting me to see probably more than anyone ever has, he is essentially a private man, and I am loath to risk upsetting him, now that this case seems to be going somewhere.

We move into the main room of the cabin where we discussed the case for the first time. On the table is a mound of documents, and I am cheered by the impression that he seems to have been working on the case. Now that Wynona is out of earshot (Chet, I notice, is much more circumspect about talking about the substance of the case than I am), it is time to get back to the main issue. I ask bluntly, "Are you willing now to go after Shane?"

Chet pulls a toothpick from his shirt pocket and begins to work at a molar as if I weren't in the room. If he refuses now, after what he has learned, I have decided I will quit the case. If it leaves him high and dry, that's too bad. We can't give Leigh a thorough and adequate defense without accusing her father. He stares into the fire for what seems an eternity. His voice gloomy, he says, "I want us to confront him first."

Abruptly, he looks up at me to see if I am gloating. I pretend to have no reaction, though inside I am about to explode with anticipation. For the first time I feel as if we have a real defense. Before I can respond, I hear the telephone ringing in the kitchen, and Wynona brings Chet a red cordless telephone, saying, "It's Shane. He says Leigh must have left the house early this morning and hasn't come back."

Chet looks as if he has seen a ghost. It is as if Shane had had the place bugged. Chet places his hand over the receiver and waits until Wynona has left the room. "I'm going to let you talk to him," he whispers. "Tell him we're coming to talk to him this afternoon." I nod, and he says into the receiver, "Good morning. Gideon is here and can answer some of your questions about your daughter."

I take the phone and awkwardly explain to Shane, omitting the reasons, that his daughter was my house guest for a couple of hours early this morning. "She wanted to talk about her case, but as you know I can't discuss that with you," I say, watching Chet's face for his reaction.

He nods, but Shane is furious that I didn't call him immediately to tell him she was all right. "Her mother and I have been worried sick since seven when we discovered she was gone."

I know the feeling. I don't mention my own daughter's absence for fear of what they will think. "I assumed she was going home after she left my house," I explain, not quite truthfully, and do not add that she has become convinced she has been living with the murderer of her husband. I know that Shane is actually angry because I won't divulge the contents of my conversation with his daughter. I would be, too. I tell him we will be out at four this afternoon to talk about the case with him.

Shane demands to speak to Chet again, and from the expression on Chet's face, it is obvious that he is receiving a lecture about his choice of a sidekick for this case. As I listen to Chet's attempt to pacify him, it hits me even harder that Shane considers himself Chet's client. Chet makes no mention of Leigh's story about the nude video, which comes as a relief. I don't know how valuable this information is or even whether it is true, but since Chet doesn't share it with Shane, at least his loyalties now seem to be clear, which is no small accomplishment.

Chet hangs up the phone with a sour expression on his face. I can't tell whether it is a result of the conversation or of pain. The call has distracted him. I know he is thinking he is betraying the man who saved his life. He says, "I wish she had told you where she was going."

I look down at my pad. I have written: *Leigh?* "I have the note at home saying she would call. She didn't say she was going home." But I had assumed it. Where else would she go? Yet, a woman like Leigh must have had many friends before she and Art quit being so involved at Christian Life. Hell, they still went once a week even up to his death. "She'll call."

But when I check with my office at nine and then ten only to find she hasn't tried to contact either of us, Chet and I grind to a halt. We can only do so much preparation without Leigh. He tells me to make sure I call Jessie St. Vrain today and get her on a plane. Shane isn't going to be the only suspect in the case. We probably won't be able to get her testimony in, but if we can, it will give the jury something else to think about. I have an uncontested divorce at eleven, so I leave promising to call him as soon as I hear from Leigh, and he does the same. "I'll get a subpoena for the secretary," I say, standing up. "What's her name?"

Chet answers with a sigh, "I already did."

I suppress a smile. I know he's serious now. "How do you want to handle this afternoon?" I ask, afraid he will tell me at the last minute he doesn't want me present.

He remains seated, staring into the fire. "Let me do the talking. If he's got something we don't know about," he says hoarsely, "I want him to have the opportunity to tell me."

I touch his arm. "I know this is tough for you."

He doesn't answer, and I go into the kitchen to thank Wynona for breakfast. Chet seems very tired already, leaving me to wonder how he will get through two days of trial. Adrenaline will take you just so far in trying a case. You need stamina to concentrate for two days of trial. The look on Wynona's face tells me that I will need to be ready. I wonder what Wynona will think of her husband when she finds out he intends to accuse Shane of murder. I know what the women in my life think.

15

As I COME through the door, Julia calls loudly, "You got a letter on the bow-wow case." The six people in the waiting room all look up to see which lawyer on the floor refers to his clients in such a charming manner.

"Be right with you," I say to my uncontested divorce client, a girl in her late teens who nudges the female next to her. The woman, her mother and witness, who will corroborate residency and grounds, rolls her eyes as if to say her daughter's taste in men hasn't improved. "Any calls?" I ask, riffling through my message box as I examine the return address: Jason's. Beneath it is a picture of Lassie.

Julia scowls as if I had asked her to disrobe. "I just talked to you a half hour ago. Who do you think wants you so bad? At this rate you're gonna want to get a car phone. Bracken probably has one, am I right?"

I motion to my client and her mother to come forward, and I glance at Jason's letter. Incredibly, there is a check for five hundred dollars made out to Wilma Chestnut. At the bottom is written: *Return of Bernard Junior's tuition.* I can't believe it. I feel like hugging the two women next to me. Jason has enclosed a short note: "In a former life, Giddy Page, I have no doubt you were a Doberman. I have found these outwardly normal animals to be the only large-size canines in existence utterly devoid of the possibilities of metaphysical growth. Your regression, as reflected in your life's work, is only natural. Very Sadly Yours, Jason Von Jason."

"This is my mom, Mr. Page," my client says, nodding at her mother, who is popping a pill into her mouth. My client's husband began beating her on their wedding night and left her six months later for a prostitute just released from prison for manslaughter. Without her bruises, Arvetta Kennedy is pretty in a wormy, underfed sort of way, but her mother's face shows the ravages of cigarette smoking and eighteen years of raising Arvetta.

"Kathy Harris, Mr. Page," the older woman says. "Arvetta is thinking of dismissing her complaint for divorce from that piece of shit. If you let her, I will make your life miserable. Do you hear me?"

Arvetta begins to sniffle. "Aw, Mom, Bobby can really be neat a lot of the time."

Everyone in the waiting room looks at me. "Let's talk about this in my office," I say, glaring at Julia to keep her mouth shut at least until I am out of her presence.

I am back from the courthouse in half an hour. (Judge Rand was in one of his moods in which he violates the statutes and judicial canons and signs the divorce decree without a word of testimony: "You're divorced; have a nice day.") I call Mrs. Chestnut with the good news. "I'm sending you a check for five hundred dollars," I say, feeling as if I had taken on Shell Oil and won.

There is a silence at the other end. "I don't think I should take the money," she says sweetly. "Bernard Junior can really try a person's patience. Just lately, he's forgetting to go to the bathroom outside, and he's four years old!"

From behind my desk I look out the window and

wonder if I could learn to be a truck driver. "I've already put the check in the mail and closed your file," I lie, holding up the check to see if it has been written in disappearing ink. "You do whatever you want."

Mrs. Chestnut's voice quivers with righteous indignation. "Mr. Von Jason was a nice man! I think Bernard Junior misses him."

Over lunch in the cafeteria downstairs I tell Dan about the last eighteen hours. Sucking on the meatless carcass of a chicken breast that is now so dry he can practically whistle a tune on it, he nods. "So Chet is finally coming around? It's about goddamn time."

Trying not to watch Dan, I sip at my coffee. I have had so much caffeine today I could begin my own coffee plantation by pissing in my front yard. "And after all this, he'll probably drop dead in the middle of the trial."

Dan finally wipes his mouth on his napkin. "The ultimate sympathy plea," he says with a grin. "What a great way to go out." He eyes the dessert section and begins to drum his fingers. He has promised Brenda to cut out sweets during the day. I know how Dan is going out. He pushes up from the table. "Don't wish for something too hard. You may get it. I'll be right back. Want some more coffee?"

"No, thanks," I say, mulling over Dan's remark. Do I really want this case so badly now that I'd wish death on somebody? Damn, am I that grotesque? Perhaps. Beginning with last night's conversation with Sarah, the last twenty-four hours have seemed like one long ache. Jennifer with a "J" is telling her friends, "I met this sad-sack lawyer last night who practically started bawling on the dance floor. I would have gone home with him but I was afraid I'd drown if he got on top of me." How can I blame Velvetta, or whatever her name was, for wanting to go back to her husband? I'm just as pathetic.

I watch Dan take a piece of cherry pie. Out of the whole bunch, only Chet and Wynona seem to have it together. How much simpler life would be if I had their faith. If I can believe my eyes, neither fears the freight train bearing down on Chet. Yet I could tell Wynona about the loneliness. No amount of faith will stop that. No child, no matter how wonderful, is a substitute for a husband or wife. Not if you were both in love. And as hard as it is to think about Chet Bracken being in love, he clearly is. Maybe that's why this case has been so hard on him. For the first time in his life he has things in perspective. Wynona. Trey. The little time he has left he can't really concentrate on a trial. In fact, he is even thinking like a human being instead of like a lawyer. That's why it has been difficult for him to suspect Shane. How can I blame him? Chet still doesn't want to believe that the man who has given him such peace may be a murderer, and it's taken him this long to face that distinct possibility.

"What the hell," Dan says, sliding the pie onto the table. The crust appears an inch thick. "I could've gotten ice cream on it."

"A man of iron discipline," I agree. "I can easily see you in a monastic order, fasting for weeks at a time. Your cheeks gaunt, your wispy body a perfectly flat line as you prostrate yourself against the cold stones of the abbey at four each morning. Toiling cheerfully for hours in the scorching sun. Your mind pure, unadulterated, your thoughts only of God and your fellow man."

Dan digs into his pie. "I'd probably become gay, all right," he muses, putting a typical Bailey spin on the subject. "Even as terrible as Brenda can be, I still get excited if we haven't done it in a while."

It. It's been a while. Maybe it's over for me. Women can obviously tell when you're desperate. I used to dream of the day Rainey and I would make love, but now it'll never happen. "Good for you," I say, meaning it. Who knows? Maybe Dan's marriage isn't as terrible as it seems. He probably makes it sound that way just to have something to talk about.

"What do you make of Leigh's story about the nude video?" I ask. Dan has been curiously silent on the subject.

The last piece of pie disappears down his throat. Three bites. And I thought Woogie ate fast. "I've been thinking about that," he says, wiping his mouth with the greasy rag of a napkin that off and on has been wedged in his crotch. "It sounds like one of those trial balloons politicians send up. She's running scared. If she thought Shane had been in on it, you or Chet would have heard it long before now. As much as she might love her old man, she's too young to take the rap for him. The last martyr even close to Leigh's age was Joan of Arc. That kind of stuff is done best by people our age whose most exciting activity is collecting coupons for arch supports and Preparation H."

I chuckle at the truth in Dan's remark. Why would Leigh want to take a fall if she's got her whole life in front of her? My problem in this case is that I don't really know the client. As I lament this fact to Dan, a light bulb finally goes on in my head. Leigh's sisters. Why aren't they here? Is there so much estrangement that they won't even be here for their sister's murder trial? Who was it who suggested I call one of them? If my memory gets any worse, I'll need to start writing down my own name.

Upstairs, I thumb through my notes on the case and, for a change, find what I'm looking for—the names of the neighbors next door. I call and am told by Ann Wheeler that Mary Patricia has never married and lives in a small town in Rhode Island. I get the number and leave a message on her answering machine. She must be at work.

At three-thirty, as I am about to head west for Christian Life, Rainey calls and tells me that she has located Sarah. "She's okay," she says. "I've seen the place she's staying in, and you don't have anything to worry about."

"Where is it?" I ask, relieved but irritated at the same time. I'll be the one to decide if I need to worry.

Her voice full of sympathy, Rainey says, "I can't tell you that. The price of seeing it was that I had to swear I wouldn't tell you."

I try to keep my voice calm, but I can't. "For God's sake," I yell, "this is my child we're talking about, Rainey!"

"I know that!" she shoots back. "Don't cut the one link you have to her right now. If I told you, and you went and got her, the next day she might be gone again and for good."

I drum my fingers on my desk in frustration, knowing she is making perfect sense. I can't lock Sarah up. "Does the place she's in have running water and electricity?"

Rainey can't suppress a giggle. "Relax. She's not fighting off rats in an abandoned warehouse. It's a very adequate apartment. The girl she's staying with is an emancipated minor and very mature for her age. She's got a job and pays her own way. Don't try to crowd Sarah too much right now, okay?"

How mature can a kid under eighteen be? I know fifty-year-olds who don't have any business living by themselves. "Is it in a safe area of town?"

"Very," Rainey says, her voice reassuring. "I even checked the refrigerator when she wasn't looking. They have more food than you do. Granted, it's mostly frozen pizzas and Cokes, but she's not starving."

For the first time in months, I feel profound gratitude to Rainey. Even though our relationship is strained to the breaking point right now, she is still coming through for me. "I take it her roommate is Christian Life?"

"Oh, most definitely!" Rainey assures me. "She's a good kid."

Not a boy, thank God. Rainey, thank goodness, can't help her social-worker mode. "Will you ask her to call me tonight?" I say, suddenly close to tears. At least she isn't facing a murder charge.

"I already did," she answers. "Try to be home about eight."

I wipe my eyes, glad she can't see me. "Thanks." For a moment I consider telling Rainey that Leigh has disappeared, but I'm already late now. I'll have plenty to tell her later tonight.

"Try to remember," Rainey advises, "that Christian Life is the most important thing in her life right now. She feels you're a threat to it."

I want to protest that I haven't prohibited Sarah from spending a single minute up there, but Rainey knows that. Intellectually, she must mean. But Sarah knows I don't know enough science to stop a case of the hiccups. Still, I suppose I represent the kind of people who do. "Why didn't she stay," I ask, looking at my watch, "and argue with me?"

Rainey says gently, "Because you don't fight fair. You use guilt, condescension, self-pity—every emotion she's never been able to deal with when you're in the picture."

Not to mention hitting her. Parents. We ought to be

killed at our children's birth to give them a chance. "I hear you," I say, but I probably don't. As Darryl Royal, the long-retired coach of the Texas Longhorns, used to say about his football team, "You dance with what brung you." As I drive out to the Christian Life complex, I meditate on what "brung" me thirty years ago out of eastern Arkansas. When my sister and I got into trouble as children, invariably we would be called in for a lecture at the foot of my parents' bed. Her *Reader's Digest* condensed book lying on her chest, our mother would take off her glasses and sigh, "Children, how did I fail you? I'm so sorry. For you to be acting this way, I must have failed you in some way. Your father's going to be so disappointed."

Our part read: "No, Mother, you didn't fail us. We're just horrible children, and we feel so bad." Did we? As I fight the five o'clock traffic, which begins earlier every year, I try to think back on how I felt, but it has been too long to recapture the precise feeling of shame that I had let them down in some unforgivable way. To Sarah's credit, she has moved beyond that. What was it she said? *I won't let you guilt me!* I wanted to turn her into a little me. Page & Page, attorneys at law. Fat chance. At this rate, I'll be lucky if she lets me come to her wedding.

Shane's office at Christian Life is big enough to put in a skating rink. If influence is measured by space, he's ready to challenge Pat Robertson as head of the religious right. My office would fit nicely in the corner where he has a couch, a recliner, and a twenty-six-inch Sony color television and VCR. It is to this area he leads me. Chet is already seated at the far end of the couch. "You have to see what your competition's doing, and these days they're on almost twenty-four hours a day," Shane rattles on nervously as I gawk at the TV.

Chet glares at me and looks down at his watch. I'm only ten minutes late.

"The traffic is murder out there," I apologize. I sit on the couch nearest the TV, and by the strained look on Chet's face, I halfway expect him to tell me he has the video of Leigh and we're all going to watch it together. Both are dressed in dark blue suits I'd be proud to be buried in. "Have you heard anything from Leigh?" I ask Chet, gathering from his expression he has not.

"Shane," he says, ignoring me, "this is as hard as anything I've ever had to do, but Gideon has made me realize that I'm obligated to ask you some questions about your whereabouts during the time Art was murdered."

Shane folds his arms across his chest and gives Chet a hard stare. "You're not serious."

Chet goes totally rigid and his head seems to disappear inside his shirt. He swallows hard and continues, "Where were you between nine-thirty and eleven-thirty the day your son-in-law was murdered?"

Shane's voice rises in anger. "You actually think I'd commit murder, Chet?"

I look at Chet, who, in all the hours I've watched him, has never appeared out of control even for an instant. For the first time he seems close. His eyes blink rapidly, and he stammers, "Answer my question, damn it."

As if he does understand what Chet is going through, Shane seems to relax. His features soften, and he smiles at him. "It's okay." He clears his throat and, trying to sound casual, says, "As best I can remember, I think I was here in the office all the time."

I have never really felt sorry for Chet until this moment. He places his hand over his mouth as if he is about to utter something unspeakable. Finally, he mumbles through his fingers, "One of the secretaries who used to work for you says that you left the office during that period and came back right before Leigh called to say Art had been shot."

Shane places his right ankle across his left thigh and says easily, "It's possible I did go out. We had a missionary from Guatemala at the church that day. I don't know. It's like trying to remember what you were doing before Kennedy was killed. You remember what you were doing when you heard the news, but not what you ate for breakfast that day. I could have gone a dozen places within a hundred yards of my office."

I wonder if I am supposed to be taking notes. This is weak. Chet said the secretary told him that Shane said he was going over to his house for a while. I glance at Chet, but he is examining his hands. I ask, "Do you recall seeing anybody or talking to anybody during that time other than the women in the office?"

Shane squinches his eyes and studies the ceiling for a long moment. "Not offhand," he says finally, fixing his gaze on Chet. "You're not going to claim in court," he asks, his voice too loud, "that I shot Art, are you?"

Chet, now slumped against the back of the couch, seems listless and broken. He spreads his hands in a gesture of hopelessness. "I may not have a choice," he says dully.

"Now, wait just a minute!" Shane almost shouts, leaning forward over his knees. "This is absurd! No jury will believe for a second that I killed my own son-in-law. As horrible a man as he turned out to be, murder never once crossed my mind. I admit I talked to Leigh about divorcing him, which may sound hypocritical as many times as I've preached on the value of couples staying together, but that's as far as I went."

I look past Norman to the large desk that sits in front

of the two windows in his office. "Your daughter loved
the man," I say, knowing I am baiting him. "She didn't
want a divorce."

"He was murdering her soul!" Shane retorts angrily.
"Leigh was a precious vessel of God's love before she
met Art."

I glance at Chet to see how he is taking these re-
marks. The back of his right hand obscures his face. His
eyes, an almost colorless light blue, show no emotion. I
am struck by Norman's use of the term "murdering her
soul." If he were on trial, instead of his daughter, before
a jury of Christian Lifers, he might argue justifiable
homicide. A father defending his child against a deadly
attacker. What person would convict a man who used
force to save his daughter? In Norman's mind, Leigh's
soul is worth more than her body. It would be far easier
to defend Norman than his daughter.

"You saw that Art was destroying Leigh, didn't
you?" I ask, believing I understand for the first time
that, given Norman's worldview, murder was the only
possible solution. What was it they said about Vietnam?
We had to destroy the country to save it. In Norman's
mind, once the corruption started, there was no end to
it. The pull of the world is too strong. Look what happened to his other daughters while he stood by. Once
you leave, you almost never go back. The world is too
seductive. When Norman doesn't respond, I ask him a
question I know he will answer. "What did you tell
Leigh about Art's death?"

Shane says in a voice so detached and automatic I
know he has thought it a hundred times since the day
Art died, "That he got what he deserved. I won't deny
that."

Biblical phrases like "reap what you sow" come into
my mind. Even if he didn't kill Art, he wished him

dead. "Since you love your daughter so much," I say quickly before Chet can protest, "you won't object if Chet suggests to the jury that others, including yourself, may have had a possible motive for murdering her husband."

Like a wounded animal, Shane roars, "You do what you have to do, but I didn't kill him!"

Remembering Chet's instructions to let him do the talking, I look over at him to see if I'm in trouble. This was his speech as far as I am concerned, but from what I've seen so far, he wasn't going to make it. He sits quietly, staring at Shane as if he is evaluating his sincerity. Finally, he says quietly to him, "It could ruin you."

Shane, now barely seated, yells at him, "You don't believe me, do you?"

Abruptly, Chet stands and heads for the door, leaving me and Shane looking at each other. I scramble to my feet and chase after him while Shane hollers futilely, "Chet!"

Out in the parking lot, his face ashen, Chet tells me shakily, "I'm going home."

Hunched over as he unlocks the Mercedes, he looks shockingly old, defeated. "Let me argue the case!" I demand. "I can do it! You shouldn't have to do this!"

"I'll do it," he says, almost under his breath as he arranges himself in the car. He drives away, mumbling something to himself.

Back home, waiting for Sarah to call, I open a beer, heat up some cheese dip, open a bag of potato chips, and sit in the kitchen looking out the window at the gathering darkness. Woogie's bowl is still half full from last night. "Depressed, huh?" I ask him as he stretches out on the linoleum by the window. "We'll hear from her tonight." I hope.

Ignoring me, he places his muzzle between his paws flat on the dirty surface. I break off a chip in the thick yellow sludge that is congealing before my eyes. I couldn't penetrate this goo if I were eating brickbats. Too tired to cook, I drink and think about Shane Norman. *Do what you have to do,* he said. What would I have said if it were Sarah who was charged and I was innocent? I don't have as much to lose as Shane Norman. His life requires that his inner and outer selves match up in a way mine do not. Yet, for all I know, preachers carry guilt inside them like everyone else, and it is only their flock that assumes that hypocrisy burdens their consciences more than the rest of us. Do I believe he is innocent? I sip at my beer. I don't know. I still have problems getting past the taboo of believing a minister would kill another human being. Yet, historically, the church has been as bloodthirsty as the rest of society, if not more so. The Crusades, the Inquisition, the persecution of Jews, religious zealots on both sides during the Civil War, white-supremacist religious groups, all stand as monuments to a barely restrained ecclesiastical violence. I think of the hatred I see in some of the faces of those people who oppose abortion on religious grounds. If that is Christian love in their faces, give me a secular humanist anytime. It is the look on Chet's face that convinces me that Norman is lying. I get out a legal pad and begin to think about what should be in an opening argument.

At nine Sarah calls, but it is not a satisfactory conversation. My supply of restraint is wearing thin, and the alcohol doesn't help. "When do you think you'll be coming home?" I ask, unable to wait her out even a few seconds.

"I don't know, Dad," she says, not bothering to conceal her own irritation. "I have to decide on what terms I want to live in the world."

What utter crap! I can't talk any further without exploding. "I'm going to bed," I say shortly, and hang up, furious at everybody I've ever known connected with religion. It is not as if Sarah had been forced to live in some brothel. She has had it pretty damn easy. Like about ninety-nine percent of the kids I know, she's spoiled rotten.

I call Rainey and unload my feelings on her. "I suppose it's just a matter of time before she will begin quoting the Bible to the effect that she has no mother or father except Christian Life. What about family values?" I complain. "Don't these so-called families have anybody in them with any sense?"

"They are talking to her," Rainey says, sounding a little shaken for the first time. "They don't force anyone to do anything."

"Well, I'm gonna go to the Prosecutor's Office when this trial is over," I yell at her, "and charge somebody with kidnapping."

"Which will guarantee that she won't talk to you for years," Rainey says right back. "Life is too short for that kind of resentment."

"Well, it's not getting any longer this way," I reply stubbornly. Miserable, I hang up and go to bed.

16

I AM AT the airport waiting for Jessie St. Vrain to get off the plane, when I hear my name paged over the P.A. system. It must be Chet. No one else knows I'm here. "You didn't have to come pick me up!" Jessie exclaims as she emerges from a stream of United passengers. She unnerves me by having cut her hair even shorter than it was last week. With the trial to begin tomorrow, it is not too late to suggest a wig. Of course, she would be highly offended.

"Southern hospitality," I say, smiling. "How was the flight?" Jessie is wearing loose-fitting brown pants under a green suede jacket. Her brown shoes look like the kind elves wear in animated cartoons. I hope she has something more appropriate in her bag. Her story is going to be hard enough for a jury to swallow without her looking like Peter Pan.

"Tricky winds out of Denver," she replies, grimacing, as she matches me stride for stride. "If we had been lower, I think we would have bounced into a mountain."

I shudder and hear my name again. Chet could have sent Daffy to get her. He and Jessie would have made a nice pair. "Isn't that you," she asks, nudging me, "being paged?"

"I get the joke," I say weakly, wondering what other

254

people in the airport think of this woman. She seems equally curious, staring boldly at my fellow Arkansans, who look pretty normal to me. "Shoes, see?"

"I was just kidding!" she practically shouts, crowding me into the wall.

Chet's message says to drop off Jessie at the Excelsior Hotel and meet him inside the courthouse at the east entrance. This can mean only one thing: the prosecutor is willing to cut a deal. We still have no idea of Leigh's whereabouts, unless in the last half hour something has happened I don't know about. When I arrive twenty minutes later, Chet is pacing around the rotunda as if he were sweating out the jury's decision.

"Jill called from her office ten minutes after you left," he says, his voice excited for the only time since I've known him. "She wants to talk."

Flattered that he has waited for me, I feel obligated to point out the obvious. "It would help if we had a client to run this by."

Chet punches the button to take us to the third floor. Six months ago he would have taken the steps two at a time. "She's bound to show up sometime. Did St. Vrain make it in?"

I nod as the elevator opens. "She's a little weird."

Chet grins. "That's what you keep telling me. Maybe we won't need her." As we ride up and walk around the corner to the prosecutor's office, it sinks in how much Chet wants to avoid this trial. His zest for trial work is such that he almost hates to cut a deal and browbeats the prosecutors until they are practically begging him to take probation. These stories are surely exaggerated, but they prove a point: Chet isn't afraid to go for an outright acquittal. Yet, why shouldn't he want to plead out this case? He isn't prepared, he is sick, and his loyalties are clearly divided. "Jill must be having some problems," I whisper as we enter the suite of offices that house Blackwell County's chief legal officer. Chet winks, as if this turn of events is too good to risk commenting on.

Jill Marymount has proved to be a decent prosecutor in her tenure in office. She can grab headlines with the best of them, but underneath all the hype is a solid record. Unlike some prosecutors after their election, she tries cases regularly instead of relying on assistants. I had thought she had political ambitions, but the rumors have died down that she wants to run for attorney general. They will be revived if she knocks off Chet Bracken. Jill sweeps through the door to the reception area, reminding me of the actress Loretta Young. She is wearing a dress instead of the suit she will don tomorrow, and she shows a mouthful of perfect teeth as if we were fans waiting for autographs. Chet, who is used to being courted in these situations, is unusually gracious, betraying his own eagerness.

Temporarily old pals instead of old enemies, we come close to slapping each other's backs as she escorts us to her office. Once there, she offers us coffee and serves it herself. It seems a miracle that she hasn't heard that Leigh has disappeared, which is a tribute to the tightness of Christian Lifers in Blackwell County. From behind her desk she says lightly, "Two against one, no fair, guys."

I steal a look at Chet, who is slouched in his chair. To be prattling on like this, Jill must have a hole in her case we can drive a truck through. But where is it? I can't see it. Chet might know, but I have no idea. Maybe it is simply her fear of the religious fundamentalists who will be on the jury and who will surely be manipulated by someone as skilled as Chet. Jill could wind up with a goose egg and have a killer on the loose in the swankiest part of Blackwell County. Chet acknowledges the truth of her remark by saying, "When Gideon and I were growing up in the Delta, we used to say, quite innocently, *'Two against one, nigger fun.'* "

Jill swallows hard as if she were a child forced to swallow a tablespoon of milk of magnesia. I don't recall the innocence of that remark, but it was a common schoolboy lament. She says, "I didn't know you were from the same town."

Our solidarity established, I clarify. "Chet's from Helena in Phillips County; I'm from Bear Creek in Lee. There's not a lot of difference."

Jill forces a smile at us. Good old boys riding up and down Main Street, looking for someone to gangbang. She has changed her office again since I was in here last. During the Andy Chapman trial, she had dozens of pictures of children on the walls. Now, painted a fresh eggshell blue to cover up the holes, I assume, the room seems empty and sterile. Jill says abruptly, "I'm offering you ten years and a plea to manslaughter."

Just a little over three years with good time. Jill's eyes are on Chet. There is not even the slightest pretense that we are co-equals on this case. Licking his lips, he doesn't so much as look at me before saying, "I'll talk to Leigh and get back to you."

I feel my insides bind. Chet barely let her get her words out. Is he selling Leigh down the river, or does he think she is guilty? I no longer have any idea. Now all we have to do is find her. Jill runs a hand through her thick, glossy hair. I don't know which of them looks more relieved. "I'll talk to Judge Grider and see if he has time to take a plea this afternoon."

Chet shakes his head. "Let me get hold of her first," he says, his voice sounding hollow against the bare walls. "If she won't take it, I don't want Grider thinking she changed her mind."

Jill begins to write on the pad in front of her. Instead of conventional legal paper, she is writing on ledger sheets. The logic of Chet's statement is unassailable, but she frowns. "You'll get back to me immediately?" she asks.

Chet stands up. "Just as soon as I can," he says, trying to sound like the Bracken of old. He is not known for giving anything away. Too bad for Jill, she doesn't know we have nothing to give. She must wonder what I'm doing on this case. So am I.

Like a slave attending his master, I pop to my feet but have nothing to say. To avoid potted-plant status entirely, I remark, "What happened to your pictures? You must have had dozens the last time I was in here."

Jill's gaze goes proudly to her empty walls as she comes from around her desk to walk us out. "They're on loan to a museum in Fort Smith."

To add to the slightly unrealistic atmosphere that has surrounded this meeting, we beam at each other as if we were busy philanthropists and patrons of the arts. "That's great!" I say, enthusiastically. Jill must wonder if Chet owes me something. She probably has heard he has cancer, but he has put the word out he is in remission so often maybe she believes it.

As soon as we are in the sunshine on the sidewalk, Chet asks irritably, "Where in the hell can she be?"

A lot of places, I think, watching an attractive woman cross the street. Like a spoiled child who isn't receiving enough attention to suit him, I feel left out. "You want me to go over and pick up Ms. St. Vrain and bring her to your office?" I say in response, having learned to answer rhetorical questions at my peril.

Chet nods glumly. "It'll give us something to do."

In the next three hours Jessie St. Vrain watches as Chet and I go nuts. At one point we get a call from Shane saying Leigh has been sighted in Lonoke County in a convenience store. Shades of Elvis. We get two calls from Jill, who is plainly becoming suspicious. "Client disappeared?" she jokes the second time, but there is little humor in her voice.

"Halfway to Brazil," I say, not certain it isn't true.

"What's going on, Gideon?" Jill asks. "This isn't an essay question."

More like multiple choice. Texas? New Jersey? Hong Kong? None of the above? I put my feet up on Chet's library table. "You should try the defense side someday. You'd appreciate us more."

Jill cuts me off. "If we have to go to the trouble and expense of impaneling a jury and then take a plea, Judge Grider won't like it."

I almost laugh. She's worried about the costs to the county and keeping a pit bull happy. "We'll pay the jury off," I say, trying to sound relaxed. "Grider will find something to do—tune in a cockfight on TV or something."

Jill giggles. She knows how much Grider likes to watch lawyers tear into each other. "Just get back to me—okay?—if and when you find out Chet's not going to plead her out."

Relegated to flunky status again, I oblige. "You'll be the first to know." I hang up and stare at the hundreds of books in Chet's library, a personal luxury few lawyers can afford. I'm pissed that I am such a nonentity on this case. During the conversation with Jill, I was tempted to blurt out that the great Chet Bracken had no idea what his opening statement was going to be just a little over half a day before the trial. She has lost her nerve for nothing.

By six o'clock Chet is so worn out he decides to call it a day, saying he will call me after dinner, but I doubt it. He is so white around the gills it sets my teeth on edge. Thank God the prosecution has the burden of proof. As little as we seem to have accomplished this afternoon, I wouldn't give even money that we will be able to prove our middle names. We have prepped Jessie's testimony and sent her back to her hotel, and that's about all. "I know it's a hell of a time to ask," I blurt, "but where is the cancer?"

The lock snaps on Chet's door. In a voice so soft I barely pick it up, he says, "At this point, it's more a question of where it isn't."

What is there to say? Go home and take some aspirin and get a good night's sleep? On this cheerful note we leave each other. I race home, hoping Woogie hasn't taken revenge on the carpet. With Sarah not there to let him out in the afternoons, he can only restrain himself so long.

Woogie races past me into the yard and cocks his left hind leg in the direction of a holly bush. Usually, he concentrates his irrigation project on my neighbors' shrubs and plants, but from the look he gives me, this is out of the question. "Sorry, boy," I apologize. At my age, I'm glad no one has asked me to make the same sacrifice. He still has one more act to perform, but this is done in a more leisurely manner on the playground of the elementary school at the end of the street. As we stroll back to the house, accompanied by howls of outrage from more law-abiding members of the canine population who are confined behind their masters' fences, I wonder in vain where Leigh has hidden herself. All afternoon long, Chet and I took message after message that she is nowhere to be found.

At home I have a message on the answering machine

from Leigh's sister Mary Patricia, who has returned my call. I wonder for a moment if Leigh could have taken off looking for a safe harbor at one of their houses, but those were the first numbers Shane called. I am still surprised that the sisters are not coming for the trial. At this rate, they would be by themselves. No telling, though, what it was like growing up in the Norman household. I should have been in touch long before now. I get her on the second ring. I am expecting a Yankee accent, but she sounds so much like her sister Leigh, I am startled. There is a softness to an Arkansas accent without the deep-fried quality that marks the speech of our neighbors in Mississippi.

"Ms. Norman, I appreciate you calling back," I say, wondering how to interest this woman in talking to me. "I should have called you a lot sooner than the day before the trial."

"Do you represent my father or Leigh?" Mary Patricia asks, without preliminaries, her voice politely suspicious.

"Mr. Bracken and I represent only Leigh," I assure her. If she knew how this case was going, she wouldn't be assured, no matter what I said.

In the background I hear classical music and wonder if this woman is as lovely as her sister. All I know about her is that she escaped the clutches of her father. "Leigh is still missing."

"I've tried to think where she might go," Mary Patricia says, "but it's been too long. Leigh and I aren't as close as we once were."

I watch Woogie lick his empty food dish. I hope Mary Patricia proves to be equally unsubtle. "Frankly, I'm surprised that neither you nor your sister are down here for the trial. Surely you know Leigh could be going to prison for life."

There is silence on the other end, and I fear I have pushed too hard. Yet, as estranged as I am from my own sister, I know she would be there for me if I were on trial for murder. Finally, her voice tentative as if she can't decide how much she should be revealing, Mary Patricia says, "I'm sure you don't understand the dynamics in our family. My other sister and I aren't close to our parents at all. In fact, my father thinks we are atheists. For my part, I think he and others like him would like nothing better than to run people like us out of the United States. Leigh would defend him to the death. I know. I was just down there a few months ago. Leigh hadn't changed a bit. We had an enormous fight, and she told me she never wanted to see me again. Naturally, I called her after I found out she was charged with murder; but she said it was all a big mistake and that Daddy would have it dismissed."

I can hear the guilt in her voice, and I try to think how I can exploit it. It will take violating a client's confidence, but over the years I've gotten better at rationalization. For the next fifteen minutes I tell her everything I know about the case, including Leigh's belief that her father may have killed her husband.

Mary Patricia listens almost without interruption and responds simply, "Daddy would never do something like that himself. He might give the idea to somebody else, but his concept of himself as a personal representative of God is too strong to allow him to kill anyone. He can preach a sermon that galvanizes a thousand people to go lie down in front of an abortion clinic, but he would cut off his arm before he would take part himself."

Finally, something clicks in my mind about who may have killed Art Wallace. I ask her, "Tell me something about your godfather, please."

Leigh's sister obviously sees this guess as something of a stretch. Her voice grows faint with obvious disbelief. "Do you think Hector could have actually done it?"

"Why not?" I plunge ahead, remembering his still keen eyesight and the trophy for marksmanship. "He was there; he was a friend of your father's; it's not as if he is a feeble shut-in."

She protests, "But he's an old man."

I remind her about his fitness and the trophies. "He seems in remarkable shape."

"You probably could say that of a high percentage of those who live on my sister's street," she responds, clearly skeptical of my hypothesis. "Hector's not a violent man."

Stubbornly, I pursue the possibility. "But he's still extremely competitive, and he could have acted as your father's surrogate. Wasn't he upset when you left the church?"

In the background now, I can hear Glen Campbell singing. I must have made her homesick. "He was horrified," she admits, "but he didn't kill anybody."

I point out, trying not to sound too combative, "You weren't the last child to fly the coop."

For the first time, Mary Patricia concedes, "And I wasn't the favorite." She adds, however, "But Daddy wouldn't talk Hector into killing Art."

"He wouldn't have to," I say, seizing on her earlier comment about her father's ability to influence other people. "Hector would get the idea."

There is a respectful pause while she apparently considers the possibility. "I just don't see Hector capable of murder."

I drop the subject, myself troubled by the timing of the events. How would this old man know things were flying apart at this particular moment? Nobody has accused him of being a peeping Tom. He did say it was odd that Leigh didn't wave. But that was all. "What about Leigh?" I ask. "What do you see her capable of?"

There is no hesitation in Mary Patricia's voice. "If Leigh were angry enough," she says, "she could have killed him. Leigh has Mother's temper, but she's incapable of killing someone in cold blood."

Mrs. Norman has been forgotten in all of this. Both quintessential Southern women. All that repressed anger beneath a boozy surface. Leigh could have had a snootful to try to relax that morning and simply exploded. Her mother's baggage. Maybe Jill's offer of ten years for manslaughter is about right. "Does Leigh drink?"

Mary Patricia answers, "Not unless Art was teaching her."

Perhaps he was. We talk for a few more minutes, but I get nothing useful except a promise that she will call me if she hears from Leigh.

I call Chet to run my latest theory by him, but Wynona tells me he had already taken a painkiller and is in no condition to speak to me. I think to myself that this case is turning into a joke. No lawyer, no client, only a single, flaky witness from California. I mope around the kitchen looking for something to eat and decide the easiest thing to do is to open a can of soup. I am beginning to have some real doubts about myself both as a lawyer and as a father. Nothing I say or do seems to make a difference. Chet apparently has no confidence in my abilities to handle this case. Perhaps he has been in touch with my old employers, Mays & Burton, who fired me. Granted, I didn't give my bosses anything to write home about, but I wasn't given much to work with either. As I open the pantry to look for the chips, the phone rings, startling me out of my growing self-pity.

"Is this Mr. Page?" It is a foreign voice, perhaps Japanese, and barely understandable.

In no mood for telemarketing, I bark, "If you're selling something, you better tell me right now." Wow. What am I going to do—hang up on them?

I hear the sound of someone clearing his throat. "There is a young lady in our motel who is asking for you. I'm afraid she is very drunk. Room 104 of the Delta Inn. Would you please come get her?" This last sentence is more of a command than a request, and the line goes dead. Leigh, obviously. Grabbing my keys off the shelf by the phone, I race out to the Blazer. It could be Sarah. Or even Jessie St. Vrain. The way the day has gone, it would be just my luck.

17

THE DELTA INN is on I-30 almost halfway to Benton. Since its parking lot is shielded from the highway, the motel offers a twenty-five-dollar-a-night sanctuary to adulterers and others who have a reason to hide their automobiles. Leigh's father claims his church members have cruised every motel parking lot in Blackwell County, but I can see how someone in a hurry would have missed Leigh's maroon Acura, which is not parked in front of the rooms but is wedged between two pickups across from the motel restaurant. I park right in front of room 104 and knock on the door a full thirty seconds before Leigh opens it and staggers back four feet to sit on the bed.

"Don't take me home," she says, her voice slurred and low.

"I won't," I promise, but I have to get her out of here before I throw up. The tiny, moldy room smells overpoweringly of mildew and bourbon and the remains of some kind of Mexican dinner that looks more than twelve hours old. A half-empty six-pack of Cokes, an empty bottle of Old Crow, and a clouded plastic glass sit on top of a dresser that looks as if it has survived a couple of fires. An entire bottle would have blottoed me. I marvel how Leigh managed to give my name to the manager. It is hard to believe such a beautiful woman can look so terrible. Matted, damp hair frames her face, which is swollen—I assume from crying and alcohol. She appears to be in a stupor, and from the phone by the bed, I dial Rainey's number.

"I need some help," I say when she answers the phone. "I've just found Leigh dead drunk in a motel, and I need a woman's touch in sobering her up for the trial tomorrow."

Rainey responds immediately. "Bring her over here."

Taking a look at the dried vomit on Leigh's sweatshirt, I gag before I can get out, "We'll be there in half an hour."

I feel like a gangster hauling an unconscious body out to the Blazer as I struggle to support Leigh's weight in the darkness. Fortunately, there is nobody else around as I half-drag her out to the Blazer. I feel keenly self-conscious about how this must look: a middle-aged guy forcing a drugged young woman into a car. She is surprisingly solid; and, to my consternation, the image of her dancing nude for the camera forces its way into my mind as I help her lie down in the backseat. There is nothing visually attractive about Leigh at the moment. I go back in, looking for any personal belongings, but find only her purse. I know myself well enough to realize that calling Rainey was the best decision I've made in a while. At moments like this, she has always been there for me, even when she is furious at me. It hasn't been too many months since my face was turned into mincemeat while I was working on a case. I was in worse shape than my present passenger in the backseat, but I pried myself loose from soft asphalt in a honky-tonk parking lot and headed like a homing pigeon for Rainey's, where she patched me up enough to allow me to go home and face my daughter.

I stop in front of the office and run in to pay the bill

and tell the man at the desk that it may be tomorrow or the next day before we pick up the car. With his distinct Asian features and his black dressing gown that could cover the side of a barn, he looks like a finalist from a sumo wrestling championship forty years ago. A rerun of the "Cosby Show" flickers on an ancient black and white TV in the corner next to a huge green safe, and I wonder briefly what odyssey has brought this man to the desk of the Delta Inn. "I think you called me about the young woman in 104," I say over the voice of one of Cosby's TV daughters, whose problems never got this seedy. "I'm taking her home."

He shoots me a look of pity. "Is the room all right?" he asks in a heavily accented voice. What the hell, I think, Henry Kissinger still sounds as if he just got off the boat, too.

"I think so," I reply, not really having checked it out. How much damage could anyone do to the Delta Inn and not be justified in calling it a part of a demolition effort? "You send me the bill if there are any problems with it, okay?" I hand him a card, as if I were the manager of a rock group that regularly trashes hotels.

"You a good rawyer?" he asks, studying my card.

Poor guy. What a crapshoot. You get one, and he's dead on his feet of cancer. I nod ambiguously. This man has probably been a citizen for longer than I've been alive, yet he'll go to his grave thinking he can be deported because he can't say his *l*'s. "I need a divorce," he confesses, near tears as he hands me a bill, showing an amount owing of fifty cents for two phone calls. "My wife—she run off with one of the maids."

I can't say that I blame her. "Give me a call next week," I say, fishing from my pocket two quarters and the room key. Somehow I don't think I'll be able to give up taking civil cases when Leigh's trial is over.

On the drive to Rainey's, Leigh stirs in the backseat but says nothing I can understand. Alcohol. It may be playing more of a role in this case than I thought. Leigh, out from under the parental thumb, may indeed be a hooch hound like her mother.

Rainey is waiting outside and helps me walk Leigh into her house. "This is my friend Rainey," I say to Leigh. "She's very discreet."

"Hi, Rainey," Leigh says, giggling loudly. "Are you his girlfriend?"

"Just friends," I say, taking Rainey off the spot. I am grateful for the darkness.

"Have you called her father?" Rainey asks as she opens the door.

At this reference to the man who has loved her longer than any other male, Leigh opens her eyes and tries to pull away from us. I tighten my grip on Leigh's arm and reassure her, "No, and I'm not going to." To Rainey behind Leigh's head, I mouth the words, "I'll tell you later."

Rainey's house, as always, is spotless. As much as she has been gone lately, I don't see how she has even had time to water the plants that abound in the living room. I have spent many pleasant hours here and feel a wave of nostalgia wash over me as Rainey walks Leigh into her bathroom. "I'm putting Leigh in the shower," she says. "You go to the kitchen and start some coffee."

Damn. Not even a little peek. I take a final look at Leigh before her transformation begins. Her stomach heaves beneath her sweatshirt as if she is about to be sick. Not exactly what I had in mind. I close the door behind me and make a right turn back into the living room on my way to the kitchen. If I had turned left, I would have walked into Rainey's bedroom. She and I must be the only two single heterosexual adults in the country who have professed romantic love to each other, meant it, had the opportunity on many occasions, but have never followed through. I remember the night I thought she was taking me to her bedroom and she opened the door onto a Ping-Pong table and proceeded to beat my brains out. Though we have played many games since that night and I have come close on occasion, I have never beaten her a single time. Some things just don't seem meant to be.

While I wait for the coffee to drip, I sit down at the kitchen table and worry that Leigh won't sober up enough to be able to discuss Jill's offer of a plea bargain. We led Jill to think it was under active consideration, but by the end of the day her patience was growing thin.

Twenty minutes later, Rainey escorts a shaky but much improved-looking Leigh into the kitchen. In Rainey's white terry-cloth robe, her dark wet hair gleaming under the bright light, Leigh looks like a bedraggled teenager who has paid the price for downing an entire bottle of Southern Comfort. I hand her a cup of coffee as she smiles uncertainly at me. "What are we going to do about clothes?" I ask Rainey. From her neck down Leigh looks almost fetching in the robe, which barely comes to her knees, but she is hardly dressed for a court appearance.

"We've been talking about that," Rainey says, flashing a Dillard's credit card and what I assume is a shopping list at me. "I'm going to run to the mall for Leigh." It is a foregone conclusion that Leigh will not be calling her father tonight.

I look at my watch. It is just before eight, and the mall closes at nine. "You better hurry," I say.

Rainey, whose salary as a social worker goes for her mortgage and not her clothes, grins. "They may be getting in a little overtime tonight." In the background I can hear Rainey's washing machine in the utility room and realize that underneath Rainey's robe, Leigh can't be wearing much. She is a good five inches taller and fifteen pounds heavier than Rainey.

As soon as I hear the screen door close, I tell Leigh about Jill's offer. "You could be out in just over three years with good time," I say, thinking about the women's unit at Pine Bluff. "I've been down there. It's not as bad as it could be." Who am I kidding? Prison is prison even if they let you get your hair done. Leigh's hands shake as she brings the coffee to her lips. She needs something to eat. "You think you could eat some toast?" I'm not much of a cook, but I can handle bread if there is a toaster around.

Leigh swallows, giving herself time to think. "Why should I plead if I'm not guilty?" she asks finally.

The implication of Leigh's remark is that she is innocent, but this is susceptible to more than one interpretation. The answer to her question is more complicated than my response, but out of habit, I give the short version. "I'm not saying you should, but you have to consider the following facts: you've lied about your whereabouts, and the prosecutor will have a field day with it; you were overheard arguing the night before the murder, and so far as we know, nobody, including the police, has found a shred of physical evidence that anyone else is a suspect. And three years and four months at your age is a lot more tolerable than spending the rest of your life in prison." Plus the fact that your lawyer is knocked out with a pain pill for the night instead of preparing your defense and will be out on his feet by three tomorrow afternoon if he lasts that long. But I do not mention this last extremely crucial fact. Why? Out of habit? Lawyers protect each other as much as doctors do. It is as reflexive as an eye blink and happens at least as often. I find a loaf of wheat bread in the freezer next to a Ziploc bag of chicken breasts and lay it on the counter to thaw. When I was a child in eastern Arkansas, the idea of freezing a loaf of Wonder Bread must have been heretical, since I was never privy to the phenomenon until I moved to the center of the state as an adult. What are bread boxes for? As warm and moist as the Arkansas Delta is, I'm surprised bread didn't turn into penicillin right before our eyes.

Leigh stares into her coffee. I've never seen her face so sad. I'm certain there is something more she is not telling me. She says quietly, "Will you call Mr. Bracken for me?"

I nod but say, "Let me ask you a question first. Were you and Art drinking that morning? You don't seem to handle alcohol very well."

"No," Leigh says, a little too abruptly. "Please call Mr. Bracken."

I shrug helplessly. Art's autopsy report showed no alcohol content. In her voice is the tone of a martyr, not a killer giving up. "I don't think you killed Art," I argue. Actually, I have no idea whether she did or not, but I can't allow her to make this decision so easily. "You don't need to sacrifice yourself for your father."

"I'm not," she says, her voice flat. "Please call Mr. Bracken."

I fight back a rising sense of panic. She may know the odds tomorrow better than I realize. Innocent people go to prison. Why spend her life there? I can't make this decision on my own and dial Chet's number from the phone in the kitchen, determined to wake him up, no matter how groggy he is. Wynona answers, and I tell her what has occurred.

"There's no point," she says. "Jill called here an hour

ago. I was able to wake Chet up just long enough for her to tell him she had withdrawn the offer."

I look at Leigh and feel my pulse begin to race from anxiety. "How did Chet react?" I ask softly.

"I could tell it depressed him," Wynona admits, "but he was pretty much out of it because of the pain pill. I'll tell him early tomorrow morning you've found Leigh."

I thank her and hang up and tell Leigh, who smiles wanly. "I guess we better get ready for the trial."

I want to grab her and shake her and make her tell me what the hell is going on. Why did she run off and get drunk and hide in a motel room? Why isn't she fighting for her life? Yet, I'm afraid if I push her, she will walk out the door just as she did at my house. I stare at her until she lowers her eyes. It was as if she were an actress who wanted to improvise for two nights before the play began but who ultimately resigned herself to sticking with the script. I test her by saying, "You realize that we're going to be arguing tomorrow that your father might have killed Art?"

She closes her eyes but doesn't respond.

I realize I am grinding my teeth and stop. Was her disappearance merely a classic case of stage fright? I can't shake the feeling she is reading her words from a TelePrompTer. What is my part? Obviously, the ambitious understudy who is willing to play any role to further his career. As I prepare Leigh for her expected testimony, I have the sense that the whole production is coming apart because the director is home in bed. In an ideal world, the judge would grant a continuance and Chet would gracefully step aside. However, at this point the outcome would be the same. I realize how little I understand Chet. Has he told me everything? I don't have a clue.

"Do I have to tell about the video?" she asks, nibbling at a fingernail while I write out questions at the kitchen table.

I glance up at her and see that she is embarrassed. She is on trial to decide whether or not she will ever have another single moment of privacy the rest of her life, and she is worried about her sense of dignity. Human nature wins out every time. I try to think about the impact this revelation will have on the jury. The police presumably know nothing about it. Jill has not breathed a word about it, which she would have been required to do if she knew anything. "Probably not," I say, thinking an Arkansas jury would want to punish her for it. What is there to argue? Somebody who knew Art entered his house during the hour or so that Leigh went back up to the church to pretend she was there all the time. Who? Shane Norman, of course.

When Rainey returns, thirty minutes later, we take a break for Leigh to look at the clothes Rainey has bought for her. Like a mother who has been on a shopping spree for her daughter, Rainey opens the boxes with a flurry of maternal excitement. "I hope you like these." She holds up a chartreuse blazer against a white short-sleeved shell and a green skirt. "I've never shopped so fast for a complete set of clothes in my life," she says, giggling, and hands Leigh's credit card back to her. Besides outer garments, she has obtained shoes, a bra, panties, and stockings. "The salesclerks thought I was wonderful."

Leigh looks through the boxes and smiles at Rainey. "They look great. Thank you."

While Leigh goes into Rainey's bedroom to try on her new wardrobe, I watch as Rainey begins to make the toast I have forgotten about. Between us is an unspoken truce. No matter how convinced she is of

Shane's innocence, she cannot help but respond to Leigh. She is too vulnerable right now, and Rainey was born rooting for the underdog. She takes eggs and turkey bacon from her refrigerator. For a few moments it is like old times. Too discreet to ask questions about the case, Rainey entertains me with gossip about the state hospital, my old stomping grounds from my days as a public defender, when I represented patients at involuntary commitment hearings.

When Leigh comes out of her bedroom, Rainey smiles and says, "You look fantastic!"

Obviously pleased with Rainey's choices, Leigh hugs her as if they were sisters. While Rainey cooks and feeds Leigh, they chat about clothes and accessories as if tomorrow were to be a normal day instead of the beginning of a murder trial. I marvel at Rainey's capacity to put others at ease. It is an art form, one alive and well in the South.

Afterward, as Leigh and I work alone in Rainey's living room, Leigh says, "There's some real chemistry between you and Rainey. I could tell just by the way you looked at each other."

Distracted, I nod, unwilling to say that it has been mostly bad for quite a while. Feeling strangely out of sync (it may be exhaustion), I drive home at eleven. So much has gone wrong lately that even though the last few hours have been better, I go to bed feeling depressed. I cannot believe this story will have a happy ending.

18

AT PRECISELY FIVE o'clock in the morning, the phone rings. It is Chet, who sounds as wide awake as I am sleepy. "I'll be at your house in an hour," he says. "How is Leigh?"

I yawn. "Resigned to go to trial. I still don't know why she took off."

Chet speaks quickly, as if he has assumed this would be the outcome all along. "What time did you tell her to meet us?"

Woogie presses against my back. "Seven," I say. "I told her I'd pick her up."

"Good," he says, after I give him directions. "I'll be there soon."

I get out of bed and stumble into the shower, thinking perhaps this case may go better than I've been thinking. Chet's voice sounded strong and determined. The rush that a jury trial of this magnitude brings may be enough to carry him through the couple of days it will take. Jill is afraid of him, and for good reason. Even ill he must seem invincible to her, and it is not beyond Chet to tell the jury that he is dying and wants to go to his grave knowing that an innocent woman has suffered enough. As I shave, I begin to miss Sarah desperately. She gets almost as excited as I do the morning of a big trial. Though she is deeply ambivalent about my profession, she usually sends me off to even a small hearing as though I were Rocky Balboa. Instead, the house is as quiet as a college dorm at six o'clock on Sunday morning. How will I handle Sarah's absence next year? Given my behavior a couple of days ago (I'm getting too old to have more than a beer or two), I'm afraid I know the answer. Though normally I am a big fan of the man in the mirror, it is obvious from the multiplying spider webs around his eyes that he has definitely passed the point of no return. Sarah, come home, he whispers, in clown face. In April she will hear about scholarship money. She wants desperately to go out of state, but without some major help it will never happen.

Dressed in my new suit, I make some coffee and try to focus on the case. With Chet sounding so good, I have to resist becoming passive. The truth is, I may not do a thing during the entire trial except hand him a file folder. I assume we will get breakfast out, but still I walk around the house straightening up. Not that Chet will notice, but who knows? Wynona keeps their place like a bed-and-breakfast waiting for its first customer. What will she do after he dies? If he is as rich as I think, maybe nothing except wait for Trey to come home from school. I see car headlights flash against the venetian blinds in the living room and check my watch. Six o'clock. It is not light yet, and I go to the door, remembering I haven't turned on the porch light. I hope Chet hasn't had to wander around.

I open the door, flip on the switch, and, in the dim light, to my horror, see him standing by the Mercedes with a pistol pressed to his temple, his jaw clenched. I scream, "No, Chet!"

An explosion rockets through the neighborhood stillness, and Chet crashes to the ground. I run down the stoop to his body but turn away as I glimpse his face.

Thank God it is still mostly dark. I am about to vomit.
I run back inside and dial 911 for an ambulance, my
stomach heaving. I have begun to sweat, and after I
complete the call, I throw up in the sink in the kitchen.
I can't bring myself to go back outside. I know I am an
incredible coward, but I just can't do it. Why? Is it the
horror of seeing him in death, his face torn and mutilated, or is it the possibility that he is still alive and that
I should be giving him mouth to mouth resuscitation?
The stillness inside the house is terrifying as I try to
imagine Chet's last thoughts. Was he thinking about
Wynona and Trey? The trial? Not surprisingly, it is still
quiet outside. Since gunshots periodically ring out from
"Needle Park," the partially boarded-up housing project
only three blocks away, my neighbors have doubtless
chosen to interpret the noise as something familiar. My
mind races frantically, until I finally realize I must call
Wynona. Why did he do this? Damn him! My real
question is, Why did he do this to *me*? But why *not* me?
He wanted to spare Wynona and Trey the shock of finding his body, but even as I think this, I wonder if there
is more.

I calm down enough to look up his number and dial
it, wondering what to say. The time it takes for her to
answer the phone seems like an eternity, but my mind is
blank. "Wynona, I've got some terrible news!" I blurt.
"Chet just shot himself!"

"Dear God!" she gasps. "Dear God! Is he dead?"

I imagine her lying in the spot where her husband's
body had been just an hour ago. I can't bring myself to
tell her I don't have enough guts to check to see if he
still has a pulse. "It looks bad," I say. "I've called an
ambulance. I'll meet you at St. Thomas." Tears running
down my face, I hang up on her, so I won't have to say
any more. Woogie, who apparently ran under my bed at

the sound of the shot, slinks into the kitchen, his tail between his legs. I should be out trying to help Chet, stopping the bleeding, something. Instead, my teeth chattering, I call Rainey. My voice shakes so badly that I wonder if she can understand me.

"It's okay, it's okay," Rainey repeats as I admit to my cowardice. "There's nothing you can do."

Her voice, soothing and gentle, touches something in me, and I begin to cry again. "I saw him do it!" I say.

"Just take a couple of deep breaths," she says. "You're going to be all right."

I realize I am panting and try to gather as much air in my lungs as possible. I hear the wail of the siren. St. Thomas is barely five minutes away. "I've got to go outside," I stammer. "I'll see you at St. Thomas." Not even for a moment do I assume she won't come.

I rush outside into the street and wave my arms as the ambulance careens around the corner toward me. Lights begin to go on all over the neighborhood. Denial can take my neighbors just so far. The door on the passenger side opens and, to my shock, the attendant is a young woman. What a job, I think. Lightheaded and dizzy, I point needlessly to the yard. "He's there. He shot himself!"

My neighbors on both sides of the house, Moses Gardner and Payne Littlefield, converge on me at the same time. "You shoot him?" Moses asks bluntly. He is an occupational therapist at St. Thomas, and is in his bathrobe with a pistol in his hand.

What is he thinking? A drug deal that went wrong? Chet's Mercedes is visible in the lights. "Fuck, no!" I say angrily. "He shot himself. He was dying of cancer."

Payne, a retired schoolteacher who can't afford to sell his house and get away from blacks, nods. "Damn," he says to Moses. We watch in fascinated horror as the female tech, using the headlights of the ambulance, checks Chet's pulse with a stethoscope and then places a tube down his throat. How she sees what to do through the blood streaming everywhere seems like a miracle. She nods, and the driver, an older black male, squeezes a bag attached to the tube. Within moments they have Chet's body loaded into the ambulance. "He ain't gonna make it," Payne says.

Great neighbors, I think miserably. More are standing in their yards watching the excitement. They probably think I killed one of the women I have brought home from time to time. "You better wait for the police, Mr. Page," the female EMT tells me. "They should be here any second."

Moses nods as if that's a load off his mind. I'm surprised he and Payne don't have me spreadeagled against my car. Woogie, my watchdog and protector, begins barking furiously behind the screen. "He's still alive?" I ask as she moves off.

Without turning around, she shakes her head and calls, "Barely."

Payne says, "They ought to just take him to a funeral home."

As they pull off, two squad cars roar around the corner and pull up in front of the house. I feel a numbness spread through my body. Well, at least, I think, as I go over to them, escorted by Moses and Payne, I won't have to try the case today. Chet accomplished that much.

Since I must give an endless statement to the cops, who seem relatively satisfied that Chet's gunshot was self-inflicted (they say the tests may be back from the crime lab before the morning is out), it is eight o'clock before I get to St. Thomas, only to find that Chet was pronounced dead fifteen minutes earlier. "You couldn't have done anything for him," Rainey whispers to me in the corridor outside the emergency room after I confess how I vomited in the sink and waited inside the house until the ambulance came. "He didn't have a chance."

Thank God. I was terrified that there was something I might have done to save his life. Rainey pats me on the shoulder. "Are you okay?"

"No, but at least I'm alive," I say, my mind replaying the moment Chet squeezed the trigger. "Where is Leigh?"

"I left her at my house," she says, looking at me solicitously. "I just called her a few minutes ago. She's okay."

I go up to Wynona and Trey, who are in the waiting room seated beside Shane Norman and presumably other members from Christian Life. As soon as I see Shane, I begin to feel anger building inside me. Why? He didn't kill Chet, but suddenly I am convinced that Chet would still be alive this morning if he had never met Norman. Though I can't put it into words and realize instantly how irrationally I am thinking, I know that Shane is somehow connected with Chet's decision to take his life. This is hardly the time for a confrontation, and I force myself to concentrate on Wynona's face, which is a mixture of shock and disbelief. Trey, the poor kid, is crying so hard he is hiccuping. I put my arms around them both, unable to think of a single word that is appropriate. After a few moments, Wynona pulls me off to the side and whispers in a choked voice, "Did he say anything at all?"

"No," I say, not up to admitting to her that I actually saw him pull the trigger, although I have told the police. "I was just opening the door to come outside."

"He left a note for me and Trey," she gasps, "but all

he says is that he loves us and that God would forgive him."

I look down at her ravaged face, realizing she is working over in her mind the same question I am. Why did Chet choose to kill himself the morning the trial was to start? What did he know that he didn't tell me? I glance at Shane, who is now comforting some old lady. He is wearing the earnest, compassionate expression of the professional caregiver. With Trey right beside her, it is not the time to ask, but I murmur, "Do you think it was related to this case?"

"I just don't understand," she says, wiping her eyes. "You know how much this case meant to him."

Trey looks at me blankly, eyes red and swollen. I can't say to him that his stepfather was notorious for having no friends, no associates, no permanent employees other than a secretary whom he reputedly replaced regularly. The truth is, I have no idea what he really thought about this case. Though finally he seemed to accept the possibility that Shane was involved in his son-in-law's death, I can't be certain of it. Did he kill himself because he couldn't bring himself to accuse the man who brought him to Christianity? I don't know. At best I was to be nothing more than an ill-prepared emergency backup. At worst I was being used in some way I can't fathom. "He was the best lawyer I ever saw in a courtroom," I say. It is trite, but I know it will mean something to Trey for as long as he has a memory. Some of the most heartfelt tributes I heard made to Rosa after her death were in situations equally awkward. I look up and see Shane coming toward me. I extend my hand, wondering if he can sense my hostility. His bloodshot eyes suggest he had a long night, too.

Wynona and Trey drift back to the sympathetic faces around them, and Shane, dressed in the expensive blue suit I saw him preach in, demands. "Why didn't you call me last night when you found Leigh?"

I had expected a question about Chet and, nonplussed, I stare at him. For the first time it hits home that, for the moment at least, I and I alone am Leigh's lawyer. "She didn't want you to know." My words come out sounding more prickly than I intend. Nothing will be accomplished by pissing off Shane Norman. It was Shane who retained Chet, not Leigh. I do not tell him his daughter has begun to take seriously the notion he may have killed her husband. "You can't represent someone if she doesn't trust you."

Shane draws back from me and says levelly, "You were only Chet's assistant."

I look about the room at the group of mourners. I do not see a single other lawyer present. I keep my voice low. "Leigh's an adult; she can make that decision for herself."

Shane somehow smiles as he says, "I insist that you tell me where my daughter is."

If I didn't feel the same way he does, I'd have less sympathy. "I'll tell her," I say truthfully, "you want very much to see her."

For the second time since I have known him, I see a glimpse of Shane's anger. With his back to the members of his congregation, his eyes narrow and his jaw tightens. "I wouldn't get too high and mighty, Mr. Page. There are ways of dealing with people like you."

Who are people like me? I wonder. Lapsed Catholics? Solo practitioners who will take any case they can get? Or fathers of confused teenagers? Clearly, this is a threat, but of what kind? I resist the temptation to ask if he is going to have me killed, too, but just barely. "I'm sorry," I lie. "I know how upset you are." Under the cir-

cumstances, he can't be a friend, but I surely don't want
him as an enemy.

He turns and walks back toward Wynona and Trey
and the members of his church. Though I cannot see his
face, I am sure he is smiling once again. At this moment Sarah walks through the double doors, her eyes
searching for mine. I have never been so glad to see
anyone in my life. "Rainey called the school," she says,
hugging me. "Dad, are you all right?"

I turn and, out of the corner of my eye, see Rainey
smiling at me. "Yeah," I manage and feel my cheeks
wet, "but I'm sure glad to see you."

"Poor Dad," she says, her voice hoarse with emotion,
"it must have been awful for you."

I guide her outside into the sunlight so I can take a
deep breath. Though she is wearing the jeans and a blue
sweater I've seen a dozen times, she looks great. Happy
to milk a little sympathy, I say, "It was pretty bad."

"I'll move back home this afternoon," she says, with
no trace of sullenness in her voice, "if you want."

I want. I nod gratefully. "And I'll keep my mouth
shut." This isn't the way I would have liked for her to
make the decision, but I am learning fast that I control
very little these days.

"For about ten minutes," she says, her red mouth
forming a familiar smirk.

I must seem okay for her to make a smart-ass remark.
If I had really looked shaky, she would have been too
scared. Just seeing her has restored my spirits. Between
her and Rainey I may make it through this week. I motion through the glass for Rainey to come out. "Rainey's been a big help," I say, thinking of last night and
this morning.

Sarah watches as Rainey nods and starts to come

toward us. "When has she not?" she says, her tone matter-of-fact. "I can't believe y'all aren't married."

I jam my hands in my pockets to keep from saying something stupid. We are covering a lot of territory this morning. If Sarah knew I had gone out to a club the night before last to pick up a woman, I'd hear no end of it. "Well, let's get poor Mr. Bracken buried first," I say, knowing this remark will bring her up short.

As Rainey pushes open the door, Sarah asks solemnly, "When is the trial postponed to?"

I wink at Rainey to let her know everything is okay. It is apparent she hasn't told Shane that Leigh is at her house. I wonder if she has finally begun to have her own doubts about Shane. Either that or she is being extremely loyal to me. Perhaps both. "A good question," I say to Sarah, wondering how long a continuance I'll get. Now that I'm going to be in charge, I'd like to take some time and figure out some things. Judge Grider, whom I reached at home, was naturally shocked by my news. He told me to meet him in his office at eleven, after I explained what all was going on. At that moment, with the police in the house verifying my story and the media and neighbors in the yard, it probably sounded as if I were having a party.

I thank Rainey and then take my daughter back to school. I am grateful beyond words that Sarah wasn't the one who opened the door when Chet put the gun to his head. No telling what it would have done to her. I'm not really sure what it will do to me. If she had been there, I wouldn't have been able to hide in the house until the ambulance came.

"Why'd he shoot himself?" Sarah asks, as I work my way through the traffic southeast toward her school. Death has a way of even turning a kid's attention from herself.

I glance over at her, wondering if Christian Life is responsible for toning down the way Sarah has made herself up. For the last couple of weeks I have noticed that Sarah was no longer wearing earrings to school or painting her fingernails. If they would let up on the dogma, maybe Christian Life wouldn't be so bad. She doesn't have to go to school every day looking like Arkansas's answer to Gloria Estefan. "He didn't want his wife having to discover his body," I say, deliberately misunderstanding her question, which, if I answer it honestly, will lead to another fight with her.

Naturally unsatisfied with this response, my daughter asks, "I mean, why, right before the trial was to start?"

Stopping at the last light before her school comes into view, I realize this is a wound that may never be permanently closed. "I know you don't want to believe this," I say, pulling over to the curb when the light changes, "but Chet had come around to the position that Shane might have killed Art. He would have had to confront him in court, and I don't think he could bring himself to do it. You must never discuss what I'm telling you."

Sarah nods, her eyes bright with tears. She asks, "Then how can you do it, Daddy?"

I glance over my shoulder to make sure I am out of the line of traffic and then back at my daughter. She is biting her lip and with her right hand is twisting her luscious black hair, a familiar sign of anxiety. I have to prove Shane's guilt to satisfy her, and unless he confesses, that will never happen. "Leigh told me just over twenty-four hours ago that she thinks her father killed her husband."

Sarah stretches her mouth tightly against her teeth before crying, "You've put this into her head! She'd do anything to keep from going to jail!"

Have I? Most definitely. That day at Pinnacle Mountain I might as well have tattooed it on her hand. A red Probe whizzes by us, violating the school zone speed limit by at least twenty miles an hour. "Would you accuse me of killing someone to save yourself?" I ask, not yet willing to admit what I've done.

"No!" she groans, wiping her eyes with her knuckles. "But I'm not Leigh. They say she changed so much, even that she's lost her faith."

Frustrated because I have no adequate response, I wheel out into traffic. "I've got an appointment with the judge," I say harshly. For an instant I wish she hadn't come back home. I need all the support I can get, damn it. I want to tell her that Rainey is now on my side, but this isn't true. Like Sarah, she has come back into my life, but both are demanding something I can't give. I'm afraid that if this case doesn't go the way Sarah wants it to, like Leigh she will leave again, perhaps this time for good. I think I could live if I lost Rainey; something in me will die for good if I lose Sarah.

As we pull up in front of her school, my daughter commits the ultimate unthinkable act (it would be if there were any kids outside to witness it) by leaning over to kiss me on the cheek. "I love you, Daddy," she says shyly. "I'll see you when you get home."

I fight a sudden urge to cry. I am closer to the edge than I thought. She will never touch me again if I get sloppy this close to her school. Still, I feel as if I have been given an unexpected present. I swallow hard and acknowledge the obvious: "I love you, too."

George Grider's chambers look less like a judge's office than the headquarters of a successful politician. His walls are covered with photographs of himself with the Arkansas rich and famous: Dale Bumpers drapes his arm around him; David Pryor is forever frozen in the act of pumping his arm as if it is one of the nickel slots in Lake Tahoe; the late Sam Walton grins as if Grider had just told him a joke about Kmart; former Arkies Sidney Moncrief and Lou Holtz flank him as if they are escorting him to the dais to be introduced as a Razorback immortal; and, directly behind his desk, the most prized picture of all—a blow-up of George with Bill and Hillary. The fly in George's impressive caldron of political soup is that, unless they were dead drunk at the time, not one of these people could stand to be around him for over five minutes. He was one of the most obnoxious lawyers in the state to try a case against, and election to the bench hasn't improved his personality. If judges were selected on merit instead of elected, he couldn't obtain an appointment as justice of the peace. But nobody with the exception of Warren Burger has ever looked more like a judge. At the age of fifty, George Grider's handsome face, noble as a Roman patrician's, is crowned by a veritable bale of cotton. A former halfback for the Dallas Cowboys for two years, George looks as if he could suit up tomorrow for the season. In a room with more than six people, he is charming, affable, even witty. Behind closed doors he relaxes completely and becomes his usual snotty, arrogant self.

"You haven't given me a legitimate reason why this case should be postponed one more day," he says to me from behind his desk. I look at our prosecuting attorney, Jill Marymount, for help. A mistrial isn't going to help her either. If she is pondering the possibility, I can't tell it, for she seems to be engrossed in the details of Hillary's dress.

"As I just explained, Your Honor," I say, speaking slowly for George's long-suffering court reporter, "Mr.

Bracken was going to try the case by himself. There were no plans for me to examine a single witness."

George handles a gold-plated letter opener that he probably picked up in a pawnshop. As a former attorney for the county sheriffs' association, he could probably provide an interesting tour of his basement. "You just said you talked with the defendant about the case just last night," George says, his voice a sarcastic whine that can't be communicated on a transcript. "She didn't even speak to Mr. Bracken. It is quite clear to this court that you were actively involved in preparing for the trial."

I suppress a sigh. "I'm not asking for a long continuance—just a week or so. This isn't a case of whether my client shoplifted a Hershey bar. She could go to prison for life."

Shifting around on a padded throne that looks comfortable enough to sleep on, Grider asks impatiently, "Why a week? You're not telling me you haven't been working on this case, are you, Mr. Page?"

What is it with this guy? Suddenly, I realize that Chet's death has released him to be the bully he is. Chet intimidated lawyers and judges alike. "I haven't prepared to be the lead counsel, Your Honor."

Grider casually pokes at a cuticle with the letter opener. "How long have you been working on this case with Mr. Bracken?"

As frustrating as it has been, it seems like a lifetime. "About three weeks," I say.

Cross-examining me as if I were a witness who could be pushed from one end of the courtroom to the other, he sneers, "You're not telling me you don't know the theory of the defense's case after all this time, are you?"

I study Bill Clinton's face. Judging by his expression, he knew what price he was paying to run for public office. Were this not a murder case, I'd risk a snide comment. What theory? So far as I know, there wasn't one. "I'm not saying that, Your Honor." I blurt, "Mr. Bracken was dying of cancer. He was in a great deal of pain and was on medication to control it. He wasn't able to prepare properly for this trial."

Grider nods as if I have conceded the matter. "If Mr. Bracken was too ill to try this case, I assume he would have informed the court. Unless you're prepared to tell me as an officer of the court that you weren't hired to assist Mr. Bracken on this case, I'm denying your motion for a continuance and we're beginning this trial tomorrow morning, is that clear?"

"Yes, sir," I say, feeling a knot begin to form in my stomach. "I take it the court won't be in recess for Mr. Bracken's funeral tomorrow afternoon?" I ask, my voice high with disbelief.

"Lawyers die every day, Mr. Page," Grider snaps. "There are far too many delays in the system already."

Jill, in a berry-and-white-striped blouse and blue skirt, is more casually dressed than she would have been if we had gone to trial. She says, "Your Honor, my office, as you know, had many cases with Mr. Bracken. I would appreciate it if the court would recess for the funeral. Some of the witnesses are from Christian Life and may want to attend as well."

As soon as the words are out of Jill's mouth, I realize that Shane will conduct Chet's funeral. How am I going to accuse him of murder on the same day he prays over the body of the man whom he hired to defend his daughter? The last thing I want is Shane Norman pontificating that day, but it is too late. Changing his mind (he knows he would be criticized), Grider says gruffly, "It's the taxpayers' money, but if that's what you want, I'll recess the trial tomorrow afternoon. I am announcing to the press, however, that the Prosecutor's Office asked for this recess so it could make sure that the man who had beaten it so often was really dead."

Grider's delivery of this zinger is so deadpan that Jill doesn't know whether he is serious or not. When I smile (there is a lot of truth in his statement) and Jill does not, Grider says to her, "Jesus Christ, I'm kidding, okay?"

In the hall next to Grider's office, Jill, speaking in a slightly lower tone, says, "By the way, I'm not renewing the offer of a plea bargain."

I wait until a couple of lawyers pass. Somehow the media has not gotten wind of this meeting or they would be standing on top of us. My hopes of some major flaw in her case disappear completely. She was purely and simply scared of Chet. Obviously, she isn't afraid of me. "You could have kept it open till Christmas," I say, with more confidence than I feel. "She didn't shoot him."

Jill looks unusually attractive. Her mane of thick dark hair in the last few months has developed a streak of white that is particularly striking. She says, with a tolerant smile, "Who did?"

Despite a natural antipathy for prosecutors, I can't dislike this woman. She doesn't have a killer instinct like some of her predecessors. "I don't know," I reply innocently. "I thought that's why we had police."

She shrugs, tossing her hair, and revealing more of the streak of white. "I didn't expect you," she says dryly, "to tell me your case."

I draw an imaginary line across my lips as if I had something to conceal. What case? I think, as I head down the hall.

During the afternoon, as I am struggling feverishly to get ready for the trial, Dan wanders into my office. He is wearing the first bow tie I've ever seen him in, which he undoes, as he stares out my window. "Have you heard the gossip?" he asks, his voice far off and distracted.

I look up from my desk from the draft of the opening statement I've been working on. People who have necks the size of Dan's shouldn't wear bow ties. It looks like a stave about to pop off a beer barrel. "That I've subpoenaed Elvis to testify?"

Dan whips off the tie and wipes his face with it. "There's crap going around," he says wearily, "that you killed Chet."

I stare at him in disbelief. "The cops didn't even take me down this morning."

"Of course not," he says. "It's not coming from Jill's office. She and the cops have already issued a statement that their investigation has concluded Chet killed himself."

My surprise is quickly turning to anger. "So who's putting that shit out?" I demanded.

"I don't know," my friend says, absently rubbing his tie on my window ledge. "A bailiff told me it was going around. You think it could be your friend Shane?"

I look hard at Dan to see if he is serious. He shrugs, as if to say, Who else could it be? This makes no sense. Even if Shane is implicated, surely he wants his daughter free. I will run this by Leigh when I go by to see her at Rainey's in a few minutes to talk about her case. "Maybe it's my old firm of Mays & Burton," I say, thinking of the client I stole from them after I was fired. "They never sued me for taking Andy Chapman from them, but they always wanted to get even."

Dan nods, "Hell, you know lawyers. It could be somebody who's jealous of you getting tapped by Chet to work with him. It could be our old boss Greta. She wasn't a big fan of yours either after the Hart Anderson murder."

Enemies, I think, wearily, supporting my face with both hands on my desk. Every decent lawyer has a million. And I haven't even begun to count disgruntled clients. "It could be my old rat-muffin divorce client. She'll go to her grave convinced I should have given her money back."

Dan pats his stomach, thinking of my client who served her husband a rat in a pan of blueberry muffins. "You should have brought in those muffins she fixed you and Sarah," Dan says, still unable to forgive me for throwing out an entire pan she brought over to my house one morning.

Who else could it be? For all I know, Jason von Jason is putting up flyers all over Blackwell County warning people to keep their dogs penned up while I am still loose on the streets. I shove my papers into my briefcase and stand up to leave. "How's this for the beginning of an opening statement?" I say and in a parody of Richard Nixon, intone, "I am not a murderer. And neither is my client."

Dan laughs, a pained expression on his face. "A real confidence builder, all right."

Shooing Dan out in front of me, I hurry from my office, wondering what Chet Bracken would make of this latest twist. From almost the beginning of his illustrious career, he was dogged by rumors that he meted out retribution to those who wronged him. Unfortunately, they were true. I rack my brain, trying to think if I offended him in any way. As paranoid as I'm becoming, I wonder if this rumor, too, is some kind of a payback by Shane Norman.

19

As I KNOCK on Rainey's door, I hear the panel of a van being slammed shut. I turn and see a cameraman and Kim Keogh, a reporter for Channel 11, hurrying up the walk. I have carelessly allowed myself to be followed. This morning, when I had come out of my house after talking to the cops, I had faced cameras from two of the three local stations and a half dozen reporters, and had refused all comment, letting the police handle the questions. Had I known someone was trying to smear me, I would have talked. "Gideon!" Kim shouts, practically breaking into a run. "Wait!"

I shudder at my thoughtlessness. I briefly became involved with Kim during my last big case. She is a lovely blonde, whose main asset as a reporter has been her sheer doggedness. Each of us knows things about the other that won't make the ten o'clock news. At this moment, Leigh opens the door and I mumble, "TV camera," and rush by her and shut the door.

Leigh, who has been in touch with me by telephone throughout the day, understands instantly and leans against the wall and sighs, "I was afraid they'd find out I was here."

"If you think today is bad," I say, wondering how to handle Kim, "wait until tomorrow. We'll need a battering ram to get you through them." Kim knocks hard on

Rainey's front door. Knowing her, she will want some kind of exclusive interview. I make a snap decision. "Let me talk to her. She knows you're here."

Leigh nods, panic setting in as it begins to hit her what the next few days will be like. Aware that Chet Bracken wouldn't have talked to the press, I open the door and step outside.

Kim is wearing a blue jade cotton knit dress with enough jewelry to open her own pawnshop. With the cameraman standing coyly off to the side, she begs, "Let me just talk to her for a minute. If you don't, every media person within ten square miles will find out she's here." The neighbors are going to love this. "Is it true she's been hiding in the Delta Inn, too drunk to get out of bed?"

How could she possibly know that? I wonder, my mind racing. "Kim, I'll promise not to talk to any reporter except you about Chet's suicide if you'll leave and keep your mouth shut," I say, "but I can't comment on the case."

Giving me a wintry smile, she turns to her cameraman and nods. "Okay, Roger." He moves in almost on top of me as Kim asks, "Mr. Page, we've heard reports throughout the day that Chet Bracken's death was not a suicide and that you were involved. Would you care to comment on that?"

I feel as if I'm being interviewed by a female Geraldo. Kim knows the police and the prosecutor do not consider me a suspect. "That's ridiculous!" I say, my voice trembling. "It's an outrage for you to even suggest that. The police have already issued a statement that Mr. Bracken's wound was self-inflicted."

"Tell us what happened, then," she says, her voice cool and professional. But her right hand, holding the microphone a few inches from my face, shakes slightly, betrays her excitement.

Damn her. It was hard enough to tell the cops. Looking into the sun, I feel my throat become scratchy and I fight to stay in control. I shouldn't have to describe how a man shot himself. "I saw the lights of Mr. Bracken's car turn into my driveway, and as I opened my front door I saw him point a pistol at his head and fire."

"Did you go help him?" Kim asks, before I can even clear my throat.

"I ran to call an ambulance," I say, hating all reporters at this instant. I can't admit that I was too sick to my stomach to go see about him. It is all too much. Tears come to my eyes, and before they can slide down my cheeks, I turn and hurry back into the house. I wish Rainey were here. She would understand what I am feeling.

Before I slam the door, I hear Kim call, "Great stuff, Gideon!"

Inside, Leigh, her eyes wide with astonishment, asks, "What did you say?"

I rummage through my pockets and come up with a wadded-up tissue to wipe my eyes. I feel terrible. The memory of Chet holding the gun against his head unwinds like a tape that can't be stopped. Why did he do it? I don't even know why I'm crying. My cowardice? For Chet? Trey and Wynona? There is no good way to exit this life. No matter how much or how little we've had, most of us want more. "To get her to agree to leave, I spoke on camera about seeing Chet shoot himself," I say, sinking down on Rainey's sofa. "I guess I'm just feeling it."

Leigh, wearing a pair of Rainey's sweats that come to just below her knees, sits opposite me on a chair that has recently been re-covered. "They're just vultures!" she says indignantly.

I think of Kim Keogh, who lives only a few blocks from here, or did, a few months ago. The night we made love, her apartment walls were covered with pictures of movie stars. She was vulnerable and insecure about her ability as a reporter, and her naked ambition had an innocent quality to it. Yet, she has become hard. *Great stuff, Gideon.* She wouldn't have said that a few months ago. Maybe I've played a part in the process. "Competition and ethics aren't in the same food group," I say, trying to joke my way onto another subject. I open my briefcase and take out a legal pad. "We've got to talk about your testimony tomorrow some more, okay?"

Even as Leigh says, "Sure," her guard goes up. "I called my father and told him I was okay, as you suggested. I didn't tell him where I am. He wants me to meet him tonight to talk."

"Not a good idea," I reply quickly. I've got to persuade Leigh to let me argue that her father could have killed her husband. If she meets with him, that may not be possible. "You left home for a reason, remember?"

Leigh brushes her hair back from her face, raising her right breast beneath Rainey's too-tight warmup top. "He sounded so forlorn."

I bet he did. Shane is running scared. Chet might not have been able to bring himself to argue that his pastor was a suspect, but I sure as hell can. "Fathers are good at that," I mutter, searching for my pen. After a certain age, guilt is the only weapon we have left. "Leigh, I've got to argue in court that he may have been the one to kill Art."

As I feared, her spine stiffens as if an electrical current were passing through it. "I can't do that."

"We have to," I argue. "You don't have a chance at an acquittal right now."

"What about the man Art cheated?" she pleads. "Art was afraid of him."

I have begun to doodle aimlessly on the pad but stop myself. "I'll argue that, but there was no forced entry, so it's weak. I'm going to call as a witness the investigator from San Francisco to give the jury an excuse to acquit if they want to, but it's a long shot." Leigh is not averse to lying, I remember, but then most people aren't if the stakes are high enough. I have told a few myself.

Leigh's right hand flies to her mouth and she mumbles, "I'll probably have to admit Art filmed me naked."

I almost snap my pen in frustration. It is as if we are back to square one. "This isn't going to be pretty!" I yelp at her. "Unless you want to sit there smiling while you receive a life sentence, you're going to have to accept the fact that you've got to be prepared to tell the truth, no matter how painful."

Leigh bites her full lower lip in anguish. "It will destroy my father!"

I lean forward with my elbows on my knees. "Not if he's the man you think he is," I argue. "You won't be the one arguing to the jury that your father may have come over while you went to the church; I will. He'll blame me, not you."

Leigh swallows hard. "But what if he's innocent?"

"He'll forgive you," I promise her. "He's not on trial. There's no evidence to convict him. If someone saw him or knew something, they would have come forward by now."

Her voice hushed, Leigh asks, "Why do you think Mr. Bracken killed himself?"

Wearily, I lean back against the sofa, knowing I may

never understand what was in Chet's mind when he pulled the trigger. It is possible that his only motive was to spare Wynona and Trey (and himself) the final weeks of agony. He had said the cancer was all over him. He didn't want to die knowing he hadn't prepared for his last case. Yet, maybe he had made a promise he couldn't bring himself to keep. Would he have told Wynona the truth? It is not difficult to believe that under the pressure he must have been feeling he simply broke at the prospect of covering up the biggest deception in his life. "I don't know," I admit. "He told me his body was riddled with cancer. For many people that is reason enough."

Leigh winces as the thought occurs to her. "Daddy will bury him, won't he?"

I look at the scores of books neatly lined up on Rainey's bookshelves. With all the wisdom they supposedly contain, they can't answer a single question on this case. "I'm sure he will," I say, watching for her reaction. My mind has run wild with theories that I can't begin to confirm. "It has occurred to me that possibly Chet knew about your father's involvement and gave him a promise he realized he couldn't deliver."

Leigh, who has been rubbing Rainey's hardwood floor with her tennis shoes like a child, jerks her head up with instant understanding. "You think Mr. Bracken knew Daddy killed Art but had told him that he could get me off?"

Mr. Bracken again, I note. Chet, who was famous for getting to know his clients better than they knew themselves, never warmed up to Leigh. "Possibly."

Leigh's face becomes stiff with fear. "Why wouldn't Mr. Bracken tell somebody that Daddy had killed Art?"

Her eyes are enormous. It is as if she realizes for the first time her situation. "Shame," I suggest. "If your father told Chet he was guilty in the context of an attorney-client relationship, Chet should never have agreed to represent you, because he was ethically foreclosed from using information that could have exonerated you. But his ego was so enormous by this time, he thought he could get anyone off. He didn't count on his cancer flaring up again. Don't you see? Nothing can prevent me from arguing your father is a suspect."

Leigh takes a deep breath, as if she needs help to absorb what I am saying. "Maybe if Daddy really did kill Art," she ponders, "he'll confess now."

I write the word "denial" on my pad. If Shane is like most people, he will shut his eyes and hope that a jury could not possibly bring back a conviction. After all, Leigh is innocent, and the case is circumstantial. He doesn't realize that accusing someone is half the battle. Regardless of the presumption of innocence, juries start off every trial believing that a prosecutor wouldn't have charged someone who is innocent. However, if Norman is the Christian he says he is, guilt will turn him inside out. Even if he can rationalize killing Art, he could never let his daughter go to jail for a crime she didn't commit. And yet, as a way to punish Leigh, perhaps he could. She had turned away from the church, had let herself be debased by lust. "Don't count on it," I say, wondering if it's worth confronting him again. "Preachers are more comfortable judging than being judged." Though, as I say this, I have the fantasy that the moment the jury comes back with a guilty verdict, he will stand up and confess that he killed Art. If Leigh is acquitted, he keeps his mouth shut. If Chet went to his grave with that secret, so could Shane.

Leigh nods sadly, as if this quip contained pearls of wisdom. She seems dazed by the day's events. Join the club, I feel like telling her. Suddenly, Jessie St. Vrain and her body mike float into my brain out of nowhere. "Maybe you should talk to your father, after all. I think I know where I can get a microphone and tape recorder this afternoon you can conceal under your clothes."

Leigh visibly flinches. "I couldn't tape my own father," she pleads. "It wouldn't be right."

I think of Jessie cooling her heels at the Excelsior. She's probably at the bar taping a conversation with some guy right now. "We wouldn't necessarily have to use it in court," I explain, "but if he says something that implicates himself or Chet, I could confront him with it before the trial. This way he'd be more likely to confess what happened."

Leigh leans back in her chair and closes her eyes. I wonder if she is praying. Finally, she says, looking down at her lap, "I need to pick up some clothes there anyway."

I suppress a smile. Only a woman would think of her wardrobe when she was on trial for murder. "We don't want to tip him off," I say, looking for Rainey's phone book to call the Excelsior. "You might want to begin by asking him why Chet killed himself. Your father might say something about him before he would implicate himself. Don't accuse your father, but give him the opportunity to talk. You may not get anything, but it's worth trying."

Leigh spreads her hands in a gesture of helplessness. "I'm not going to know what to do."

As I dial the Excelsior's number, I smile and say, "I know just the person to teach you."

Twenty minutes later, in Jessie's hotel room, I introduce the two women to each other. If they were from opposite sides of the planet, they couldn't be more different. In her borrowed tight sweats and sunglasses, Leigh, with her voluptuous body and striking ebony

hair, looks like a Hollywood starlet not trying very hard
to appear incognito; Jessie, in baggy jeans and a newly
purchased Razorback sweatshirt, grins like a twelve-
year-old boy playing hooky from school. After they
have sized up each other like rivals for the lead in a
high school play, Jessie winks at me. "Get out of here
for a few minutes, Gideon, while I show Leigh how to
wear this thing." She opens her hand and shows me the
equipment. I marvel at the tiny microphone. "The way
you're built," she says to Leigh admiringly, patting her
own flat bosom, "you could hide an entire recording
studio in there."

Leigh giggles and turns crimson. As far as I am
aware, Jessie knows nothing about the video Leigh
made. Not even for an instant can I imagine Leigh taking off her clothes before a camera. Her sensuality is essentially unconscious and must be coaxed. Art, I think,
not for the first time, must have been quite a guy. "I'll
go down to the lobby and call my office."

"You do that," Jessie says, escorting me to the door.
"We'll be fine."

Standing alone in front of the elevators, I feel slightly
cheated and wonder again about Jessie's sexuality. For
all I really know, she could be a man. Damn. If I lived
in California, I'd be too confused to get out of bed.
From the lobby I call Julia and am told a half-dozen reporters have called. So has Shane Norman. Good.
Shane, my man, I think, we are about to set the hook
for you.

"Have you heard the rumor going around," Julia says,
not lowering her voice at all, "that you shot Chet
Bracken in your front yard?"

I rub my head. I might as well hire a sound truck and
broadcast it all over Blackwell County or simply let
Julia ride around in the back of a pickup and talk in a

normal voice. "I've heard it," I whisper. At the next phone, with his back to me, is a guy in a dark suit and sunglasses who is either almost asleep or doing more listening than talking. "Do you believe it?" I ask sarcastically.

This is the wrong question to ask Julia. "I dunno," she booms in my ear. "What I can't figure is why you'd pick your front yard. I know you're the kind of guy who shits in his own nest, but that's ridiculous."

"Thanks for that vote of confidence," I say, exhausted by this conversation. "Is Dan in his office?"

"Naw, he's off trying a million-dollar lawsuit," Julia says, snorting at her little joke. "Of course he's here. He's too fat to go anywhere. Speaking of heavyweights, there's this enormous Oriental man wearing a black shroud who insists on waiting for you. I can barely understand him. He's sitting here crying his eyes out. Poor thing."

The motel manager. I tell Julia to put him in the empty office across the hall and have him pick up the phone.

"Mr. Page, I'm so sad. So sad. My wife she not coming back. Please help me. I can't wait no more."

I don't even know this guy's name. "You'll be seeing my assistant, Mr. Bailey. He'll take care of you." I tell him how to switch me back to Julia.

Julia comes on the line and snaps, "You've got to help this poor man. I mean it."

I'm moving right after this trial. I don't care if I have to open an office on the sidewalk. "Do you mind buzzing Dan? I'll ask him to see him."

"I'm paid to keep you guys happy," she says, and puts me on hold.

Finally, Dan comes on the line and says, "How's it going, buddy?"

"You want to sit at the counsel table with me tomorrow and make some notes?" I ask. "We're gonna be flying by the seat of our pants."

"Sure," Dan says loyally. "I've got an uncontested at ten, but I can postpone it. Want me to come over tonight to go over the case?"

Good old Dan. I think he'd amputate his right arm to help me. Too bad he can't cut off his stomach. Paranoid about the man next to me (he hasn't said a word in a minute), I don't go into what's happening above me in Room 542. Without asking for details, Dan also agrees to pretend to be my assistant and interview the motel manager, and we set a time for him to come to the house, and then I take the elevator back to the fifth floor.

Upstairs, Leigh and Jessie are fast becoming friends. "Leigh'd be great undercover," Jessie says dryly, "up to a point."

She is studying Leigh with unconcealed admiration. I ask, "And what point is that?"

Jessie nudges Leigh in the ribs. "I don't get many requests to take off my shirt in my line of work," she says. "I suspect Leigh would."

Leigh giggles unexpectedly, and for the first time since I've known her, I get a glimpse of the woman inside the stiff, frozen mask. I have mistaken fear for haughtiness. Jessie tells a story about an arson investigation she conducted in Southern California involving a building owned by a nude sunbathers' association. "I swear to God the owner talked to me buck naked. She looked so comfortable I would have joined her if I hadn't been wired for sound."

Jessie, even as she entertains us, remains sensitive to Leigh, who must have confided in her while I was downstairs. "He won't suspect a thing if you just act natural," she says, patting Leigh on the shoulder as we talk to her about the conversation she will have with Shane. I tell her to call him and suggest they meet in his office. If her mother is there, Shane won't implicate himself.

When Leigh calls and reaches him at the church, I notice a flicker of uncertainty on her face. I wonder if this idea will backfire. Shane has spent a lifetime dominating her. The possibility that she may put him on the defensive seems remote. Jessie, to her everlasting credit, invites Leigh to spend the night in her room after I tell her that I was followed to Rainey's. I do not trust my old friend Kim Keogh or her cameraman not to reveal where Leigh is staying. As Leigh and I leave the room together to drive to the Delta Inn to get her car I make her promise to come by my house after she has talked to her father and picked up her clothes from her parents' house. I advise her not to go back to Rainey's. Sarah can run over there for her clothes. "We have a lot of work to do tonight," I tell her.

She nods, but I can tell she is already thinking about meeting her father. I wonder how I would feel if I suspected my father had murdered my spouse. My father's own suicide in a mental hospital when I was fourteen left me with questions that will never be answered. As we hit the freeway traffic, I am forced to admit to myself that Leigh may be conning me. Yet she seemed so innocent in the hotel room with Jessie that I was convinced for a moment I was representing a person incapable of murder. Maybe the jury will think so, too.

20

"Do you want me to go with you to Mr. Bracken's funeral?" Sarah asks from the couch where she is scratching Woogie. Our dog, who is on his back with his legs in the air, seems as happy as I am that his mistress has returned and moved back into the house with all her belongings. Unlike myself, Woogie had no one to assuage his grief at her temporary abandonment. Jason Von Jason could make a fortune in this country treating animal depression.

"There's no need," I say cautiously. "I'm sure Dan will go with me." For the longest time I have tried to shield Sarah from death, as though the loss of her mother was a quota that must not be exceeded. I slice the sausage pizza that has just arrived from Domino's. I sense a reluctance on her part to come to terms with what happened in our front yard only a few hours ago. I can understand her feelings. I'm not sure it has completely sunk in on me. I check my watch. Seven o'clock. Leigh should have been here by now. "Come wash your hands and let's eat before this stuff gets cold."

Sarah smirks at Woogie as if to say, "When will he learn not to treat me like a kid?" but obediently comes into the kitchen and scrubs her hands in the kitchen sink. I give her a graceful way out. "Do you have any tests you'd be missing?"

"Actually, I do have a couple," she says, drying her hands on a dish towel she has taken from the counter by the sink. "I guess I better not. Did you like him?"

I open the refrigerator and take out a couple of Coke Classics and hand one to Sarah. No booze tonight, though I could use a couple of beers. Did I like Chet? A good question. "I think I would have if I had gotten to know him better and hadn't been working for him." As we eat at the kitchen table I tell Sarah about Wynona and Trey. "The kid was crazy about Chet," I conclude. "That was obvious."

"Most children go through a stage where they worship their parents," Sarah says dryly, wiping her mouth on a paper napkin.

Trey was a stepchild, but I won't quibble. "I haven't exactly felt worshiped lately," I say, getting a smile out of my daughter. "How do you feel about Leigh coming over here tonight?" I add, realizing I haven't given a moment's thought to Sarah's reaction. For some reason I don't fully understand I won't be content until I have rammed this case down my daughter's throat. I know I risk further alienation, but I'm determined that she see the other side. Even if she is guilty, Leigh seems more human than her father.

"Weird," Sarah confesses, "but a little curious. Our house seems to attract death these days."

I try not to react while I absorb her remark. She's absolutely correct. What a great father I've been lately.

There is a knock at the door and, of course, it is Leigh. As I glimpse her face in the glow of the porch light I realize that I had been afraid she wouldn't show up. I invite her to share our pizza, but she tells me she has eaten with her parents. She follows me into the kitchen, and I introduce her to Sarah.

As they exchange pleasantries, I am struck by how much they resemble each other. Leigh is taller, not as dark, but her ebony hair and delicate facial structure make her look like Sarah's older sister. She has discarded Rainey's sweats for a white turtleneck sweater and red skirt, making me fear she intends to spend the night in her parents' house. Smiling, Sarah informs me she has to study and takes her pizza and Woogie to her bedroom. Leigh takes Sarah's seat at the kitchen table, and as soon as we hear Sarah's door shut, she says, taking the tiny tape recorder from her purse, "My father doesn't say a word on the tape that would make anyone suspect he was involved in Art's murder."

I try to mask my disappointment. I had naively been convinced that he would implicate himself. After the trial he might, perhaps, but not now. If he confesses to Leigh before she is tried, there is no telling how she might react. She pushes the "on" switch and I hear Shane's voice scolding her for not telling him and her mother where she has been. Ruefully, I recognize the tone: manipulative, judgmental, perfectly calibrated to induce a sense of pity and guilt. Sounding defensive, Leigh says she was "afraid," "ashamed," "exhausted," but in no manner explains her refusal to call her parents. Shane does most of the talking but says very little of substance, making me wonder if my conversations with Sarah are equally one-sided and meaningless.

Leigh admits to taking a room in a motel and gives its correct name but omits to mention her state of drunkenness. On tape she sounds no older than Sarah. Disappoint her father? No more than necessary, even if he might have murdered her husband. For the first time she reveals to her father that she had allowed Art to photograph her dancing naked. I had encouraged her to bring this up to get Shane's reaction. "How could you take off your clothes and dance nude in front of a camera?" Shane exclaims, his voice boiling with righteous indignation. I listen hard to gauge his sincerity. If we knew he somehow had found out about her little performance, Shane would have even more of a motive than he already had. He sounds angry, but there is a professional tone to his words as if he were preaching in church. Leigh does not immediately answer, giving Shane an opportunity to give further vent to his outrage: "What did you get from displaying yourself naked like that? Is your lust so out of control that you'd do anything to gratify it?"

Leigh no longer sounds like a woman but a child as she attempts to explain. "I loved him, Daddy. Nobody else saw. He said that he wanted to capture my beauty forever. It didn't seem wrong. . . ."

"Not wrong?" Shane shouts. "How can you say that? You were made in the image of God, Leigh. Have you forgotten that? How can you hope to reflect the love of Jesus Christ when you let a man satisfy his nature by taking your picture with your legs splayed apart like some drug-crazed whore?"

Leigh's voice is teary but stubborn. "He was my husband. *'Wives, be subject to your husbands.'* Don't you remember saying that in your sermons?" Though she has set up an argument, one not without its own internal logic, her voice pleads for forgiveness.

I glance at Leigh, but her eyes are shut, her lids fluttering with each blow as she relives each moment. It is as if she has forgotten why she went over to see him. "God has given you a free will, Leigh," Shane says severely. "You can't justify your own sin by hiding behind your husband."

"You won't try to understand," Leigh says. "I wanted to please him because I loved him. Didn't God give men and women this nature to please each other?"

I listen, fascinated as always by the topic of desire. The official line at Subiaco, of course, taught that sex was for procreation. If you were married and were trying to make a child, it was okay to like it. The practical absurdity of this dogma was apparent to every boy old enough to masturbate. The first joke at Subiaco I ever learned was couched in the familiar language of the catechism: *Why did God give Adam two hands? So he wouldn't wear one out.* Shane can't, or won't, shed the role of preacher. "He gave us our nature to please Him," he says, his voice didactic and cold. "And making ourselves objects of lust does not do it."

Leigh's face is now buried against her knuckles. Unless she is willing to argue that evolution has dictated the female form to be an object of sexual desire, she is fighting a losing battle. Shane holds all the cards. Ethics, morality, and religion are all on his side. Biology is on hers, but it is a weapon she cannot bring herself to use. She does not respond, and he continues to rant until he realizes that she will not answer him.

She clicks off the tape when he insists that she eat dinner with her mother and him. "What was that like?" I ask, allowing myself to speculate about Shane's own sex life. Surely no man is more tempted to stray than a minister. Women of all ages at all hours of the day and night wanting assurance that they are lovable and that their lives have meaning. I would be only too happy to assure them.

"Horrible," Leigh says, finally raising her eyes to meet mine. "Mother cried the entire time; Daddy alternated between a grim silence and lectures. He kept demanding that I ask the judge to postpone the trial and allow me to get a new lawyer."

I stare out the window into the darkness. Not a bad idea. I'm not even capable of getting a week's continuance for her. "Did he say why?"

Leigh, her voice a mixture of indignation and embarrassment, straightens her spine and looks me in the eye. "He said you were just Mr. Bracken's flunky—that he checked your record out and you've never won an acquittal in a big case."

I see the beginning of panic in her eyes. She wants me to tell her that I am a great lawyer, another Chet Bracken. I ask, "What did you say?"

"That I trusted you!" she says sharply, as if the emphasis in her voice justifies her decision.

Instead of gaining confidence, I feel more burdened than ever. I didn't lose much sleep over the convictions of the drug dealers, rapists, pimps, and killers who made up the clientele at the Blackwell County Public Defender's office. I will if Leigh goes to prison. I realize that the fact she was willing to tape Shane has convinced me of her innocence. If she really does trust me, now is the time to find out. "Despite the fact you didn't get anything on tape," I say, challenging her, "you know I'm going to have to argue in court tomorrow that your father may have killed Art."

Leigh drops her eyes, her long lashes a temporary screen against reality. Finally, she raises her head. "I know."

Mightily relieved, I resist the urge to go over and hug her. This moment has been a long time coming, and though I am exultant, I am forced to wonder what has changed her attitude. Was there something in his tone that made her doubt him? As if reading my mind, she clicks the tape back on and lets it run until I hear her voice. "I don't believe anymore, Daddy. I just don't think every word in the Bible is true. Art was right. The world is older than six thousand years. The Bible was written by men who couldn't know what we know today. They just didn't know."

As if from a great distance, I hear Shane's voice, more sad than angry. "Don't you see what you let happen? He stole your faith, Leigh. Just as if he were a robber breaking into your house, he stole the most precious thing you'll ever own. It doesn't mean much to you now, but it will. Your sisters couldn't wait to disown their faith, and what do they have? Nothing of value. If you go to prison, and you probably will, you'll need your faith more than ever. But it's hard to regain it once you let someone convince you that reason holds life's key. You see what happened? Art made you his slave. Only faith in God's Word can prevent what the world does to people. I failed you. You, whom I loved best. It wasn't that I didn't love Mary Patricia and Alicia. I did, but I tried so hard to keep you pure that I grew to love you more than them. And now you're just like them!"

I hear Leigh cry, "Daddy!" but then nothing more except the sound of her crying and her car starting. Then the tape stops.

Leigh now cries silently into her hands. Guilt. Shane has dumped a ton of it on her, and yet she has finally fought back. I am proud of her and yet amazed she could do it. "The argument that Shane may have killed Art probably won't be enough by itself," I follow up. "But with the rest of our case it may be enough to cause a jury to find reasonable doubt."

A sustained hammering at the front door announces Dan's arrival. Sarah and Woogie, who is barking furiously, usher him into the kitchen and retreat immediately to her bedroom while I explain to Leigh that it will be helpful for me to have another lawyer at the defense table tomorrow to help listen to the state's testimony. In no position to object, Leigh forces a smile at Dan, who barely manages not to leer at her while I introduce them. Since his stomach is mostly concealed by a jacket he declines to shed, he does not look too bad, and I seat him next to me at the kitchen table and hope he keeps his smart-ass cracks to a minimum. In the last few minutes Leigh has begun to look shaky and does not need Dan's irreverent wit.

Perhaps chastened by my serious expression, Dan asks deferentially, "Where do you want to start?"

A good question. First assuring Leigh that Dan is ethically obligated to keep his mouth shut, I reprise for Dan my conversation tonight with Leigh, knowing it will become apparent to her that he knows a lot about her case already. "Our defense obviously has to be that practically anybody, including Shane, could have killed Art during the forty-five minutes she was gone from the house."

Dan stares across the table at Leigh, who has cradled her beautiful face in her hands. Knowing Dan, I realize he has probably volunteered to help me as much from the desire to be this close to a looker like Leigh as out of friendship. He turns to me and says, "You have to consider the fact that if Leigh testifies, it could play right into Jill's hands by giving her the opportunity to show the jury how bad Leigh was feeling about her father. The jury may knock the charge down to manslaughter if they think that Leigh decided to kill Art in a moment of guilt and anger after her father called, but it could just as easily come back with first degree."

I pull out a legal pad and begin to make some notes. "Jill will get most of this out of Shane anyway," I say, glancing at Dan's beefy face.

Dan nods and looks up at my cupboards—he probably would like a snack—but again fixes his gaze on Leigh's bowed head. "And she's got to explain why she lied to the cops," he contributes.

"She's prepared to do that," I say for her.

Leigh looks up and nods bravely.

"It's going to go well," I say, kicking Dan under the table. He sounds too pessimistic. Leigh has to appear confident, or she won't have a chance.

At ten I send Leigh on to the Excelsior and tell her I will see her at 7 A.M. in the restaurant. By two o'clock, Dan and I are finished or probably so exhausted that we just quit. We have conversed as much as we can. Leigh will testify, and her credibility will be the ball game. In bed, trying to get comfortable, I begin to have doubts about Leigh's innocence. Mary Patricia's words come back to me in the darkness. Shane wouldn't have killed anyone, but he could have talked someone into it. Who? Leigh obviously. He might have incited Leigh to do what he didn't have the guts to do. After Leigh and her father finish testifying, that might be plain as day to the jury. It might also be obvious that I have been set up by both of them. The last thing Dan said as he was going out the door was that Mr. Woo, our motel manager, had said that I was a "great rawyer." At least I've fooled somebody. I flatten my lumpy pillow and try to sleep.

21

"JUST KEEP SMILING and don't answer," I whisper to Leigh as Dan bullies his way ahead of us into the courthouse through the media and the onlookers. I don't have to worry. Although she appears almost regal (her hair is swept up and gorgeous), she looks too scared to speak. If ever I wanted some publicity, I've got my wish. All I can do is hope that when this trial is over, the headlines don't read: "Bracken's Replacement Blows Big One." Though it is a beautiful spring day, my T-shirt is already drenched with sweat and my heart is pounding as if I had never tried a case before. I haven't, not like this one.

Inside, the action is considerably quieter. Jury selection could take quite a while, and with the trial recessing for the funeral this afternoon, Dan and I will have the weekend to work. Judge Grider's courtroom is relatively small, and I'm a little surprised, publicity hound that he is, that he didn't ask to switch with Judge Raferty, who would have readily yielded his territory for the asking.

Grider, each white hair perfectly in place, gets started with an announcement that stuns all of us. His docket is crowded, and he wants to work on Saturday. Why didn't he tell us yesterday, the bastard? I had counted on the weekend to work on the case.

Dan whispers, "I hear the Judicial Department has rapped his knuckles recently for letting his criminal cases stack up. He's supposed to have an opponent next year."

Jill, dressed in a funereal black double-breasted suit, rises quickly to address the court. "Our office has no problems with Saturday, Your Honor, but I am concerned that some otherwise qualified potential members of the jury may have some scheduling difficulties."

I pop out of my chair, pissed at Grider but more irritated at myself for letting Jill beat me to the jury. One of the first rules a trial attorney is supposed to learn is to show the jury he cares about their problems so they'll be more sympathetic to his client's. "Your Honor, a lot of folks might have been planning to shop for their Easter outfits tomorrow," I improvise. Good Baptists aren't supposed to care about their holiday wardrobes. Actually, the problem is that Easter is still two weeks away.

"Mr. Page," Grider says snidely, "why don't we let the panel tell us whether they will be inconvenienced if we work on Saturday instead of you making that judgment?" He turns to the panel members and quizzes them. Only two people raise their hands.

"Damnation!" Dan says in amazement. "They want to be around to hear the dirt." Why the hell not, I think gloomily. Chet's suicide, Leigh's beauty, and Christian Life's prominence have made this trial the hottest ticket in town. Grider excuses them on the spot, and we get down to the business of winnowing the panel down to twelve jurors through the process of voir dire, which permits the lawyers to ask questions of prospective members.

I watch carefully as Jill runs through her questions. One of the trickiest problems is how to handle the six

people on the panel who are members of Christian Life.
If I have to make the argument that their minister killed
Art Wallace, I have no doubt how they would choose
up sides. I wish I could hear Shane conduct Chet's service before I had to make any decisions. I lean over to
Leigh and say, "Chet's notes say you know a couple of
these people personally."

"Just slightly," she says, her warm, minty-flavored
breath in my right ear.

I needn't have worried, because Jill seems more concerned than I am and makes a motion that all six be
stricken for "cause," which would automatically elimi-
nate them if the motion is granted by Grider.

I stand and argue against it, knowing Jill will be
forced to use all but four of her peremptory challenges
if I am successful. Grider summarily denies her motion,
holding that if any of the six contributed to Leigh's bail
or signed an affidavit on her behalf, he will strike that
person for cause, but church membership alone is not
sufficient.

The two women who know Leigh personally admit to
Grider that they gave a few dollars for the bond, and
Grider tells them they are excused. They seem disappointed. Jill returns to the prosecution table and flashes
a smug smile at Dick Harvey, her main deputy, who is
second-chairing the case. Obviously, she has no inkling
that I would love to argue to the jury that the wrong
family member is on trial.

By eleven-thirty we have seated a jury composed of
six Baptists, two African-Americans who belong to an
AME church, one Charismatic (according to Chet's
notes) Catholic, and three who attend other so-called
Bible churches in Blackwell County. As Grider dismisses the other panel members, I have second thoughts
about Chet's position about who should serve on the

jury. It is deeply conservative and will be shocked if
Leigh admits to the video. They may forgive her but
still send her to jail. Until now, I never questioned
Chet's strategy. Too late, I wish I had chosen the most
liberal jury possible. Dan was right. If Chet had told me
that he was going to recite the Gettysburg Address as
part of his opening statement, I would have told him it
sounded like a good idea. In retrospect, Chet wasn't
thinking clearly about this trial, and I should have chal-
lenged him. For all I know, it was deliberate.

I ask the court to break for the funeral, which is at
three, but Grider instructs us to give our opening statements now, saying he wants to complete the trial by tomorrow afternoon if at all possible. Jill seems about to
protest (Grider has us both off balance), but comes forward to the podium and tells the jury that while this
case is circumstantial, the lies told by the defendant will
convict her of the first-degree murder of her husband.
Standing calmly in front of the jury rail, Jill, without a
single note, tells the jury that it won't be able to understand this case until it understands Leigh's upbringing,
and begins by tracing Leigh's devotion to her father and
to Christian Life. "The defendant's parents will tell you
what their youngest daughter was like before she met
the victim. As a child and as an adult until she married
Art Wallace, the defendant was devoted to her father
and his church, making numerous trips overseas with
him to help those less fortunate. . . ." As Jill catalogs
Leigh's Christian virtues before she met Art, I watch
the faces of the jury, who already seem intrigued by the
story. Tales about the Devil's work fascinate all of us,
and this is where I assume Jill is going with it.

"However, the defendant began to change," Jill continues, "after her marriage. Pastor Norman will tell you
that her husband turned out to be something other than

a devout convert to Christian Life. In fact, only weeks
after his marriage to the defendant, Art Wallace began
to withdraw from the church, and soon so did his wife.
Christian Life, Pastor Norman will tell you, is a way of
life. It's not just a matter of showing up on Sunday.
Laura Partrain, a member of the defendant's 'church
family,' as they are called in Christian Life, will tell you
also that a few months after the defendant's marriage,
Leigh Wallace not only quit her job in the church office
but participated less and less in the activities in the
church to the point where she only saw her on Sunday
mornings, when before she had seen her four or five
times a week. Mrs. Partrain will tell you that more than
once she confronted Leigh about her absence but was
met with a defensive and guilty attitude. Her father and
mother, who, by the way, will tell you they believe their
daughter is innocent, will also tell you of many conversations with Leigh on the subject of her husband and
their near total withdrawal from church activities. Their
daughter's reaction over several months was one of denial and excuses, which brings us down to the night before Art Wallace was murdered."

Having effectively set the stage, Jill retreats behind
the podium, where she has her notes, and begins to
summarize the testimony of the witnesses, beginning
with the next-door neighbors, the Wheelers, who "overheard the defendant from a distance of several feet ad-
monish her husband to quit saying ugly things about her
father."

The jury noticeably reacts to this bit of information.
Several shift in their seats and lean forward as if they
are about to hear some particularly juicy gossip. "The
afternoon after her husband of less than a year is shot to
death in his study with a twenty-two-caliber pistol without a sign of any forced entry suggesting an intruder,

the defendant is questioned by the police. She tells them a series of lies designed to mislead them into believing she had actually been at Christian Life at the time of the murder and only discovered her husband's body when she brought home an older acquaintance to have lunch."

Jill stops speaking and walks quickly over to a chalkboard and writes in a large clear hand: "Lie #1—what the Defendant told her father the day before the murder." Walking up to the jury rail, she drops her voice almost to a conversational tone and tells the men and women, who are listening as avidly as children to a ghost story, that Shane will testify that he had encouraged Leigh the day before to come the next morning to a workshop led by a Guatemalan missionary and she had assured him that she would. Returning to the chalkboard, Jill writes: "Lie #2—Defendant's story to the police." Now, moving slowly from one end of the jury box to the other, Jill recites Leigh's story to the cops and summarizes the testimony of each witness who will contradict it.

Jill concludes by hitting hard at the absence of signs of forced entry. "Forensic investigators have been all over the house and study where the victim died. They will testify they found absolutely nothing to suggest that anybody was there that morning except Leigh Wallace and her husband. The only reasonable conclusion you can come to, ladies and gentlemen," Jill winds up, leaning on the jury rail, moving her head from side to side, "is that Leigh Wallace, perhaps in anger, perhaps for some other undisclosed reason, walked into her husband's study and shot him through the heart with a twenty-two-caliber pistol. Then, disposing of the pistol who knows where, she drove to her father's church, where she pretended to have been all morning. To divert suspicion from herself, she invited an unsuspecting friend home to help discover her husband's body, and thus began the web of lies I've just told you. . . ."

As I get to my feet, I fight the usual temptation to begin arguing the case, which, of course, is not permitted in the opening statement. Concentrating primarily on the most sympathetic-looking member (a Mrs. Holland seated in the middle of the second row and the only Catholic), I announce to the jury that Leigh will admit that she lied to the police but that she did not kill her husband. "Leigh will tell you her reasons for her deception, and you will learn they had nothing to do with the murder of her husband. In some respects, Leigh's testimony will be similar to what you've just heard the prosecutor say her father and other witnesses will tell you. It is true that Leigh grew less active in the church due to her husband's influence, and Leigh herself will tell you that she felt guilt over this, but none of that proves she's a murderer. Unfortunately for Leigh Wallace, her husband was not what he seemed when she met him. You will learn that Mr. Wallace had recently stolen two hundred thousand dollars from the owner of a video store in San Francisco that specialized in pornography. You will further hear a taped conversation with an investigator from a fire insurance company in San Francisco that the owner of the same video store in San Francisco hired an individual to burn the store of a competitor. And Leigh Wallace will tell you she was afraid for their lives as a consequence of her husband's theft."

I pause to let this sink in and move over to the blackboard and take the eraser and wipe out Jill's questions. I have decided not to mention Shane in my opening statement. I want to keep him guessing. When I finish, I write on the board, trying to make the words legible: "Who wanted Art Wallace dead?" "The point is, ladies and gentlemen, that Art Wallace had enemies who played rough. The medical examiner will put his death no earlier than ten-thirty that morning, and it is undisputed that Leigh wasn't even at home most of that time. Leigh will tell you that she was frightened for herself and for her husband, but that she loved him and wanted to please him. She will also tell you that she loved her father and wanted to please him, too. Neither action makes her a murderer."

I walk to the front of the podium and scan the jury. Every one of them has secrets, Chet pointed out the night we worked on jury selection. The trick, he said, is to get as many as possible to identify with some part of your client. We've all done shameful things, but those acts don't make us murderers. According to Chet, if a couple of people can imagine themselves in your client's situation, you're halfway to an acquittal, no matter how bad the evidence appears. I home in on Mrs. Holland, a solidly built woman in her thirties with large brown eyes that seem to melt a little every time she looks over at Leigh. As a nominal Catholic, I know she is familiar with guilt. "The evidence will show there is no record that either Leigh or her husband owned a gun. If she shot Art," I slip in, though it is argument, "where did she hide it in the few minutes between the time her father talked to Art and her appearance at Christian Life?" I discuss the lack of physical evidence and then sit down, knowing I have done a less than impressive job. Perhaps I should have gone right after Shane in my opening statement. Dan had me convinced about midnight last night that I had no alternative. Yet, once Shane hears, as he surely will, that I have not argued he killed his son-in-law, his guard will be down during cross-examination.

Dan whispers as I sit down, "You blew it."

I smile as if he is congratulating me on the best opening statement he has ever heard from anyone besides Chet Bracken.

At Chet's funeral, the huge sanctuary at Christian Life bulges with members, lawyers, the media, and perhaps even a couple of members of the jury. Dan and I squeeze in ten rows from the front on the right side, next to Amy Gilchrist, whom I haven't seen since my last visit to Christian Life. "Hi, guys," she whispers, unable to suppress a grin despite the solemn occasion.

The three of us were pals in night law school, and then, after graduation, we all went to work for the county, Amy on the opposite side. Just the sight of each other stirs a host of memories. I lean across Dan and say, "Remember the day Chet stormed out of Phil's office when Phil showed him those pictures of his client naked with that woman? He nearly kicked Phil's desk in."

Amy wrinkles her slightly pug nose in disgust. Her boss then, the former Prosecuting Attorney of Blackwell County, didn't have a murder case, and she knew it. "I tried to crawl into the wall that day," she says, her hand on Dan's knee, as she leans over to talk.

Dan wheezes softly. "Rub it a little, Amy. It's getting stiff."

I grin but catch the disapproving eye of a man on the other side of Amy and put my finger to my lips. I wonder what she's heard in the last twenty-four hours. Now isn't quite the time to ask. Fortunately, Chet's casket, squarely in the middle of the sanctuary at the front, is closed. I don't want to dwell on what his face must look like and turn my head to view the church. Its stained-glass windows seem conventional enough, though I would be hard pressed to name the Biblical characters represented in them. As Dan observed on the way in, "Once you've seen one stained-glass window in a church, you've seen them all." At my level of appreciation, this heresy has the ring of truth.

The immense walls are unpainted concrete blocks. The effect is one of strength, not ugliness, which is perhaps a reflection of my own lack of architectural taste and inherent miserliness. Yet, although I was raised a Catholic, the wealth of the Vatican has always seemed to me a scandal. As a senior at Subiaco in Christian Doctrine, I dared to offer this criticism to one of the monks, who cracked, "Jesus was poor, and look what happened to him." Money talks in any age. Poor suckers like me keep forgetting that.

At the front of the church above the pulpit and hanging from the ceiling is the largest cross I've ever seen. Were it to fall during a Sunday service, Shane and half the choir would be killed. As these thoughts flit through my overheated brain, Shane, carrying a white Bible, appears from the left, walks to the middle of the sanctuary in front of Chet's casket, and signals us to stand. Apparently there will be no choir. I cut my eyes to the left and glimpse the pallbearers marching past me. Curiously, my feelings were a little hurt that Wynona did not ask me to be one. I remind myself that I was not a close friend of Chet's. Still, he chose to end his life in front of me, and somehow I have the feeling that entitles me to some public acknowledgment. I do not know any of these men. Perhaps they were members of his "family." Behind them in a solemn procession follow his relatives. Trey and Wynona, who is biting her lip and visibly trembling, walk hand in hand to the front row. There must be twenty other members of Chet's family, presumably from Helena. After they are seated, Shane, today dressed in a gray suit, briskly climbs three carpeted steps and from behind the pulpit opens his Bible and reads, " 'Whoever hears my words and believes him who sent me has eternal life and will not be condemned; he has crossed over from death to life. I tell you the truth, a time is coming and has now come when the dead will hear the voice of the Son of God and those who hear will live.' " Shane closes the book, and booms, "Chet Bracken, I tell you, brothers and sisters, heard the voice of God and today is alive in heaven."

Shane takes the microphone from its stand and moves around to the right side of the pulpit. He stands at parade rest except for his right hand, which is grasping the microphone at the bottom as if it were a stick of peppermint candy. Smiling, and his voice as conversational as that of a talk-show host, he says, "Chet, for those of you who didn't know him, became a Christian less than a year ago. It seems like just yesterday I had the privilege of baptizing him in the name of Jesus Christ in this very church. Right now I ask the members of his 'church family' to stand and be acknowledged." I crane my neck and watch, as in different sections of the congregation about twenty-five people of all ages, including all of the pallbearers, stand. Ten rows in front, Wynona and Trey, their heads bowed, rise as one. Even as enormous as this church is, it is hard to avoid a feeling of intimacy as Shane takes a moment to explain the significance of church families at Christian Life and then says simply, "You were Chet's real ministers, and I share your grief.

"Let us pray," he says, and raises his left hand, which had been behind his back, as a signal to the rest of us to rise. "Dear God, through your Son Jesus, comfort us in our bewilderment and pain. Like Job, we do not understand human suffering. You send the rain upon the just and unjust. Those you raise up to be your servants, you seem to strike down, even at that time when we need them most. Our human hearts futilely cry again and again for a reason, as if it were given to us to comprehend Your divinity and majesty. . . ."

As his prayer continues in the same vein, I try to understand what I am hearing. Is he saying that Chet's suicide was God's will? I know nothing of the theology here, but I am reminded of my own religious confusion, which was never cleared up by the monks at Subiaco. If Jesus was God, what is this talk about the Son? "My God, my God, why hast Thou forsaken me?" Who did Jesus think He was? No wonder they didn't want us reading the Bible by ourselves.

When he finishes, the girl I recognize as a song leader from my earlier visit enters from a side door onto the platform, and Shane says, "Sheila will lead the Christian Life members present in 'A Green Hill.' "

Sheila, whose blond hair comes halfway down her back, receives the microphone from Shane and without benefit of musical accompaniment begins on a note impossibly high for any male over the age of thirteen. Around me, some people raise their arms and close their eyes as they sing. Without a song sheet to follow, the words are lost to me, but the melody soars, and by the third verse I hear Dan, who had been worried the roof of the church might fall in on him, humming along.

After Sheila departs, Shane follows with more Scripture. "But if it is preached that Christ has been raised from the dead, how can some of you say that there is no resurrection of the dead? If there is no resurrection of the dead, then not even Christ has been raised. . . ." My mind wanders to Sarah, and I wonder how much she really believes. Is it the absolute certainty of a life after death that attracts her to Christian Life? I don't think so. Shane reads, "If only for this life we have hope in Christ, we are to be pitied more than all men."

Sarah, for sure, would reject the notion that Christians, whatever their beliefs about heaven, are to be pitied. Christian Life provides meaning for her in the here and now. Children her age do not think about death, anyway. In my work I can't seem to avoid it.

Shane follows with a eulogy, and I listen closely to see if he will lay down any clues about Chet's death or his own possible role in Art's murder. Once again, I realize, Chet's death can be understood as a conscious decision not to betray Shane. Is that why he killed himself? After recounting an anecdote about Chet's boyhood in Helena, Shane says, "Almost immediately after becoming licensed, Chet established himself as one of the better defense attorneys in the state, and within a decade my lawyer friends tell me he was without equal in his chosen field. Now, I'm sure, like a lot of you, I have questioned the value of so many lawyers in our society. The very afternoon after I baptized him we were sitting in my study and I asked him how he could continue to represent people who are considered the lowest form of life in our society—drug dealers, pornographers, murderers, child abusers. And you know what he told me? He said, 'Pastor Norman'—I couldn't get him to call me Shane back then—'what you can't really know is that these people are not always guilty, as the public thinks they are. Most of them are poor; some are addicted to drugs or alcohol; many are without education; but all are at the mercy of the system when it cranks itself up and decides to get rid of them.' He said, 'Pastor, you know much better than I do that it was the prostitutes, the thieves, the despised, the sick in mind and body that our Lord and Savior cast his lot with during his ministry. I can't turn my back on these people, especially now that I have such joy and hope in my own life. . . .' "

Dan nudges me sharply in the ribs and whispers, "I give you two to one, now he's gonna mention Leigh."

Shane pauses to take a sip of water from the glass on the lectern. "And, lo and behold, my own daughter, in the eyes of society, not the members of this church, praise God, became one of the despised Chet talked about that day. As everyone here knows, Leigh, my youngest and gentlest child, has been accused of murder. Unable to find the killer of her husband, the authorities have pointed their fingers at her. So, finally, brothers and sisters, my own arrogance and assumptions about persons accused of crime have dropped away, because I know my daughter is innocent of murder. And, as many of you already know, Chet volunteered to undertake her defense free, out of gratitude, he told me. So it was an enormous shock to me personally when yesterday, on the morning Leigh's trial was to begin, he took his own life. So that we can put the gossipmongers to rest, Wynona Cody, Chet's widow, has authorized me to state that Chet was suffering from terminal cancer and was in great pain that was no longer being completely controlled by medication."

The overflowing congregation (folding chairs have been placed in the aisles) sits rapt as Shane stops to swallow more water. I wonder if he is more nervous than I realize. This story can't be easy, even if he has conducted a thousand funerals. "Even as my heart aches for Wynona, Trey, Chet's family and friends, and for my own loss because I considered Chet a personal friend," Shane says, almost shyly, "I have not been able to avoid worrying how his death will affect my daughter's defense. Again with Wynona's permission, I am going to ask Mr. Gideon Page, if he is here, to stand."

When I hear my name, it almost doesn't register that he has asked me to get to my feet. How can he do this in a funeral? But it is his church. He can do anything he wants. Will he ask me to speak? Agree to refuse to try the case tomorrow? I try to fight down a rising sense of panic that I will be humiliated if I acknowledge my presence. Dan's elbow stings my ribs again. "Get up!" he whispers. "He obviously knows you're here."

I push myself up, sweat pouring down my sides. I feel as though I were in one of those dreams I've had where I am naked in front of other people but can't quite seem to get my clothes on. Shane says, "Mr. Page's daughter, Sarah, has begun coming to our services and been assigned a 'family,' so I feel he is almost a member himself. Please bow your heads."

What is he doing? I close my eyes, almost expecting to be shot. Instead, Shane offers a simple and eloquent prayer for my efforts on Leigh's behalf. When he concludes, he nods for me to sit down and when I have done so, his voice slightly apologetic, he says, "I think Chet would have wanted us to pray for Mr. Page."

While Shane continues in a more traditional manner, mentioning Chet's family in Helena by name and telling a couple of anecdotes obviously supplied by his family, Dan mutters out the side of his mouth, "Talk about slick! He's boxed you in tighter than a rubber on a donkey's dick."

Hoping no one has overheard this pearl of wisdom, I nod, so he won't feel compelled to repeat himself. Is this what Shane was after? I concede the possibility. How could I dare stand up in court tomorrow and accuse him of murder? No wonder Leigh refused to come with me. He would have had her come up and stand beside him. Yet, the sincerity I have heard in Shane's voice leads me to believe otherwise. When he began to

speak, he seemed like a man caught up in events entirely out of his control, admitting he had no more ac-
cess to the mind of God than his congregation. All he
can do is pray. Hardly a diabolical act, since that is
what preachers do.

After more prayer and Scripture, the service ends,
and I am surrounded by people, wishing me well on
Leigh's behalf. So many people speak (none I know), it
takes a full ten minutes to move from the sanctuary to
the front steps. I get a glimpse of Jill walking to the
parking lot and wonder if it ever crossed her mind to investigate Shane. I tell Dan to wait for me in the car, because I should speak to Wynona and Trey. Chet will be
buried in Helena, which is more than two hours to the
east, so Dan and I will not be going to the graveside
service.

It takes another ten minutes in line to work my way
up to the black limousines where mourners are consol-
ing the family. Tongue-tied as usual in these situations,
I simply hug Wynona, who squeezes me hard against
her. She and I are the last persons who saw Chet alive.
Wynona, surprisingly dressed in gay colors (red and
green) rather than the traditional black, whispers, "Call
me when the trial is over." I nod, and she does not say
more. I turn to Trey, who is standing beside her. In his
little suit with his hair slicked down, he looks like one
of those small-town-looking kids Norman Rockwell
used to draw for the *Saturday Evening Post*. If Chet has
sinned by taking his life, it is against Trey. By his expression he doesn't have a clue.

"Hi, Mr. Page," he says, his face brightening when he
sees me, offering his hand to me the way his stepfather
would have wanted him to. "I hope you do good in the
trial," he says. "I wanted to come, but Mom won't let
me."

My hand swallows his, but I let him squeeze, remembering the pressure of his previous handshakes. I can't imagine he even knows what he is saying, but maybe he thinks he would see Chet's ghost instead of a pale substitute. "Gotta do what your mom says," I tell him. "I'll come out and see you and her next week, okay?"

"Great," he says. "Maybe we can play some catch. It's almost baseball season."

"Yeah," I tell him, amazed at this child's aplomb. "That'd be fun. We'll do that."

Riding back downtown to the office with Dan, I have the feeling I am fighting to wake up from a dream. I tell Dan about Trey, and his face softens. He would like to have a kid in the worst way. "What a little trouper," he says admiringly, as he barrels down the freeway at seventy miles an hour.

"For sure," I agree, thinking of Rosa. You can do all right for a while, but sooner or later you have to go home and the person you loved is not there.

22

WHEN I ARRIVE home at seven, Sarah, shadowed by Woogie, is in the kitchen. "Some woman just called long distance," she says, handing me a notebook sheet of paper before going over to the refrigerator to take out a frozen pizza. "She said it was important."

I smile at my daughter and vow silently that after the trial I will sit down with her and talk. She is on automatic pilot around me for the time being. The same goes for Rainey. I've clearly exhausted my line of credit with each of them. I take the paper and squint. The call shouldn't be from Leigh, since I have just talked to her. As usual, I have gone off and left my reading glasses at the office. I make out "Mary Patricia" followed by a strange area code.

I call from the kitchen and get her on the first ring. "This is Gideon Page," I tell her, realizing again how much she sounds like Leigh and wondering what the other sister must be like. "My daughter said you just called."

Mary Patricia's soft voice sounds as if it is coming from the next room instead of Rhode Island. "I've just thought of something that may help, if it's not too late. I know the trial has already begun."

I scramble to find a pen and paper on the shelf by the phone. She may not have come, but she is certainly keeping in close touch. "No, it's not too late," I assure her. "What do you have?"

"Do you recall our conversation the other night when you thought it could be my godfather who shot Art?"

"Hector Tyndall," I say finally, my mind fumbling for his name. As soon as I had realized that he had no way of knowing what was going on inside the house the morning of the murder, I had dismissed him as a suspect and not given it another thought. "What have you found out?"

Mary Patricia, sounding slightly impatient, says, "I haven't found out anything, but I remembered something that might be of help to Leigh."

Let her talk, I tell myself and begin to doodle on the pad. "What's that?"

Mary Patricia pauses as if reconsidering, then says, "Hector's retired now, but at least until a few years ago, one of the businesses he owned had to do with surveillance equipment. I remember when I was a teenager, he showed me all these listening devices. It always gave me the creeps, but he used to say that if people weren't doing anything wrong, they didn't have anything to worry about."

I write the words "Hector" and "video" on the pad. Mary Patricia must have been in touch with Leigh and gotten the story out of her that she had been dancing naked for Art's camera the morning he was shot. "So you think your godfather could have planted a bug in their bedroom and was listening in that morning?"

Somewhat breathlessly, Mary Patricia adds, "I bet if you searched his house you might find the video Art made of Leigh."

Below Art's name I write "Shane." If we are going to

speculate, we might as well go all the way. "Do you think your father put Hector up to this?"

There is no pause. "He might have," Mary Patricia says, her voice harsh for the first time. "Privacy isn't Daddy's strong point."

I nod, wondering what my limits are. If I suspected Sarah was on drugs, I realize I wouldn't hesitate a minute about searching her room. Would I listen in on her conversations? If her life was at stake, I would. To Shane and Hector perhaps Leigh's life was on the line. We talk for a few more minutes but I learn nothing more and, after thanking her, hang up so I can call Dan and run this by him. Even as I dial his number, I begin to admit to myself how thin the possibility is that we will be able to prove any of this.

Dan, his mouth obviously clogged with food, has to listen but agrees, "Grider won't stop the trial and let you search Tyndall's house. He'd laugh this one into the next century."

I kid Dan, "You want to volunteer to break in there tonight?" As I listen to him chew (it sounds as if he is trying to gnaw through a plastic freezer bag), I doubt if a tape is lying around, but there should be some surveillance equipment.

Dan smacks his lips. I hold the phone away from my ear. He says, "I can see the headlines in the *National Enquirer:* Fattest Thief in Country Nabbed: Claimed He Was Looking for a Home Video. You need to take a couple of sleeping pills and go to bed early."

Is there ever a time when he stops eating? "You're a lot of help," I complain. I smell sausage pizza from the oven. I was hungry until now. "I know somebody who'll do it for me," I say, thinking of a conversation I've had recently on this subject. "Jessie St. Vrain."

"You're kidding," Dan growls. "I thought you said she's a flake."

I can't help but smile as I think of Jessie and myself walking back to my hotel after dinner. I was terrified. "I'm not contemplating a long-term relationship. She says she can turn off a burglar alarm and crack a safe."

Dan doesn't take much convincing. "You really think she'd risk getting caught?"

From the little I know of her, she'll think it's fun. "Obviously, she isn't going to want to testify. Jill would charge her with breaking and entering as soon as she stepped off the witness stand. I gave Sarah a Polaroid for Christmas she could use and then I could confront Hector with the pictures if she finds anything."

I hear a swallowing sound as Dan chokes something down. "Why not send her over to Wallace's house and let her look for bugs?"

I look over at Sarah and realize she has been listening to this conversation. "Too risky," I say, watching Sarah's face, which is registering disapproval. "Grider would put her under the jail for tampering with the crime scene."

Sarah is shaking her head. I tell Dan I'll call him back and get off the phone.

Leaning against the stove, Sarah says incredulously, "You'd even involve me?"

Stalling for time, I take a Coke out of the refrigerator. I got so caught up I forgot she was there. "We don't really have a choice," I say, knowing I sound defensive. "This is important."

Sarah puts her hands up to her face as if to shield herself. "Is there ever a time," she says in a choked voice, "when the ends don't justify the means with you?"

"Let me call Jessie," I say, looking up the Excelsior's

number, "and I'll discuss this with you." I should have stayed at the office. I'm about to get another lecture about how I use people. I can't make her understand how limited my options are. As I dial the number, it occurs to me to leave Leigh out of this. So much for trusting my client, but I don't want her to have the opportunity to sabotage me. When Jessie answers the phone, I tell her to make up an excuse and go down to the lobby and call me.

Sarah takes the pizza from the oven and sets it on the counter. "I can borrow a Polaroid from anybody," I tell her.

"Then you'll have to," my daughter says, her voice constricted with emotion as she takes a knife from the drawer and begins slicing the cheese. "Don't you realize that you're doing the same thing you're accusing that man of?"

I lean back against the wall by the phone. She has no idea what is at stake. "The situation is not even remotely comparable," I say as evenly as possible. "Mr. Tyndall may have listened in on Leigh and Art Wallace in the privacy of their own bedroom."

My daughter won't even look at me. She takes our ancient spatula from the drawer and scoops out a slice of pizza. "The principle is the same."

I will myself into silence for once. Sarah is right to be stubborn. If anyone should be an idealist, it should be someone her age. She'll find it won't be so easy when she's older. With everything else that has happened though, I worry what this will do to our relationship. Rainey has already made it clear how she feels. Yet surely I have a duty to Leigh to do everything I can to win this case. So why am I not calling her? If I can't even trust my own client, this case has more to do with my own ego than the lawyer's canons of professional responsibility.

The phone rings. It is Jessie, who says, "Leigh's in the shower. I'm downstairs." As I tell her what I want, Sarah, with pizza in hand and Woogie at her heels, walks out of the kitchen.

"How do I get there?" Jessie asks without a pause.

I marvel at the excitement in her voice. I wouldn't go out my front door when Chet was shot until I absolutely had to, and she's willing to break into a house on the spur of the moment. "I'll park in the garage across from the courthouse and leave my keys and directions for you at the front desk. A camera with film will be in the front seat. Put the pictures in an envelope, and Dan will walk across the street during the trial and pick them up. I don't expect you to testify that you broke into his house."

"Thanks," she says dryly. "All of the witnesses are supposed to be in the witness room by eight-thirty. How do we get him out of his house?"

I look at the pizza cooling on the stove and begin to get hungry again. I haven't thought of that. "You know how old people are; he'll probably be thirty minutes early," I say. "He's got a red Saturn. If it's not in his driveway, he's already left. If you can't find anything in fifteen minutes, forget it and come on down. If you're only a few minutes late, he'll never suspect it was you." I describe his house as best I can remember and answer her questions about what to photograph to set up the initial questions and then get off the phone so I can track down a Polaroid.

I shouldn't have been worried. "I'll rip off Brenda's and meet you at seven in the Excelsior parking garage," Dan says after I call him back.

Dan's main worry, like the concern of most of the

human race, is with getting caught. As we discuss the
case and how I will try to use the photographs, I wonder if he and Brenda have used the Polaroid to photograph each other naked. I can't imagine it. Yet, who
knows, as the song says, what goes on behind closed
doors?

At ten the phone rings again, and I fear it is Jessie
backing out. Instead, when I answer, Pearl Norman's
boozy voice says, "Mr. Page, neither my daughter nor
my husband killed my son-in-law. . . . I'd like to talk to
you."

Where is she calling from? I wonder. Surely Shane
wouldn't be putting her up to this. I hear the sound of
water running and realize she could have a portable
phone in her bathroom. "I can't talk to you, Mrs. Norman," I say. "As a witness in the case you've been in-
structed not to discuss it with anyone. Don't you
remember the judge telling you that this morning?" I remind her. Grider will have me disbarred if he thinks I
have tried to influence a witness.

She mutters something incomprehensible and hangs
up, and I kick myself for never having tried to follow
up with her. Does she have some information, or was
this the drunken call of a pathetic alcoholic who is sure
to lose something tomorrow? Either her daughter is going to jail or her husband's reputation will be irrevoca-
bly harmed, or both. It occurs to me that I never
checked out her alibi, but the truth is that I haven't ever
been able to make myself take her seriously. What did
Leigh say? She has been out of the loop ever since she
was born. Still, tomorrow when she testifies, she may
say more than she intends to, and that may be what this
phone call was all about.

Sarah's light is off when I lock up the house at midnight. I hope she will be there when I get up the next

morning. In bed, I have trouble getting to sleep. My daughter is right. I use people. I used Jessie and even Dan tonight. Maybe when this case is over I need to think about the direction my life is taking. Yet, with a little luck, I can win this case tomorrow. I know I can.

23

JILL BEGINS HER case with the two octogenarians Leigh originally claimed she spoke with at the church between nine and eleven-thirty and follows with Nancy Lyons, who also contradicts the story Leigh gave to the police. All we can do right now is pretend we are not being hurt by her lies. During the middle of their testimony I send Dan across the street to the Excelsior with his briefcase to pick up what I hope are some pictures of the inside of Tyndall's house. Ten minutes later he comes back and nods, and it is all I can do to resist tearing into the envelope he lays beside me on the defense table. For the last hour I have imagined I could hear sirens, but my strange friend Jessie St. Vrain must have carried out her crime undetected. Hurray for the West Coast, I think, as Dan whispers, "She got a few halfway decent shots of some equipment and the interior of his house."

Watching the jury as Jill zips through her witnesses, I think about Tyndall's possible answers. If he doesn't authenticate the pictures, they will be useless. Leigh, beside me in a beige suit that sets off her magnificent black hair, has a quizzical expression on her face, but I shrug as if Dan merely went out to get some routine documents. Since Chet's death, I have not been able to read her. If she has been participating in some kind of

340

cover-up involving her father, Chet's suicide is not a part of it. If anything, she is more perplexed than I am by his decision to end his life. Understandably, she is so nervous today she can't keep still and stirs impatiently at almost every question. "Try to remain motionless," I remind her. "If you move around too much, some of the jurors will take it as a sign of guilt."

She nods solemnly and clasps her hands in her lap. Her testimony will be the key, but all she can do now is wait.

Jill puts on the cops who took Leigh's statement, follows with the pathologist who fixes the time of death at between ten and eleven-thirty, and then calls Mrs. Sims, who found Art's body. As I listen to this poor old lady babble about the crime scene and how she burst into tears, I find it unlikely that Leigh would have picked a weepy, frail old woman in her seventies to discover Art's body. Yet, that unlikelihood could have been part of a desperate attempt to cover up his murder. I waive my chance to cross-examine the witness lest I reinforce the impression she is making. Between sobs, she has volunteered that Leigh, like herself, became hysterical. Beside me, Leigh tears up, possibly from guilt at what she put the old lady through. I don't discourage her, and during this emotional moment, I take a peek at the pictures. They could help, but everything depends upon Tyndall's answers. As I quickly flip through them, I see that Jessie has done about as well with the Polaroid as I could have hoped for. Though the quality isn't terrific, she has managed to get various pieces of equipment, including a tiny microphone similar to the one she wears, next to a photograph of Tyndall and a young woman, who may well be Mary Patricia.

Ann and Bobby Wheeler prove to be more nervous witnesses than I would have expected, given their wealth and sophistication. Holding herself stiffly erect in a spruce-green cotton knit dress which is overlaid with expensive jewelry, Ann, so warm and sympathetic before when I interviewed her, answers in a tense, clipped voice. She is more forthcoming than her husband and establishes that there was, indeed, an argument between Leigh and Art the night before he died.

"Did you check out their alibis?" Dan asks, during Jill's examination of Bobby.

"Hell, no," I mutter. Moments before, Bobby Wheeler barely acknowledged that there had been a little unpleasantness in the neighborhood that day. Still, Dan is right. We should at least have made a phone call or two. Ann, her gold bracelet clanking against the arm of the witness chair, tells Jill she was playing tennis at the "club" all morning. If I had been able to establish that they, too, had actually been at home at the time of Art's death, Leigh's odds might have improved. But as fastidious and career-driven as Bobby appears to be, I can't form a mental picture of him taking off a morning to murder anyone or even to screw his wife. These people are simply embarrassed to be here.

Hector Tyndall strides briskly to the witness stand as if he is anxious to begin a marathon. Jaunty in gray slacks and a blue blazer complete with red handkerchief, he doesn't act as if his goddaughter's sister has been charged with murder. But then, in my presence, he never has. The day I interviewed him, he didn't volunteer a word about his closeness to Shane and his family. Why not? But, if he had murdered Art, wouldn't he have pretended remorse or at least concern?

After Jill briskly takes him through his story about seeing Leigh on her way home the morning of her husband's murder, I begin by asking him why he didn't tell me the day I interviewed him that he was a godfather to Leigh's sister.

"My goodness!" he exclaims, his voice strong and clear of an old man's foggy rasp. "You claimed to be Leigh's lawyer. I figured you knew that already."

Behind the railing that separates the trial participants from the spectators, laughter rolls toward me like a faint peal of thunder. What kind of fool does Leigh have for a lawyer? Yet Tyndall's attitude doesn't wash. That day he seemed too removed, too self-centered. Granted, it was months after the incident had occurred. But a family friend would have showed more emotion. However, people are weird, especially this guy. He may be no more capable of showing his feelings in front of another person than a robot. "Mr. Tyndall, you're a member of Christian Life?"

Tyndall smiles benignly. "I told you that day that they even let old men go."

Behind me I hear more titters. The spectators love the guy. From the grin on his face, Tyndall loves it, too. He is getting to go one on one and winning as usual. "In fact, you were a founding father of Christian Life, isn't that correct?"

Before Tyndall can answer, Jill pops to her feet and in a bored voice says, "This is irrelevant, Your Honor."

I respond, "I should be permitted to get at Mr. Tyndall's relationship with Christian Life for the purpose of showing bias."

Grider's face takes on an amused, superior expression. "Mr. Page, it seems to me as if you are about to convince the triers of fact," he says, cutting his eyes to the jury, "that Mr. Tyndall was biased in favor of your client, not against her."

For an instant I feel as if I am back in trial advocacy in law school, being hung up to dry by one of the trial lawyers who double as adjunct professors. I listen for more titters, but there are none. Perhaps the spectators have become embarrassed for me. "I'd like to run that risk, Your Honor," I say, trying not to sound as if I am pleading.

Grider shrugs as if it makes no difference to him if I screw up. "Go on," he says, "but I'm not going to let you waste the jury's time with a lot of this."

Quickly, I get Tyndall to confirm that he and Shane have known each other for over thirty-five years and have remained good friends. If Tyndall knows where I am heading, his eyes don't betray him. Scratching at the padding on the armrest of the witness chair with a thumbnail, he seems like a rooster pleased to take his turn in the chicken yard. "You were aware that Pastor Norman wasn't at all happy with his son-in-law's efforts to influence Leigh's participation at Christian Life?"

Tyndall says dryly, "It was common knowledge. Leigh had always been the apple of his eye."

Tyndall's smoothness is distressing. I had hoped that he would try to minimize his knowledge, and that I could expose his lack of truthfulness through Shane, who is waiting to testify out of his hearing. The problem with my theory is that Tyndall, despite his spy equipment, may not have anything to hide. There isn't a shred of evidence he killed Art or even taped a single conversation. "You used to be in the surveillance business, didn't you, sir?"

Out of her seat, Jill roars, "Objection! This is totally irrelevant, Your Honor."

Grider rubs the bridge of his well-shaped nose as if a headache has settled in. "Answer his question, Mr. Tyndall."

Confident as ever, Tyndall nods. "And I sold it five years ago for a nice profit."

"Just one moment, Your Honor," I say, delighted with this answer. I walk over to the desk and pick up the envelope and take out the pictures and show them to Jill, who whispers, "What are these?"

"Souvenirs left over from the business," I say, taking them from the table.

Jill stiffens, but there is nothing she can do. I walk back to the lectern and hold them up for Tyndall. Though he is too far away to identify them, he should be guessing what is in my hand. "Actually, you have some surveillance equipment in your house this very morning, don't you, Mr. Tyndall?"

Tyndall pauses, and I feel my heart in my throat. If he denies that he does and then says the pictures don't fairly and accurately depict the scene in his house, I'm stuck with his answer.

Finally, he answers, his voice sullen, "That's true."

Chet's comment that Christian Life people won't lie to cover up for Leigh comes back to me, and suddenly I know that if I ask the wrong questions he may implicate Leigh. It's a risk I have to take. "In fact, you knew what was going on in the Wallace household the morning Art Wallace was killed."

The old man's jauntiness disappears completely. The expression of confidence on his round face has been replaced by fear and embarrassment. "Let me explain," he says in a low voice.

"By all means," I reply, tapping the pictures against the podium.

Tyndall clears his throat. "After Leigh and Art's involvement with the church began to drop off, we were all worried about Leigh. Because of his deception, I was convinced that Art might be involved in other forms of wrongdoing, too, and I tapped their phone. After I discovered that Art was trafficking in pornography, I bugged their bedroom as well because I was afraid he would try to involve Leigh in it."

The old man stops and waits for me to ask him a question. He doesn't want to volunteer. Jill or even the judge will continue this line of questioning if I don't, but I want to control it. "Who knew about you tapping their phone and placing the bug in their bedroom?"

"Her father knew," he admits, "but only about the phone tap."

Tyndall is nothing if not loyal. He has begun to sweat. "Did he ask you to tap their telephone?"

Tyndall nods.

"You have to speak up," I direct him, "so the reporter can record your answers."

"Yes," he says, "but the bug in their bedroom was my idea. He didn't know about that."

I steal a look at the jury to see how they are taking this information. Every one of them seems frozen in place. "What did you hear the morning Art Wallace was murdered?"

Tyndall swallows with some difficulty. Plainly, he is not happy with what he is about to tell us. "I didn't begin listening that morning until I saw Leigh returning home." He pauses to clear his throat and takes out a handkerchief and wipes his mouth. "I heard her husband tell her he wanted her to dance nude while he filmed her. She agreed."

I glance over at Mrs. Holland, my Charismatic Catholic. Her eyes are the size of dinner plates. "What happened after that?"

Mr. Tyndall blinks rapidly. "I called Leigh's father at the church and told him what I was hearing."

Damn! I should have figured that's what Shane's phone call was about. I ask, "How did he respond?"

"He was upset I had been listening in," Tyndall says. "But he said he would handle the situation from here on in and for me not to listen anymore."

I stare at the jury. If that doesn't get their attention, nothing will. "Is that what you did?"

"Yes," Tyndall says. "I was ashamed at what I had done, so I erased the tape and spent the rest of the morning in the den watching television."

The old man looks as if he is about to cry. I wonder if he is lying about having destroyed the tape. "And yet you never told the police any of this?"

Tyndall shakes his head. "They never asked," he says, his voice defensive. "They asked if I had seen Leigh that morning and I told the truth."

I can't let him get away so easily. "But you knew," I insist, "information that was material to this crime."

Tears slide down Tyndall's cheeks. "I was embarrassed," he says with great difficulty. "Pastor Norman swore to me that neither he nor Leigh was involved in Art's death, and I believed him."

Sure. And I'm going to start growing hair on my bald spot. "Did he say who he thought killed Art?"

Tyndall, clutching his handkerchief, wipes his eyes. "He said he thought it might be some guy Art cheated."

As farfetched as that conclusion seems right now, I do not belittle it. I'll take all the suspects I can find. "Can anyone verify," I ask, "that you stayed home watching television the rest of the morning?"

The old guy launches into a fit of coughing. Even if he is innocent of murder, he knows the rest of his life is stained. "No," he says feebly.

"You were quite a marksman at one time, weren't

you, Mr. Tyndall?" I ask, remembering the trophy in his den.

Tyndall, now restless as a caged animal, says, "Yes, and I own some guns, but I didn't kill Leigh's husband, if that's what you're getting at."

I lean against the podium. "You've shot a twenty-two-caliber pistol before, haven't you?"

Cornered, Tyndall becomes belligerent. "Of course!" he snaps. "But I don't own one."

"No more questions," I say. I will not even bother to try and introduce the pictures into evidence. I want the jury to remember the look of anger on his face.

Clearly surprised, on redirect Jill covers much of the same ground. Tyndall adds a few details and admits breaking into the house while the Wallaces were on vacation, but essentially repeats his story and looks a decade older as he leaves the witness stand. As he is led out of the courtroom, I ask Leigh, "What did your father say to Art when he called?"

Leigh insists, "What I told you before. He didn't say a word then about what Hector had done."

Jill calls the name of Shane Norman, and I, along with everyone else, watch as he is brought into the courtroom by the bailiff. Shane looks like a preacher who is disappointed with his flock and manages only a weak smile for his daughter. He can't know what is coming. I wonder how Jill will handle him. If he lies, her case, as far as Leigh goes, is dead.

Jill wastes no time in confronting Shane with Tyndall's testimony, but if he is surprised, I can't tell it. With amazing aplomb, he explains what happened. "I knew I wanted to get Leigh out of that bedroom, but I didn't want to admit to Art or her right then that their conversations in their bedroom had been taped. Art answered the phone and said Leigh was at the church. Of course, I knew this was a lie, and I lost my temper and called him a son of a bitch. I hung up then and tried to think what to do. I had to get out of my office and so I walked over to the house to try to think everything through. I went back to the office after a while and was there when Leigh called to say she had found Art's body."

Stunned by his coolness, I think back to my conversation with him. He had lied to me, but his story today just might hang together. Jill is plainly furious that he has not come forward with this story before and berates him, "Why didn't you tell the police this story when they interviewed you?"

Shane responds forthrightly, "My daughter is on trial for murder. I didn't lie to the police, but on the other hand I'm not going to embarrass her or help convict her. She's my daughter and I love her."

Abruptly, Jill switches gears and leads Shane down memory lane; and we hear, as she promised in her opening statement, of a father's boundless love for his daughter. I can hear snuffling behind me from the spectators as Shane talks about Leigh's accomplishments in the church and his obvious pride in her. While Leigh steadily wipes her eyes, Dan whispers, "Do you believe this horseshit?"

I don't know what to believe, but I can't wait to cross-examine Shane. As Jill lets Shane run on with story after story of Leigh's perfect life before she married Art, I whisper back, "Jill is setting up her argument on closing that it was Leigh's guilt that led her to kill Art."

Shane is preaching a sermon to the jury whose subtext is forgiveness. "Her faith strengthened my own," he tells the jury. "There were times on these trips when everything imaginable would go wrong, and I'd look up and see Leigh holding a filthy, love-starved urchin on her lap as if the child were her own. Then I'd be certain that we were right to have come."

Gently, Jill brings him to the day that Leigh told him that she was going to marry Art, and before our eyes Shane changes into a figure out of the Old Testament. His whole manner, from his glowering expression to the barely suppressed rage in his voice, tells the jury that Art was the Fallen Angel. The jury, composed of men and women who know a preacher when they see one, sit fascinated. Though Shane has no pulpit to pound, his message is ancient: good corrupted by evil, and now that the evil has been banished, if we can't very well rejoice, at least let his daughter get on with her life very soon, if not today. He turns his head to Leigh and then back to the jury. "This was a child who time after time had followed me in faith and love all over the world. This man was scum, and he had possessed her so completely she was willing to humiliate herself in any way he demanded."

Dan nudges me so hard he bruises my ribs. Cupping his hands against my ear, he hisses, "He's begging you to go after him!"

I look over at Leigh, who is hiding her head in her hands as Jill sits down after a few more questions. I half expect her father to confess now, but he doesn't. If he is directly asked if he murdered his son-in-law, surely he will admit it. I begin my questions as I rise from my chair. "When you went to your home after speaking to Art," I ask, to make sure Pearl isn't going to suddenly turn up as an alibi for him, "where was your wife?"

Shane, who is perched on the edge of his chair, says blandly, "She was in Benton visiting her mother that morning."

I nod. "So she can't testify she was home with you?"

Obviously trying to relax, Shane pushes back in his chair. "Hardly," he says dryly.

I stand by the side of the podium and ask him why he had taped Art. Each time Wallace's name is mentioned, anger flows into his voice. It is obvious that he felt personally betrayed by the man. Turning directly to the jury, he talks about how Art deceived him. Art's acceptance of the Scriptures seemed as genuine as anyone's he had ever witnessed. "If he lied about that," Norman says, "I knew he was a liar about other things, and I wanted to find out what they were."

I goad him. "Leigh defended him, didn't she?"

Norman's eyes flash. "That's why I know she didn't kill him," he says firmly. "He had her fooled completely, too."

"How did you feel," I ask, "when Mr. Tyndall called and told you about Art having Leigh dance nude in front of him?"

Shane set his jaw. "I was absolutely furious. My first thought was that he was going to use the film for some kind of pornographic video. That's the kind of man he was."

"Were you mad enough," I ask quickly, "to kill him?"

Surely expecting this question, Shane gives me a bitter smile. "An angry Christ drove the money changers from the Temple, but he didn't kill them."

I stare at Shane. "We're not talking about Jesus, Pastor Norman. Throughout history, angry Christians have killed thousands of their enemies. Were you angry enough to kill Art Wallace?"

Defiantly, Shane says, "Yes, yes, I was angry enough to kill him! But I didn't! As God is my witness, I didn't kill him and my daughter didn't either! Leigh is totally nonviolent. When we were leaving to go to Peru on a mission trip some time back, the Shining Path had just murdered ten people. Leigh wanted us to go to minister to them."

This is welcome testimony, but what else would a father say? I ask him a few more questions and let him step down.

After a brief lunch recess, Jill calls Pearl Norman to the witness stand. As she comes through the door, it is obvious that she is drunk. "Hoo boy, she's looped," Dan marvels, as she lurches toward the witness stand. "She must carry a flask in her purse and drink in the bathroom."

Indeed she must, because anybody over the age of three knows something is seriously wrong. Beside me, Leigh flinches as her mother slurs her own name. For the first time since I've known her, she looks sloppy. Her lipstick has missed the mark, and her hair isn't quite combed. Jill asks sternly, "Have you been drinking, Mrs. Norman?"

Pearl Norman nods and bursts into tears. Leigh tugs at my arm and whispers, "She doesn't know anything." I stand and ask Grider for a conference and he motions me and Jill to the bench. We approach and, with my back to the jury, I say quietly, "Maybe we can stipulate to her testimony, Your Honor. I understand she has a real alcohol problem."

Grider looks at Pearl in disgust and turns to Jill. "What do you want out of her?"

Jill shakes her head. "I want her to tell what she knows about this case!"

For the first time Grider seems to be on my side. "Haven't you already interviewed her?" he asks sharply. "Does she help the State's case?"

Like a child being questioned by her father, Jill shifts her weight from side to side. "I don't know what she's going to say under oath, Your Honor. We've had a few surprises already," she adds dryly.

I look over at Leigh and suggest to Grider, "Why don't we go ahead with her direct testimony? I'm not afraid of her."

Grider looks past us at Pearl and says harshly, "Are you too drunk to tell the truth to this court?"

Pearl smiles foolishly at him. "No, Judge."

Irritably, Grider snaps, "I should hold you in contempt of court. Let's get on with it."

As expected, the next few minutes are a waste of time. Either Pearl cries, rambles, or gives such vague answers that the jury, now that its initial titillation at her condition has worn off, grows visibly restless and bored. All that Jill shows is that she is a strangely pathetic creature who is an embarrassment to her husband and her youngest daughter. When Jill is through with her, I let her sit down without a question. She seems so relieved it is impossible to avoid wondering if she is hiding something after all.

Jill concludes her case by calling Laura Partrain, who reinforces Shane's testimony about the changes in his daughter caused by Art Wallace. A pillar at Christian Life, Mrs. Partrain speaks of her own personal efforts to keep Leigh involved in the church. She makes real the anguish experienced by other church members. "No matter what we said or did," the woman, an attractive redhead, laments, "Leigh came to church less and less. Her husband was a terrible influence on her. Leigh had been such a joy, too. We hated what was happening, but nobody could do a thing about it."

I let Mrs. Partrain go without a question, and after Grider summarily dismisses my motion to dismiss the charges, I begin our defense. Daffy is my first witness, and, as strange as he is (thank God he is wearing shoes instead of sandals), he does a decent job of piecing together Art's scheme to launder the two hundred thousand dollars he swindled from Jack Ott. Grider gives us an unexpected break when he allows Jessie St. Vrain to play the tape in which Robert Evatt confessed that Jack Ott had hired him to torch a rival porno dealer's store. Over Jill's vehement protest, Grider permits the recording to be admitted into evidence because Evatt said on tape he was supposed to burn up the dealer as well. However, the recording is difficult to understand and Evatt sounds like the drug-crazed loony he was.

If the jury is impressed, I can't tell by their expressions. Jill and the cops have already emphasized to them that there was no forced entry and no sign of a struggle. If Art feared for his life, why was he sitting at his desk when he was killed? It all sounds too far out and crude for the rich neighborhoods that overlook the Arkansas River. As she steps down, I smile at Jessie, who has done as well as she can. Although she has surprised me by keeping her promise to wear a dress, she still looks like a young boy, but she is close enough for the jury to give her the benefit of the doubt. Turning to smile at the jury as she steps off the witness stand, she seems as unlikely to have just committed a break-in as Pearl Norman.

I look over at Dan and he shakes his head. Don't put Leigh on the witness stand. But I have to. Credibility is what this case is about. Shane has made too powerful a witness on his own behalf for me to believe that Leigh is safe. Shane may well have convinced the jury of his own innocence, but if he is telling the truth, there is no way he can save his daughter. He wasn't there. Leigh will have to save herself.

Leigh takes the stand, and I have her tell her story. In a tense, anxious voice she sounds so much like her father I wonder if I could tell their words apart if I were reading their transcripts. Without apology, Leigh admits she was a daddy's girl from the time she was born, and listening to her words, no one in the courtroom can escape the conclusion that they adored each other. Her one defiant act was marrying Art. "His personality was a lot like my father's," she volunteers, as if it weren't obvious. "He was very determined and gave me a lot of attention."

To make plain to the jury how much control Shane exercises, I ask about Pearl. "How did your mother figure in the picture when you were growing up?"

Leigh gives me a bitter smile. "As you saw today, my mother unfortunately has a drinking problem and has had for many years. I'm sure she's been very lonely at times. My father has gotten attention all his life, and she has received very little. He is such a dominant personality it has been hard for her to find her own niche. I really haven't been very close to her."

I nod, content with her answer. The jury has to feel the bond between Leigh and Shane if they are going to believe her story of why she lied to the police. "I felt enormous guilt for not going to the church as regularly as I had before I married Art. The church was my whole life, and I felt terrible when Daddy would comment about my not being there."

For the next ten minutes I get Leigh to explain her actions the morning of the trial. "I had told Daddy that I would come hear a missionary from Guatemala. Art wanted me to stay home, so I went up to the church twice that morning to make Daddy think I had been there all the time. I know it sounds pathetic, but I always felt so bad when he asked me to come to the church."

Knowing Jill will ask this question if I don't, I say,

"Did you relieve those bad feelings by killing your husband?"

"No!" she exclaims. "I loved Art. He was the smartest man I've ever known. And he made me feel like a person and a woman for the first time in my life."

I steal a glance at the jury but can't read anything. A new Art is emerging from Leigh's lips. Gone is the terrible deceiver who seduced her away from Christianity. She is free-lancing with this version, but intuitively she must know that if she gives the impression that she had begun to hate him, the jury will assume she had a reason to kill him. Cautiously, I go with this new, improved model. "You loved him despite the fact," I ask, giving her a chance to explain, "that he was a thief?"

Leigh responds earnestly, "He took the money from pornographers. I was worried about our safety, but I wasn't upset at what he did."

"Did you feel threatened?" I ask, watching Leigh carefully. She is fighting for her life now, but she is on thin ice.

"Of course," she says, "but we couldn't very well go to the police."

I have no choice but to ask her about the video. It is a double-edged sword, equally a problem for her as well as her father. "Why did you let your husband film you naked?" I ask, wondering how closely she will stick to the script. Whatever I argue to the jury in my closing statement about Hector and Shane, the jury will be asking itself if Leigh suddenly blew up.

Her face colors, and her voice drops into a lower register. "I was always taught that the husband is the head of the household," she says softly. "Sex generally was a taboo in our house. I suppose you could say Art was trying to teach me that the body didn't have to be dirty."

I am impressed at how manipulative my client has become. If Leigh had a self-destruct button, it is no longer apparent. After a few more questions, to which she reiterates her innocence, I sit down and watch Jill's assault.

Jill begins by forcing Leigh to admit the name of each person she deceived. Beginning with her father and the women in the church down through the police, it makes an impressive list. "Isn't it a fact," Jill asks harshly, "that in this case you've lied whenever it was convenient for you to do so?"

Leigh pauses and finally admits, "Yes."

Jill covers much of the ground I have already been over in an effort to reinforce how guilty Leigh must have felt during the last two years. Jill's contempt for Leigh is palpable. Though surely it is part of the prosecutor's bag of tricks, Jill truly does not like Leigh. I wonder how much of it is rooted in disdain for her apparent hypocrisy. Jill pushes Leigh on her decision to dance naked for Art. "Were you embarrassed when he turned on the camera?"

Leigh ponders the question. To be consistent, she must answer yes. Instead, she answers, "It was in the privacy of our home."

Dan nudges me. "She's trying to be cute. The jury has got to believe her. Jill will crucify her on closing if she doesn't cut this out."

"So your testimony is that," Jill badgers her, "you weren't embarrassed when you danced naked for your husband?"

In preparation for her testimony I have begged Leigh not to try to outsmart Jill, but even the most astute clients make that mistake. Jill will make her look as though she is incapable of presenting a consistent image to the jury. "Art said it would never leave the house."

Jill bores in on her. "Isn't it a fact that just the night before you and your husband had had a fight in which you told Art to quit 'bad-mouthing' your father?"

"It wasn't a fight," Leigh says defensively.

"And isn't it a fact that the next morning an hour before your husband's death," Jill asks, "you were upset with him because of an angry conversation he'd just had with your father?"

"Just because I was upset," Leigh says, "doesn't mean I killed him."

"Are you saying," Jill asks bluntly, "your father shot your husband?"

Leigh shakes her head. "I don't know who shot my husband."

Jill asks grimly, "What about you, Mrs. Wallace? You're capable of telling repeated lies. But are you just too sweet and pretty to kill anybody?" Before Leigh can answer, Jill turns her back on her and goes to her seat. I remain where I am. I don't want to hear the answer.

After Grider instructs the jury on the law of the various degrees of murder, Jill begins her closing argument by summarizing the testimony of each witness and its significance, then goes to work on the crucial hour and a half between Shane's phone call and the discovery of the body. "What happened, ladies and gentlemen," she asks rhetorically, standing in front of the jury rail, "after Art Wallace put down the telephone after speaking to the defendant's father?" Jill looks back over at Leigh for an instant and then says conspiratorially, "You know as well as I do what happened. The defendant was feeling a crushing sense of guilt. Her entire life had been centered around her father. From the time she was born until this very moment, her father adored her, and she adored him. No relationship was more important in some ways to either of them. She made trip after trip with her father to foreign lands; after graduation from college she worked for him in the church. It is not too much to say that Leigh was as much inspiration to this tireless minister of the Gospel as he was to her. And why not? She was willing to try to convert the Shining Path, the Maoist guerrilla group terrorizing the country of Peru. And the defendant reveled in her father's love. What daughter would not? Inevitably, this beautiful woman was bound to attract the attention of other men, and perhaps, understandably, she probably thought they were all as wonderful as her father."

Jill pauses here and then says dryly, "Well, Art Wallace was not. With a persistence that bordered on the fanatical, he began to chip away at the defendant's relationship with her father and her church until one devastating morning Leigh Wallace found herself lying to her father, lying to her friends, and dancing naked in front of a camera. Of course, we know what happened next! The police have told us there was no forced entry, no evidence of another soul coming into that house until the defendant brought Mrs. Sims back with her to discover her husband's body."

Jill raises her voice slightly as she taps her right hand above her left breast. "Guilt and anger, ladies and gentlemen, guilt and anger are a deadly combination of emotions, and Leigh was experiencing them both when she frantically began to get ready to drive to the church so she could pretend she had been there all along. She felt guilt because of everyone she had betrayed, and she felt anger at herself and the man who had debased her. Her husband, we know, got dressed and went into his office and sat down behind the desk and turned on his computer. What happened, ladies and gentlemen, was that Leigh took a twenty-two-caliber pistol and walked

into her husband's office and shot him through the heart
and killed him. She then drove to the church, pretended
she had been there all morning, and invited a friend to
lunch so she could happen upon her husband's body.
There is no evidence in this case that supports any other
explanation. . . ."

Leigh's body is practically rigid beside me as she listens with her left hand placed firmly over her mouth. It
is as if she is stifling a scream. Jill's explanation is so
reasonable, so obvious, that it is impossible to resist a
wave of depression. As I stand to make my closing,
Leigh begins to weep, hardly an encouraging send-off.
I walk quickly to the jury rail to draw attention away
from her. What are her tears if not an admission of
guilt?

"Ladies and gentlemen," I begin hoarsely, and stop to
clear my throat. I know I sound nervous and try desperately to relax. If I had not begun to feel Leigh was
guilty, this would be easier. Starting again, my voice
still scratchy, I say too loudly, "What the prosecutor
wants so badly is to have you ignore the obvious conclusion that there is no evidence in this case at all—
there is no evidence whatever that Leigh Wallace shot
her husband. There is no murder weapon, no eyewit-
ness, no physical evidence at all. She has offered no
motive except emotions that those of you on this jury
feel every day. If there was a murder every time someone felt guilt and anger, there wouldn't be a person in
this courtroom." I slap the rail in front of me and pretend to scoff, "Talk about making a virtue of necessity,
and necessity being the mother of invention! The prosecutor has invented her theory because she has no
facts." I turn to Jill and point at her. "What proof did
the prosecutor offer that Leigh Wallace killed her husband? A magician couldn't distort reality any better," I

say, and turn back to the jury. "The prosecutor practically tells you that Leigh has been the victim in all of this and then, in the time-honored fashion, where there is no evidence to support it, she blames the victim!"

I back away from the rail to give the jury some time to digest what I have said, and lower my voice. The hoarseness is gone, and I almost believe what I am saying. "Who killed Art Wallace? Unlike the prosecutor, I don't pretend to know beyond a reasonable doubt. It very well could have been an out-of-town hired gun. Professional killers know how to slide back locks on doors; they know a well-placed twenty-two-caliber bullet makes someone just as dead as the bullet from a deer rifle. On the other hand, the murderer could have been anybody in Blackwell County. For all we know, it could have been Hector Tyndall. He lived only a few doors down and has admitted he was at home all morning. He knew the agony that Shane Norman was going through as a result of his son-in-law's actions. And if you want to suspect someone who felt the emotion of anger toward the victim, you might as well add Shane Norman to the list of possibilities. He could have easily gone to his daughter's house and invited himself in on the pretext of talking things out with his son-in-law and then shot him to death."

I stop speaking and walk back to the podium. "Do you see how easy it is?" I thunder, leaning against the lectern as if I were a world-weary veteran with a hundred murder trials under my belt. "If the system wants to, it can make anybody appear guilty! Opportunity does not make someone a murderer! Motive does not make someone a murderer! Nor do the two together make a murderer in our system of justice, because, as we see, there is no end to the number of theoretical suspects in this case. As Hector Tyndall told you, it was common knowledge within Christian Life what was happening to Leigh. And if you ask every one of those people where they were the morning Art Wallace was murdered, and assuming they could remember, I'd bet my house that some of them would not tell the truth the first time they were asked. . . ."

As I sit down, Dan whispers, "Chet would have been proud." I wonder what he would have said. What he had that I lack is credibility. I have no idea whether the jury believed a word coming out of my mouth.

Jill gets to her feet and smirks at me as if I were the worst con artist in the world. "Ladies and gentlemen," she says, turning to the jury, "Mr. Page wants you to suspend your common sense. He wants you to forget the facts of this case and pretend you are looking for a needle in a haystack. That is absurd and your common sense tells you it is. Where did the police tell us they discovered the victim's body? On the floor in his office beside his computer, which was still on when the police came. Art Wallace didn't bring his killer into his house and go back and sit down and start working again. You've heard investigators tell you how they went over every inch of the house and there is no evidence his body was dragged or moved after the victim was shot. . . ."

The last word. How I wish I had it, but even Chet told me that he had never finished a trial where he hadn't wished to say something more after the prosecutor sat down. The fact that the computer was on when he was shot proves nothing. But people know that from their own experience. If his killer was somebody he knew, he could easily have brought that person back to his office and sat down at his desk to talk. Trials have to end somewhere though, and all the wishing in the world isn't going to make anything different.

Leigh sighs heavily as the jury files out. "What do you think?" she asks as the door shuts on the last one.

I slump in my seat, exhausted. It is six o'clock. Food will be brought in while they deliberate. Chet wouldn't have made it. Maybe he knew he couldn't have lasted long enough and simply couldn't bear the thought of not being able to see the trial through. "I don't know," I say honestly. I glance at Dan, who is quietly gathering up the papers on the table in front of him. A bad sign.

Dan volunteers to go out for hamburgers and takes Sarah with him, leaving me to visit with Rainey as the crowd dwindles rapidly. If the jury doesn't come back with a verdict by nine o'clock, they will be sequestered over the weekend. Rainey and I sit at the defense table and watch Leigh and her mother and father talk in the back of the courtroom. I'd like to be a fly on the wall during this conversation. Pearl looks better but not by much. Rainey smooths down her flowered spring dress and says, "If they convict her, I don't think it will be first-degree murder."

I rub my head, which has begun to ache. If Rainey is thinking conviction, we are in trouble. "Good," I say weakly, wishing for a moment that Chet had been well and had tried this case. But that feeling passes quickly. I wanted to try this case in the worst way. "They didn't have any real evidence."

Rainey smiles, but it is not reassuring. Get real, I think. Men and women commit acts of violence against each other every day. Why should Leigh and Art be any different? The jury, composed of faithful believers like herself, may well decide, as Rainey undoubtedly already has, that once the bonds of her church were loosened, there were no restraints on her behavior. I kick myself again for not questioning the strategy of seeking a jury of Bible thumpers, but then Chet's logic hits me as I stare into Rainey's face. He was convinced that Leigh was guilty. Maybe he knew she was. In choosing a jury, he was thinking about the length of her sentence, not the question of her guilt or innocence.

"You must be exhausted," Rainey says, smiling sympathetically.

"I'm a little tired," I admit. "When I signed on for this case, I didn't know what I was getting into."

"Poor Gideon," Rainey says, patting my shoulder and in the process touching me for the first time in over a month. When was the last time we even kissed? I can't remember. It is hard to believe we used to neck like teenagers on her couch. What will become of us? I have no idea. Maybe it is true that friendship is better than love, but I'd rather have both.

Dan and Sarah come back with food from McDonald's, reminding me of the night we waited for the verdict in the Andy Chapman case. No acquittal in that case either. Dan wanders off to visit with a friend from the sheriff's office, leaving me alone with Sarah and Rainey. My stomach is too nervous for me to eat, and I sip at the chocolate milkshake Sarah has handed me. Standing in the doorway of the courtroom, Sarah stares at her minister, who is still seated at the back of the courtroom with his wife and daughter. "After all this, do you really think Pastor Norman could have killed Leigh's husband?" she asks. "Or were you just using him as an example of the fact that just about anyone could have done it?"

I look around to see who else might be listening and say under my breath, "I'm afraid he might have. Though I can't prove it, I suspect there was a lot more to this case than ever came out in the trial."

Sarah whimpers, "He couldn't have ever done that."

"No, you're wrong," Rainey agrees. "That's impossible."

"I didn't say he did," I respond defensively, but from the looks on their faces I may have changed their lives forever. A priest at Subiaco used to warn my Christian Doctrine class that faith for some of us would be a rudderless ship subject to the strongest wind. With my words, the storm that lately has been energizing the lives of my daughter and girlfriend may have ebbed. I'd be lying to myself if I didn't admit that I hoped it was so.

"The jury's coming back!" Grider's bailiff yells at me from across the courtroom. My heart thumping, I look down at my watch. It has only been an hour, a terrible omen. The longer they're out, the better. I hand my cup to Sarah and wave at Leigh to come down front.

Coming toward me, she looks stricken, obviously reading the fear on my face. I try to speak, but no words come out. I can hear the comments tomorrow: the jury was barely out an hour. Maybe the Arkansas Supreme Court will reverse because of incompetence of counsel. I wonder if I can get back into social work. As the jury files back in, I have given up pretending I can read results on the faces of jurors. I scan their faces, but they merely seem anxious to get home.

Leigh unexpectedly takes my hand and holds it as Grider silently reads the verdict form. Her fingers are rigid as she digs her nails into mine. The room is so quiet I can hear Dan's slightly asthmatic breathing. Thank God, Jill didn't go for the death penalty. I hold my breath as Grider begins reading. And then, suddenly, it is all over—acquittal on all charges. As Leigh cries against my shoulder, I feel as if a huge metal ball has rolled off my back. Although I am not much of a believer in an afterlife, I can't avoid the thought that somehow Chet Bracken is also breathing a sigh of relief.

Standing in the courtroom moments later with Rainey and Sarah, who are both bubbling with excitement, I watch Leigh's celebration with her parents and the crowd (presumably from Christian Life) gathered around them. It is hard to escape the sobering thought that a murderer is rejoicing.

24

"I THOUGHT YOU said you used to play when you were a kid, Mr. Page," Trey calls as he watches me bend down to pick up the third ball I have dropped.

Beads of sweat from my forehead drop into Chet's old glove. Maybe I am imagining all those Little League games in Bear Creek. The first ball ever hit to me in a real game went between my legs. I haven't improved with age. "I guess I'm pretty rusty," I say, glancing over at his mother, who is watching us from the deck. Wynona smiles gratefully at me. It has been only a week since her husband's funeral, and it is nice to see her smile. It is glorious out here behind the house in the April sun. New life is bursting from every tree, every blade of grass. This is the kind of day that must make Chet's death particularly hard to bear. Yet the air is so soft and the morning so clear and bright with the rich promise of a long Arkansas spring, it is impossible not to feel alive.

After a few more minutes, Wynona tells her son, "That's enough, Trey. Let Mr. Page rest. I need to talk to him in the house."

"What about?" Trey asks, throwing the ball up and catching it. I used to do that by the hour in Bear Creek, pretending I was Mickey Mantle.

"He just needs to help me go through a couple of

things," Wynona says gently to her son. "You play out here by yourself." On this warm Saturday morning she is wearing a pair of loose-fitting shorts and a man's workshirt. Chet's, I suppose. Good legs, I notice. Trey waves me into the house. I'm no Brooks Robinson, his grin says, but I'll do until the real thing comes along.

"Thanks for playing with him," Wynona says, her voice still mechanical with grief as she leads me into the kitchen. "It's going to be particularly hard for him. He and Chet were amazingly close."

She is talking about herself, I realize, as well as her son. A plain-faced woman in her forties with a kid, her prospects for remarriage aren't bright. Yet she found Chet, and, I assume, had been married before him. Some women are better at finding men than others. "I'm afraid it will," I say bluntly, thinking of myself and Sarah. "But he'll survive. We all do."

Wynona stands on tiptoes and pulls down a gray metal lockbox from behind a wooden panel above her refrigerator. From the left pocket in her shorts she extracts a key and opens the lock. On top of what appears to be several envelopes is one with my name on it. Wynona reaches in and picks it up. "Chet said for me to read this to you, but not to give it to you. Why don't you go sit at the table?"

Dreading what is coming, I choose the same chair I sat in when I had breakfast with them. Wynona opens the letter, which is not sealed, and begins to read in a clear, patient voice.

Gideon:

I hate to leave you by yourself with Leigh's trial, but there is no way I can pull this off, knowing what I do. I feel terrible about deceiving you, but I let myself get sucked into an agreement I know now I never should have made. When Shane first asked me to represent Leigh, he didn't tell me the truth. He knew Leigh was not her husband's murderer. Knowing my reputation, he was convinced I could get her off. He didn't know then I had cancer. I took the case thinking I had more time, and frankly, given the evidence Jill had, I thought I could win it, too.

Here in my final hour of life, I know better than most humans that pride is the mother of all sin. Because of what Shane had done for me, I agreed. Instead of admitting how little energy I had, I convinced myself that I could last through March in good enough shape. You know, of course, what a joke that was.

As I began to investigate the case, it became clear that Pearl Norman knew more than she was telling. Always an alcoholic, she went off the deep end and really crawled inside the bottle. Initially, I thought it was a reaction to the charge against Leigh, but gradually it dawned on me that she might have killed her son-in-law. Finally, in January, after I confronted her, she admitted she went to the house drunk and killed Art after Shane called her from his office and told her that Art had gotten Leigh to dance nude for him. Pearl knew by then about Art's scam and somehow assumed he was going to turn Leigh into a porn star. She swears she never intended to shoot him when she went there, and I believe her. Knowing his influence on Pearl (and all of us), Shane felt totally responsible for her actions, and begged me to try the case without revealing what I knew. Leigh, of course, was in on all this as soon as Shane came up with the idea. What is most incredible to me is that the disease of hubris contracted through continued success had reached such an advanced stage

*that, like a damn fool, I agreed. Even as sick as I was,
I believed I could pull it off.*

As you know now, we went to elaborate lengths to
make you believe that Shane murdered Art and that I
was being brought around to make that argument,
which presumably you made at the trial. Leigh hated
this tactic, but Shane and I had finally convinced her
that it was the surest way to an acquittal. Much of
what I did was to try to keep you off the scent of Pearl.
What you cannot know is how much Pearl means to
Shane and to Leigh. They love her very deeply. Both
have always felt guilty about her alcoholism and her
isolation in the family. Recently, Pearl has been diag-
nosed as having permanent liver damage. With her
prognosis, Shane couldn't bear the thought of her
dying in prison.

I apologize for having deceived you. Though you will
try the case without knowing all the facts, you will not
be engaging in any act of fraud on the court. I would
have, of course, and this is what ultimately I could not
do.

What I counted on was your own ambition. You
wanted to become the next Chet Bracken! It has taken
me a lifetime to realize how much vanity has played in
my life. I was an ugly, jug-eared runt from Phillips
County who was determined to make something of myself, and I never got past that. Even after my conversion, I never brought my ego under control. But it has
helped me understand you. And exploit you. I do not say
any of this to hurt your feelings (you have the potential
to be an outstanding lawyer) but merely to explain why
I have acted as I have.

I have made my peace with God, and firmly believe
in an hour I will be in a far better place. If you can
bring yourself to do it after what you have learned,

please look in on Wynona and Trey occasionally. They
deserve far more than they have received. I am no ad-
vertisement for Christianity, but they truly are. Chet.

It is only with these last few sentences that
Wynona's voice breaks. She wipes her eyes with her
wrist. Too dumbfounded to move, I watch as she
shreds the letter, forces it down the drain, and turns on
the faucet and the garbage disposal. Pearl Norman! If
Jill had asked the right questions, would she have broken down and confessed? No wonder she was almost
hysterical. As Wynona turns off the switch on the disposal, she says, "I'm sorry, Gideon. I hope you can
live with this."

Like a stroke victim who has lost the power of
speech, I find I can only nod at her. I leave, but not before promising Trey I will return in a couple of weeks
to take him to an Arkansas Travelers baseball game. A
Cardinal farm team, the Travs haven't been very good
lately, but, who knows, maybe we will discover another
Brooks Robinson.

On the winding road back east into town, my mind is
a blur of images. I think back to the day Chet showed
up in my office and told me that he thought Leigh was
probably guilty. I was being set up from day one! I feel
my face burn as I remember that I never got around to
checking out Pearl's alibi. Why did I do such a poor job
of thinking about this case? The reason is obvious: I
wanted to discredit Shane. He was stealing Sarah and
Rainey. How pathetic of me! Chet had me eating out of
his hand, and so did Leigh. I fell for every lie they fed
me. Why didn't Chet simply ram down my throat that
we were going after Shane? I would have bought it. Obviously, because there was a conflict. I was supposed to
figure it out gradually and insist on Shane's culpability

after they all rubbed my nose in it. I bought everything, even the taped conversation between Leigh and Shane. They set me up every time. Leigh must almost have cracked, though, at one point. When she ran off and got drunk, she must have scared Shane and Pearl to death. And yet, even with Chet's suicide and Hector's unexpected testimony, Shane never missed a line or cue. He went right on as if he had a script in front of him. How could I forget to what lengths families will go to protect each other? Driving too fast, I have to brake hard on a curve, reminding myself that accidents can happen. Maybe Pearl didn't intend to kill Art, just threaten him with a dramatic gesture. Poor Pearl. Those phone calls. She wanted to confess to me, I think, but I wouldn't listen. Her daughter and her husband wouldn't let her take responsibility for her life. The American Way. Why? Easier to make excuses and keep her out of sight. Perhaps I should go to Jill with what I know, but, without a shred of proof, I'm pretty sure I will wait. Chet's letter to me is part of the Blackwell County sewer system, and doubtless, precautions have been taken to firm up Pearl's alibi. If she is dying, what would be the point? As traffic halts at the entrance to the freeway that will take me home, I realize that the case, as it stands now, has generated a lot of favorable publicity. There have been a couple of nice articles that mentioned my name. No one has yet claimed that I am Chet's heir apparent, but it is nice all the same. I speed on the freeway, practically begging to be arrested, but there isn't a cop in sight. Ah, the practice of law.

"Hold still!" I command my dog, who is shaking as if he is about to be electrocuted instead of being given a bath in the backyard. "You can turn on the water!" I holler at Sarah, who is wiping beads of sweat from her forehead as she stands over the spigot with a pair of pliers. She turns the handle, and water runs from the hose onto Woogie's back, as he begins to shiver all over again. It is sweltering, and it isn't even June.

Sarah walks over to us and bends down to take hold of Woogie's collar. "What a terrible year for Pastor Norman," she says. "First his daughter is charged with murder and then his wife dies."

I nod in agreement. "I can't imagine having to live through both events in the same year." Unbeknownst to Sarah, I feel Pearl Norman's death last night has lifted a weight from my back.

"Though I'm sad for him, I don't quite feel the same way about Christian Life," Sarah admits, holding Woogie as I soap his back. "Since the trial, there's been so much dissension that it doesn't seem the same place. There's talk of a big group of people leaving to form a new church."

I rub the bar of soap against Woogie's belly. He looks at me as if I were holding a gun to his head. I grunt, "I noticed you haven't been going much lately." Though Sarah was angry at me again after the trial, the main casualty has been Rainey. I have seen her only a couple of times the last two months. My daughter is more forgiving. After all, I am her flesh and blood.

"Do you still believe the Bible word for word?" I ask, trying to sound casual. I rinse Woogie off and pretend to admire his fur in the glistening water and bright sunshine.

"I don't know," Sarah says irritably, perhaps betraying that it is a battle she can't win. "That's really important to you, isn't it?"

I reach down on the grass for the ragged yellow towel I keep beneath the sink for this occasion and begin to rub Woogie briskly. "I guess while some people have a need to believe," I respond, "I have a need not to, unless I can understand it."

Sarah's mouth puckers as if she were tasting something that does not agree with her. She has already forgiven me for going after Shane but wants to have the last word. "You miss a lot that way," she says, petting Woogie's head to calm him. "It's almost over, boy."

"Probably so," I concede as I dry Woogie's legs. You miss a lot of nonsense. But I do not say this. I've got my daughter back. Now is the time to be relatively magnanimous.

"I could never be a lawyer," Sarah says and stands up.

She is saying this to hurt me because she knows someday I'd like to see "Page & Page" in the Yellow Pages. "I know." She has plenty of time to change her mind. Woogie, freed from the towel, squirms around on the grass on his back. He'll show me, by God.

"Everything is always the ends justifying the means," Sarah says unnecessarily. "I don't see how you can live like that."

Our dog runs in circles and then plops down on the grass again. "There are really a lot more rules than it looks like," I call after Sarah as she goes over to the spigot to turn it off.

She doesn't say anything, and after turning off the water, she marches inside. I sit down on the grass and watch Woogie take a tour of the backyard. There is a lot more I could say, but I won't. For starters, I could tell her that my ego nearly did me in, but I escaped. Not with everything. Rainey is gone. I suppose she could come back, but the last time I talked to her she said that she wanted to see if I was the only kind of man she was attracted to. "What kind of man is that?" I asked. She didn't smile when she said, "The kind who always does what he wants to and expects the woman to be there to fix everything."

It is hot out here. I call Woogie, who is happily sniffing the fence that separates my property from my neighbor's, "Let's go inside!" He follows.